Lords of Destiny

Reap the Hurricane

STEPHEN RICKETTS

ISBN: 9798618419574

This is a work of fiction. Names, characters, places and incidents either are the product of the author's imagination or are used fictitiously, and any resemblance to any actual persons, living or dead, events or locales is entirely coincidental.

Story – S Ricketts
Cover design – S Ricketts & Destiny Productions
Editing – S Ricketts & J Aellen
Destiny Books
www.destiny-books.com

15/04/2020

For my sons

CONTENTS

The Lords of Destiny series so far

Exodus

War Storm

Zodiac

Firebird

Reap the Hurricane

The Realm of Eagles
The Eagle Lord: Davos Saberlund
Banner: A white Eagle with outstretched wings and reaching talons on an emerald green background
Army: The Eagle Warriors
Sword: Aquilavesica (Eagle's Claw) the Eagle Blade

The Realm of Lions
The Lion Lord: Arc Saberlund
Banner: A red Lion raised up on its back legs on a yellow background
Army: The Lion Warriors
Sword: Leovesica, the Lion Blade

The Realm of Dragons
The Dragon Lord: Axan Saberlund
Banner: Black Dragon with its great wings spread over a red background
Army: The Dragon Warriors
Sword: Dracovesica, the Dragon Blade.

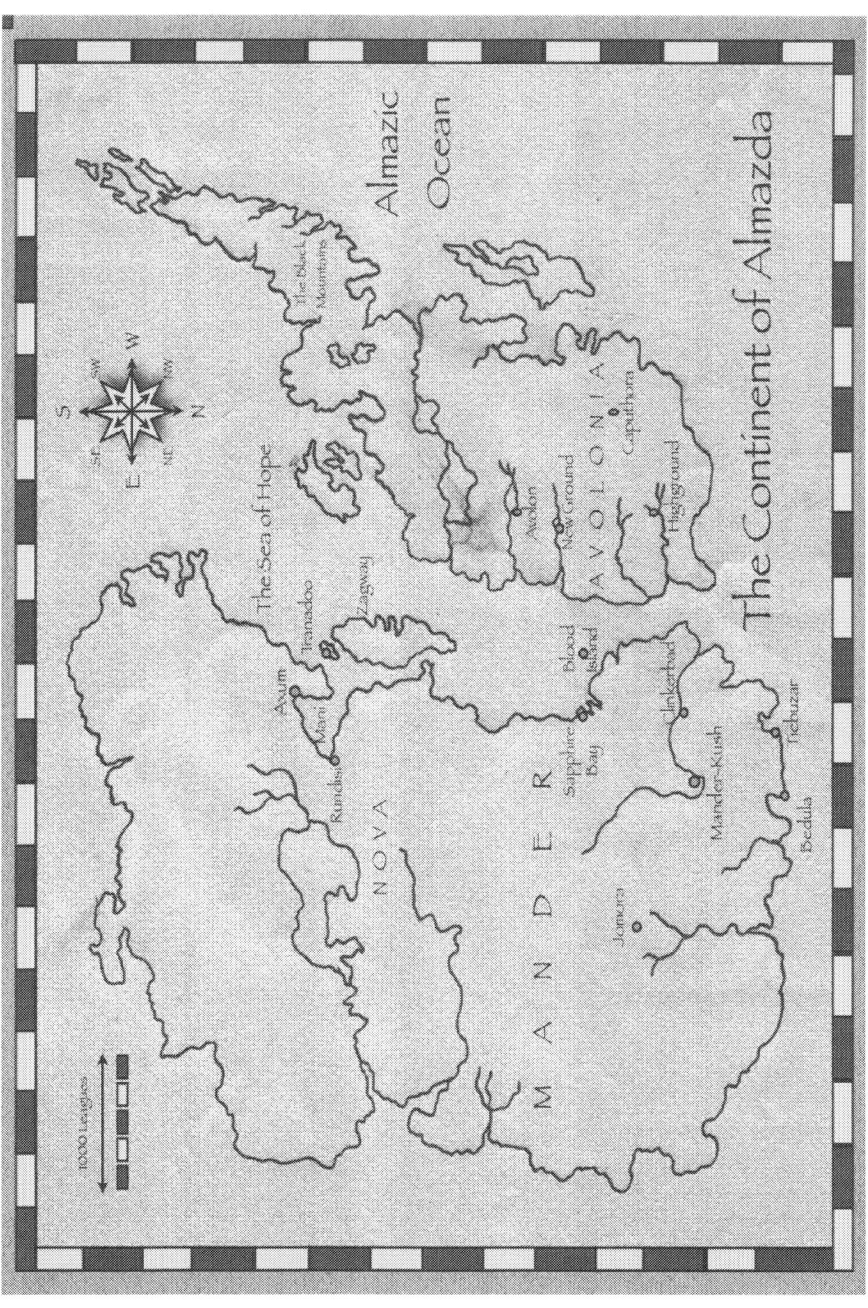
The Continent of Almazda
Almazic Ocean
The Sea of Hope
The Black Mountains
A V O L O N I A
Avolon
New Ground
Highground
Tranadoo
Zagway
Axum
Mani
N O V A
M A N D E R
Sapphire Bay
Blood Island
Jomora
Mander-Kush
Tiebuzar
Bedula
1000 Leagues
N
S
E
W

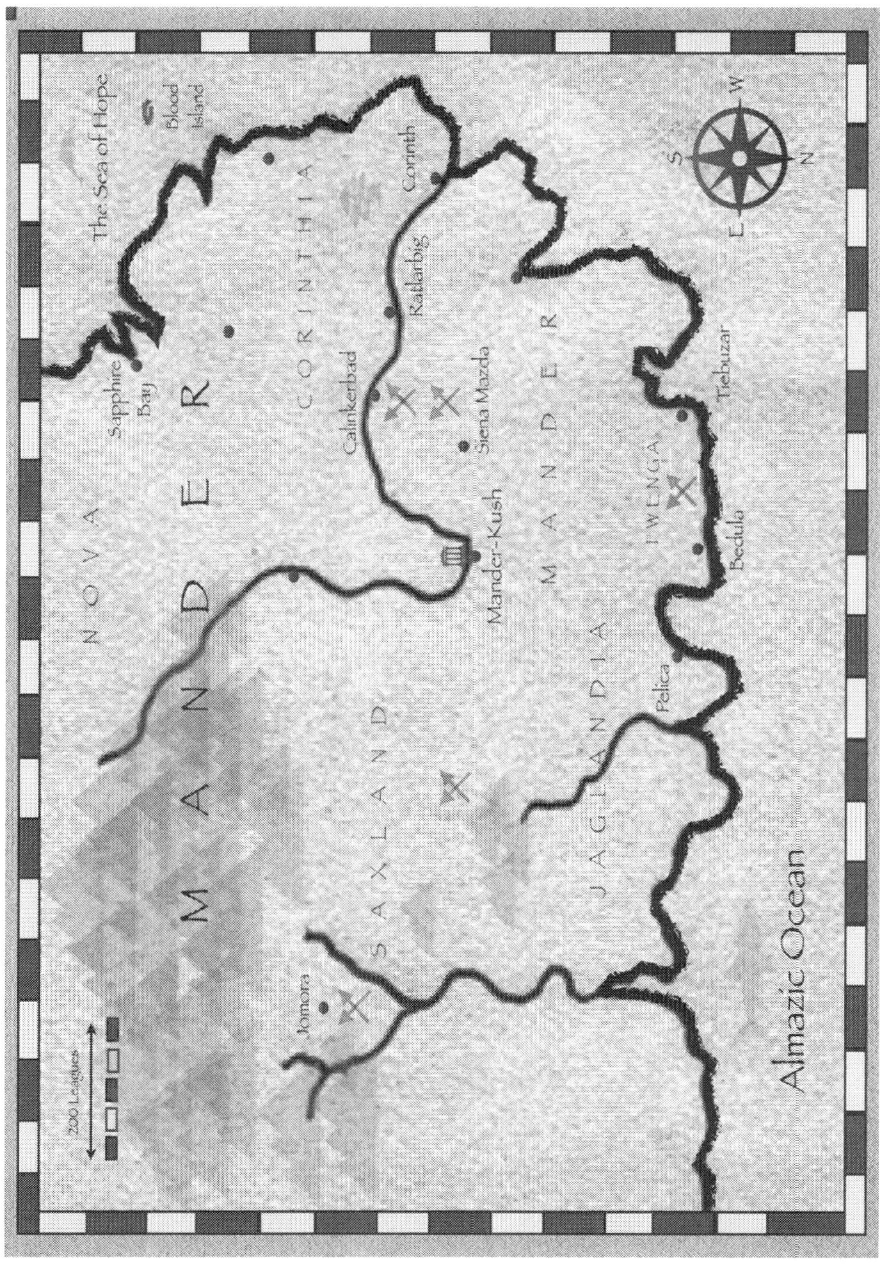
The Sea of Hope
Blood Island
Sapphire Bay
NOVA
MANDER
CORINTHIA
Corinth
Ratlarbig
Calinkerbad
Siena Mazda
Mander-Kush
MANDER
EWENGA
Trebuzar
Bedula
Pelica
JAGLANDIA
SAXLAND
Jomora
200 Leagues
Almazic Ocean
N
S
E
W

Prologue

The story so far

It was the dream of men that three lords with one destiny would one day come to lead the world into a utopia, free of cruelty and oppression. Foretold in ancient times, was the story of three brothers who would become lords. A prophecy passed down through the ages by Pathfinders, who guide the world towards their vision of destiny. From the shadows, by the side of kings and queens, and with a hand in most things that come to pass, the last three Pathfinders toil to see the prophecy fulfilled.

The Lion's blade has swept a thousand souls from this world of mortals. Arc has cut and thrust his way into the history of Almazda. From humble beginnings as a captain in Highground's City Guard to the Lion Lord of Avolonia, leading a crusade across Mander, he has survived against all the odds.

Rising through the ranks of his enemy, Arc led Mander troops to victory, and became the Lion Warrior. He returned to his homeland, followed by the brave warriors he had led in the east. He found his two stepbrothers, and together they defeated the Merron hordes to become the three Lords of Destiny.

As the Lion Lord, Arc led the Avolonians into a new land. He built cities, bringing peace and order to a wild land. But the Mander came, led by the Prince who had been Arc's patron during his days in service to the Empire. Arc defeated Atropolis' forces at Caputhora, turning the tide of the battle by charging the enemy on his great black warhorse, Shadin.

The Lion Lord may have been victorious at Caputhora, but his heart died on that battlefield. Atropolis had Arc's youngest daughter slain in a bitter act of vengeance. A cold flame of hate and revenge was lit within the Lord, and he vowed to destroy Atropolis and his father's empire.

Arc left his fledgling nation in the hands of his stepbrother, Davos, to lead the Lion Crusade across the Sea of Hope. He has lost his home, his wife, and his youngest daughter to Mander cruelty and oppression. The Lion Lord has risen against the white-fanged beast of Empire. His warning echoing through every town and city across Mander. '*You have sown the winds of tyranny, now you shall reap the hurricane of retribution.*'

The Lion Crusade has clawed its way along the blood-soaked path of vengeance, to reach deep within the Mander homeland. Every victory dragging Arc deeper into the realms of darkness, where hatred and loathing wait in the shadows to pick the flesh from his soul. With their shackles of oppression left lying in the dust, a freed people have risen to join Arc's crusade. Victory or death. There is no longer room in this world for both nations to exist. In the end, there can be only one... that is their inevitable... Destiny.

Chapter 1

The Lion Crusade

Enola

Gavara carefully made his way down the stony path leading to the opal-coloured water of the mountain lake. He used one hand to steady himself on the rocks while he negotiated the more substantial steps with his frail, stick-like limbs. No one knew how old the Pathfinder was, and he had no intention of revealing such secrets. He was the keeper of much darker mysteries than the conundrum about his age.

Once he had reached the remote lake's side, Gavara sat on a smooth rock, watching the lithe figure swimming. He smiled as the young woman burst through the surface of the lake, only to fold her naked body and dive back down into the depths.

Enola was aware of the old man watching her, of course. She was a warrior of great renown, and little escaped her observation. Enola laid her head back in the icy water and allowed her body to float. She felt the warmth of the sun on her face and breasts, as she allowed her mind to swim in the same kind of tranquillity her body was experiencing.

Gavara watched her calmly floating towards him. He admired her womanly beauty, not in a sexual way, those thoughts were something that no longer troubled him at his age. But he did love beautiful things, and Enola had that something different, something unusual, that captivates the imagination.

'I knew I would find you here,' Gavara called out, as Enola floated to within a few strides of his rock.

She rolled onto her front and let her feet drop to find the pebbled bed of the lake. She sauntered towards the shore, the water level dropping lower on her body with every stride of her long legs. Enola made no attempt to hide her nakedness from the old man. Even if he had not been like a grandfather to her, she was confident and accustomed to being naked around men.

Gavara marvelled at the muscle tone of her body, she was like a racehorse. She was a warrior, toned on the training grounds, but she retained enough femininity to be desired by any man. The old man felt a morsel of pity for the young woman. She would have been the most beautiful person he had ever seen were it not for the scar down the left side of her face, that shaped her eye into a perpetual squint. Yet even that disfigurement added to her unique attractiveness and made her more alluring.

Most of the women men found attractive these days were soft and skinny with large breasts. When Gavara did think about that sort of thing, he preferred something with a little more meat on the bone. Enola had the correct shape for modern preferences, but was hard and muscle toned. She didn't look quite right in the flimsy dresses women found fashionable at the moment, but in her warrior's attire, she was a goddess.

'You are a creature of exorbitant beauty, my dear,' Gavara told the young woman while watching droplets of water roll over her chest and down her flat stomach.

'You're a dirty old man,' she said, smirking. 'I should have my father cut off your head so there's one less pervert in the world.'

Gavara huffed. 'I am no such thing, and you are very capable of cutting my head off yourself, without having to run and tell tales to your father.'

Enola dried off with a blanket and dressed herself, hitching her leather kilt over her hips, and pulling her cotton tunic over her head.

'Did my father send you to smooth things over?' Enola asked with cold assuredness, as she came to sit alongside the old man.

'You know better than that,' Gavara replied, placing a comforting hand on her leg, below the hem of her kilt, her flesh still icy cold from her swim. 'Your father does not smooth things over. If he gives an order, you take it or leave it, but you don't negotiate with a force of nature. You may as well ask the rain to stop falling or the birds to stop singing. No, I am here because I know you are your father's daughter. He may have banned you from entering the leadership contest, but I know you. You are likely to get yourself seriously injured or killed trying to defy him.'

Arc was gathering together his best warriors to form an elite strike force. A multitude of tribes, races, and creeds had flocked to his banner, each with their own heroes and elite fighters. They currently fought separately as sections, but Arc hoped to bring them all together under one banner. He knew to do that successfully, he could not just choose a leader as it would show favour to one faction and be resented by the others. So, Arc had announced a contest. The winner would take command of the new elite force.

Gavara had designed a course full of obstacles and challenges. The best warriors from all factions were invited to take part. The course had many dangers, and more than one of the obstacles were life-threatening. The winner of such a contest would indeed be worthy of leading an army's elite troops. As a commander in her father's Lion Warriors, Enola jumped at the chance to take part, but Arc had denied her that right, forbidding her to enter.

Enola laughed at the old man. 'You may be clever old man, but if you think you can talk me out of it, you're not as clever as I thought you were.'

Gavara gave her a kind smile. 'As I said, you are your father's daughter, and I know better than to waste my breath telling the rain to stop falling. No, I am here to make you an offer. If you are determined to compete, then I will train you.'

Enola laughed again. 'My father will cut your balls off if he finds out. Anyway, what makes you think that I need your training?'

Gavara tried his best to frown. He had spent his life manipulating the fate of others. His intention on this occasion was more about keeping the young woman he was so fond of alive, rather than influencing the outcome of the competition.

'Your father will find out, undoubtedly. Luckily, I have no use for my balls anymore.' Enola threw her head back and laughed. Gavara enjoyed her amusement for a moment, before continuing. 'I have designed a course that will put fear into warriors who previously feared nothing and nobody. I will teach you the skills you will need to survive, and I will hear no more about it.'

Arc

Slim clouds drifted across the azure heavens, shifting shadows over the baked ground. Out in the open fields, away from the sour-smelling camps, the air tasted of jasmine. The Lion Crusade had attracted over a hundred thousand followers, and that did not come without its problems. Multitudes of people living on top of each other in cramped conditions created a melting pot of disease.

Arc made sure he kept the Warriors' tents separate from the followers'. They were laid out with military precision, with well-dug latrines and cesspits. Plenty of clean water and good sanitation kept sickness at bay. But Arc could not stop the men from visiting the followers' camps, to see their wives or other camp women. It was on such visits that warriors picked up the stomach sickness. The longer the army stayed in one spot, the larger the epidemic became.

Gavara advised the Lion Lord to keep the army moving. 'People need to leave their foul maladies behind,' he had protested.

Arc did not find it easy to follow his old friend's advice. After a battle, men needed time to recover. Provisions had to be gathered, and newly liberated provinces reorganised so that they would not fall back under Mander control as soon as the army moved on. People who had lived under Mander oppression all their lives were only too happy to join the crusade and maintain their newfound freedom. But there were others who had thrived under Mander rule, and they would always present a danger.

Arc had won over many of the indigenous leaders, persuading them to join his cause of freeing the world of Mander oppression, and bringing their fighting men under his banner. Decades of taxes and segregation that the Mander had inflicted on their occupied lands made Arc's job all the easier. The people had been left with nothing to lose, whole regions seethed with an undercurrent of hate and desperation. Change of any kind was seen as salvation, and welcomed with open arms, even if it meant dying for one's freedom.

Today, everyone had come out to witness the trial to select the leader and officers for Arc's new modern army. The hills around the grasslands were smothered with spectators. Warriors stood in lines on the perimeters of the open field, waiting to show their skill with bow and javelin. Gavara wanted the first round of the trials to include equestrian skills, but Arc had deemed it too risky for the precious horses. He knew all too well what cumbersome brutes some of the infantry officers were, and he would not see good horse stock damaged to prove that.

Excited children scrambled and played around the ropes marking out makeshift arenas where contests of sword and wrestling would take place. Each contestant would have to win in both before moving on to the main event. The loser of either game was instantly eliminated. Only the one hundred best of the day would make it to the race.

Gavara had set out a course that would test the contestants' strength, stamina, speed and agility. The challenges would also test the bravery and cunning of the participants, with many problems to solve and many fears to face. Every entrant who finished the course would be guaranteed a commission in the new army. It would be respect well earned.

Enola

Enola took her place in the lines. There were other spear-maidens entered in the contest, so she tried to blend in amongst them. Over fifteen hundred entrants stood ready, all eager to be tested, all dreaming of leading their own army. Every man and woman there could taste the honour, feel the admiration of the soldiers that would worship the ground they walked on. Egos were swollen, and the air reeked of ambition.

The Lioness made short work of the bow challenge. The equipment was standard army issue, and hugely inferior to her own hand-crafted bow, but Enola had learned to shoot at a young age. Stann, her guardian during the time she was separated from her father, had taught her to hunt with a bow in the forests around Ribbelstead.

The challenge was to hit a fist-sized bull's-eye on a target one hundred paces away with one of three arrows. Enola missed the bull's-eye with her first shot, but after adjusting her aim for the crude weapon's limitations, she slammed the remaining two shafts bang into the centre.

'Nothing less than I'd expect from our lord and master's daughter,' the sergeant manning the archery station commented, as he took the bow from Enola, and passed it to the next in line. 'What on earth are you doin' here, missy?'

She lifted a finger to pursed lips, her wide eyes communicating her desire for him to make less of a fuss.

'Oh,' he exclaimed, in realisation. 'Good on ya, missy, and best of luck.'

Enola smiled at the sergeant as she took the ribbon that would get her through to the Javelin challenge.

More people recognised the Lioness in the next line, and a small crowd gathered to watch her throw the javelin. This was a standard training bolt, the sort Enola had thrown a thousand times before. The challenge was to throw the weapon over a set length and within a set corridor. Enola's technique was flawless, and while she may not have achieved the longest throw of the day, it was easily the straightest. The javelin pierced the ground ten paces beyond the distance marker and slap bang in the middle of the corridor. The crowd applauded her efforts, and she quickly took the ribbon and moved on.

Halfway through the morning the sword contests got underway. Enola was pitted against a young corporal from the auxiliary units. At first, the young soldier looked confident when he realised he would be fighting a woman, a mistake many of the younger men make. His expression soon turned to one of concern when he realised who she was. He was suddenly more concerned about avoiding humiliation, as a crowd rushed to his arena to see Enola fight.

He was right to worry. Dozens of men before him had been humiliated by Enola's speed and skill with a blade. The corporal stood tall and proud as Enola came in low, swaying from side to side. He never even saw the first strike coming, or if he did, he was too slow to react. His humiliation was complete when the next two attacks came just as fast, and he was out of the contest without scoring a single hit on the Lioness.

Fifteen hundred had been whittled down to four hundred, and the sword contest had seen that number reduced to two hundred. The wrestling challenge would see the contestants reduced to the final one hundred. Enola was pleased to see that more than a dozen spear-maidens had made the cut, and a couple of those looked like they would have any man there for breakfast.

Antona and Eric joined Enola on the hill where the contestants watched the wrestling bouts while waiting their turn. The three of them sat on the grass, Enola in the middle, flanked by her two oldest friends. They had known each other since their cadet days, and the siege of Yalta. It was in that ancient bastion that Enola had killed her first man. Ever since then, her two friends had been by her side. Both had been her lover at one time or another, but they had come to realise that they were nothing more than sparring partners in her journey of self-discovery. Their friendship had survived through the years, and the two young officers were dedicated to protecting Enola. Both of them carried a torch for her that burned as brightly as ever.

'What number do you have?' Eric asked showing the black one hundred, and thirty-six daubed onto the underside of his forearm. Antona showed his eighty-four, and Enola her twenty-nine. 'Oh dear, you could end up facing either of us,' he pointed out to Enola. 'They are pitting odd numbers against even numbers.'

Enola laughed. 'I should be so lucky as to draw one of you two no-hopers.'

Eric looked hurt by her comment, whereas Antona just smirked.

'Doesn't matter who you face,' Antona stated. 'Your father is going to kill you for entering.'

'I'm not his little girl anymore, I'm a grown woman, and I have proved myself on the battlefield time and again,' Enola argued. 'He will respect my decision, once he has seen me qualify and earn my place in the race.'

It was Eric's turn to laugh. 'You will always be his little girl, but even you don't get to defy the Lion Warrior and get away with it.'

They did not have to wrestle each other, all three would face strangers in the arena. Enola took particular interest in the women's bouts. They all faced larger men, except for Enyo and Elektra, two sisters who were bigger than most men competing. Elektra smashed a brute of a man to qualify, breaking his arm in the process.

Enyo fought Hals, one of the favourites to win the contest. She did well at the beginning of the bout, making Hals work hard to gain the first submission. The match ended when Hals broke her fingers and twisted her into a choke hold. Enyo, named after a little-known goddess of war and fury, had to be carried out of the arena unconscious, her windpipe probably damaged.

Antona won his bout without conceding a point, with one fall and a submission gaining the two points needed out of a best of three contest. Eric had a much harder time of it. His bout was drawn one all, and the final score was contested fiercely. In the end, he won on a technicality, but the contest had taken a lot out of him.

'I told you to lay off the pastries and wine, and stick to the meat and milk, like me,' Antona teased his friend.

But Eric, red in the face and drenched in sweat, was too exhausted to come back with any rebuttal.

It was now noon, and the day was getting warmer. Enola watched on, as only two other women made it through the wrestling round before it was time for her to compete. She glanced at the thunderclouds forming on the horizon, as she stepped into the arena. The growing clouds seemed to be calling out an ominous message to her, giving her an uneasy feeling. Enola knew better than to let doubt find its way into her thoughts. Positivity would win the day, and she would not allow herself to think about anything other than a successful outcome.

Enola pursed her lips into a tight smile when she saw her opponent. He was a head taller than her and had arms as thick as her legs. She threw a little curse at the Gods for not giving her the luckiest of draws. She let out a sigh and accepted her fate, dropping low and opening her arms to show that she was ready to start.

'Go low,' she told herself, as the brute took his first steps towards her.

Maximo had been a wall builder before joining the crusade. He had spent his days lifting heavy rocks and now trained every day as a warrior. The big soldier was accustomed to throwing larger men around. He grinned like an idiot, unable to believe his luck, when he saw who his opponent was to be. He swaggered towards Enola, his guard down, inviting her to attack.

Enola sprang like a panther at Maximo's legs, thrusting her arms around his knees, and pumping her legs in the hope of driving him back and off balance. It was like running into a tree. With all her efforts, Maximo took no more than one step back. Enola grunted and pushed until she was red in the face, but Maximo stood his ground. He reached down and placed his shovel-like hand at the back of Enola's neck, trapping her against his legs. Then the tree fell, but not as Enola had intended.

Maximo came down on the back of Enola, driving the wind from her lungs. She was trapped against the dry ground with Maximo's full weight on her back. She could not breathe. She held out as long as she could, eventually having to tap out in fear that she would pass out. The crowd cheered, some even jeered at the ease of which Maximo scored his first point.

Enola brushed herself down and drank some water. It took her several deep breaths to recover. When she turned to face Maximo, he was already waiting, smirking, eager to finish the contest. She wiped the sweat from her brow, and to the delight of the growing crowd, she took her place.

Enola could hear Gavara's voice in her head, recalling what he had taught her.

'Bend like the branches of a willow tree swaying in the wind,' she heard him saying. *'The windweaver tree is the last thing standing after a great hurricane,'* Gavara had told her. *'The Mighty oak ripped up at the roots, and the solid pine broken in half because they stood firm against the storm's fury. The willow's flexibility is its strength, letting itself bend and fold until the wind tires and moves on.'*

'What do you know about fighting?' Enola had challenged her tutor.

'I once taught gladiators their art,' Gavara had replied. *'A philosophy of movement and forces. When an unstoppable force meets an immovable object, there is no more than a collision of force, but when one uses the power of the other against itself, the impossible can happen.'*

Maximo grew impatient, eager to please the crowd he advanced. Enola let him come on and rolled out of his first attempt at a grip. Again, and again she turned out of his arms as he tried to enclose her in his grasp. Maximo's anger was quick to surface and he lunged without care. Enola guided him past her each time, using his own momentum to throw him off balance. He fell into the dust twice and was furious to hear the crowd cheer.

It was Maximo who was now red in the face and panting. His heavy build favoured a quick finish and he knew it. He bounded towards Enola, determined to trap her in his grasp. Enola was cornered on the side of the fighting area. She waited until Maximo's eyes lit up with the thought that he had her then, like a small bird taking to flight, she made her move.

Enola wrapped herself around Maximo's waist and slithered around the back of his legs. He grasped frantically at the serpent twisting around him, but he could not get a grip. Before he knew what had happened, Maximo was tumbling out of the arena and crashing into the crowd. He hit the ground hard, taking several of the spectators with him.

The biggest cheer of the day so far went up from the spectators. It was a technical fall and a point for Enola.

The grass felt crisp underfoot, as Arc strolled across the top of the hill to where Gavara had erected a rostrum for himself and the elite of his military staff to watch the day's events. In front of the mound, a large arena had been laid out on the flattest area. This would be where the final games would take place. From the benches of the tribune, Arc and his guests would have a grandstand view of the proceedings.

A flock of Almazic starlings swooped and twisted in the sky above the arena. Hundreds of individuals moving and changing direction in unison as if they were one. The birds, with their intricate displays of folding patterns and varying shades, entertained anyone who turned their gaze skyward.. Arc found it difficult to take his eyes off the flock as they performed their aerial dance.

Gavara was already sitting on a bench in the centre of the tribunes when the Lion Lord arrived. With him were Edius-Max, Grand Master Razor of the Jagger Knights and several other generals. They had all taken their seat early, not wanting to miss any of the day's excitement.

'Good day, gentlemen,' Arc announced, making sure he had everyone's attention. 'I'll bet there is not a man amongst us that would not rather be down there competing.' He knew each man had a favourite from their own legions, so amused himself by poking a stick into that hornets' nest. 'Who do we favour to take the day?'

'The wise money is on Hals,' came the first suggestion from Edius-Max.

'You would say that as he is your legion champion,' Razor retorted. 'Maximo is about to fight. He's from the new auxiliaries, built like a stone outhouse. I've seen him throw men across the training ground as if they were bundled rags.'

'Dozens of the auxiliaries are built that way, and as strong as oxen. I think they feed them lion's meat from birth,' one of the generals chipped in.

'They do grow them big around here, must be something in the water,' another spectator commented.

'You're all missing the point' Gavara interrupted, sounding defensive. 'It's not all about strength. Today is about the ability to overcome all odds, and that will take more than brute force.' A cheer interrupted Gavara's explanation of the contests priorities. He quickly continued in a raised voice, attempting to regain everyone's attention. He knew full well that the cheer came from the arena where Enola was wrestling and wanted to distract everyone. 'It will take intelligence and great skill to win this day.'

No one was listening to the old man. All eyes had turned to the arena where the excitement came from. The crowd was thick around the field and the spectators in the stands could only manage a fleeting glimpse of the contestants.

'What about you, Cid?' Arc called out to the imposing figure of a Jagger Knight, who sat with his head in hands watching the contest. Cid sat up and turned to face his commander. 'You would be my best guess and favourite to beat any man out there.'

Cid grinned. 'I'm a Knight of the Jagger order, through and through. Why would I want to command your legion of misfits and inbreeds?'

Arc laughed. 'Bloody snobs you Knights, all of you.'

Razor gave Arc a disapproving sideways glance. He was looking old for his age and more so since the battle at Fwenga. He had been gravely injured in the fight to defeat Salamanca and his Mander Army. The Cid, as he was known, had pulled him from the clutches of death. Razor was slowly recovering his strength, but it was doubtful that he would ever ride into another battle at the head of his army.

'He will be Grand Master when my days are over,' Razor told Arc, his statement laced with pride. Cid was Razor's nephew, and the finest knight in the Jagger order.

'I'd give my newly acquired hand-crafted Arian saddle for a chance to test myself against that lot,' Cid told everyone listening. 'But it is Jagger blood that flows through my veins, and until my uncle is well the order needs me. Is that not correct, Grand Master?'

Arc leaned forward and slapped Razor on the back, causing the ageing general to wince. 'You have a fine one there. You can retire with the knowledge that your Knights are in good hands.'

'Retire, don't be ridiculous,' Razor blustered. 'There is a whole bundle of things I need to teach the lad before he's ready.'

Not a man there thought Razor would ever return to actively leading the Knights. It was the hope of most that the Grand Master would remain in nothing more than an honorary role from now on and leave the leadership of the Knights to Cid.

'And I am ready to learn, Uncle,' Cid called out, in unashamed support of Razor.

Another cheer went up from the crowd below, and everyone in the tribunes stood up to get a better look.

'That spear-maiden in the arena looks incredibly like Enola,' Edius-Max pointed out. 'Is she entered?'

Arc looked across at Gavara, his anger plain for all to see. 'I'll have your balls for this, Gavara'

'Funny you should mention that, I thought about bringing them gift-wrapped for you.'

Arc's expression flicked between anger and confusion, finally settling on the latter. 'Explain yourself, you old witch.'

Gavara rolled his eyes at the insult. 'She has your stubborn blood running through her veins, and she possesses the skills and abilities of any man here.' Gavara took a deep breath, puffing himself up. 'And what's more, she has the strength and courage of a lion. To refuse her entry would be like standing in the way of her destiny.'

'By the gods, man. She is a warrior who rides into battle alongside the best of them. I don't think letting her compete in some games will cause her much harm,' an Arian general called Memfis pointed out.

'When I want your two bits worth of silver, I will ask for it,' Arc snapped, regretting the put down as soon as the words had passed his lips.

Gavara did not know whether to be pleased for the general's support or annoyed because he had called his contest 'some games'.

'She has every right to enter, and by pulling her out now, you would destroy the credibility of the contest. You must let nature take its course.'

'He's not wrong,' Edius-Max said, trying to be helpful. 'Anyway, I have seen some of the obstacles in the race, no woman is strong enough to complete the tasks on that course.'

Arc's face was a picture of turmoil. If he withdrew Enola, it would not only lose credibility for the contest, but also the respect Enola's warriors had for her. The commander in him knew what had to be done, but the father in him was dancing around with anxiety.

'As you have said to me many times,' Arc turned to Gavara, 'I can no more control a free spirit like Enola than I can control the clouds in the sky. You have left me no choice, old man. But if this goes wrong, if...'

'Yes, yes I know,' Gavara butted in, 'my balls. If this goes wrong, you will have my balls. I may as well carry the blasted things around in a jar.'

Razor laughed, 'I don't think you will have to worry too much about her getting to the race, that's Maximo in the ring with her. He will fold her inside out and hang her from his belt.'

'Want to make a wager on that, Uncle?' Cid asked, with a glint in his eye.

Enola

Maximo bellowed like a wounded bull, his rage showing in his eyes. He was eager to finish off his opponent, but he hesitated while his feeble mind strained itself to work out if he was overlooking any advantage the spear-maiden may be hiding. His ego soon overcoming his wits he rushed in. The spectators cheered, their eyes wide with excitement, the thrill of the moment whipping them into a frenzy.

The score was one all, the next fall or submission would be the decider. Most of the other wrestling bouts between closely matched men had been fought in a constant embrace or rolling around on the ground, like a beast with two backs, until one or the other gained a technical advantage. Enola against Maximo was a different affair, something more exciting for the crowd. Enola knew that if Maximo managed to get her into a grip she would be finished, so this was a match of moves and counter moves, cat and mouse.

Enola made no attacking moves, she got Maximo to overshoot, overbalance and even to trip by moving with him instead of against him. He brought the power, and she guided it, like the windweaver willow tree, guiding the hurricane through its branches. Maximo was tiring, and his frustration grew with every humiliating stumble. Enola remained calm and patient, waiting for the soft underbelly to be exposed before she dared to strike.

Luck threw Maximo a bone. As he rushed at Enola, all fury and sweat, she turned her ankle on a stone.

Momentarily stunned by the pain, she was slow to react. Maximo howled with relief as he felt her lithe body trapped in his grasp. He immediately levered one arm under hers, securing his grip, and wrapped the other around her neck. Enola was locked fast in a choke hold. She could feel the blood pumping into her head as she tensed every muscle in her neck and shoulders to resist the pressure.

The crowd cheered the turn of events, not favouring one contestant over the other, but rather thrilling to the excitement of the contest. The mood of the spectators soon changed when they realised this could be the end of the drama, and many of them screamed frantically at Enola to do something. It seemed unlikely that the encouragement would be of any help, Enola could feel the life draining from her, and she gasped for breath to no avail.

Maximo was grinning like an idiot, and dribbling like a dumb hog as he enjoyed feeling the strength drain from Enola. He didn't expect the blow to the face, that seemed to come out of nowhere. Enola folded like a pocket knife, her legs swinging upward, delivering a mighty blow to Maximo's head. The brute was shocked, but his grip did not slacken. Enola hung onto his arms with both hands and swung again. This time her feet connected with his nose and broke it.

Maximo's grip slackened just enough for Enola to shift her weight. She swung her legs up again, but this time gripped his bull-like neck between them. She locked her ankles behind his head, ignoring the pain it caused her, and began to choke him. Maximo released his grip on Enola to prise her legs from his neck, but before he could, she swung her body up to wrap her arms around the back of his head. The momentum of the move sent Maximo staggering backwards. He was so top heavy with Enola attached to his head, that even his great strength could not hold him up. He toppled backwards, and crashed to the ground, his shoulders pinned by all of Enola's weight.

The crowd were stunned into silence. Enola felt Maximo's powerful arms start to lift her. She tightened her grip on his head and twisted her whole body to get it to rotate at an angle, as Gavara had shown her to do. The force vanished from Maximo's arms, the nerves that brought them strength pinched in the twist of his spine. The marshal called out a hold, and the spectators went berserk, cheering and shouting. Enola had triumphed.

Ninety-seven winners of the preliminary rounds paraded past the VIP grandstand. One-hundred had successfully made it through, but three had sustained injuries in the wrestling round that prevented them from racing. Many of those in the parade were limping, or clutching an arm, or rubbing their neck. All but a few looked tired already. Enola tried to keep her chin up as she passed the stern gaze of her father. She expected to hear his voice at any moment, calling her out of the procession. Arc remained silent, and Enola was allowed to join her friends at the start line.

Antona looked as fresh as a daisy and was hopping around like a fly on a hot stone, to keep his blood up for the race. Eric looked more like a man who had just finished a race, than a man about to start one.

'I know how you feel,' Enola greeted the red-faced Eric.

'There'll be no stopping Flash here,' Eric swung his thumb towards the bouncing Antona.

'Oh, don't worry about that one, all thunder and no lightning,' Enola chuckled to see Antona frown at her.

'More like all fart and no turds,' Eric added, unable to prevent himself from laughing at his own wit.

Antona raised an eyebrow to show his contempt, rather than chomping at the baited conversation obviously intended to distract him.

Enola stopped laughing, as she felt a heavy hand on her shoulder. She turned, expecting to see one of the many muscle-bound officers she knew. It was Elektra. The man-like woman stood a head taller than her and at least twice as wide at the shoulders.

'I saw you fight Maximo, mam,' Elektra blurted out, with the admiration of a little girl swooning over her idol.

Enola felt the heat of her face reddening with embarrassment. 'It was nothing.'

'No,' Elektra quickly disagreed, the veins in her neck standing out and the muscles in her chest twitching. 'No, he was my training partner. I could never have done that to him. You used your head. The likes of me and Maximo don't have the brains of the likes of you. We are blunt clubs, swinging at loose vines, fighting someone like you.'

Enola could see the giant woman was trying to make a point, and struggling to reach her objective. 'Thank you, you are too kind. You and your sister are the strongest women I have ever seen.' Enola could hear the condescension in her voice as she spoke and hoped it did not offend.

Elektra shook her head. 'Strength alone will not win this contest. Power and cleverness need to work together.'

Enola furrowed her brow, trying to fathom what the spear-maiden was trying to say.

'Flippin' heck,' Antona butted in. 'She is offering you an alliance in the race.'

Elektra nodded vigorously. 'That's it. I know I don't have the brains to lead like you do. Let me be your power. I would follow you anywhere. You must win this contest.'

Enola gazed into the surprisingly gentle eyes of her new ally, not knowing whether to be flattered or insulted by her statement. 'So, you think I cannot win this alone?'

Elektra looked hurt, realising the offence in her words. 'I meant no insult, it's just,' she paused, 'I helped bring the logs we must carry through the forest.' The race was divided into several parts, a run, heavy log carrying, a rock climb, a swim and finishing with a second run. 'I could just about carry a log,' Elektra explained herself. 'You will never be able to lift it over the river crossing and the obstacles. You must win,' she pleaded. 'I will carry your log for you and return for my own.' She added the last part to show that she had no intention of giving up the race. She would help but still wanted to finish.

'No alliances are allowed,' Eric pointed out, thinking that if it were that easy, they would all be helping the Lioness win.

Enola gave a tight smile and nodded. 'He's right. Gavara designed this contest as something that needs to be overcome, not powered through. Thank you for your offer, and I will remember it, but I must find my own way through.' Enola reached up to place a hand on her new friend's shoulder, surprised at the size and hard tone of the muscle she gripped. 'You must do your best for yourself. If I win this, I will need good officers like you.'

Elektra grinned, happy at the thought of being an officer, and delighted that the Lioness would want her. She turned to leave, but not before pulling a threatening face at Eric for pointing out the flaw in her plan.

'If?' Antona questioned. 'If you win? Is that a sliver of doubt showing in the Lioness' confidence?'

Eric laughed. 'That would be a first.'

'Shut up you two, or I will get my enormous new friend to snap you in half.'

The sudden blast of a horn grabbed everyone's attention, and contestants made their way to the start line. The buzz of anticipation was palpable. The hum of excitement made hairs stand up on the back of necks, and eyes widened as if exposed to new light. Enola, Eric and Antona made a circle, gripped each other around the shoulder, and put their heads together.

'For us, if for no one else,' Enola spoke the saying they used as a good luck charm before battle.

'For us,' the other two repeated.

Several passers-by patted them on the back while they were in their huddle. The three friends parted and headed towards the line, swept along with the throng as if floating with the current of a slow flowing river. Silence fell upon the hopefuls while the rules were read out. Marshals on the course would ensure that contestants participated within the rules. Anyone disqualified would be sent back to their regiments in shame, and any rank forfeited. All those who finished the course in the spirit it was intended would be guaranteed a higher position in the new army. Only the first six back would be eligible to go through to the final two stages, which would decide the senior officers and the commander.

Another blast from the horn started the race. The crowd surged forward, all elbows as contestants jostled for position. The group soon thinned out as they entered the woods. Some weaved between the trees, leaping over fallen tree trunks and crashing through the undergrowth. Most kept to the trails, content to join the long lines that snaked their way through the woods.

Enola watched as both Antona and Eric became frustrated at the slow pace of the line they were in, and bolted into the trees to try and reach the front. Enola knew better. The race would not be won or lost in this first section. She would save her energy in the line, she would need it for the next stage, the log carry. Gavara had been clear about this first challenge. *'Slow and steady will not win the first stage, but it will help you win the race. Let the young bucks burn themselves out fighting through the undergrowth.'*

At the end of the run Enola felt tired enough. She joined the scramble for logs. Some of the bigger men were already crossing the river with the cumbersome trunk up on one shoulder. Enola stepped around one of the other women in the race who struggled to get a grip on her log. She tried to lift it twice and then gave up, deciding instead to drag it towards the river. Enola frowned at several of the men who made fun of the woman's efforts. At that moment, Elektra arrived, grabbed a log with her shovel-like hands, and hoisted it onto her shoulder.

'Well, don't just stand there gawping, that logs not going to carry itself,' Elektra called out as she sped off with the trunk seeming to cause her little if no hindrance.

Enola grabbed at a log, instantly shocked at its weight. She dragged it from the pile into an open space, like a wolf would drag its prey into the open to be devoured. She managed to get it up onto her shoulder, but after a few steps had to drop it. Twice more she tried, and twice more she dropped it. She tried to hold one end and drag it, but the log was pulled out of her hands every time the end of the log on the ground hit an obstacle. Every four or five steps, the trunk was torn from her grasp, it seemed useless.

'Brains, not brawn,' she told herself. She had seen Elektra run off with her log and saw the other two women wrestling the trunk in the same way she was. The river

suddenly looked a very long way off. Enola squeezed a memory from her mind. She thought back to how her father had once lifted a whole army, including the horses and artillery, up a cliff face using winches and harnesses. She unstrapped her belts, fastening one tightly around the end of the trunk, and using the other as a harness between her and the log. She hoisted the strap over her head, so that it sat on one shoulder, and heaved.

The log slid along, bouncing over obstacles instead of getting stuck, and Enola was able to make headway towards the river crossing. She was now at the back of the field and desperate to catch up. By the time she reached the river, most were already crossing. She saw one man thrashing at the water in frustration, his log floating downstream and his race over. A second man caught her attention. He was trying to drag his log across, but the water was too fast and pushed angrily at the end dipping into its current. He was a strong warrior but the river was stronger. He yelped as the log was wrenched from his grasp and taken down the river. He jumped in after it, but the trunk was carried further and further away from him.

Enola watched several more men lose their logs in the same way and admired those who successfully crossed with the trunk carried on their shoulder. The crossing was the only shallow part of the river, but the fast-flowing water cascading over the stepping stones made it an impossible hurdle for Enola. She looked to the cliffs down the river, they would be the third challenge. *'If only I could get there,'* she thought, *'I would, at last, have an advantage over the muscle-bound brutes.'*

Watching the river flow past her was hypnotising to Enola. She felt the urge to jump in and let the flow of water carry her away from her troubles. *'The only reasonable solution to this problem is unreasonable to me,'* she told herself. *'What would Gavara say about that?'* She laughed. *'Come on Gavara, you have a saying for everything.'* It hit her like a lightning bolt. *'When reason fails, look to the unreasonable.'* She heard Gavara in her head and decided what she must do.

Enola heaved her log down the river bank, letting it roll into the water. The current grabbed the wood pulling Enola off her feet and into its flow. At first, she scrambled to keep her head above water but then ducked under to get her head out of the harness. She wrapped the leather strap around her right arm and grasped hold of the log with her left. Each time she tried to clamber onto the wood, it rolled her off. She tightened the strap around her arm so that it was pinned to the log so tight it was cutting the blood supply off. It did the trick. Enola heaved herself up one more time, and the log held steady. Once she was up and had a tight grip on the wood, she kicked with all her strength to push her raft away from the near bank.

The river was like a dog with a stick, it pulled and pushed at the log, never releasing its grip, continually twisting and turning. Enola fought to keep straight enough to paddle across the flow. She could see the opposite bank rushing by. The cliffs were almost level with her, and she was not even halfway across. Enola began to doubt her decision, thinking she would inevitably be swept far too far down the river ever to come back to the cliffs.

The flow in the centre of the river was considerably lighter, and Enola was able to paddle across. She spotted an outcrop in the far bank further downstream, and paddled frantically into the faster current. The wilder water spun the log around, making Enola twist and tug to try and regain control. The whirling current won the battle and pulled her under the surface. Enola kicked and pushed, but each time her head broke the surface, she was instantly pushed under again. She held her breath until she thought her lungs would burst.

There is a sense of calm once you accept the inevitable and give up the fight. But Enola had done all but give up. She could not get her head above water, but she still had a grip on the log, and she could again kick. The rapid current pulled and twisted Enola who sensed the end was close, as she fought for her life, cursing the decision to tie herself so tightly to the log. Her last chance was to free herself, but she could not.

There was a violent thud as Enola's face was slammed against the log. The pain of the impact caused her to push out with both legs. Her feet slammed into the shingle coated riverbed, and her head was forced through the surface, and out of the water. She took an enormous gasp of air, expecting to be dragged back under. She was not. The log had stuck fast in the roots of overhanging trees growing on the outcrop of the riverbank. Enola had made it. She was across, half drowned, coughing and spluttering, but still in possession of her log.

Arc

The Lion Lord watched as his daughter disappeared into the crowd of runners. It felt strange worrying about her. He had watched her ride into battle, seen her cut his enemies to pieces, but in his mind she was still the little girl who would often climb onto his lap like a cat and fall asleep in his arms. A hand on his shoulder disturbed Arc from his memories.

'Lord, we must go,' it was Gavara. 'The Corinthians are here.'

Arc wanted nothing more than to follow the race, to watch his daughter and his elite warriors competing. Instead, he would have to be content with entertaining Odexsius, chief of the Corinthians, and his overbearing son, Tyezore. They were the guests of honour. Odexsius was a chief in exile, his kingdom governed by Mander. His family had ruled for generations, puppets of the Empire. When Odexsius had protested against Mander taxation without representation, the Emperor, Al-Din simply replaced him with his more agreeable brother.

Arc led a procession of his generals over to the lavish canvas structure Gavara had designed and built for the occasion, it was like a ship stranded a thousand leagues from the sea. Great sails slowly turned in the breeze, casting shadows over a vast decking to protect it from the midday sun. Tables filled with all kinds of foods covered three sides of the wooden flooring. On the fourth side was a raised platform with the Lion Lord's ivory throne, sitting in the centre.

The throne had been taken from the Palace of Tibuzar, as spoils of war. Great white tusks from giant elephants, long since hunted into extinction, curled in all directions to form the back, sides and seat of the throne. Arc hated the chair, said it smelt like ghosts, but he had to admit it looked awe-inspiring, and today was about impressing. Arc wasn't fond of the rest of the furnishings, either. Colourful, upholstered sofas in the Corinthian style were scattered about in clusters.

'Where do you find these things?' Arc asked his old advisor while using his foot to test out the cushioning of a baby blue sofa.

Gavara stepped in to brush off the dusty footprint. 'Odexsius' aids brought them. He will bring his wives, and apparently his concubines, with him. They are accustomed to relaxing in comfort and have every intention of doing so while your generals woo them.'

'Woo the women, what kind of treaty are we planning to make with these people?' Memfis asked.

Gavara waved his hands about, as he did when he was pretending to be annoyed at being asked an obvious question but was really glad to be given a chance to showcase his knowledge. 'Understanding a man's culture is the key to understanding the man. The Corinthians are spiritual people. They believe the wise spirits of their ancestors reside in their women and the brave spirits in their men. Odexsius would not contemplate making a decision about an alliance with us without the approval of the wise spirits.'

'So, if the Chief's wives and whores don't find us charming, the deal's off?'

'That's about the size of it,' Gavara pointed out.

Arc studied his old friend. It had been more than a decade since they had met, and he was trying to decide if he looked any older. Gavara still had the same long, wispy, white hair and beard. His face was as sharp, wrinkled and noble as it ever was. He had returned to wearing the long, thin, white robes that let the light through to reveal his bony silhouette beneath.

Arc let out a laugh. 'You haven't aged a day in the fifteen or so years I have known you.'

Gavara gave his friend a puzzled look. 'What on earth has that got to do with anything?'

Arc was about to answer when a fanfare announced the arrival of Odexsius and his Corinthians.

'Take your places, gentlemen and ladies of the court,' Arc followed his command with a warning. 'Eat what you wish, but only indulge in the watered wine, we have a purpose this day.'

Arc took his place on the ivory throne, Gavara at one side, and Edius-Max and Razor at the other.

Odexsius strolled majestically through the shadows cast by the many sails above his head. Two gargantuan guards flanked him, their stature daunting and their expressions murderous. In contrast, Odexsius was smiling, his dark complexion absorbing the brightness of the day, revealing a gentleness that comes with age. His tightly curled and oiled hair shone when he passed through fingers of light poking through the gaps in the sails. He wore a lion skin cloak, the beast's head resting on the Chief's chest, fastening the two halves of the garment together with its great teeth.

Arc could see that the Chief had once been a warrior. He still had the broad shoulders and the muscled arms gained by training, but his midriff had ballooned from years of overindulgence, and absence from the training grounds. Odexsius carried himself in a way to give the impression he was still the warrior he had once been. In his mind he may have believed he played the warrior role well, in truth his appearance was one of a typical politician, an old one at that.

Following directly behind his father was Tyezore, his expression as stern as the guards'. He carried a ceremonial spear and looked every bit the warrior his father did not. He wore the skin of a beast, like his father, but his was a leopard's skin. Arc knew the type well and was not looking forward to negotiating with him. Behind Tyezore followed the usual mix of ambassadors, generals and a surprising number of women. These were the wise spirits: wives, concubines and even daughters of the Chief.

Gavara made a big fuss of the introductions, making all sides sound as grand as he could. Odexsius, along with his two main wives and Tyezore, joined Arc on the platform. They sat on the Corinthian sofas and were joined by Gavara, Edius-Max and Grand Master Razor. Arc sensed warm and friendly energy emanating from the old chief. He could see a severe danger in Tyezore's eyes and detected very little from the two women.

It turned out that they were not his wives. One was his sister, and the other his head concubine. The two women were almost indistinguishable, other than by the colour of their swarez, Corinthian traditional dress. It took generous amounts of silk to make a swarez: one long sheet of lushly coloured silk was wrapped around the woman in a way that elegantly displayed her curves and rounder figure. A headdress made of the same cloth, wrapped the woman's hair into a beehive shape, suggesting an extensive mass of locks beneath, although not a single strand was showing.

The sister wore a baby blue swarez that almost matched the sofa she was perched on. Light blue was a royal colour and therefore reserved for those with royal blood coursing through their veins. The concubine wore a green swarez. Both women were the same size and equally decked in jewels. Arc could not tell them apart and found in them a type of beauty he was unaccustomed to. The women had voluptuous figures, round faces with large eyes, a button nose and lips that were every bit as voluptuous as their figure.

The rest of the Corinthians and Avolonians spread out and mingled. It was not long before the hum of small talk filled the afternoon's warm air. Food was served, and wine poured in vast quantities. A lot depended on the day and Arc was not going to let a lack of hospitality spoil it.

Razor opened the conversation with some small talk. 'It is commendable, Chief Odexsius, that you have so many of the fairer sex here today. Women are obviously thought of as equals in your society.'

The Chieftain let out a roar of laughter. 'No, we do not,' came his reply. 'We don't think of women as equals. No, no, what nonsense. On the contrary, we know that they are superior in every way.' He laughed again, making Razor more than a little uncomfortable. 'We men are stumbling children in their wake, destroyers, killers, pretenders. Whereas women, on the other hand, build and nurture.'

'How so?' Razor found himself asking, out of natural curiosity rather than any kind of challenge to the Chief's proclamation.

Odexsius took a deep breath and made a theatrical sigh. 'Give a woman your manly seed and she will turn it into a child. Give a woman food and she will turn it into a meal. Give a woman a house and she will turn it into a home. Isn't that correct, my dear?' he said, turning to his concubine and patting her on the thigh in a condescending manner as if to contradict the integrity of his own words.

The woman kept a stern face as she gave a reply of her own. 'Give a woman your affection and she will turn it into love. But give a woman your scorn, and she will turn it into a storm.'

Odexsius let out another belly laugh, more amused at the woman's response than he should be.

Gavara broke the uncomfortable silence that followed. 'Maybe we should stick to the matter at hand and save the small talk for later in the day.' It was not in the Pathfinder's nature to be so pushy on diplomatic occasions, but he was very aware of the differences in culture and worried there may be disagreements if one side accidentally offended the other.

Arc was offering to reinstate Odexsius to the throne of Corinth. If the Mander were ousted from Corinth, Odexsius could field more than ten thousand trained warriors with a fearsome reputation. Gavara thought that Corinth had been too long under Mander rule to rebel. They had become subservient to the Empire, ever proud to be a part of it, but Odexsius wanted his throne back, and that was an opportunity not to be missed.

'What kind of man is your brother?' Arc asked Odexsius. 'The man who sits on your throne.'

'He is a weasel,' Tyezore answered for his father.

Odexsius shook his head. 'No, he is a frightened man who does what he thinks is best, even though in his heart of hearts he knows what he does is wrong. It is my fault,' he went on in a gentle tone. 'He was the youngest of four brothers. I put his two older brothers to the sword, to claim my crown, as is our custom. But he was just a small boy then, I had not the strength to take such a young life. Now the ancestors punish me for my weakness.'

'Will he fight?' Arc asked.

Odexsius shook his head again, sadness showing in his eyes. 'He is not a fighter; the warrior's spirit has never found a way into his soul. It is his Mander masters that will put up a fight and bring retribution onto my people for a rebellion.'

'Shaka hasn't even taken the spirit of the beast,' Tyezore blurted out, his disdain for the puppet king evident in every syllable of his words. 'The Blood Lion is back in our lands and it roams freely, to steal cattle and men. No one rests well at night, in fear that the red devil will take them in their sleep, and that coward hides behind my father's throne.'

Odexsius noticed Arc's confused expression, and it made him smile. 'Our customs must be strange to you,' Odexsius leaned forward, clasping his hands together and pressing a finger against his full lips in a thoughtful manner.

Arc leaned in, feigning interest in the story his guest was clearly eager to tell.

Odexsius kept his hands clenched in front of his face, the knuckle of his forefinger pressed against his top lip. His silence was monumental, and when he finally spoke he had the attention of everyone around him. 'You see the skins of the beasts my son and I wear upon our backs?' He paused and looked around at everyone nodding their answer. 'It is a royal blood's birth right to take the soul of the beast. The lion is for kings and the leopard for warrior princes, no other man may kill the beasts. Only a king or his eldest son may take the male lion. I took the soul of this beast with my own bare hands,' he struck the lions head with his fist. 'Now the power, courage and ferocity of the animal are joined with my spirit.'

Razor was clearly fascinated with Odexsius' monologue. 'If the male lion is reserved for the king and his eldest son, then why does Tyezore wear the skin of a leopard?' It was an honest question. 'Is he not your eldest son?'

The concubine at Odexsius' side let out an involuntary screech and quickly raised a fist to her mouth to stifle any further outbreak.

'Kane, my first born, now walks with our ancestors,' Odexsius continued his story. 'He went after the Blood Lion alone, armed only with a lion spear and his dagger, as is our custom. The devil took his spirit and ate his flesh. By the time my men found him, he was no more than a skull and a few bones lying on the blood-stained ground. The beast that did this to my son has returned to our lands. He is a man-eater, and my brother allows him to terrorise the herdsmen of the plains because he is too afraid to face his destiny.'

It was Odexsius' sister's turn to lean forward. She reached out and placed a hand on Arc's thigh. He was not sure how to react, so he did what came naturally. Placing his own hand on hers, Arc gave it a squeeze to show his acceptance of the gesture.

'My name is Shakana, and I brought up that boy as if he were my own son. I died inside the day that devil beast took his spirit. The beast must die by man's hand to claim back the spirit of Kane. My baby brother, Shaka, is too afraid, so another must challenge the Blood Lion.' Shakana grasped Arc's hand in both of hers, her eyes wide and pleading. 'You are a God to your followers. You can kill the beast. You can free Kane's spirit.'

Odexsius gently moved Shakana back into her seat with his arm. 'My sister is right. The wise spirit in her has shown us the way. If you kill the beast in a way that will please our ancestors, my people will accept you. They will follow you against the Mander. This is the way. Kill the beast. Kill my brother, and when I am back on the throne of Corinth, my people will follow the Lion Lord to freedom.' The Chieftain turned to the other woman. 'Your silence is deafening me, Latana. Do you not think this is an excellent idea?'

Latana pursed her lips, holding back her reply until she had the right words. Her thoughts danced in her sparkling eyes. 'That beast is elusive. He may have other ideas than to throw himself on the lion spear.'

Arc expected to see irritation in the Chieftain's expression, but was surprised at the calm and kindness in his voice when he spoke.

'I can see a thought poised on your lips.' Odexsius said, with a wry smile. It is like the hummingbird hovering in front of the open flower, waiting for just the right moment to dart in. Will you not share it with us?'

'We have ways of cementing alliances,' the thought entered the petals. 'A marriage of royal blood has always been our way. The people will trust that.'

'But all my daughters of marrying age already have husbands, so I have no daughters to offer.' Odexsius replied.

'And I have no sons,' Arc added.

'I do have two sons who are or are just about to reach manhood,' the Chieftain continued. 'I have heard of your famous daughter, is it not time she took a husband and made you some grandchildren.'

Arc felt his temple throb, he had to stay silent until he could suppress the pain enough to respond calmly. Gavara noticed his friend's discomfort and understood the situation.

'It would be a joyous idea,' Gavara replied for Arc. 'But the lady Enola already has a husband.'

Arc was still speechless, but he managed to turn to Gavara and give him a quizzical look. It was true that Enola had married Huwel, but Arc had refused to accept the marriage. He had no intention of marrying off his daughter, even if he could force her into such a thing.

'There is another way,' Latana said, glancing at Shakana. 'There is your daughter, Sonaji.' Shakana stiffened on hearing her daughter's name. 'The great Lion Lord has no wife.'

Odexsius burst into laughter. Wiping a tear from his eye, he calmed himself enough to speak. 'That girl has refused every prince or politician we have paraded in front of her. Even two of my sons were foolish enough to ask for her hand, knowing full well it is forbidden to marry such a close relation. You will need the luck of the Gods with that idea. She could kill the sacred lion herself with one of her cold stares.' The Chief burst into another fit of laughter, suddenly stopping himself, and changing his expression to one of deep thought. 'Is your daughter here?'

'She is,' Shakana replied.

Odexsius turned back towards Arc. 'No harm in introducing you two. Bring her over.' Odexsius clapped his hands, and an assistant disappeared into the crowd to do his bidding.

Arc slowly shook his head. 'There are no slaves in my camps, and no one is forced to marry another against their will.'

'Fear not,' Shakana said, leaning closer to Arc again. 'Sonaji will never marry against her will. Our traditions are different from your life experiences, I don't doubt. Odexsius has many wives who are no more than his friend.'

'And many lovers who are forced to serve him,' Arc countered, without worry of the offence his words may cause.

It was Latana's turn to stiffen. 'A concubine in our culture is not a slave, nor forced against her will. She is a free woman who has fallen in love and chosen to dedicate her life to one man.'

Arc regained his diplomacy, realising he was escalating the situation into a cultural debate. 'Excuse my ignorance, my lady. I meant no offence.'

The conversation was quickly forgotten as the guests in front of the platform parted to allow Sonaji through.

The young woman, slim and elegant was dressed in a yellow swarez. Her eyes were bright, her cheekbones high, and her full lips were painted the lushest shade of red. Sonaji's dark skin seemed almost reflective, and her beauty was astonishing to witness.

'Close your mouth,' Gavara whispered into Arc's ear.

The Lion Lord was stunned by the young woman's elegance and beauty as she glided up the steps. She stopped just a few paces in front of the ivory throne and gave the smallest curtsy imaginable as a greeting. Sonaji never once broke from gazing into Arc's eyes while she was being introduced.

'Sonaji is Corinth's cultural ambassador to Mander,' Shakana described her daughter with unashamed pride.

Razor could not help himself and said out loud what most were thinking. 'Are you not a little young for such a responsible role?' he asked, instantly realising how offensive the question might be. 'I mean, you must find it a great responsibility on your slender shoulders.'

'I am older than I look,' Sonaji answered. Her tone was not angry, but it had a confident sternness that surprised the Grand Master. 'My shoulders may be slim, but I can assure you that spiritually they are as broad as any man's here.'

Odexsius filled the air with his infectious laugh and slapped his thigh. 'Careful gentlemen, this one has teeth. Sonaji, you have walked this earth for almost thirty summers. You have no husband, no children. I think it is about time you plugged those holes in the circle of life. The great Lion here has no wife.'

Arc was about to speak and put an end to the ludicrous notion that he would marry this woman who looked almost as young as his daughter, but Sonaji beat him to it.

'I am sure the leader of the Avolonian crusade has less use than I do for a relationship and all its baggage. I have no need for a husband and have seen little in men to make me think I will ever find one worthy.'

Arc felt some admiration creeping into his impression of the woman. She was astonishingly beautiful, and he desired her as any man would. But she was right, he had no need for a life partner nor the time for courtship. He lived for one purpose and one purpose alone, to destroy the Mander Empire.

'Would a man be worthy if he wore the pelt of the lion, and had the spirit of the great beast in his soul?' Shakana asked.

Excitement flashed in Sonaji's eyes. 'Such a man would be truly worthy of consideration,' a hint of a smile turning up the corners of her mouth revealed that she was well aware of her mother's little trap. 'It is a pity that no such man is present. No man here has slain the great beast with his own hand. Other than you, of course, Uncle.'

Shakana gave her brother a stern look as if warning him against a thought he had ventured to think once before.

'This is all irrelevant,' Arc could hold back from saying no longer. 'No offence, Sonaji. Marriage for political gain is not our way. I will hunt and kill the man-eater to show your people I am worthy of their following. I will place you back on the throne of Corinth, Odexsius. Marriage though is not on the negotiating table.'

Arc regretted the finality of his words. The man in him found it difficult to close the door on his desires. The leader in him had learned long ago that slamming shut the door of temptation was the only way to stay firm, striding towards his purpose.

At that moment, a young warrior came running into the centre of the decking and announced that the contestants were on their way back to the arena. Everyone immediately put down their drinks or plates and headed towards the grandstand.

'Shall we?' Gavara asked, holding a hand out to help up one of the ladies.

'Will you at least escort me to the spectacle you have arranged?' Sonaji asked of Arc, holding out her delicate hand. 'That may at least lessen the heartbreak I am consumed with due to your rejection.' Her words were laced with irony, and her face painted with a charming smile that Arc had no defence against.

As they all made their way over to the arena, Gavara hung at the back of the royal procession with the generals, while Arc, with Sonaji on his arm, and Odexsius on his other side, led the way.

'Looks like someone is going on a lion hunt,' Gavara told Edius-Max and Razor, chuckling to himself at the irony of the Lion Lord on a lion hunt.

'I think more than one lion is being hunted,' Razor replied, nodding to point out to the others how flirty Sonaji had become.

Enola

It was only a hop, skip and a jump to the base of the cliff from the river, not that Enola could do any of those things while dragging her log. She was drenched, and water dripped from her hair and squelched from her sandals, even though the midday sun was rapidly drying her. Enola gasped with relief as she dropped her burden against the pile of tree trunks already gathered at the base of the cliff. The marshal painted her shoulder with a red mark to indicate she had completed that section of the race.

Several contestants were already picking their way up the craggy rock face. Enola had to lift a hand to shade her eyes from the sun so that she could see the highest climber. It was Hals. Gavara had made her climb this rock for three days in a row. She had almost fallen several times trying to change lines half way up. The old man's voice echoed in her thoughts, *'The fastest way up is to stick to one fault line for as long as you can. The fastest line to the top is Snake Crack to the ledge and then Lightning Crack to the ridge.'*

Enola had almost ripped her fingernails out of her flesh trying to hold onto the ridge to get from one line to the next. The memory of the pain made her fingers tingle. Heavy footsteps behind her jolted Enola into action, and she hurried to find foot holes, and pull herself up the fault line she called Snake Crack. She was less than two men high from the ground when she felt the grasp of a hot hand around her ankle pulling her down. Enola looked around to see a large warrior she did not recognise, grim-faced and pulling at her leg. Her grip was faltering, and she kicked aimlessly at the man.

Enola was unable to hang on any longer. The man was about to succeed in pulling her from the rock when she heard him cry out, and felt his grip release. She looked over her shoulder just in time to see Elektra slamming her assailant into the rock face, and then knocking him to the ground with a sledgehammer punch. The colossal spear-maiden looked up at Enola, a massive grin on her face. She urged her new friend on with a wave. Enola acknowledged and thanked her with a curt nod and a smile before continuing to climb.

The Lioness was no more than a third of the way up the cliff face when she heard a desperate cry. A rock, the size of a fist, hit her on the shoulder, knocking her hand free of the cliff. Enola managed to hold on with the other hand but was swung around. She flinched as the man who had cried out fell through the space where she had been a moment before. He hit the ground hard. Enola could not take her eyes off the fallen man. The marshal and a contestant ran to his aid, but he was silent and still. Enola took a deep breath and continued her climb.

Her training had served her well and she made short work of the rest of the climb, overtaking two others on the way up. Her fingers bled from crossing the ledge to reach the Lightning Crack fault line. 'A small price to pay,' Enola told herself as she scrambled onto the grassy summit. She could see those contestants ahead of her gathering on the far side, and she hurried to join them.

The men were shuffling backwards and forwards, looking over the cliff to the green water far below and trying to gather the courage to jump. Enola peered over the edge into the abyss. 'Clever little man,' she thought to herself about Gavara, when she saw the fear and hesitation in the men around her. She could see Hals had already jumped and was swimming towards the bank.

One man suddenly found his courage and sprinted off the cliff's edge. Enola watched the man descend, his arms and legs flailing on the way down. He overbalanced and entered the water leaning back. There was an almighty thud and water fountained into the air. The man disappeared below the surface, thousands of bubbles rushing up marking his entry point.

The bubbles faded and the man did not reappear. Two of the men on the plateau instantly took off down the long route, following the sheep path down to the base of the escarpment. Another started to climb down the rock face to find a lower point to jump from. Enola stood on the end of the cliff, stretched her arms out wide, arched her back, went up on her tiptoes and dived.

She entered the water like an arrow, clenching her fists tight to break the water's surface, and tucking her head between her outstretched arms to protect it. She let herself be taken into a forward roll to limit how far she penetrated the depths, and kicked for the surface, taking a giant breath as she launched into the clear air. Enola had practised diving from many cliffs this high. First diving from halfway up, then two-thirds, before finally diving from the highest point. Her body had learned how to maintain balance and correct itself on the way down.

Instead of swimming to the bank, Enola plunged back beneath the surface and kicked towards the bottom of the lake. It was deep, and the pressure built quickly in her ears. She pinched her nose and blew to release the pain before kicking for the darker water at the bottom. Lake grass grew tall between the rocks, reaching out for a taste of the sparse sunlight above. Enola saw a cloud of mud rise up from between the stones where a perch had been startled by her sudden appearance.

Two loud thuds echoed through the water, one directly after the other. Enola looked up to see two bodies, arms and legs flailing, surrounded in a cocoon of bubbles. Her lungs were starting to burn as she looked around, desperately trying to find the man who had sunk. She was about to push for the surface, to take another breath, when a shadow caught her eye. She swam towards it, hoping she had found the drowning man.

As she neared, the shadow became a figure in the darkness, and she rushed towards it. She could make out the arms, outstretched and floating lifelessly, but the body was hard to distinguish, it seemed to be rippling in the darkness. Enola reached out to grab the man. Shock hit her like lightning as she grasped a slimy, tube-like body. Teeth flashed in her face, as the beast turned on her and wildly snapped its jaws. Enola reeled backwards to escape the eel, emptying her lungs in the panic. She dropped like a stone to the bottom.

A hand grabbed Enola's tunic at the back of her neck and pulled her off the lakebed. She was being pulled upwards and kicked furiously to help. Her lungs felt like they were turning inside out, fighting the urge to gasp. She hung onto the thinnest thread of consciousness long enough to burst from the surface. She could finally gulp in the air she so desperately needed, splashing in the panic to keep her head above the surface.

'Enola!' a voice cried, the sound drowned out by the noise of splashing. 'Enola!' it called again. 'Calm down, or you will drown both of us.

It was Antona. He held Enola above the surface of the water, receiving several blows to the head and face for his trouble, before she calmed down.

Once Enola had regained her senses, she coughed up the water out of her lungs and gestured towards the man below.

Antona shook his head. 'You saw the eels on him, he's done for,' Antona also coughed up some water. 'He's half eaten by now, they were all over him.'

Enola coughed again, spat out the mixture of lake-water and phlegm before swimming for shore. The two friends scrambled onto the bank and rolled over onto their backs, side by side.

'That's the second time today I have nearly drowned,' Enola blurted out.

Antona laughed. 'Yes, I saw your little stunt crossing the river. You are the least sane person I know,' he slapped her on the chest, accidentally hitting her breast.

'Ouch!' she cried out, more in annoyance than pain. Come on, there are several already in front of us. We are out of this if we don't catch them.'

The two friends squelched and plodded their way to the last marshal station before the finish. There they were each handed a heavy, circular oak wood battle shield, and a long pike. As Lion Warriors, both were accustomed to marching at double pace with such equipment, even jogging for great distances. Both of them knew full well that they were no match for the common soldier at this drill, as officers they had spent too much time in the saddle.

'How many ahead of us,' Antona barked at the nearest of two marshals.

'Just what you can see out there,' he replied, waving at the figures running into the distance, and making no effort to hide the sarcasm in his voice.

'Six,' the other marshal offered, embarrassed at his associate's rudeness.

Enola and Antona gave each other a worried look and instantly took off in pursuit. There were only places in the final games for the first six across the finish line.

'Only you,' Antona timed his words with his breathing, 'could risk the contest,' he breathed in, 'by trying to save….,' another breath, 'save someone.'

Enola was focused on hunting down the nearest trail of dust in front of them. 'Save your lungs,' she timed her words in the same way. 'Shut up,' she breathed, 'and run.'

It was a long way to the finish, and the two friends slowly reeled in the other runners. Enola listened to

Gavara's advice in her head, *'Trust in your pace, and be patient.'* She was doing that and, although she had halved the distance to the next runner, she worried that the finish line would come too soon for her to overtake.

'What's that?' Antona gasped.

There was something that looked out of place on the ground, amongst the grass. The wild grass was thin and only about knee high, stretching across the long meadow it seemed denser than it was. The seed heads waved gently in the breeze, balanced on the slender stalks holding them up. Insects hopped and flew in their multitudes above the ocean of grass.

As they drew closer, they could see it was a man slumped on a shield. As they passed the forlorn figure he glanced at them with tired eyes and tried to get to his feet. He fell awkwardly back to the ground, and was soon left behind. The man had run himself to exhaustion, spurred on by the dream of commanding his own troops.

'Only you,' Antona said, then took a breath and finished with, 'to beat now.'

Enola pushed her friend with her shield and increased her pace. *Match this*, she thought.

Enola quickened her pace, keeping the man in front firmly in her sights. She was relentless in her pursuit and gained at a rapid pace. As she caught up with him, the man glanced sideways at Enola, a worried expression fixed on his face. The man visibly dug deep only to be shocked at how easily the Lioness was passing him. Enola did not look over her shoulder, she knew that anyone overtaken in a long race rarely had the strength of body or mind to reverse the action.

The finish line grew out of the grass as Enola drew closer. Many flags on long poles marked the end of the race. She could hear the crowd over the constant thudding in her ears of her overheated blood rushing through her veins. She found a renewed energy as she crossed the line, holding her head high in case her father was watching. Handing over her shield and spear to a marshal, Enola turned just in time to see Antona win the race with the man she had passed. Both men staggered and fell as they crossed the line, casting their shields and pikes to one side in their struggle to stand up.

Enola snatched at the water skin that was offered to her and drank as if there were flames in her stomach that needed to be dowsed in an instant before they burned her alive. She stopped only when she was forced to take a breath. Her skin tingled as she poured the cool water over her head and let it wash across the hot flesh of her back and chest. She drank some more, and then splashed her face before walking over to Antona and handing him the skin.

The crowd were cheering the first four back who were pacing up and down in front of the tribune Enola gestured to Antona, and the two of them joined in the celebration. The six finalists were given bridles, and they watched as a dozen horses were herded into one of the arenas. A horn sounded to silence the crowd who were now excited, in anticipation of finally being able to see the action.

A large officer bellowed out the details of the next event. It was to be a hestathlon, a horse and rider event, 'hest,' meaning horse. The six finalists would choose their mounts to take them eight laps around a track. On each lap, they would have to shoot an arrow into a target from the saddle, and then dismount to hit a second target a greater distance away. If they missed a target, they would have to complete a penalty loop. The first two that completed the course would be the finalists.

The men ran in to choose their horses. Hals bellowed at the two men racing ahead of him to slow down before they spooked the beasts. Enola and Antona just laughed at the men's lack of equestrian prowess. It was too late, the horses panicked. Wide-eyed and skittish, the beasts struggled to get away from their pursuers. Hals was obviously going for the largest black stallion. He raised his hands to calm the animal which responded by rearing up.

Enola glanced into the crowd, looking for Gavara. She knew everything that he did was for a reason. He knew that by having the men race in to compete for the best horses, it would cause havoc. She took another look at the horses that were not clustered with the central group. She made eye contact with a beige mare. Keeping eye contact, Enola lifted her head twice while walking at an angle past the horse. She finally broke off her stare and turned her back on the beast to stand still with her arms tucked into her body and her head lowered.

She waited, listening to the commotion going on behind her. She kept perfectly still for what seemed an age. Her patience was rewarded, and she felt the weight of the mare's muzzle on her shoulder. She slowly lifted a hand and stroked the beast's nose, its hot breath on her hand. Enola carefully turned, placed the bridle she was carrying over the horse's head and led her to the edge of the arena to be saddled.

Antona brought over a chestnut gelding that was sleek and looked fast. 'You're supposed to choose the horse, not let the horse choose you,' he told his friend.

Enola smiled. 'She chose me because she likes me. She sees my spirit, which means she will ride hard or do anything else she can to please me.'

'You sound like Gavara,' Antona said, looking to the crowd to see if he could see the old man.

Odexsius leaned over to Arc. 'Isn't that your daughter?'

'She looks very strong,' Sonaji commented.

'She looks magnificent,' the Chieftain added. 'I'll bet a lamb's head against a duck's head that she is like a young Lion Lord at that age, only with a bosom.'

Arc knew they meant no offence, they were only trying to be complementary. Enola was magnificent, every bit the slender athlete he had been at her age, but he did not see himself in her. He saw hints of her mother hiding behind the scarred face and muscles. It was marginally hurtful that they did not comment on his daughter's beauty, knowing that Enola did not worry about such things. She was a warrior and a leader, wanting to be seen for the things she had earned, like her strength and courage, not to be judged and measured by her attractiveness.

Cubb, the daughter Arc had lost, found her way into the Lion Lord's thoughts. He remembered how much she looked like her mother. Jem was always telling him how much Cubb took after her, and Fawn took after him. Fawn was Enola's childhood name. She had taken her adult name from the comet which had been burning across the skies of Avolonia at the time.

'She is more like her mother,' Arc spoke softly. 'The strength she gave herself. The bloody-mindedness it took to do that, and her good looks, are all her mother.'

'Nonsense,' Gavara interrupted. 'From what I have heard about Jem, Enola probably has a resemblance in the face and sharp mind of her mother, but she is her father's daughter that one. She has the spirit of a warrior and the ruthless determination of a lion. No, she is not the gentle soul her mother was, she is every bit as stubborn and pig-headed as her father.'

Arc raised an eyebrow at his old friend and could only frown to show his disapproval. He had no comeback to Gavara's comments, the old man was right, as always.

'Look, they are about to race,' Sonaji leaned in and grasped Arc's hand tightly. 'Are you not afraid for your daughter?'

Arc shook his head. 'She is by far the finest rider in the field. She had the best teacher.' He looked back at his old friend again, but this time gave him a smile.

Enola avoided the centre of the line and the jostling for position that involved. She did not have the fastest horse in the field, but she thought her mare was the steadiest. She stayed to the side, and let Hals and his large black stallion bully the centre. She had been given a quiver of green flighted arrows, Antona had yellow flights, and the other contestants had a mix of blue, black, red and white. Each contestant wore a headband and an armband with their colour.

The race started with a ceremonial blast from the horns. The spectators cheered as the horses sprang forward. Hals took an early lead, as expected. He pushed the stallion up the straight and was three lengths ahead by the first corner. Enola let her mount set its own pace and tucked in behind Antona's chestnut gelding. Two riders were almost unseated at the first corner, their mounts struggling to keep their footing as they tussled with each other around the bend.

Hals, Enola, Ebruc and Antona, all hit the first target on the hoof, and sped on, to the thunderous excitement of the crowd. The two others had to slow to almost a complete stop to draw the string and hit the target. One missed and instantly rushed off around the penalty lap, leaving the other to try and make up ground.

Ebruc was a Simterian, born in the saddle and drawing on a bow in his cradle. Enola had been the Avolonian Army's equestrian champion for the past few years, but that was before the Simterians joined. She now saw Ebruc for the threat he was and urged her bay mare on.

'Come on, girl,' Enola slapped the beast's neck. 'Good girl,' she told the mare, as she sprang from the saddle.

While sprinting across to the archery range, Enola nocked an arrow, drawing the bow as soon as her toe hit the chalk line. She was momentarily distracted as in her peripheral vision she saw Hals's blue flighted arrow hit the target. Antona's hit next, and when Ebruc's arrow slammed into the target, Enola let loose hers with more haste than she had intended. She did not need to wait and see if the arrow flew true. She knew instinctively that the shaft was on target, hearing the thud of it striking home as she ran back to her horse.

Hals opened up a substantial lead by the third lap, pursued by Ebruc and Antona. Enola concentrated on sparing her horse while not letting the leaders get away from her. There were eight laps and the big stallions of Hals and Ebruc had been pushed hard from the start. She imagined Gavara sitting amongst the spectators and grinning. *'Manage your animal well. Eight laps are too far for a stallion to maintain a blistering pace,'* She heard Gavara's voice in her head. *'The short rests at the archery range are deceptive, the bigger beasts will not recover in such a short time, but the smaller mares will. The bigger animals will tire late in the race.'* Enola was not sure if Gavara had actually told her that, or if she just knew it and imagined Gavara saying it to give her faith in her own strategy.

After four laps it became a four-horse race, with the two others left so far back they were no longer competitive. It was on laps six and seven when Enola's smaller horse started to gain on the leaders. Hals had been out in front but Antona had caught up with him, his lighter gelding's stamina holding out better than the big black stallion's. The two beasts were neck and neck down the back straight. White foam covered the animals' overheated bodies and formed around their mouths.

Antona was starting to edge ahead to take the lead. Hals reacted by swerving his larger mount into his adversary, forcing Antona wide on the bend. The chestnut gelding was a well-balanced horse, but lost its footing and stumbled trying to push back against the bigger stallion. The beast's head went down, and it took every bit of resolve and skill for Antona to stop himself from being launched over the neck of his mount. The gelding survived and managed to stay on its feet, but it was injured and pulled up limping. Hals raced on to the penultimate target.

There was a twist for the final round, a new challenge; not only would the riders have to hit the target while speeding past but the target itself would also be moving. A cloth sack stuffed with straw swung on a chain. It would take a skilled archer to hit it with a standing shot from thirty paces, the riders would have to do so at speed. Hals's arrow hit the sack dead centre, to the crowd's delight.

Enola pushed her mount hard, and the bay mare responded by giving everything she had. Enola narrowed her eyes against the dust and lowered her head. The two of them soon came alongside Ebruc's tiring stallion. Ebruc was already nocking an arrow as they flew past Antona's limping mount. Enola drew an arrow from her quiver. Ebruc had been waiting for that moment, it was why he had drawn his own arrow so early. He forced his stallion over into Enola while she only had one hand on the reins and was twisting to reach to her quiver.

The mare was not going to let some brute of a stallion unseat her rider. As Enola was thrown to one side, the mare instinctively swayed to re-centre Enola before she fell. The Lioness was furious. She steered the mare into the stallion and held her there while she nocked the arrow. They all reached the target locked together: man, woman, mare and stallion, a speeding mass of flesh and determination, grappling for position. Both riders let fly their arrows at the same time, and the force of impact flung the sack up into the air.

Ebruc swerved his mount away from Enola. The mare, caught off balance, could not avoid stumbling. Enola was hurled out of the saddle. Hanging onto the pommel, and with one foot still in the stirrup, she pushed and pulled her way back onto the horse. The mare had instinctively tried to keep going but was forced almost to a stop by her unseated rider's attempts to hang on. Enola cursed to herself as she watched Ebruc disappear behind a wake of dust.

By the time Enola reached the final target, Hals's arrow was in the bullseye and he was holding his bow above his head in triumph. The crowd were yelling their approval. Enola watched Ebruc shoot his last shaft into the noise filled air as she raced to the line, hoping against hope that his arrow would miss the target. Without hesitation she let her arrow fly, instantly knowing it flew true, allowing her aspiration to stay afloat one moment longer only to be sunk by the sound of Ebruc's arrow slamming into the target.

Enola's arrow hit the target dead centre, but she was not watching. Nor was she watching Ebruc celebrate. Her head hung down, she closed her eyes and sighed. It was a sigh of resignation, a tired sigh that expelled her disappointment and hid her rage. She did not know if she was angry with herself for losing or at Ebruc for the unsporting way he had won. She decided on herself, knowing there was no point in looking for blame or excuses. She did not see Antona walking over to her with one of the marshals following him.

'Don't let your head go down now,' Antona said, placing a hand on his disappointed friend's shoulder. 'It's not over until it's over.'

Enola looked up in time to see Antona casually loose his final shaft into the air. His eyes traced the arrow through the sky until it hit the target. Enola didn't know if her friend was trying to be sarcastic, his words were not making her feel any better. She felt her anger bubbling to the surface. Antona saw the perplexed look on his friend's face and nodded towards the race marshal before the fury he knew was coming could be unleashed.

The marshal carried the stuffed sack that had been the moving target. Three arrows hung from it, embedded in the straw content. Enola could see Hals's blue flight, Antona's yellow feathers and her own green ones. What she could not see was a forth arrow with Ebruc's black flights.

Antona's grin widened as he saw the realisation on Enola's face. 'Do you want to tell him, or shall I?'

Neither of them had to tell Ebruc that he had failed. The marshals marched across to him and dangled the target that did not contain his arrow in front of his face. Ebruc shook his head vigorously at first, eventually covering his face with his hands and dropping to his knees. Even Enola felt a pang of sympathy for the man, but that was short lived as Antona pushed her arm up in triumph and led her towards the spectators.

'You must be proud,' Tyezore called up to Arc. 'Even if it is all for the show. Your daughter has done well.'

Arc felt the sting in the general's words. 'What do you mean, all for the show?'

Odexsius shot his son a look of reproach, but he ignored it.

'It is the sign of a great leader,' Tyezore went on, 'that even in fierce competition his subjects love him so much that they would step aside for his daughter rather than risk his displeasure or her wellbeing.'

Arc felt his anger growing. He was about to unleash his wrath when Gavara stepped in.

'I am sure the Chieftain's son is not suggesting there is anything untoward going on. He does not know the skill and determination of the Lioness as much as our people do.' Gavara explained. 'This final test is out in the open and for all to see.'

At that moment the crowd cheered as the two contestants were brought forward and handed a shield and a sword.'

Tyezore huffed. 'I am sure we will all see a great deal of skill from the finalists, but you can't expect me to believe that girl who is dwarfed by her opponent could win if the poor man were not afraid for his life. I'll bet the swords are even blunted. He can't win: if he kills her, you will kill him. There is no way this is being fought to combat rules with sharp swords.'

Arc glared at Gavara, knowing from the old man's expression that Tyezore was correct. He knew he had made a mistake. If Tyezore saw it that way then many others would see it that way too. Arc knew he had to do something. His army was held together by a thin thread of respect, if that was lost it would fracture and disband. He stood up and pushed his way down to the arena where his daughter and her opponent were warming up.

The spectators' roar quietened to a hum of intrigue as Arc strode out into the arena. He paused to speak to one of his elite bodyguard who was standing in the row of sentinels between the crowd and the field. The guard left his place in the human barrier to attend to whatever errand Arc had sent him on. The Lion Lord continued to the centre of the arena, stopping only when he was between his daughter and Hals.

Both contestants stood to attention and banged their shield with their sword as a salute. Arc held his hand out towards Hals who was unsure at first what was expected of him. When it dawned on the warrior that it was his sword his commander desired, he flipped it in his hand, catching the blade and offering the hilt to Arc. The Lion Lord took the grip with his right hand, wrapping his left hand around the blade he squeezed.

The Lion Lord looked at his hand and held it up to show the crowd that there was no blood. Groans of disappointment skipped through the mass of spectators, and Arc was reassured he had been right to intervene. He took Enola's sword and threw both blades to the side of the arena.

The guard came trotting back from his errand carrying two swords. One was Enola's golden blade, Leo-fang. The other was Hals's own blade which was broader and more substantial than Leo-fang, but didn't look as well made or as well balanced as Enola's weapon. But what sword would look as well made as a blade made of gold?

Arc had taken the precious weapon, and a second identical blade, from the dead hands of a Nomad leader he had killed in one-on-one combat. He had given the second blade to his loyal friend Arcilus. The sight of the golden sword reminded Arc of the friend he had left behind to protect the newly formed nation of Avolonia. He missed the old general, and more than once had wished him at his side on the crusade to destroy Mander.

Arc handed Enola her familiar sword, but before he handed Hals his, he squeezed the blade with his hand and then held it up so that the crowd could see the blood.

'No training blades to decide the victor in a contest as imperative as this one!' Arc bellowed out to the crowd, in a voice that was accustomed to being heard in the chaos of battle. A cheer went up, filling the air with a mixture of accord and excitement. 'Honour of Combat rules apply!' he roared, to the approval of the masses. 'Submission, domination or death!'

The crowd knew the rules. First blood was not enough to win a contest with combat rules. To win, one or other would have to admit defeat and surrender, be unable to continue or die. Enola and Hals were brought metal grieves to protect their forearms and shins, and each was given a simple battle-helmet.

Arc sensed the spectators' excitement, like a flock of birds taking off. He waited for them to settle before speaking again, but mostly he waited to gain control of the pain in his head. He took a deep breath and held up his hands to get the attention of the masses. The pain persisted and Arc decided he would have to endure while he spoke.

'We live by a code of honour!' Arc called out, the pain in his head making his words seem angry. 'Any man or woman amongst you can prevail on their own merit and only by their own merit.' The crowd listened intently. 'No favouritism will be shown here today, and no one has to fear that there will be any retribution resulting from their actions. My daughter, the Lioness, Enola is a warrior of her own worth. She would be appalled and dishonoured should I ease her path of accomplishment.' He drew the Lion Blade and pointed it at Hals. Leovesica was like no other sword, its folded steel blade was made with the skills of a bygone age, the technology lost in the past. 'You are protected from, and absolved of any outcome you think offends me.' Arc spoke loud so that enough of the spectators would hear his words and then share them with those who did not hear. 'Do your best and let the warrior known as Enola contend with whatever wrath you can muster. I offer you only one piece of advice. If you are not afraid, you should be. It is not for you that I invoke the rules of combat, it is to unleash powers Enola does not yet realise she has.' Arc turned to walk away, but stopped nearer to the edge of the arena. He turned on his heels, pointed his sword at Enola, and said, 'Remember, you have nothing to fear except fear itself.' Turning back to the fascinated crowd, Arc raised his hands again and addressed them directly. 'If not them, then who? If not now, then when? Those about to die salute you.' He had adapted Hillel's ancient verse of combat to suit his needs, but it did the trick, the crowd went into a frenzy of cheering and excitement.

The roar from the crowd vibrated in Enola's chest, making her heart quicken. She felt the weight of her well-balanced sword in her hand, drawing comfort from its familiarity. She remembered the verse of combat, written a millennium before by Hillel, and taught to her by Stann, her guardian in Ribbelstead when she was a child separated from her father. She would chant the words over and over again when she could not sleep, hoping to dream about acts of courage when she finally did fall into slumber. Enola slowed her heartbeat by saying Hillel's verse to herself.

'Those about to die, salute those about to live.
If not us, who?
If not now, when?
If not for honour, what?
If not for victory, why?
If not by the blade, how?
Those about to live, salute those about to die.
May the Gods see our valour.'

Combat rules, or battle rules as they were sometimes known, were the code of conduct used to referee duels, fights of honour and dispute settlements. By following the code of honour, a warrior could earn great esteem on the battlefield. Duels between officers and even generals before a battle were commonplace, with one side trying to gain a psychological advantage over the other. Better to die by the code than survive in disgrace. The fights on the field of combat were almost always to the death, whereas fights to settle disputes, more often than not, ended when one opponent submitted. Combatants still died in such fights, but usually because of an accidental wound.

Enola and Hals had no reason to die, but neither had any intention of suffering the embarrassment of defeat. They had both been blooded in battles fought on the Lion

Crusade, seen the horrors of war and survived all attempts to snatch away their existence. They were warriors and losing was not in their nature. Both banged their blades against their shields to signal the start of the contest. The spectators cheered.

Taking confident, powerful strides, Hals moved in on Enola. He was a lot bigger than the Lioness and judging from the grin on his face, obviously thought he was the apex predator and she was his prey. Even the most significant and most robust predators fear injury from their smaller quarry. They play the game of death by the rules: caution, manoeuvring, patience, waiting for the clean kill. He eyed the golden sword, thinking of it more like a serpent's needle-like fang than the big cat it was named after. He regarded it as little more than a sting, but he would have to neutralise it before he made his kill.

Enola moved with grace and balance, her sinuous muscles tensing and easing as she stepped from foot to foot. She kept moving, changing direction frequently to keep Hals off balance. She smiled when she saw him twitch as her blade darted out, even though he was well out of range. Hals felt his anger rising, knowing he was being frustrated into making a rash attack. He picked his moment carefully, then made his move.

Shields crashed like the coming together of two ibex rams butting heads in the mating season, their giant curved horns colliding with great force. Enola leaned into her shield, stretching out her back leg, thinking she could hold her ground. She realised in an instant that she was no match in strength to the man who was a head taller and probably a third heavier than her. Enola rolled away, twisting at an angle so that she held her shield above her head.

At the moment Enola broke away, Hals took advantage of the weakness and chopped his blade down into space where he anticipated she would roll. The sound of steel on gold rang out, confirming that the Lioness had covered her retreat well. Hals grunted with frustration, for a split second he had thought he was about to make a quick kill, but now scolded himself for his foolishness. A wave of exasperation washed over the spectators who, like Hals, had underestimated Enola's speed and foresight.

A wicked grin spread across the width of Hals's face. He realised that he only needed to continue using his superior strength over and over until Enola made a mistake, then he would finish her. He swaggered forward, showing an invigorated confidence that the crowd lapped up. They cheered every time Enola escaped a killing blow or was knocked to the ground by the power of it. She was back on her feet with the speed of lightning before Hals could finish her off. She knew that each time she sprang from the ground, she was a fraction slower than the time before, and so did the grinning Hals.

Enola's arms had gone numb from the relentless pounding against her shield and sword. The scales of domination were securely tipped in Hals's favour, and she had to find some way to balance them, soon. She could not survive such an onslaught of power for much longer. In the next attack, Hals drew first blood. Enola did not feel the blade slicing the flesh of her shoulder as she rolled away from the pressure of the hulking man's shield. The crowd went wild at the sight of blood.

All eyes on the tribune turned to Arc, their expectant gaze revealing that they thought he would call a halt to the mismatch. Arc's gaze never faltered. He remained calm, unaffected by the drama. Inside he was bursting with rage as if amid a battle. He wanted to draw the Lion Blade and cut his way through the crowd to slay the enemy threatening his daughter. But it was not an enemy, and he had ensured he was powerless to intervene. So, he had to hide his fear and stay calm in the face of this self-made adversity.

Enola felt the warm blood running down her upper arm. She would not give her advisory the satisfaction of seeing her look at it, so she kept her eyes firmly focused on his. Hals jutted out his broad chin in the direction of the wound as if pointing it out and silently asking if that was enough to decide the outcome of the contest. Enola ignored the gesture, causing Hals to drop the grin from his determined face and continue the attack.

Their shields clashed again. This time Enola tried something different, she did not break off and separate the shields, even though she was being forced backwards. As long as they were locked together, Hals could not get his blade into an angle that could harm her. She would force his shield up and then step aside to throw him off balance. As Enola pushed upwards, Hals countered and used his power to press the shields in the opposite direction.

Enola felt herself panic, if her shield were to be forced down, Hals could stab at her over the rim. The Lioness could not do the same, as she was now using both hands to resist the move. Her heart sank when she realised the shields were dropping. Enola heard her opponent laugh a split second before she felt the most indescribable pain in the centre of her face. Her legs gave way, and although she was unaware of it, blood had sprayed out of both her nostrils to hose over the rim of her shield. The hot sticky fluid coated Hals's chest.

As she lay bleeding on the ground, Enola knew she was finished. The earth swirled and her senses were in complete disarray. All she could hear was the roar of the crowd, and all she could see was the blurred shape of Hals standing over her. He had smashed the pommel of his sword into the bridge of her nose the instant he could reach over the shields. In a battle, he may have waited a moment longer and stabbed the point of the blade into his enemy's face. Luckily for Enola, he had gone for the faster and less deadly option.

Hals looked at the bright blood covering his chest and curled his lip in disdain. He did not rush to finish the fallen Enola, seeing how disorientated she was. Instead, he savoured the moment.

'That will put an end to your pretty looks,' Hals laughed, referring to the angle of Enola's broken nose. 'Now yield, bitch!' he called out, as he stepped in to pin her to the ground with the tip of his blade at her throat.

'Bitch!' the word splashed and kicked in her thoughts like a drowning woman in a stormy sea. The insult triggered a response in Enola that was no less than superhuman. Clarity was thrust upon her in an instant, her movements faster than a twisting polecat. Before Hals' blade could trap her, she rolled out of its way and darted the golden blade between the startled man's legs. The sharp edge sliced over the greave protecting the shin of his right leg but continued on between his stance to cut the exposed flesh at the back of his left leg.

Hals yelled out. He danced away from the pain, giving Enola time to spring to her feet. Blood gushed from her nose. She reacted quickly by ripping a strip of cloth from her tunic and stuffing it into her nostrils. She sniffed, and almost choked on the amount of semi-clotted blood that rushed to the back of her throat. She stood there without her shield. Hals thought this to his advantage, but to continue without the cumbersome protection was Enola's intention.

Hals once again advanced on his prey. The difference this time was that he limped. The wound had not cut deep enough to hamstring him, although it had almost done so. Enola's vision was still blurry through watery eyes, but she now saw her objectives clearer in her mind. She moved like a striking cobra: her blade reaching further and faster than seemed possible, like the serpent's spraying venom. The first thing Hals knew about it was the cut to his shoulder.

Enola did not stop there. In three more rolling and sweeping passes at speed, she cut his cheek, the shoulder again and a shallow stab to the upper chest. Hals bellowed as he twisted and turned to try and counter the attack from a woman he thought he had already defeated. He was losing blood and tiring quickly. He rushed in to close his attacker down before he lost his strength. Enola allowed her limping opponent to catch her. She held one hand out against the shield, placing just enough resistance to force Hals to push. When he did, she released and sidestepped the juggernaut intending him to fall past her.

Hals staggered forward, crashing to the ground on top of his shield. He rolled into an upward facing position but the wind had been driven out of him and he was too slow to be able to defend himself. The next thing the felled warrior knew was the weight of Enola's foot on his sword arm and the tip of her blade at his throat. His reaction was automatic, and he used his immense strength to swing his shield at Enola's legs. She resisted the blow, but the pain fuelled the rage already erupting from her.

Hals realised his mistake when he saw his attacker's eyes widen with determination and fury, the pressure from the blade increasing on his windpipe. Enola braced herself and placed her free hand on the pommel of the golden sword to ram the blade home, unable to control the rage within. It was then she saw what no other had ever seen before. Fear in Hals's eyes. He was a man who feared nothing. All his life he had been faster, stronger and more determined than any adversary he had faced. That had all changed in an instant when he experienced Enola's wrath. He realised his fear, taking control of it so as not to lose his dignity at the moment of his death.

The sound of the crowd rushed into Enola's ears. It gave her back a little composure, enough not to complete the killing thrust.

'Do you yield?' she demanded.

Hals nodded, and Enola lifted her foot off his sword arm so that he could raise a hand to show the crowd his submission. They let out a cheer that must have deafened the gods up in their heavenly realm or awoken the dead from a thousand years back.

Hals was quick to his feet, unwilling to allow his embarrassment to last a second longer than it needed to. He took Enola's free hand and held it up in triumph. The spectators were ecstatic, rushing forward to raise Enola onto their shoulders to carry her at least ten times around the field. Against all the odds, she had been victorious in front of her people, her gods and her father. No one could deny her the position at the head of her own troops.

Chapter 2

Arc

Fires lit the night sky in all directions, as far as the eye could see. The Corinth plains were ablaze, burning the fields and meadows to make way for and to encourage the growth of new grass. The Corinthians were herders, keepers of livestock and the animal they valued most was the ox. Vast herds of the humpbacked beasts roamed the grasslands for three seasons out of the four. In the winter, all but the pregnant cows and prized breeding bulls were slaughtered. Old cows were turned into dried slivers of jerky. The young gelded males not already butchered by winter, spent their last few days in the slaughter lines. The prime cuts of succulent young meat were devoured by the Corinthians who fattened themselves up in preparation for the sparse winter months ahead.

The young men of Corinth made good warriors because they were hardy. They had lived out on the plains since an early age, tending to the family herds. They slept out in the open; surviving off a mix of milk and blood. They were brought bread when the family came to slaughter a calf or a young gelding. They were always left a limb of the butchered animal to chew on for the following week or so, until the maggots started crawling out of the pickings left on the bone. The rotting meat was not wasted or discarded, it was hacked up into smaller pieces and boiled into a broth, maggots and all. The bone marrow and larvae gave the soup an extraordinary taste that the boys craved for, even years after they had left the savanna. Sucking any remaining marrow out of the boiled bones was regarded as the second highest treat in the young herders' lives, surpassed only by finding a beehive in a rotting tree and stealing the honey filled-combs from within.

The night air was acrid and stifling, drained of oxygen by the fires' smoke. Arc opened the flaps at either end of his tent to try and keep the air flowing through. He drank another cup of wine in an attempt to wash the smoke out of his throat and to stave off the pain he sensed creeping into his head. He had come to Corinth in the hope of killing a big cat, wooing the people and marching out with an army. That had been weeks ago. The lion was proving to be evasive, and the game of politics between Odexsius and his brother had reached a stalemate. There had only been one thing preventing him from giving up on this fruitless escapade, and as he felt her warm breath on the back of his neck and her cool hands embracing his shoulders, he let the frustration melt away.

Sonaji had not rushed into the Lion Lord's bed. She had first played an elusive and cold game of intolerance and disinterest in him, while being her most alluring and charming with those around him. She blew hot and cold around the Lord, disapproving of his jokes and questioning those who spoke of his fame, and then leaving him to wonder about her alluring smile as she parted, or the gentle, almost accidental stroke she gave to his arm or the back of his neck. Only when she was sure that Arc was confused by his conflicting emotions and her mixed signals, did she finally strike. She chose a night when he had drunk too much and followed him to his room in the Chieftain's palace.

Arc did not hear Sonaji slip through the heavy teak door. She moved silent and agile like one of the silver-grey house cats which roamed the palace grounds. Arc knew nothing of the intruder until her hand reached from behind him, slipped into his tunic, and toyed with his chest hair. Arc's warrior instincts and senses were sharp. Normally, he would have reacted swiftly and violently to fend off the possible danger. On this occasion he did not react to the unexpected invasion into his private space. His subconscious mind unwittingly expected the intrusion, while his conscious thoughts thrilled in the excitement and possible danger. She turned him around and moulded herself into his body, as if she were the soft cushions of the sofa he lay upon. No words were exchanged between them as she guided him to the sleeping mats on the floor.

Since that night, Sonaji had been elusive and cold towards Arc in the daytime, avoiding any suspicion of their intimate relationship, but she spent every evening in his chambers. Sonaji knew all too well how palace tongue wagging could turn into political situations. She had her own most trusted bodyguards assigned to watching over Arc and the corridors leading between his chambers and her own. The trusted guards were essential, not only to keep her night-time affairs secret but also to protect the Lion Lord. Arc had ten-thousand Lion Warriors camped within a day's ride of the Corinth capital. If anything were to happen to Arc, a bloody war would instantly ensue.

Now that Arc had moved out to the grasslands, their romance was more straightforward. Sonaji had her new lover's tent lavishly furnished and placed behind her own. Her guards kept prying eyes at a distance, ensuring the couple's privacy. Sonaji was not a silent or restrained lover, but her bodyguards knew better than to ever eavesdrop on the bedroom activities of their Princess. They kept their distance, which enabled them to keep a straight face when they had to stand before their mistress in the daytime. Sonaji had ordered the flogging of more than a few of her guards for accidentally smirking in her presence and revealing their opinion of her private affairs.

Arc watched the flames through the open tent flap, facing towards the eastern horizon. The fires were bright in the dark night, making the distant hills appear like the slopes of a volcano with rivers of lava snaking their way downward. He listened to his own breathing and the wheezing in his chest caused by days of breathing smoke polluted air.

'When are they going to put out those blasted fires?' Arc tightened his grip on the naked Sonaji as if to wake her to hear his question.

She was already awake, her head on her lover's chest listening to that same gentle wheeze as he drew in each breath slowly so as not to cause her any discomfort.

'It's been three days now. If the winds are favourable, the flames will blow themselves out in a day or so.' Sonaji pushed herself up onto one elbow. 'Shaka is still hiding behind his palace walls. The coward still refuses to fight Odexsius, man against man, royal against royal. He would rather thousands die in a power struggle than one life be taken for the good of all. He gathers his warriors around him.'

Arc was admiring her breasts as he listened to her words. He was mesmerised by the glittering effect of his perspiration on her dark skin. She did not sweat from the heat of the humid nights like he did. Sonaji's skin was dry to the touch, like soft linen. She stayed cool as she slept, while Arc suffered droplets of sweat meandering their way down his back. Only when Arc took her to the physical limits of their passion did her body release its dew, showering her lover with droplets of perspiration.

'Why doesn't he just kill him?' Arc traced his finger over one of Sonaji's soft nipples, to wipe away the remnants of his own perspiration, and caused it to stiffen. 'He has the right, and your laws allow it.'

She shuddered. 'It's not that he is afraid. He wants to fight his brother. I think he fears that in the wrong situation he will end up fighting the royal bodyguards rather than Shaka. Shaka is cowardly enough to hide behind them.' It was Sonaji's turn to idly draw a finger over a sensitive part of her lover's body. She smiled at the reaction she induced. 'Or, he is afraid he will lose the support of his warriors and the people.'

Arc frowned, his impatience with the situation showing in his expression. 'His warriors would never be displeased with a bold action that meant seizing power. The people who were doing well under Shaka's rule will protest, but they have no real power.' It suddenly hit Arc that Odexsius was not afraid of upsetting his warriors or the people of Corinth. He was keeping his options open with the Mander. If he killed his brother, the Empire would send troops against him. But that was the point, Arc wanted that irreversible commitment, and Odexsius was trying to sidestep it.

That thought would have to wait until the morning, his attention had been captivated by Sonaji, all his senses seduced by her sexuality. He pulled her leg across his body and lifted her easily by the waist, sitting her on his lap. She let out the tiniest of gasps, as he lowered her onto him.

Their eyes met and she gave the wickedest of smiles as they joined. Now Arc would have the satisfaction of seeing his lover sweat.

The next day word came that the Blood Lion had been sighted, a day's ride to the east. The smoke was blowing to the south, away from the camp, and there was a hint of sweetness in the air.

'Your uncle is playing a dangerous game,' Arc told Sonaji, while they shared breakfast.

'What do you mean?'

'He is attempting to keep his options open. That wasn't our agreement. He commits to the crusade or I will march on him and his brother.'

Sonaji's eyes widened at the force of Arc's words. She quickly calmed herself before speaking in her uncle's favour. 'He is just being prudent, to retain his popularity with the army and his subjects.'

'No. The people and the army will not hesitate to stand behind him. He did not need me to overthrow his brother. He needed a threat at his border to make the Mander believe his seizing of power from his weaker brother was a necessity.'

Sonaji thought carefully. She was aware that the fate of her homeland hung in the balance. They were about to be wiped out by the Lion Crusade or forced into the fight against the might of an empire. She considered the lesser of the two evils.

'Odexsius is just being overcautious.' Sonaji took Arc's hand in hers. 'You go kill the lion. At least give Odexsius the time it takes you to do that. I will return to the city and make him aware of the urgency.'

Arc's instincts warned him against allowing a possible enemy more time to organise against him. Corinth's warriors would be a grand prize for his army, but he could not afford to face them as part of the Mander war machine. They would either join him willingly or be forced to bend a knee as a defeated foe. In the end it was the doe-eyes of Sonaji's pleading expression and her gentle persuasion that made his decision for him.

'Very well then. He has until my return to tip his dead brother out of the Corinthian throne, or it will be him the Corinthian nation will be grieving for.'

It had been several days since the Blood Lion had killed a young Corinth herder. While he slept the boy had been dragged from the ring of thorn bushes meant to protect him and the escaped calf he had retrieved. The Ghost Cat, as he was known in this area, had ripped the boy to pieces, eating only the succulent organs and leaving the rest for the vultures. The beast had then carried off the calf. The lion was known to roam a vast area as its territory. When game was plentiful to the south the cat never troubled the herders. But in times of shortage the beast patrolled the northern borders of its range, and that brought it into contact with the Corinthian herders.

Arc and Lincon, the captain of Arc's bodyguard, walked with the Corinthian guides followed by the bodyguards and the caravan of bearers and pack horses.

'The Ghost Cat is moving east,' the guide in charge had told Arc and Captain Lincon. 'The villages in all directions around the place the boy was murdered, have tied calves to a stake as bait. The one to the east was taken two nights ago, so we go east.'

Arc was fascinated that the guide called the beast's killing of the boy, murder. These people thought the cat's actions as premeditated, as if the lion was a serial killer or a hater of men.

'Why does the beast have so many names?' Lincon asked Figgis, their guide. 'I have heard it called the Ghost Cat, the Blood Lion, the Devil Cat or Lion, and my favourite, the Shadow Cat.'

The guide instinctively touched the charms hanging around his neck as Lincon spoke the beast's aliases. 'Those who claim to have seen him, say he has a red mane that looks like it is stained with his victims' blood. He is a cunning beast. He covers his own tracks, misleading wise trackers like myself.' Figgis looked nervous talking about the lion. 'The Ghost leads you in one direction, and then appears in some place in the opposite direction. He returns to a kill several times in one night, using more than one path to approach and leave, making it impossible to decipher which was his final choice. I have followed his trail several times, only to come to a dead end. It is as if the Shadow Cat simply disappears.' Figgis hung onto his charms as he spoke the next words. 'He is the devil, a cunning beast with a twisted soul, sent here to punish us for the wrongs we do.'

It was still long before noon, but the heat of the day was starting to take its toll on the small column. Arc's gaze was drawn to three trees, the like of which he had never seen before. They looked like giant mushrooms with green tops. They had thick knobbly trunks from the top of which sprouted twisted branches in all directions. These branches were veiny with a dome of green spikey foliage above them.

'Dragon blood trees,' Figgis told them. 'They have a blood like sap that has many magical properties. It heals many ailments, and can even be turned into wine, I make it myself.'

A group of grassland fowl protested at being disturbed. A big female bird was silenced with an arrow shot by one of the younger guides. The other fowl took flight, landing just outside of arrow range as if it understood the limitations of the weapon. The caravan stopped under a group of marula trees, their leafy branches providing shade from the hot sun. A fire was made, the bird was roasted, and everyone took the opportunity to relax. The ground they laid on was scorched, but already new shoots of green grass were sprouting through the blackened earth. Ants scurried in lines up and down the trunks of trees, and across the ground, carrying pieces of leaves cut from the marula.

'You are a fine guide and a hunter, Figgis,' one of the bodyguards with sharp features and a stern expression pointed out. 'Why have you not killed this beast?'

'It is forbidden,' Figgis replied flatly.

'The Ghost only comes here at this time of year, and not every year,' the younger guide who had shot the bird told them. 'The fires drive away his food, so he comes to take ours. We just try to drive him away. Only those of royal blood can take a lion. Figgis is a great hunter, but if he were to take the Ghost, our ancestors would be displeased.'

Figgis laughed. 'And after he had burned my village for killing the royal beast, the Chieftain would cut off my balls and hang my naked body upside down from a dragon blood tree for the crows to pick out my eyes and the ants to strip the flesh from my bones. No, we don't hunt the Ghost, just chase him away.'

Arc was the first to his feet. 'Come on. If I am to get ahead of this monster we need to get moving.'

Enola

One hundred and five officers were chosen from the competition, one hundred and six if you counted Enola. The Storm Legions were formed. Four new legions called Hurricane, Typhoon, Cyclone and Tornado. The warriors in all the legions would be known as Spartikens, taking their name from Spartik, the God of Storms. Eighty Sergeants were charged with finding two-hundred and fifty of the best warriors for their units. Each legion was to be made up of three thousand heavy and light infantry, one thousand heavy and light cavalry and a mix of one-thousand archers, artillery and engineers. Gavara had organised them into units of two hundred and fifty of the same types: infantry, cavalry, archers, etcetera. They were designed to fight as a legion and not as individual units. Other parts of the Avolonian army were compiled in a different way, so that each unit of two hundred and fifty could operate independently from the mass of the legion.

Arc had different expectations of the Storm Legions than for those of the rest of his army. They were to be a battering ram for significant battles. Collectively the Storm Legions would operate as one big powerful weapon to strike fear into the enemy; individually, as the Hurricane, Typhoon, Cyclone or Tornado legions, they would be a tactical weapon of immense ferocity operating together on the battlefield or in different battles at the same time. Gavara had designed their structure specifically for the Lion Crusade and the task that lay ahead. Every man, woman and beast in the Storm Legions would need to be well-trained, the finest, and bravest there is to create a force that even the Gods would fear to face. Gavara would make sure the new troops bonded and felt the loyalty and pride that would hold them together or spur them on in a battle. Already they had a motto, 'No retreat.'

Enola chose five generals to be her staff. General Antona would command the Hurricane Legion. It was never in doubt that she would want her trusted friend to be on her staff. To lead the Tornado Legion, Enola selected General Hals. Elektra was her choice to lead the Typhoon Legion. The Shieldmaiden had tried to turn down the commission, protesting that she would be happy to be a captain rather than a general, due to her lack of experience. Enola would have none of it; she saw something special in the big female warrior and insisted she joined her staff as General Elektra of the five thousand strong Typhoon Legion.

General Ioniedas was the final choice for the last legion. Enola wanted General Cid of the Jagger Knights to take command of the Cyclone Legion, but he was never going to be allowed, nor would he want to step down from leading the Knights. It was only a matter of time before Cid would take over from the ailing Razor as Grand Master. Ioniedas did not take part in the competition, as he was a Lion Warrior. Arc had banned any of his elite force from entering the competition or selection for the new legions. Gavara had persuaded him to make the one exception. Ioniedas had proved himself beyond a doubt in the ranks of the Lion Warriors. Gavara suggested him to Enola because of the experience he would bring to the all-new legions. The distinguished officer had been reluctant to leave his beloved Lion Warriors, but Arc had made it clear that it was his will and Ioniedas' duty.

Eric was chosen as the last of Enola's staff. He did not do very well in the competition, but Enola trusted him and knew he had an analytical mind that was exceptional at problem-solving. She made him the general in charge of supplies and logistics. It may not have been the commission that would fill his world with glory, but it did allow Enola to make her good friend a general with real purpose.

Every blacksmith in the army was put to work on making new weapons and armour. The uniform was to be bronze armour, as the elements for the metal were plentiful in the region and it was easy and quick to shape. Also a crimson tunic and cloak that would not show blood. Every warrior was to carry a bronze shield with their legion's letter in black on the front, H, T, Ty and C. The letters were shot through with crossed lightning bolts, which was to be the symbol for the Storm Legions. They were all given a curved sword known as a kopis, a short sword with a hoplite blade, and a dory-tipped spear. The archers had their bows instead of the spear, but carried the two blades strapped in a cross on their backs like every other warrior in the Storm Legions. The swords, spear tips and arrowheads were all made of the most modern steel. Bronze was too soft a metal to hold up against Mander steel but would work well as armour. In addition to their bronze shields, the warriors of the Storm Legions would have a breastplate, a helmet with cheek flaps and a nose piece, and greaves for the shins and forearms.

Gavara sat beside Enola on the rocks crowning the hilltop overlooking the training fields. Twenty thousand warriors of the Storm Legions trained with swords, or linking shields in a phalanx to practice advancing as one unbroken line, or riding their cavalry mounts in twisting and turning formations. The Commander and her trusted adviser were joined by her five generals. Antona and Ioniedas were both stereotypical-looking officers. Their chiselled features and bulked up, lean bodies, toned by thousands of hours spent on the training grounds and years of hard military campaigns, gave them the same look as the bronze statues which had been cast in the likeness of Gods or great heroes of the past. The only thing distinguishing them from each other was that Antona wore his hair short, and, as most of the Lion Warriors did, Ioniedas wore his long to show he was a free man.

The Lion Warriors had once been an auxiliary legion in the Mander army, and Arc had risen through the ranks of that same army to become a Mander general. The Lion Warriors had been treated no better than slaves until Arc came along, giving them pride and the honour they deserved. When Arc left the Mander army after leading them to victory at Jomora, every man of the Lion Warriors deserted to follow him. Since that day in the deserts of Saxland, the Lion Lord had led his warriors into many battles. The first was against the Merron Hordes at Ribbelstead before leading them halfway around the world to fight the Mander forces of Atropolis at Caputhora.

Ironically, Arc had faced Edius-Max at Caputhora. Before that fateful day, Arc had led Mander troops against his now trusted general, when Arc himself had been a general in the Mander army serving under Atropolis. After being defeated at Jomora, Edius-Max and his surviving troops were conscripted into the Mander army as auxiliaries and marched west to face the Avolonians. In the battle of Caputhora, Edius-Max had helped turn the tide of the fight against the Mander. He, and the auxiliaries he led, betrayed Atropolis by refusing to fight. Edius-Max and all the men he led had earned their freedom that day and followed Arc back to Mander to destroy the Empire. Arc and his elite warriors had almost come full circle in their bid to bring that retribution. Mander had put them in chains, killed or enslaved their families, and taken their lands.

Antona and Ioniedas are both above average height and well built, but they looked small next to Hals and Elektra. Eric sat on a rock adjacent to Enola. He had what was probably an average amount of body fat but, in the presence of such a lean and well-trimmed group, he looked plump.

'Have you all recruited the numbers you need?' Enola asked, her words sounding nasal. Her eyes were a little black and puffy, and there was still some swelling of the broken nose Hals had given her in the final round of the competition to become commander of the Storm Legions. It had been a bad break, making the nose crooked and angled. Enola had toyed with the idea of keeping the disfigurement and ridding herself of her good looks. She was not convinced that being an attractive commander was going to be an advantage. Gavara had persuaded her otherwise and to let him straighten her nose. Now that the swelling was going down, it was apparent what a good job the old surgeon had done.

'Getting the numbers is not the problem,' Antona answered. 'What is taking the time is swapping out the duffers.'

Hals laughed. 'General Memfis is none too happy.' Enola gave him a puzzled look. He laughed again. 'He gets all the rejects. We take his best warriors, and he gets back what we don't want.'

Gavara sighed. 'I fear that Memfis has the hardest job of us all. His troops are made up of rejects, farmers and refugees; they will always be the weak link in our army. He will rely on numbers.'

'They don't need to be skilled warriors. They will do what they always do, and hide behind the trained troops,' Elektra said, as she found a comfortable place to sit on the rock. Two finches scattered from behind a boulder, complaining loudly at being disturbed as they flew across to the next outcrop of rocks.

Gavara shook his head. 'If only that were true, we could advance directly on to Mander-Kush. But I fear they will need to be in the front ranks or our line will be too short, and we will be outflanked and engulfed when we face the vast numbers the Mander can bring to the field of combat.

'Then let's hope my father can bring the Corinthians back with him,' Enola added. 'We have advanced as far as we can through lands that have a grievance with the Mander. From now on we are entering regions loyal to the Empire. Between here and Mander-Kush we will face people who are of Mander origin; who think of themselves as loyal citizens of our enemy; who will see us as invaders, not liberators. The easy days of liberating and moving on are behind us. What lies ahead is a wall of resistance and a fight to the death.'

Gavara agreed. 'What has made Corinth so wealthy is its location. As well as having a tradition as a warrior nation, it has grown wealthy on trade. The Mander have swelled their own coffers by heavily taxing the Corinthians. Their territory is a crossroads of all the main trade routes. If they side with us, we will have all the supplies we need.'

'And their much-needed spears in our phalanx,' Ioniedas added.

Two serving girls appeared over the brow of the hill. They carried one wine jug and one water jug each.

'I thought we could do with some refreshments up here tonight,' Antona told the gathering, with a wry smile.

The girls poured wine for everyone, handing out cups and olive bread from a bag each of them carried over their shoulder. They made a second round, adding a little water to the wine already in each cup. Enola was captivated by the beauty of one of the girls. The woman was about one, no more than two years, older than the Commander, with mousy hair and a full figure. Both girls were pretty, but there was something about this one's face that Enola found pleasing.

'What's your name,' Enola asked, as the girl poured some water into her wine.

The young woman was surprised to be asked a personal question by someone so far above her social status. She smiled at the Commander and replied, 'Jenaliena, Mam,'

Enola was instantly mesmerised by Jenaliena's opal-blue eyes and seductive voice. She felt an unfamiliar type of attraction and realised she was beginning to flush.

'Is everything ok, my lady?' Jenaliena asked, worried about the strange expression on Enola's face and the uncomfortable silence that had followed her answer.

'Yes,' Enola was startled into replying. 'Yes, and it's sir, not mam or my lady,' she replied more sternly than she had intended. 'In the military, all female officers are sir. Mam or my lady is for the wives of the male officers.'

'Sorry mam, I mean sir. I should have known better. I'll remember in future.'

'Jenaliena, bring some more of that wine over here,' Antona commanded, knowing he was rescuing the girl from an awkward situation.

Elektra had also noticed the altercation and was intrigued by what she had seen. 'Pretty, isn't she?'

'No more than the hundreds of other serving wenches around the camps, gold digging for a rich officer husband.'

Elektra grinned at the sharp answer, seeing it for what it was, Enola's attempt to cover up her embarrassment of being attracted to another woman. Enola did not notice her General gloating at her, she was too distracted by Antona laughing and joking with Jenaliena. She suddenly felt enraged when she observed Antona take a handful of the serving girl's buttock and squeeze it a couple of times without being rejected or reprimanded.

'Leave us!' Enola called out. 'We have business to attend to here,' she added, to leave no doubt that she meant the serving girls.

'Leave the wine,' Antona politely demanded, as both girls made a hasty departure.

Gavara drained his cup and placed it on the rock. Ioniedas saw this and raised an eyebrow.

'It's only water,' Gavara defended himself when he saw the General's expression. 'We must agree on a code of conduct to be taught to the Storm Legions.' This was the main reason Enola had gathered her Generals on the hill. 'We have gathered together many races and cultures. They all think individually and value different traits. We must change this at once. If we are to have any chance against our oversized enemy, they must think and behave as one.'

'Gavara is right,' Enola threw her weight behind his point. 'He has a lifetime of knowledge and experience in the art of war.'

'More than one lifetime,' Ioniedas cut in, 'if the myths are to be believed.'

Gavara frowned and made several dismissive gestures. 'The legions must be a machine: a killing machine; a machine of war; a living, breathing entity that acts without thinking. Every man must be equal, taking the same level of responsibility for the success of the many. There can be no acts of individual heroism. We must stamp out any thoughts of suicidal recklessness in the pursuit of glory. There must be no berserkers. The warriors of the legions must value life above all else. They must see the valour in those who fight with the will to live, over those who care not if they die. They must fight with a calm determination, avoiding rage or anger, this way they can preserve the phalanx and destroy anyone who dares to stand against them.'

When Gavara stopped speaking, there was silence on the hillside. Shouting from the training grounds came floating up to the hilltop. The metallic rhythm of blacksmiths' hammers pounding out Avolonian steel could be heard in the distance, as the Generals sat and contemplated Gavara's vision for their troops.

'It is a bold notion,' Antona stated. 'But how do we make the variety of individuals we have into your army of conformists?'

'Ioniedas, as an officer in the Lion Warriors, you have some experience of this.' Enola pointed out. 'How do the Lions achieve that invincible shield wall we have all seen is so effective in battle?'

'Training, training and more training,' Ioniedas replied without hesitation. 'Training until every action becomes instinctive, without thought.'

'Yes, yes,' Gavara said excitedly. 'But, what is it that binds every warrior to such discipline?

The young general struggled to comprehend what it was the old Pathfinder wanted him to tell. 'We fight for each other,' he said, hesitantly. 'It is the highest dishonour to break the link with your neighbour's shield and leave him in mortal danger.'

'Honour and dishonour, that is it!' Gavara exclaimed, his enthusiasm reaching a new high. 'How is that instilled?'

Ioniedas' expression lightened, suddenly realising what was expected of him. 'Every warrior makes a pledge to those he serves with. He promises to fight for the men by his side. He promises never to think of himself as anything other than their equal unless they ask him to lead them. He swears to train as hard and as long as every other Lion Warrior. No excuses. It is a dishonour to miss training, and not to maintain our weapons or armour. A dropped shield, a dull blade or tarnished armour are all reasons for disgrace. We don't boast. We tread lightly and use few words.'

'Exactly the code of honour we must instil in the Storm Legions. But, tell us, how do you remain calm and keep your composure in the heat of battle?' Gavara asked.

Ioniedas smiled. 'You know very well, old man. It is the singing you introduced that works so well to calm the men. We sing calming songs as we march into battle.'

'The song of the dead,' Enola butted in.

'Yes,' Ioniedas nodded. 'The songs slow the heart, calm our nerves. Any recklessness that would endanger the phalanx would be dishonourable.'

'There you have it,' Gavara told the Generals. 'A code of honour. The fear of letting down their fellow warriors. The fear of being seen as not training hard enough. Do not banish warriors from the legions for their inadequacies, banish them for any infringement of the code. That's how we turn these legions into fighting machines. They will live and die by their honour.'

'And songs,' Antona added.

'And songs,' Gavara agreed.

The rest of the warm night on the hillside was spent drinking too much wine and the telling of stories from battles like those at Caputhora and Fwenga. Enola was troubled by her feelings towards the serving girl and decided she was missing her friend and lover, Huwel. He was with his pirate fleet, and it had been too many moons since she had felt the press of his body against hers. She turned her attention towards Ioniedas. He was young and handsome and had the potential to fill in romantically until she could be reunited with Huwel.

It was not Ioniedas' attention that presented itself to Enola at the end of the night. It was Elektra who made a pass at the her under the full moon. The imposing spear-maiden had noticed how the servant had affected Enola. She misread the situation, thinking her Commander shared her own sexual preferences. The consumption of far too much wine made the new General brave enough to act on her impulses. With her huge, man-like hand on Enola's naked thigh, she asked if the Commander would like to join her in her tent for some more wine. The hand was swiftly removed and the rejection brutal. Enola left alone, for her own tent.

Arc

For two days Figgis led Arc from the edge of the grasslands into the deep bush territory. They had left the others behind in a small village, which was no more than a few huts and some cattle pens. An angry red sun sat on the horizon, setting the dusk sky on fire with amber tones. Arc made camp under a marula tree. Figgis left with his spear and bow in hand, a long knife tied to his waist and a water sack over his shoulder. He returned not long after dark, with a full water sack and an arm full of buffalo meat.

'Make a fire,' the little guide ordered Arc. 'This will be the last night you will be able to cook. The smell of burning wood will drive away the game and the beast you seek will not come near if he smells smoke.'

'What makes you think he will come here?'

'This is his way home. Over there,' Figgis nodded towards the horizon, now nothing more than a silhouette against a sapphire sky filled with countless stars, 'is the only waterhole in the area. I have left the carcass of the buffalo on the bank and hung its guts in a tree. The smell of that should draw him in. This is no ordinary creature. He is a beast of fate, an old spirit. If his soul is tied to your destiny, he will come.'

'Thank you,' Arc said, with genuine gratitude. 'I could not have done this without you.'

'But you must. You must do this alone,' Figgis said with conviction. 'Cook the meat and we will share a last meal together. Then I must leave and you must bury the ashes and take the lion spear and hunting knife to the waterhole. It would be foolish to come all this way and then miss the beast because you are sleeping on a belly full of meat,' Figgis chuckled to himself. 'I will wait for you at the village with the others. The next time I see you, you will carry the spirit of the beast within you, or you will not return because he has eaten you. I will come back here to find the spear and any bones the lion did not like the taste of, as I did with the Chieftain's eldest son.'

The meat began to crackle on the fire, so Arc turned it over. 'Any advice for me?'

Figgis showed all his perfect white teeth in a huge smile. 'Yes, my friend. Kill him.' Every wrinkle on the little man's face deepened as he roared with laughter. Abruptly, he stopped laughing. 'Do not run from him, he will chase you down. Do not climb into a tree, he will pull you out. Do not hide from him, he will find you. Once he has seen you, you must kill him or he will surely kill you.'

They shared the buffalo steak. The meat was tough, and Arc found the taste unpleasant. Figgis had no such issues, he wolfed the steak down with evident pleasure. Just before he was about to throw the last of the meat into his mouth, Figgis suddenly froze.

'What is it?' Arc asked.

The Guide gently made a shushing sound, and pointed to the sky, cocking his head to listen. Arc could hear nothing but the grasshoppers chirping. Then he heard it, a deep guttural sound like the cough of a dying man, faint and almost nothing more than a hint of sound on the breeze.

'That's him,' Figgis confirmed. 'He is far away, but he will come.' He got up to leave. 'Bury the fire and go to the water. I must leave.' A look of concern crossed the old guide's face. 'Be careful lord, something else is stalking us out here. I have felt it since we left the village. A man has no future without one eye on the unexpected.'

Arc was unfamiliar with the expression, but he got the meaning.

Figgis reminded Arc of one more thing before he left. 'Remember to eat the beast's heart. You can't take his soul if you don't eat his heart.'

Atropolis

A silver wedge of light forced its way between the silhouette of the distant hills from the receding night sky. The birds in the royal garden celebrated the approaching day with a dawn chorus of melodic calls. The daily contest between the peacocks and the blue jays started earlier than usual, their calls increasing in volume as they tried to outdo each other. Atropolis stood naked on his balcony watching the silver splitting the blue as dawn came to life and pushed the new day forward.

As the High Priest of Mander, Atropolis was second only to his father, the Great and Exulted Al-Din, the Bringer of Light, the Granter of Life. In truth, High Priest was a dull-bladed title. He shared sovereignty over the church with another, while his older brothers led the Empire's armies. His eyes narrowed as he watched the lower quarters of the city, outside of the Jade Palace's grounds, come to life. He wondered how many heathens and believers of false gods roamed freely through the streets of the Holy City. With the dawn of each day, there was an energy that raised itself within the High Priest. Atropolis welcomed the feeling rising within him, the hate and loathing of the heathens, the desire and determination to see the world united under the one true God, his God.

The Questerus demanded obedience and absolute faith. He would see the scriptures obeyed in their purest form, not the modern dilutions that welcomed tolerance, diversity and even the education of women who were neither high born nor priestesses. The world had become sick and diseased, he was the cure, the world's antidote against blasphemy and agnosticism. Today he would take the first step towards the Final Solution, one world under one religion. Today he would give his dream teeth, he would ordain the Immortals into his church and embrace them to the bosom of Kush.

The Immortals were his father's elite forces, a sort of royal bodyguard. Al-Din kept his Imperial Army close to the capital city, and the Immortals were the best of the best of those troops. Through shrewd negotiation and political wrangling, Atropolis had persuaded his father that they should be the warriors of God.

'All our warriors fight for God,' his opposition had argued.

Atropolis stood firm in his beliefs and referred to the teachings of the Questerus and its accounts of a vast army of priests who had carried the blades of reckoning to cleanse the world of sinners. The Immortals were destined to be the reincarnation of that holy army, and Atropolis would be the High Priest to ordain each and every man into the priesthood and the Army of God. He shuddered at the thought of a million blades hacking sin out of the world. His mind was ready for the day, he would now prepare his body before he attended his father's court.

Al-Din sat upon his throne, as he always did. What was different about this day, Atropolis noticed as he entered the Jade room, was that his father was dressed in his armour. Generals crowded to the divine leader's right of the steps that led up to the throne. Clerics and chancellors of the state clamoured for a position on the left. There was a constant stream of voices, and Al-Din looked like he had tuned out from the white noise of debate.

Atropolis felt his blood begin to boil as a result of what he witnessed. He stormed towards the throne. Al-Din saw his son approaching and his spirits lifted. He saw the look on Atropolis' face and held up a hand to quash the rage he saw coming towards him.

'Enough!' Atropolis bellowed as he bounded up the steps towards his father.

Al-Din's eyes widened at his High Priest's outburst. Atropolis noticed how weary his father was looking. The Lion Crusade had taken its toll on the Empire's Divine Ruler, and there would be no better time for Atropolis to assert himself. The tirade of voices resumed, fuelling the wrath that grew in Atropolis. He knew he could not let that angry demon loose; the last time he let it free it destroyed the Disciples of Kush, obliterating their souls with the Lord's vengeance.

'Silence!' he yelled, to let out some of the steam that was building.

General Pompieum was the only one from the military side brave enough to challenge the High Priest. 'Don't overstep your authority. You have no idea about the latest developments that are threatening the very core of our Empire. Go back to rutting your harem of priestesses and leave the war talk to the real warriors.'

Atropolis instinctively placed a hand on the golden dagger in his belt. He dressed like a priest, but he had the body and strength of a formidable warrior. He took a deep breath and suppressed his anger.

'If the good General spent less time chasing young boys and more time dealing with our enemies, the Lion Lord would probably not be amassing his forces on the borders of the Old Lands.' The venom was still recognisable in Atropolis' words, but he succeeded in keeping a level tone. 'Never in a thousand years has an enemy dared come so deep into Mander. Can't you see how your failures and your excuses are draining the life out of our Lord and Master?'

'That's ripe coming from the one who lost the Western Army and brought about this blasted crusade against us,' Pompieum spat at the High Priest.

Atropolis could no longer contain his anger. 'Get out! Get out, all of you! I will speak with my father alone!'

Mesteroph stepped forward on the side of the clerics. 'You have no authority to dismiss court.' He was the Chief Cleric who shared religious authority with Atropolis. 'Trading insults here will not vanquish our foes.'

'Out, I said! Now!' Atropolis' voice had risen to a screech.

Both Pompieum and Mesteroph looked towards Al-Din. The Emperor looked disinterested and waved a hand to dismiss court. A suppressed smile twitched at the corners of Atropolis' mouth. He had won this round and would whisper the foundation of his Final Solution into the ear of the one man who had the power to help him make it a reality.

The colossal bronze doors to the room groaned as they came together like two old men complaining, and finally closed with a clash not too different from the sound of the metal drums used by the palace musicians. Atropolis wasted no time in turning to his father.

'Do not underestimate this man, this Lion. If you run to face him, he will destroy you.' Atropolis poured some water from a jug sitting on a small table by his father's throne and handed the cup to the Emperor.

'What then do you suggest? The Lion Crusaders are in our land, at the borders of the old country. Every thief and peasant from the coastal provinces has taken up arms against us. I cannot be seen as hesitant or weak. I must destroy him before he takes one step into the heart of Mander.'

Atropolis shook his head. 'That is Pompieum talking, and what the Lion wants. Do not underestimate him. Send for the Southern Army, and gather your forces from the east and west. Stall him, trap him and starve him. Frustrate him every step of the way until you are ready. Then show him the might of a million warriors in the field. Crush him with the fist of God, and then march on to take his lands in the name of Kush.' Atropolis was finding it hard to suppress his anger. He had once thought his father to be the chosen one. The one named in the Questerus as the second coming: the divine entity that would place the word of Kush on the lips of the world. He now thought him weak, surrounded by fools and those with only self-advancement in mind. 'You are the Divine, the earthly embodiment of Kush. You have a duty to follow the Questerus in its purest form, and it says to bring the word of Kush to the world, not just Mander.'

Al-Din looked at his son with eyes that gave away his inability to think straight. 'Your brother, the Third

Prince is bringing the Northern Army to Siena Mazda. He is already on his way. Xarius is expecting me to bring the Imperials there, to join our forces and stamp on the Lion's neck.'

'They are all your forces,' Atropolis said, offended by his father's suggestion that he needed to join up with his arrogant older brother. It just made the High Priest more convinced his father was weakening with age. 'Excellent! Xarius can cut off their supplies and ambush them at every opportunity. He will give you the time you need to assemble the true might of your army.'

There was a sudden glint in the Emperor's eye. 'Yes, you are right. Xarius will save the day. He will hold the Lion by the tail, while we ready for his destruction. Send for Xerces and his Southern Army. The earth will tremble when our armies march.'

Atropolis felt the spice in his blood racing through his veins. There would be no more conforming or empire building to swell the coffers of the Mander Aristocracy. The world would embrace Kush or take its steel through the heart.

'I will make it so,' he told his father as he left. 'Rest, don't let your wives wear you out.'

Enola

The day started calmly with the expectation of passing from dawn to dusk as uneventfully as the day before. As is often the case, drama erupted to shatter that calm. Light clouds hovered over the Avolonian camps, shading them from the sun but making the air humid and heavy. The day was just about at its hottest when the news came that the Mander were on the march. Two armies, both estimated to be over one hundred thousand strong, were snaking their way west to Siena Mazda. One was the Imperial Army from Mander-Kush, led by the Emperor Al-Din. The other was the Northern Army that had marched south towards the city. Half that force had broken off and turned west in the direction of Calinkerbad.

'They aim to cut us off from the best supply route through Calinkerbad, while securing the defence of Siena Mazda,' Antona pointed out to Enola, and the other Generals gathered to discuss the news. 'Half the Northern Army have broken off and are heading for Calinkerbad. That number of troops could hold the port city indefinitely. They have enforced a scorched earth policy on the lands between where we stand and Siena Mazda. They must have marched hundreds of thousands of civilians, livestock and supplies east.'

Edius-Max let out a slow whistling sound. 'They can't have moved everyone and everything from what must be an area two hundred and fifty leagues long and five hundred leagues wide.'

'They can, and they have,' Cid of the Jagger Knights confirmed.

'I have seen this before,' Edius-Max went on. 'They hope to stretch our supply lines so far back that we cannot defend them. They will starve and weaken us until there is little fight left in us. Then they will strike at our core.'

'Al-Din knows he has time on his side.' Memfis looked around the room for any opposition to his statement. 'I hear that with enough time he can easily field another half a million warriors against us. In addition to the two hundred and fifty thousand he will have gathered in Siena Mazda.' He added the final sentence intending to focus everyone on the task at hand.

'We can use this against them,' Enola said. The room was quiet while the Generals gathered their thoughts about what Enola meant. 'We split the army in two,' Enola went on when no one else offered anything. 'We send our main force to block the half of the Northern army heading for the port. The others can then take Calinkerbad. Once we have secured that supply route, we can combine against the Emperor's army at Siena Mazda. They have hundreds of thousands of mouths to feed, and if we take Calinkerbad they will suffer,'

Edius-Max rubbed the stubble on his chin, a thoughtful look on his face, with a hint of worry. 'Your father is against splitting the Army for any reason. He thinks we must maintain our strength while picking off each of Mander's smaller regions until they are forced to face us toe to toe on the battlefield.'

'Well, events have overtaken us. Their scorched earth policy means there are no smaller regions remaining to be overcome. If we don't act fast, they will gain all the advantages.' Enola narrowed her eyes. 'This way the Lion Lord will get his wish, we will be facing the might of the Mander Army at Siena Mazda sooner than expected.

'Your Storm Legions are not ready for battle, they need more training. We should wait for your father's return,' Edius-Max argued.

'My father is not here, and the Mander have left us without time to wait for him. The Storm Legions will train as they march. I will take Calinkerbad with them, they are trained enough to take a city. They have all been in a battle before.'

Edius-Max was not yet convinced. 'What if you can't take the city quickly? I can hold the breakaway faction, but I doubt I can hold back the Imperial Army and the rest of the Northern Army if they advance from Siena Mazda.' He thought for a moment. 'If you get stuck in a siege, it will not matter how many troops I have, the Emperor will have time to crush us and then advance on you. I will feel happier if you take two of the Lion Warrior Legions to get the job done quickly and get back to us before the Mander can react.'

Cid joined the debate. 'My knights will come with you. You can concentrate on the city, and we will watch your back.'

Enola smiled at her friend. 'That will be appreciated, Cid. Will that satisfy you, Edius?' She did not wait for his reply. 'Memfis, will your troops be able to keep up with Edius' Lion Warriors and auxiliaries if you join him to block the Northern Army?'

'I doubt it,' Memfis said sulkily. 'I'm left with an ill-equipped rabble after the trials for the Storm Legions.' He rolled his eyes and made a dramatic sigh. 'They will keep up, they will have too.'

Enola was not concerned with gaining her father's praise for taking Calinkerbad and foiling the Emperor's plan to starve their army into submission. She was more afraid of his scorn for not acting quickly to counter the threat. Her quick action would put the Mander on the back foot, and give the Avolonians a foothold deep in the Empire's centre. She would have liked to consult with Gavara, but he had set off to join Arc in Corinth. She would send word to them of her plan, and ask them to bring the Corinthians to join her at Calinkerbad, if they had won them over. She would also send word to Huwel and his pirate fleet, to ask him to advance up the river and start bringing supplies to Calinkerbad as soon as the city was taken.

'Then that is the plan. Edius-Max will lead the army to...' she looked at a map in the middle of the room and placed a finger on a point between Siena Mazda and Calinkerbad. '….Gala, there is a river in the Gala area. Hold the Northern Army there. Memfis will bring the numbers to give your line width, and the Lion Warriors and Saxish Auxiliaries will have the experience needed if it comes to a fight. You will have a force of close to seventy thousand; it will not come to a fight when the Mander realise that so many are facing them. I will take my four legions and the Jagger Knights to Calinkerbad. Once the job is done there, I will join you,' she looked at Edius-Max, 'and we will be ready to face the Mander on our terms.' Enola felt a sense of pride in her decisiveness, and no one disagreed with the plan. Edius-Max had his reservations, but even he could see the need to react quickly to the new situation. With a sigh of satisfaction Enola ended the meeting. 'To war then, Generals, to war.'

Enola lay awake, the excitement of taking her new legions into action proving too much for her mind to think about. She finally gave up on sleeping and sent for some wine and olive bread. The order was based on a craving, but she also thought the food and drink would help her sleep later. A servant girl brought a tray. The girl looked sleepy, having been disturbed from her own slumber. Enola recognised the girl, it was Jenaliena. She poured the wine and placed the bread along with some dips on a table next to her.

'Jenaliena, isn't it?' Enola asked.

'Yes sir,' came a faint answer.

'You remembered to call me sir.'

'Of course,' Jenaliena had now woken up enough to be her usual flirty self. 'I said I would. Are you still angry with me?'

The question took Enola by surprise. 'I was never angry with you, just stressed with the situation. Through no fault of your own, you were a distraction. I didn't care for General Antona taking the liberty of groping you.'

Jenaliena laughed. 'He has taken more liberties than that. A proper liberty taker that one.'

'Tell me more,' Enola requested, her interest evidently awakened. 'No. First, pour yourself a cup of wine and join me.'

Jenaliena hesitated.

'Come on,' Enola said, patting the seat next to her. 'I need the company.'

The young woman shrugged, poured herself a cup of wine and slumped down on the sofa next to Enola.

'So, you and Antona are an item?'

Jenaliena giggled at the question. 'I have let him bounce around on me a few times, but these days he is more interested in my friend, Plenty.' She had to pause to let out a little laugh and took a gulp of her wine before continuing. 'He likes Plenty because she gives plenty.'

Enola was pleasantly surprised at how quickly the girl had relaxed, and how freely she talked about her private life. Enola had mostly grown up around men. Serious and self-important had been the standard. The closest she had come to gossip and self-criticism was the way that the less charming of the warriors she had grown up around put each other down. One warrior would make fun of another's mistake or shortcomings. The offended party would then highlight his insecurity by coming back with a more elaborate insult or put down, and the whole thing would escalate until it became a feud or a brawl.

'You actually have a friend called Plenty?' Enola was visually amused by the fact. 'And, she gives plenty. That is typical of Antona. I spoiled him,' she gave her new companion a mischievous look. 'I was his first. Did he tell you that?' Enola had grown giddy with the thrill of sharing her intimate secrets in such a light-hearted way.

'He did not. I should have guessed. He adores you. I thought it was respect for your leadership, but I will bet a silver chip that he carries a torch for you.'

The two women emptied the jug of wine, laughing and gossiping through the night. By the time they fell asleep, they knew each other's secrets and all the dirt on the people they liked or disliked. Enola forgot all about her troubles and the heavy burden she now carried as commander of the Storm Legions. She fell into a deep sleep on Jenaliena, using her new friend's breasts as a pillow. Jenaliena traced a finger over the scar that ran from Enola's forehead, through her eye and over her soft cheek, and gently stroked her hair until she also fell asleep.

Arc

The lion did not show himself at the watering hole on the first night or the following two nights. Arc heard the beast calling into the night, but the sound did not seem to be getting any closer, and he feared the lion was passing him by. He lay in the tall grass at the base of an outcrop of rocks where he had a clear view of the buffalo carcass, and his back was protected. Arc kept one hand on the thick shaft of the lion-spear. He would have preferred his trusted sword and a shield instead of the cumbersome weapon, but tradition dictated.

The smell of the buffalo's rotting flesh was unbearable. Arc had watched for days as birds, small animals and a constant swarm of flies had feasted on the carrion. Disappointingly, nothing significant had come to dine. The Lion Lord was relieved when the wind changed and carried the stench away from him. The night air was suddenly so sweet that he felt its aromas relaxing him to the point where he was in danger of falling asleep.

His mind wandered, turning to thoughts of Sonaji and how she kindled emotions in him that had been a long time dormant. Arc's heart had been closed to romance for too long. There were women, companions to lie with him through the long nights, but they were never more than a solution to his urges. He was pursued by guilt when women were affectionate towards him. The love of his life had been Jem. As a teenager he had not chased around after the popular girls in the city, trying to inflate his ego by making conquests. Jem was the only one for him. He had adored her, growing more and more in love with her as they aged together. She gave him the most beautiful daughters he could hope for, and they were happy until the Mander came along.

Arc's mood darkened at the thought of losing Jem. He had knelt, helplessly watching, as she was dropped from a city wall with a rope around her neck. The look she gave him in the final moments of her life had haunted him ever since, his heart had ripped in two as he watched her fall, holding her gaze until the very end.

He had eventually taken revenge on her murderer. But in the time that passed between Jem's death and the knife being drawn across her killer's throat, he had let another into his heart. Sefra was a slave girl who had drifted into Arc's life at a time when he had lost all memory of who he had been. They became lovers and he cared for her. She was the first tenderness in his life of hardness and cruelty, since being captured by the Mander. Arc had arranged for Sefra to be freed from her bonds of slavery, when tragedy struck. She took her own life after being raped and abused by Al-Jin, the same monster that had executed Arc's wife. The kind-spirited young slave was unable to face her existence as a slave any longer. She died without knowing she was on the brink of freedom.

Arc felt anger rising in him as he remembered finding the young slave girl, naked in a pool of her own blood, her body beaten and violated by Al-Jin and his henchmen. Arc had hunted down the fiend responsible and inflicted a bloody revenge for taking away from him the exquisite souls of Jem and young Sefra. He clung onto the anger he was feeling and enjoyed remembering slitting Al-Jin's throat and watching the life drain out of him. Arc calmed his anger by thinking once more about Sonaji. She brought him peace and was fast becoming his safe haven in the turbulent storm that was his life. He doubted he could ever love again, but Sonaji was starting to bridge the gap between the cold-hearted warrior he had become, tortured with an obsession for revenge, and the man he once was.

The moon was at the highest point of its arc when a gust of wind swept around the rock behind where Arc was hiding. As if on cue, all the grasshoppers stopped chirping at the same time and the night was left in silence. The hairs stood up on the back of Arc's neck. The silence was deafening, and he did not dare move. He just listened. His heart was pounding as if it was trying to climb out of his chest. He struggled to breathe in silence. Then he heard it: a low rumbling sound coming from the rocks behind him.

There was light scuffing of claws on the granite. A small rock tumbled down to land in the grass by the side of Arc's foot. His ears filled with the sound of panting. The beast was right above him on the rocks. He heard the rumbling sound again. It was a deep throaty sound as if the lion was roaring in a whisper. Arc's heart was beating faster than he had ever known it could. He wanted to turn his head to look, but found himself frozen to the spot.

There was a sudden scramble and Arc braced himself, sure that the beast was about to drop on him. The lion leapt from the rock and landed several paces in front of where Arc lay. Dust spurted up from under the beast's massive paws. It flicked its tail and shook its huge head, causing the dark mane to fluff up. Arc was no longer aware of how fast his heart was beating, he was mesmerised by the size of the animal. The great beast hunched its back, opened its enormous jaws and let out an earth-splitting roar. Arc's body trembled with the sound.

The beast turned its head and looked directly at Arc. Its demonic eyes reflected the moonlight. Arc was sure the creature could see him, and even more convinced it could smell his sweat-coated body. Surely it would attack at any moment. He tightened his grip on the spear, but the beast turned away. The lion strolled over to what remained of the dead buffalo, sniffed at it a few times, and then slumped down next to it.

Arc just watched as the beast chewed on the flesh. The lion grunted as it pulled off strips of meat and let out crackling roars that Arc could only assume were roars of pleasure, even though they were an angry sound. He let the beast fill its belly with the remains of the buffalo. He decided that a lion with a full stomach would be easier to kill than a hungry beast disturbed from its meal. He did not want to wait until the lion had finished entirely and risk it taking off into the bush, so he kept his patience until he thought the beast was coming close to finishing.

The lion stopped chewing, raising its head to lick its blood smeared snout. It closed its eyes and curled back its black lips to bare its giant fangs, as if sniffing the air. The beast's eyes suddenly opened wide and it froze for an instant. It sprang to its feet, dust scattering in the shuffle of its paws. The beast faced the trees to Arc's left, snarling and threatening towards the darkness. Arc did not know what had spooked the lion, he just knew that if it bolted now he would never get another chance to face it.

Arc jumped to his feet with the lion-spear in hand, its great long blade aimed at the beast. The lion turned its head and froze with surprise when it saw the pale figure standing there. There was a moment of indecision in the animal, which ended swiftly when it focused on Arc. It arched its back and sprang at him, covering half the distance with one bound. Dust spurted up under its massive paws. It let out a mighty roar, baring its yellow, dagger-like fangs at Arc. The beast's fury knew no bounds, its anger terrifying. It charged directly at him.

Arc dropped to one knee, rammed the butt of the spear against the rock and lowered its fearsome point at the beast. The lion ran onto the razor-sharp blade. It kept on coming as the point sank in, its colossal bulk unstoppable. Arc held tight onto the small crossbar a third of the way down the spear's shaft. The impaled beast hit him with such force that Arc was battered to the ground. The lion tried to claw at Arc's stomach with its hind legs. It missed, catching its claws in his leg instead. Arc cried out with pain as the beast's claws dug deep into his flesh.

Arc did not know if the lion was dying or would live long enough to kill him. He heard the spear's shaft cracking. In a panic he grabbed the hunting knife from his belt. The beast had now wrapped its front paws around Arc's back and was trying to pull his head into its large gaping jaws. The creature let out an earth-shattering roar into Arc's face. A fountain of boiling blood sprayed over him, into his open mouth and over his chest.

The beast was suddenly limp, its immense weight crushing Arc. He lay still, holding the unused hunting blade at the ready in case the creature revived. But the savage blade of the lion-spear had split the beast's heart and flooded its lungs with its own blood. Arc lay motionless until he could no longer bear the bulk of the lion. He pushed the beast's body off enough to wriggle free. He stood up, panting, shaking and covered in the lion's blood. He looked at his leg, cringing at the three deep bloody claw marks he saw. The lion was bigger than he had ever imagined. He had never known such power and fury could exist in one creature.

Arc crouched down to stare more closely at the magnificent beast. Even in death, the great lion had a majesty that had to be admired. He contemplated the best way to skin the creature, but first he would attend to the wound on his own leg. The lion's claws would be laced in poison. Dried blood and the rotting flesh of its victims coating the vicious talons would cause any scratches they left to fester and corrupt.

As Arc stood up it felt like he had been hit in his side by a hammer. He was spun around and stumbled backwards over the lion. He hit the ground hard. Lying still for a moment, Arc realised he had been hit by an arrow. If he had not stood up when he did, it would have caught him in the throat or chest, a killing shot. His mind raced as he realised that someone was there and they intended to kill him. He snatched up the hunting knife he had dropped when he fell over the lion and struggled to his feet.

Two men emerged from the treeline at the far end of the waterhole. Arc held onto his waist. The arrow had skewered him, so that the wound, with the shaft still in, bled at the front and the back. He tightened his grip on the knife and let his anger distract him from the pain of his wounds. One of the men held a bow aimed at the Lion Lord as they approached, an arrow nocked and the string drawn. The other man carried a warrior's sword and shield. They were both Corinthian warriors, big men with the physique of seasoned fighters. Their black skin reflected the moonlight as they carefully made their way towards their prey.

The man carrying the sword was grinning from ear to ear, whereas the man with the bow wore a severe look, concentrating his aim on Arc.

'Who are you?' Arc asked, not knowing what else to say.

'The men who will kill you,' came the gleeful answer from the man with the sword.

Arc's warrior mind weighed up the situation, taking in every angle, looking for any opportunity. The drawn bow ruled out any attack on his part unless they came too close.

'That's close enough,' the warrior with the sword said, putting an end to any hope Arc had of them stepping into his killing zone. 'I just want to be close enough to see the fear in the eyes of a great leader as his life comes to an end.'

'Who sent you?' Arc demanded, more to stall for time than out of curiosity.

'Not something you need to worry yourself with. Who benefits from your death is a matter for the future, and you have no future,' the sword warrior was happy to point out. 'All you need concern yourself with now is the manner of your death. Will you piss yourself as you die? Will you beg for your life? No, you are a great warrior. I saw you kill the lion, there is no fear in you. I think all you have to worry about is how many shafts it will take from my friend to put you down. Then I will come over there and take your head.'

Arc was furious. He wanted to dash at the men and cut them down, but they were smart enough to stay a safe distance away. The bowman would have time to fire at least two arrows before he could reach them.'

'I will not die a coward, but what about you? Will you fight like warriors or will you hide behind that bow?'

The sword warrior launched a laugh into the night sky, which tapered off into a snarl. 'Nice try, but we are here hunting for glory. You should not have come to our lands. You should never have imagined yourself leading our warriors. There is a new regime coming to Corinth, and there is no place in it for you, Lion Man,' his smile dropped away to be replaced with a mask of hatred. 'Kill him.'

Arc braced himself as the bow creaked, drawn to full stretch. The earth suddenly began to tremble and the bowman slackened his pull on the bow to see what was happening. From the cover of the long grass adjacent to the waterhole, burst a mass of fury and anger, another lion. The beast charged directly at the two warriors, snarling and roaring with every bound it made. The speed and intensity of the creature was shocking. It covered the distance between its hiding place and the warriors in the blink of an eye.

Arc was frozen to the spot as he watched the lion lunge at the warriors. The beast hit the bowman, bowling him over. It wrapped its forelegs around him in a deadly embrace, driving its claws deep into the flesh of his back. The massive creature brought its back legs up repeatedly, clawing great gouges into the man's body. His stomach was ripped open and his entrails raked out. The other warrior yelled a sound that was beyond fear and ran for the trees. The lion was now standing on top of the bowman, biting down on his head and shoulders. Arc could hear the cracking and crunching of bones. The beast opened its enormous jaws and snapped them shut, driving its dagger-like fangs through flesh and bone like a knife through soft cheese.

Arc tried to drag the spear out of the dead lion, but the shaft had been cracked and it broke away in his hands. He was left holding a broken pole without a blade. The lion stopped mauling what was left of the bowman and looked up at Arc. The beast looked at his dead sibling: they had been brothers. He then looked up at Arc who was holding the splintered shaft. Arc stood utterly still and tried to look as defiant as possible. The beast let out a roar that shook the night air and trembled the ground. Arc felt it shake his bones. He did not know if the creature felt grief for its dead sibling or had the capability of desiring revenge, but he could see the torrent of anger and fury flowing from the beast.

The lion suddenly looked away from Arc, distracted by movement in its peripheral vision. It was the Corinthian warrior running for the trees. The beast's predatory instincts took over. It was unable to resist prey that fled. The lion charged after the running man, closing the gap in two shakes of its own tail. All the wrath and vengeance of hell streaked across the trampled earth towards the fleeing warrior. From a cloud of dust, the lion pounced onto the man's back. The warrior let out a blood-curdling scream that was silenced when the beast's fangs closed around his throat. The lion shook the full-grown man as if it were a dog shaking a rabbit.

It was over in seconds. The beast carried the warrior by the throat, the lifeless body trailing along the ground between the animal's legs. The lion looked menacingly towards Arc, its eyes reflecting the moon like two large yellow stars. Arc wondered if the waterhole was deep enough for him to swim away from the beast or if he could reach the bow before the lion covered the ground to reach him. His thoughts suddenly gave him the strangest experience. He found himself laughing. He had seen the speed and ferocity of the creature, neither the water nor the bow would protect him. He recalled Figgis' advice, *'Do not run from him, he will chase you down. Do not climb into a tree, he will pull you out. Do not hide from him, he will find you. Once he has seen you, you must kill him, or he will surely kill you.'* He added a line of his own, 'And don't fire arrows at him, you will just piss him off.'

Arc decided to stand his ground and stare the lion down. It made no difference. The lion just gave Arc a puzzled look before trotting away with the warrior still held in its mouth. The beast did not care how many battles Arc had won, how many men he led or how brave he was, it would just kill him if it got the chance. For now, the death of his brother forgotten, the beast had a meal and he would enjoy it in undisturbed seclusion.

Arc let out a sigh of relief. He could feel himself shaking. Facing these magnificent beasts had been nothing like fighting amid a battle. The battle rage was a different thing. There, he was the beast. He remembered his wounds. First, he peed on the claw marks in his leg: they would have to be stitched, but he would wait until he could coat them in sap from the dragon's blood tree. Then he pulled the shaft from his waist. He bound the wound with some cloth and a leather strap to stop the bleeding. It was only a flesh wound and didn't worry him.

He looked at the dead lion. He was tired and wanted to sleep, but he knew he had to work fast. The dead lion's twin could return at any moment. Arc would have to skin the beast quickly. He limped over to the tattered remains of the bowman to collect the bow. His stomach turned when he saw the amount of damage the creature had done in only a few moments. The man was unrecognisable as human. His body had been turned inside out, his limbs shredded and his head crushed. Arc collected the bow and the few arrows that were not broken from the quiver.

He decided that his best protection would be to light a fire. He limped around, gathering as many as he could carry of the dead branches scattered about the ground. He piled them by the corpse, stuffed them with dried grass and used his flint to set the fire. Once the flames reached a satisfactory height, Arc set to work on the lion. He cut out the heart. It was much bigger than he had imagined, too big to eat in one sitting, he thought. He held the massive organ tight, the dark blood washing down his arms as he took a bite of the raw meat. Once he had taken his bite, he placed the rest of the lion's heart on the fire to cook, and set about skinning the beast.

Sonaji bathed Arc's leg with warm water mixed with birch bark and forest plant essences that would disinfect the wounds. She washed away the crusted coating of dragon's blood sap that Arc had applied himself into the open claw marks.

'You are lucky,' Sonaji told him. 'There is no significant infection in the gashes. I can stitch them for you.'

'No luck about it,' Arc replied. 'Figgis told me of the healing properties of the dragon's blood sap. Without that stuff poured into the wounds I'm sure I would have lost my leg.'

It had taken Arc three days to get back to the small village where the others were waiting. After the night he had killed the lion, he had walked at dawn and dusk when it was not too hot but light enough to see. He had rested in the dark and in the heat of the afternoons. The nights were cold. Arc had decided the second lion was long gone and no further danger to him. On the other hand, he could not be sure that there were not others, like the two Corinthian warriors, hunting him down. So he had thought it wise not to light any fires which would give his position away.

Once he reached the village he used a swift horse to get himself back to Sonaji's camp. Gavara had been waiting for him there, and after a warm greeting had taken the lion skin from him for tanning.

'There is good news from the city,' Sonaji told Arc, while she stitched his wounds. 'My uncle marched into the palace, fought off two of Shaka's bodyguards and killed him. The state burial is today. Odexsius rules Corinth once more.'

Arc was gritting his teeth, dealing with the discomfort of the needle being pushed through the tender skin of his shin, but he nodded his approval.

'Does he have control of the army?' Arc was finally able to ask, while Sonaji was threading her needle with a new thread.

'He does. They debate whether to join your crusade or if it would be wiser to sit on the side-lines and let the two juggernauts fight it out.' Arc stiffened as Sonaji pushed the needle into the lip of the last wound that needed closing. She could see he was about to speak and she did not want to be interrupted. 'Don't worry. Odexsius killed two of his generals that were against joining the crusade. He knows that our best chance of survival is for the Mander to suffer defeat.' She paused to concentrate on a difficult part of the wound, which had a lateral tear. ' He could do with your presence at the palace to help sway the people's support towards your cause.'

'He is a good man; a strong leader, they will follow him. But, if it makes a difference, I will go to him. My Lion Warriors will parade alongside the Corinthian Army through the streets of Corinth. As long as we then march east together. We have wasted enough time already.'

'Did the men who attacked you say who had sent them?'

'No,' Arc replied, unable to say any more as Sonaji pulled a part of his wound closed.

'It must have been Shaka. Who else could it have been? My uncle wants you alive and well to destroy the Emperor.'

'I wouldn't trust that son of his. He has murder in his eyes and contempt in his words every time I meet him.'

'Tyezore? No, he may be an ambitious and ill-mannered man, but he is loyal to his father. It was Shaka, I am sure of it, and he has now paid the ultimate price for all his sins.'

Arc was wrong. He would not march his warriors through Corinth or even travel there himself. Just as Sonaji was bandaging Arc's leg, Gavara returned with news.

'Enola has marched the Storm Legions to take Calinkerbad,' he told Arc, his white hair and beard tangling in the breeze. Arc looked unconcerned. 'Edius-Max has taken the rest of the army to intercept the Mander Northern Army. It has splintered between the directions of Calinkerbad and Siena Mazda. She says she is acting to keep open the line of supply through the port city.'

Arc's expression rapidly changed. 'It's a trap.' He looked at Gavara, who nodded his agreement. 'Send word to the Lion Warriors. We ride for Calinkerbad, immediately.' Arc turned to Sonaji. 'Go to Odexsius. Tell him to bring his army to Calinkerbad.'

Gavara left and Arc got up to follow him. A thought struck him, and he turned back towards his lover, kissed her as if it were of great importance and left her with a single word. 'Hurry.'

Arter & Hurcan

A dust cloud one league long hung above the land the legions marched through. They were determined to maintain a pace of forty leagues a day to reach the walled city of Calinkerbad in good time. In the mornings, the warriors of the Storm Legions sang in time with their steps. In the evenings they were silent and grim-faced, conserving their energy for every step that would take them closer to the fortieth league and an end to the day's toil.

Arter coughed and spluttered as he staggered along, the dust choking him. He sweated and stumbled his way through the march. His back hurt from carrying his shield. His legs ached, and he felt like he could drop at any moment. He looked at the men around him. They all seemed to be enjoying the experience of being pushed to the edge of their physical endurance. He admired them, giving each of his fellow Spartikens a smile when he caught their eye, only to receive a frown or a derogatory look in return.

The men of the Hurricane Legion were strong, robust and fit. Arter knew he was, compared to the rest of the warriors in his unit, somewhat lacking in those qualities. He had dreamt about being a Lion Warrior ever since Arc brought the crusade to his homeland. Arter had been there when Arc gave his famous and rousing speech, to rally to his cause the people, tribes and states of Northern Mander. He could close his eyes and still hear the inspirational words of the Lion Lord. *'They have sown the winds of tyranny, now they shall reap the hurricane of retribution.'* Arter was inspired, and from then onwards he knew his calling was to fight by the great Lion Warrior's side. Ever since that day he had followed in Arc's wake with pride in his heart and a rusty old blade hanging from his belt.

When he heard the Storm Legions were to be formed, Arter was at the front of the recruiting lines. The officer in charge had sent him away, saying he was too skinny and to come back when he had put some meat on his bones. He thought it just as well when he heard about how many hopeful recruits were rejected and sent back to their own units, carrying with them the shame of falling short of the legion's requirements. Arter already lacked the respect of the men in his former unit. They treated him like a servant. He was the unit's dogsbody, fetching and carrying for everyone. His patience finally snapped when his Sergeant called him a useless bastard once too often. He stormed back to the recruiting officer of the Hurricane Legion and demanded to be allowed to try out. He was determined to show everyone that he was made of sterner stuff than they gave him credit him for.

Arter was about to be refused again by an angry officer who did not take kindly to some upstart making demands of him. Luckily for Arter, a passing Sergeant overheard the altercation between the two men and was amused by Arter's determination.

'Send the lad to me,' the Sergeant had shouted. 'I'll open his eyes up to what it takes to join the best of the best.'

'He won't last the day,' came the answer. 'But if you want him he's yours, just get him out of my face.'

No one had been more surprised than Arter when he made it through the first week and was issued with his kopis blade and a shield. He was the worst at almost everything the warriors had to do. There were only two things that got him through each day: he had lightning quick reflexes, and he was smart. He soon learned that obeying the Storm Legion's code of conduct carried more weight than winning a sword bout or a race to the top of some hill and back. He still had to put up with the jibes and bullying from the men in his unit who openly thought he was not good enough to serve with them. But what he lacked in strength and skill he made up for in effort and determination.

When the legions stopped to make camp after the third day of forced marching, Arter had fallen to his knees, exhausted. He was forced to suffer a barrage of abuse, as the men around him set about making camp.

'Quit, you bloody fool, before it kills you,' one legionnaire shouted at Arter as he struggled to his feet.

'He's making a laughing stock of our unit,' another one shouted.

A hand suddenly grabbed Arter's tunic and hoisted him up. 'Come on, lad, best we make camp quickly,' a stern voice, but one not lacking in compassion, told him. 'We have to practice our drills at first light before we march, so the sooner we get some food in us and a good night's sleep, the better.'

The kind words came from Hurcan, a big man of great strength. He was a man born to fight, muscles of stone and shoulders like boulders. His face was bulbous, his nose, lips and eyes swollen as if he had just been in a boxing match. He had white hair. The colourless hair was not from age, he claimed it had always been that way. Hurcan was admired for his strength and skill in a fight, but he too was ridiculed by the other warriors for his slow wits.

Atropolis

The Immortal warrior was stripped to the waist, his upper body glistening with the sweat from the exertion. Blood ran from the young man's nose, and from a cut to his forearm as he stood in the centre of the training area staring in bewilderment at the High Priest. Salik felt as if he was being punished, but knew he had committed no wrong. It was just his turn to spar with the Priest, as someone from the ranks of the Immortals did every morning at dawn.

Atropolis returned the man's gaze with disappointment in his eyes. He had heard that this warrior had shown promise with a blade, beating several more experienced Immortals in the arena. In the grey light of dawn, the young warrior had not lived up to expectation. The sun climbed over the walls of the training area to shine on Atropolis. He looked like a bronze statue in the cold light, naked except for a tightly bound loincloth and his sandals.

'Give him water,' Atropolis ordered. 'And a shield.'

Salik gulped the water down, holding his breath until he had finished. Drawing in a deep breath, the Immortal turned to the man holding a shield and took it from him. He felt invigorated. With the newfound energy came a wave of anger. He had been warned to stay calm, to keep his head, but the need to redeem himself for the humiliation of the morning was too great. Salik ran at the Priest, sword raised and yelling his battle cry.

Atropolis did not flinch or step aside from the attack. Instead, he took a step forward and dropped his shoulder into the centre of the shield. For Salik it was like running into a stone wall, his neck jarred and his teeth smashed together. Before he had time to recover or react, he was being forced back under a barrage of sword strokes. Atropolis pounded on the shield with his blade, purposely overexerting to give himself a workout. He battered the Immortal's shield relentlessly, only breaking off momentarily to knock Salik's sword down each time he made a feeble attempt to use it.

Eventually the shield was battered from Salik's arm. He was forced to lunge at the Priest to protect himself. He took a blow to the side of the head for his trouble. Atropolis came at him with several skilful thrusts and strokes that should have disarmed or defeated him, but he hung onto his sword and held out. He saw the killing rage in the Priest's eyes and panicked when he realised a stroke was aimed at his head. He reacted by putting his hand up to protect his face. The blade took the top off three of his fingers. Salik gasped with pain as the fingers fell to the ground like figs dropping from a tree.

'Fool!' Atropolis cried out and hit Salik in the middle of his forehead with the hilt of his sword.

The Immortal's legs buckled and he fell to the ground.

'He dropped quicker than a whore's knickers on soldiers' payday,' the officer observing said with a chuckle.

Atropolis was not amused. 'When he wakes up, have him sent back to the infantry. He is not worthy of the Immortals.

Two priestesses rushed forward to wipe the light coating of sweat and dust from their master's body and dress him in a silk tunic and riding leggings. The women's perfume lingered in the air for a moment after they had walked away. The sweet aroma of jasmine and nut oil was a temporary relief from the bitter taste of smoke lacing the morning air.

The previous night a man had been burned at the stake by order of the High Priest. The unfortunate had been the lover of one of Atropolis' priestesses. She and her unborn child had died on the altar as her lover watched, his limbs having been broken and his body beaten by the guards holding him. The execution had been a test of the Raven Queen's loyalty to Atropolis. In an orgy of sexual indulgence and cold-blooded murder, Rave had shown High Priest the blackness of her heart and the malevolence of her soul. He felt the salivation in his mouth as he remembered the sight of the Raven Queen drawing the blade across the throat of his unfaithful disciple. He relived the bittersweet joy of feeling the life drain from the priestess while their bodies remained entangled in a sexual embrace to the death.

The Raven Queen had a dark and twisted soul, but her mind was sharp. She had been hardened by the trials and tribulations that came with ruling and war. Her husband, the Wolf King, was proving to be a weaker ally than Atropolis needed in Avolonia. Rave was strong and influential in the Wolf State; those traits would serve her well when she brought the light of Kush to the heathen lands. She would be a sharp edged blade for him to unleash upon his enemies. She had come to the High Priest as a hostage, but she would return to Avolonia as his weapon of retribution. Her new-found belief in Kush would bring the word of the one true God to her own lands, paving the way for the holy crusade that was to come.

Atropolis knew there was something afoot as soon as he passed through the giant bronze doors of the Jade Court Room. *'Was the air filled with the heavy fumes of corruption and deceit?'* Atropolis asked himself. *'Or was it that he was just sensitive to the body language of those men already in the room?'* He could see both General Pompieum and Mesteroph flanking his father, all three of them in deep conversation. Military men ran up and down the steps to Al-Din's throne, carrying parchments and maps. Atropolis made his way directly to the throne, ignoring the other members of the court who seemed to be skulking in huddled groups and doing their best not to make eye contact with him.

Three pairs of eyes gave Atropolis a cold welcome. Mesteroph, as if he had just detected a sudden stench in the room, turned up his nose and frowned when he saw the rival priest.

'Ah, my son arrives on cue,' Al-Din suddenly burst into a warmer welcome. 'You save me the trouble of sending for you.'

Atropolis did not reply, he looked in turn at Mesteroph and Pompieum. The smirk on the General's face almost sent him into a rage. He suppressed his anger, instinctively knowing that the damage had already been done, and losing control of his emotions now would only make him seem weak.

'So, I take it you have decided against my counsel, Father?' Atropolis did not know whether to be more annoyed at his father, those who had swayed him against his plan, or his own spies for failing to inform him of the treachery.

'I have decided on another path, yes,' Al-Din seemed more confident than of late. He was once more an imposing figure of power and strength. 'It seems to me that calling back the Southern Army from our conquests in the south would be weak and futile. There is unrest in Nova, and Prince Xerces is gathering his forces to invade Axum. It is time for me to show my loyal subjects that they have my protection, and that I will strike down with my own blade any enemy daring to threaten our borders.' Al-Din turned to his two advisors and made a sweeping hand gesture towards them. 'With the help of these wise gentlemen, I have devised a plan to starve and crush this Lion's plague that crawls across our lands on its belly, infecting our provinces.'

Rage was clawing its way into Atropolis' mind, like a demon climbing out of the underworld full of revenge and retribution. To contain the beast, he built a wall of calmness across his thoughts. He would find an advantage in his father's foolishness. Mesteroph and Pompieum would regret the day they sniggered in the dark corridors of the palace in a conspiracy against him.

'If this is your decision, Father, then I am but your humble servant and will do what I must to support you in this venture.' Atropolis spoke calmly, with even a hint of affection in his voice. Internally a battle raged to hold back any sarcasm and the desire to take a dig at this ludicrous course of action. 'Please allow me to offer but one caution.' He waited until he was sure there would be no objection before continuing. Everyone was too shocked at the High Priest's compliance to take exception to the offer. The Emperor's advisors were disappointed that Atropolis had not flown into his usual rage. They were counting on it, knowing the only outcome would be to alienate the Seventh Prince from his father and strengthen their own positions. The room was all ears. 'Never forget that you are facing one of the greatest military minds of our time. Going toe to toe with the Lion Lord and slugging it out will be stepping into his den. Respect him enough to know that numbers alone will not triumph over him.'

Pompieum huffed. 'This Jackal, Lion or whatever he chooses to call himself, may be one of the few leaders to defeat a Mander force in the past one hundred years, but the honour of the title "Greatest Military Mind of our Times" belongs to the great and exulted Al-Din.'

The Emperor smiled at the compliment, but Atropolis knew it was far from true. His father had little experience in leading troops. Since he came to power, his sons had led his armies. Even as a prince, Al-Din had only led one campaign against a small uprising in Corinth. To have Al-Din lead his armies against the Lion Crusaders and Arc would be like sending a lamb to kill a wolf. Atropolis knew this all too well, having faced the Lion Warrior on the battlefield at Caputhora, capital of the Invelta in Avolonia. Arc had destroyed Atropolis' greater force and vanquished his mercenary allies, sending the Prince home, a broken man.

Mesteroph was only too happy to remind Atropolis of his military failure. 'You fear the Lion because he bested you on the field of combat. We have no such fear, and have faith in our leader to crush the threat with no more effort than you would use to swat an annoying fly.'

Atropolis had to pull tightly on the chains that restrained the furious beast that was his anger, to stop it bursting out. He won the struggle with his rage, but his expression gave away the conflict within. 'I humbly recognise my own limitations and have atoned for my failings every day since that fateful day when I felt the Lion's teeth at my throat. It is the understanding that tragedy brought me that enables me to say to you now with confidence, do not go rushing into those unforgiving jaws.'

'Of course not,' Al-Din interjected. 'I plan to divide him, cut him deeply and then crush him. It is not just enough that I defeat the Lion, but how I do it. I want a victory so complete that it will echo throughout our history.' Al-Din looked towards Pompieum. 'Tell him of my plan.'

The General let it pass that the Emperor was taking credit for the plan he had devised. 'We will split his forces by sending troops to block him from Calinkerbad. We will empty the borderlands of food by scorching the earth of crops and livestock so that there is not even a diseased rat left for them to eat. Their lines are stretched too thin for them to be able to defend supply lines, so they will have to head for the port city, or they will have nothing to survive on.'

'Arc would never split his forces,' Atropolis insisted.

Pompieum raised an eyebrow at the interruption. 'Our spies tell us that the Lion is not with his armies. He has travelled to Corinth. We will strike while he is away.'

'I will lead the Imperials against him,' Al-Din spoke with childish pride.

Atropolis looked confused at his father's announcement.

Pompieum felt the need to explain. 'When the invaders send a force to Calinkerbad, they will be surprised to find it is heavily garrisoned with our soldiers. While they are trying to fight their way in, our great and wise Emperor will march the Imperials against them. They will be trapped between our greater force and the city walls. They will be annihilated. Then the Imperial Army can turn east and trap the Avolonian main force between them and Prince Xarius' Northern Army. Crushed between two great armies is what they will be.'

Atropolis had to agree that the plan could work, but he knew the Lion Lord too well. He would find some way to upset this perfectly stacked apple cart.

'Father, you should not be the one to go chasing around,' Atropolis saw an opportunity. 'As Emperor, you should be at the head of the main force. Travel directly to meet up with my brother, Xarius. Let me lead the Imperials on the more laborious task.'

'You are right. I should lead the main force,' Al-Din said, and then shook his head. 'But I want you and your Immortals here, guarding the city. Pompieum, you will lead the attack on Calinkerbad.'

The General could not help smirking as he watched the Emperor's seventh son wrestle with his emotions, hoping he would lose control of his temper at any moment. Atropolis wrapped both hands around the chains restraining his anger and heaved on them to choke the beast. He knew that there was no changing his father's mind now. He would stay behind, but he would find a way to turn this to his advantage. For the first time, Atropolis saw his father as a threat to his plans. He knew now that he was the only one with the vision and resolve to fulfil the demands of the Questerus. His father was not the second coming of the profit that had been prophesied.

Atropolis realised in that moment that it was down to him to raise the sword of Al-Charmagne. He alone would be the one to ignite the world in a war between the Children of Kush and the heathens of the earth. A prophesy written in the Questerus spoke about the coming of a second prophet, Al-Charmagne, a sword baring priest. It told of the world burning in a continuous battle until Al-Charmagne had slain every last non-believer. Atropolis knew what he must do, his fate was as clear to him as the brightest sunrise.

Atropolis said nothing more. He turned and left, ignoring the look of triumph on Mesteroph's and Pompieum's faces. A greater destiny was calling him.

Chapter 3

Arc & Enola

Artillery machines creaked and swayed as they threw stones at the ancient walls of Calinkerbad. The rocks made little impression on the vast walls that were twenty paces thick at their base. A pattern formed from chips and divots could be seen on sections of the walls where the fire had been concentrated, but it caused no more than a little irritation to the city's defences. Arc rode directly to where Enola had her command centre, a thousand Lion Cavalry following him.

Enola felt a little relieved to see the Lion Army's red and yellow banners fluttering in the wind as the warriors rode up the shallow incline leading to the city walls. She was also somewhat disappointed. The Lioness hoped she would have had more success by now or been in the city by the time her father returned from Corinth. His approval was now the least of her worries; Enola knew she had marched into a trap, and would need every drop of her father's military prowess to get her new legions out of this fix.

The ground shook and the air was filled with the thunder of hooves. Arc was preceded by a cloud of dust that rolled on as the cavalry came to a halt. He took off his helmet and slammed it on the table where Enola had a mock-up of the city laid out. He shook the dust from his hair and brushed some of it off his arms.

'Report!' he demanded, without taking any time for a formal greeting.

Enola felt disrespected and it angered her. She let one of her Generals respond.

'The Mander Imperial Army is bearing down on us,' Antona stepped forward to report. 'But they are slow moving due to their number. We have attacked the walls twice already, but the defenders on the wall are too numerous.'

'And your plan, should they arrive before you gain entry to the city?' Arc asked without looking up from the table.

Enola now felt calm enough to reply to her father's question. 'We have preparations in place for a swift retreat. We shall link up with Edius-Max and the rest of the army.'

Arc slammed his fist down on the table, his anger suddenly filling the room. 'I said not to split our force!' He swept aside the wooden blocks used to make the model on the table. One hit Elektra and the others scattered across the floor. 'It's already too late to retreat. The Mander will send cavalry to shatter your marching columns. They want us to run. We will then be surrounded by their well-positioned army in Siena Mazda and another marching against our backs. You're not getting into that city, it's full of troops sent here weeks ago.'

'Then we face the Imperials and fight,' Hals stated, as if it were the obvious solution to their dilemma.

'As soon as our back is turned, the troops will ride out of the city and cut us down. It is what they are waiting for,' Arc shot back at the General.

The room was uncomfortable and no one wanted to speak next. Several of Arc's officers arrived, nodding curt greetings as they brushed off the dust covering them. Arc took a water jug from the table and drank directly from it before passing it back to the officers.

Enola sighed before breaking the silence. 'We can't retreat, or Al-Din has us trapped. We can't get into the city because it's full of troops. And we can't stand and fight because we will be outnumbered and flanked by the troops in the city before any battle can even get started.' She looked to her father. 'So who do we have to kill to get us out of this mess?'

The Lion Lord frowned, which was the closest his face ever came to a smile these days, so his daughter took it as a good sign.

'We fight,' Arc said, some calm returning to his voice. He noticed the puzzled look on Antona's face. 'Have you something to add?'

Antona turned his thoughts over in his mind. 'You are aware of how many we face?' he asked cautiously, and then offered the information. 'The Imperial Army is over a hundred thousand strong, with numerous cavalry and artillery. Not to mention how many hide behind the walls of the city. We could be facing over a hundred and fifty thousand, and we have just about a quarter of that number.' The young General hesitated before making a suggestion, knowing that he was a child playing soldier with a stick for a sword, while Arc had been fighting real battles like this one. 'Would we not be better to pull everyone back until we can regroup?'

'Regroup?' Arc shouted, and then calmed himself. 'We fight because we must. If we pull back now, we will be pulling back until they drive us into the sea. We can't give up the forward momentum we have worked so hard to achieve. There will not be another chance like this one.' He looked to Hals. 'Build me a wall around the city, just out of arrow range. Build it as a palisade, it's quicker; and build it across the city's gates first. We don't want them riding out on us until we are ready for them, now do we?'

Hals acknowledged with a salute, banging his fist against his chest. 'Around the whole city?'

'Riverbank to riverbank,' Arc answered, and then turned to one of his own Generals. 'Julius!' The Lion General stiffened and saluted in the same way as Hals. 'Build me a second wall, riverbank to riverbank, fifty paces further from the city than the first wall. Bring the wood from the forests to the west, and position gates to the east and west of the palisade.' Arc then turned to Ioniedas. 'Build me defences outside the walls to the east and west. Leave the centre open. You know the type of obstacles I want.' Ioniedas nodded. 'Make them cavalry-proof.' Arc knew the younger General well from his days as a Lion Warrior, and trusted he knew what he meant.

Arter & Hurcan

Fires lit the night in two long curved lines following the workings around the city. The humid night air hummed with the sound of tools digging the ground or cutting logs for the palisades. The legions started working at dusk, worked through the night and continued through the dawn until the sun was high overhead. It was too hot for this kind of work in the middle of the day, so that's when the men slept. It was a race against time. The Mander Imperial Army drew closer with every day that passed. In only two days the men and women of the Storm Legions and the Lion Warriors had built walls that reached halfway around Calinkerbad, from the river to the east of the city. They needed two more days to complete the defences, and no one believed they had that much time.

The Jagger Knights did not get involved in the construction. They patrolled along the city walls in case of an attack and scouted the outer areas for any sign of the enemy. On the third day, Arc planned to order Cid to send half of his Knights to work on the outer wall. It was a risk he would have to take if he was to finish the walls before the Imperials arrived. The men doing the foresting were already working through the heat of the day to harvest enough trunks for the palisades.

Arter used his pick to lever out a stone, then scratched the excess dirt out of the hole so that the trunk could be levered into place. Hurcan bound the lower half of the log with a hemp rope and then scurried up a ladder to secure the top half.

'This is bloody worse than the marching,' Arter said, smudging dirt onto his forehead as he wiped away the sweat.

His skin glistened in the firelight. Nights were humid in this part of the world, so even in the middle of the night a man sweated as he toiled. Luckily there was a plentiful supply of water close by.

'Spartikens don't complain,' Hurcan called down from the ladder.

Arter's comment brought the attention of the Sergeant. He was not a very patient officer, but he was usually fair. He was called Kurgin and came from Tiebuzar on the Fwenga coast.

'Is all this digging ruining your soft hands, Arter?' Kurgin did not wait for an answer. 'Fetch the water buckets. The real men are thirsty.'

It was easy popularity points from the men for the Sergeant to pick on Arter, he was the outcast and fair game for any of their ridicule. Hurcan was the closest he had to a friend, and he did not say much. Arter stood his pick against one of the metal baskets containing fire, added a log and went to fetch the water.

'We are building a bloody great coffin for ourselves here,' Erwin, the mouthiest of the Spartikens pointed out. 'We will have plenty of water in, but what are we going to do when we run out of food? Ask the lovely Mander to throw us some over?' Several of the men laughed, but Erwin only got a frown from the Optio. 'Yea, yea, I know. Spartikens don't complain.'

'He is right though, sir,' another legionnaire chipped in. 'We can't hide behind these walls for very long. For one thing, they're not strong enough.'

The Sergeant scratched the stubble on his broad chin, trying to think of an answer that would make him look good. His mood soured when he couldn't think of anything. 'I'm sure the Lion Lord has a plan, that's why he leads a crusade, and I get to lead you bunch of latrine overspill.'

'He is nullifying the Mander's superior numbers by forcing them to attack two killing zones,' Arter told them, as he scooped out the water from his bucket with a ladle and filled the eagerly held out cups. 'The inner wall neutralises the threat from the city while the outer wall prevents the much larger army from outflanking us and rolling us up.'

'Get this clever bastard!' Erwin shouted. 'If only he could fight half as well as he can think, we would all be saved.' Several of the Spartikens laughed. 'Get some of that water over here to me before your heart explodes from all that thinking.'

'Head explodes,' Arter said, as he brought the bucket to where Erwin was digging.

'What?'

'Head explodes,' Arter repeated himself. 'Everyone knows that your thoughts come from your head and your emotions from your heart, so it will be my head that explodes, not my heart.'

Laughter came from the Spartikens again, but this time at Erwin rather than with him. He did not like that and stuck out his foot to trip Arter as he moved on. Arter hit the ground hard. His bucket tipped over, and the contents rushed out, darkening the ground. Roars of laughter came from the Spartikens. Humour at Arter's expense was their favourite type.

Hurcan helped his friend up. 'Spartikens look after each other,' he told his comrades, looking directly at Erwin.

'Back to work!' Kurgin yelled. 'The bloody Mander will have been and gone before you lot finish this wall.'

Arc

The Imperial Army lined the horizon for the second day. The silhouette of their shield-covered bodies bristled with spears. The entire army just watched, their numbers so vast that their line stretched as far as the eye could see. The Avolonians hurried to complete the palisades and to strengthen their defences. All week, raids had come from the city to try and slow down the work on the walls, but they had been nothing more than a nuisance. They had killed dozens of the Spartikens before they could be driven off, but no major offensive had come.

Arc and his officers stood on one of the structures that had been built for the giant crossbows. From there they could see out over the palisade. The sound of hammering, sawing and the general commotion of the work sites surrounded the group of officers.

'Why don't they attack?' Cid asked no one in particular.

'They are waiting for something.' Arc gave the simple reply, explaining no more than they already knew.

'Or someone,' Gavara called out as he reached the top of the platform.

Arc allowed the corners of his mouth to twitch with the hint of a smile to welcome his old friend. 'Are the Corinthians coming?'

Gavara had come directly from Corinth. 'They are coming, but not in time for this showdown.'

'Then we are on our own,' General Antona stated.

Cid laughed. 'If you call being trapped inside a cage of our own making with thirty thousand warriors, alone, then yes we are!'

'How many are they?' Hals asked.

'Ninety thousand, that we can count,' Eric gave an answer. 'We have no idea how many they have in the city or how large their cavalry is, as their mounts are hidden in the forest to the east.'

'Your best guess?' Arc asked.

'One hundred and thirty thousand or more. Give or take ten thousand.'

'Give or take ten thousand,' Elektra blurted out. 'I hope it's take.'

Arc turned to Gavara. 'Can you get me into that city without me having to lose ten thousand brave souls climbing those damn walls?'

'And I suppose you expect this to happen before the Mander break through your palisade, which they will.'

'I do. I know you well, old man. You always have something up your sleeve.'

Gavara noticed that his friend's hand trembled. He had already seen the black circles around Arc's eyes and the dark shading of the indentation at the side of his head, the old wound that would have killed him were it not for the Pathfinder's skill as a surgeon. Arc realised that Gavara was taking an interest in his hand and gave it a rub, attempting to stop the shake.

'Are you sleeping at all?' Gavara asked.

Arc let out a nervous laugh. 'I've been chasing wild beasts and readying an army. Not much time for sleep.'

'I will make you a sleeping draft. You must get some rest, or there is no telling what your body will do.' Gavara sounded concerned for his friend.

'None of your sleeping potions while the enemy is at our gates.' Arc let out another ironic laugh. 'The last one you gave me had me asleep for two days. Unless you can get me into that city, it won't matter anyway, we will all be dead.'

'You at least need to drink more water,' Gavara told him. 'Ah! There you are,' he suddenly exclaimed, as he caught sight of a young Corinthian striding towards them. He reached out for the sack the boy was carrying. 'This is Ethus,' he told Arc, 'He has been most useful these past few days. He will be my new assistant.'

A smile beamed across the boy's face, his white teeth and bright eyes standing out against his dark skin. Gavara took hold of the sack. His twig-like arms were dragged down by the weight of the sack's contents and it hit the ground with a thud.

Arc frowned. 'Didn't do him any favours bringing him here.'

'Nonsense,' the old man protested. 'He has brought you something that will cheer you up.' Gavara handed his staff to the boy and opened the canvas sack. After rummaging around for an annoying amount of time, he grunted and hoisted out a lion's head. The bag dropped, revealing the beast's long mane. He huffed as he tried to pass the trophy to his friend, but it was too heavy for him to lift any higher. 'The head has been stretched over your war-helmet. It will tighten and stretch as it dries out.'

Arc reached out and took the head, scrutinising the helmet inside. His mind flashed back to when he felt the heat of the beast's breath on his face. Those demonic eyes, full of rage and terrifying were now replaced with black stones. Its deadly fangs bit into the steel rim of the helmet, and its face stretched over the dome. Arc opened the two silver cheek pieces and tried it on.

'It's too heavy,' the Lion Lord made his judgment, tilting his head from side to side. 'It will restrict my movements.' He tried wrapping the skin around his chest in the same way he had seen the Corinthians wear their animal skins.

'You will not need to fight wearing this, lord,' the boy finally found the courage to speak. 'Your enemies will flee in terror at the sight of the Lion God.'

Arc raised an eyebrow at the boy's use of the word "God".

'He's correct. This is about how your own troops see you, as well as how the enemy sees you. You lead them on an impossible mission. They need to see more than just a man. Your enemies must see you in their nightmares, and I'm sure you agree that the features of that terrifying beast will haunt them in a multitude of ways your ugly mug won't.'

Arc handed the helmet to Ethus. 'Keep the mane but cut off the skin, so that it is just a helmet and not a robe. Bring it to me at the wall.'

The boy nodded, placed the skin back in the sack and left to return to where he kept his tools.

'Drink plenty of water,' Gavara insisted, as he started to leave. 'I'll get you into those walls.'

It was late in the afternoon, when the sky was turning red, that the white sails appeared on the river. It became apparent why the army had been waiting. The Emperor's barge, shrouded in white sails, anchored in the channel of the river before it reached the docks of Calinkerbad. A flotilla of smaller boats and barges surrounded the giant craft. The soldiers on land reinforced the area around the riverbank, and boats started to ferry men and supplies from Al-Din's barge.

Arc watched as a ferry carrying a white stallion disappeared around the hill that blocked his view from where the Mander had built a pier. Several more boats came and went from the pier before the Emperor himself was transported from the barge to shore. It was the first time in over a decade that Arc had seen Al-Din. He remembered very little about their last encounter. Arc had been recovering from his head injury at the time. As the ferry neared the shore, Arc realised it was not the Mander ruler on-board. He did not recognise the man dressed in clothing that would not be out of place on the Emperor, but he was sure it was not Al-Din.

'Turn the catapults and scorpion bows towards the gates of the city! Watch, at the ready for an attack from that direction!' Arc barked the orders loudly, but with a resolute calm. 'Every other man get to fixing the outer wall. They will attack at dawn.'

The Avolonians sprang into action at their leader's command. Work that had stopped while the troops gazed at the arrival of the Emperor's barge was resumed. Men who had been at rest took up tools and joined their comrades at the outer palisade. The inner palisade still had significant gaps in it, but the Watch gathered at those openings to make a wall of shields and spears.

As Arc had anticipated, a Mander offensive spewed through the city's colossal gates. The predictable action cost them dearly. Bolts from the scorpion bows slammed into the densely packed cavalry as they were channelled through the gates' opening. The fearsome shafts went through horses and men, each bolt taking several lives at a time, causing pandemonium. Man and beast had no warning of death's approach, their lives snuffed out before they were even aware of the danger.

The projectiles from the catapults were not as effective on their first volley. Only one of the giant boulders hit its target, but even the crushing hand of a god could not have been more devastating than that one bolder. To the onlookers, it looked as if a swathe of men and horses had instantly disappeared. An open space appeared in the throng, the ground smeared in red goo. Eyes and minds had to adjust before the carnage of shattered bodies and the terrified screams of the dying could be grasped.

The artillery ensured that nothing more than a broken force reached the inner palisade. The Lion Warriors forming the Watch made a bloody mess of their attackers. They hacked at the disorganised attack with swords that rose and fell in unison. Some Mander riders were impaled on spears, while others had their mounts cut from beneath them. The losses were terrible on the Mander side, while the Avolonians suffered no more than a few deaths and a dozen or so injuries severe enough to take the warriors out of the line. Only one more attempt at an attack came from the city that night, but when it suffered the same fate as the first attack, the gates of the city remained closed, and its ramparts silent.

Work went on through the night, and men rested in shifts. Arc wandered the ramparts of the palisades trying to see through the darkness beyond his defences, hoping to gain any knowledge he could about his enemy's movements. He stared out over the top of the wooden wall as the faint glow of the wolf dawn backlit the horizon. His heart beat a little faster as he recognised the shapes of warriors and horses gathering at the centre. Arc ordered men to pass through the palisades and start digging ditches and defences in front of the centre.

The officer in command of that section looked confused. 'But sir, it's too late. We will have done little more than scratch a few lines in the earth by the time they attack.'

'Then get scratching!' Arc called back.

The officer knew better than to challenge an order for a second time. He sent men through the small openings they used to pass in and out of the wall. These openings would be sealed before the attack to make the wall secure.

The officer grabbed one of his men by the arm just as he was about to duck through the opening with his shovel. 'Pass the word around the men to be ready to get back in here sharpish. I'm not sure what this madness is, but I don't want to lose good men to a Mander raiding party.'

The engineer nodded and then ducked through the gap.

Enola joined her father on the wall. 'An afterthought?' she asked, referring to the troop of engineers digging in front of the wall.

'Why do you think I have taken the time to build defences on the flanks but left it too late here, at the centre?'

Enola took little time to think about her reply. 'The Mander know we cannot hide behind these defences for long, especially with an aggressive city at our backs. Eventually he will get in, and we will be slaughtered. He knows we must face him in open ground, here, at the centre. You have defended the flanks so that we can retreat behind the walls if we need to, and use those defences to keep his cavalry from cutting us in half as we do so.'

A stork flew across the top of the palisade, only a little higher than where Arc and Enola stood. They watched it fly gracefully towards the river. The bird looked as if it was about to land, changing its mind when it saw its favourite fishing spot occupied by Mander soldiers. As the bird flew on to cross the river, Arc stopped watching and turned back to his daughter.

'You have a sharp military mind and so does our opponent, so we use that against him. Make his decisions for him. Control his forces as if we were giving them the orders ourselves.'

Enola listened to her father but was still unsure of his meaning. 'You intend to draw him down the centre by making it our weakest point?' She thought a little more about it. 'He will see that as plain as the nose on his face. You can't trap him here, he will have countermeasures in place. He will be ready and waiting for us whichever way we turn.'

'Exactly,' Arc replied. 'He knows we have no choice than to face him here. He will have considered all the options, as you have. Today will not be about what we should do, it will be more about what we don't do.'

The Lioness placed her hand on the hilt of her sword, finding the touch of the cold steel reassuring. She didn't understand her father's meaning and decided to evade showing her ignorance.

'Today is about you, father. The great Lion Lord. Your troops will follow you through the gates of Hell if they have to. With you leading them, our army has strength and conviction that the Mander lack. The sight of you in the front line gives our warriors the courage they need. You only...' Enola's praise for her father was cut short by yells from below.

The engineers ran for their lives as a squadron of Mander cavalry pounded across the open ground to where they were digging. There must have been about three hundred men digging out there. The small passageways to safety in the wall were instantly blocked as men scrambled to squeeze through. The men digging furthest away from the walls were cut down by the riders before they could make it back.

'Archers!' Arc yelled.

The first Avolonians to respond threw their spears down at the attackers. They missed the riders, hitting one of the horses in its flank, and piercing one of their own men through the leg. The speared engineer was finished off by a Mander horseman with a sword cut to the neck. Archers rushed up the ladders to the platform that ran the length of the wall, but in the time it took them, the damage had been done. The Mander raiding party had been fast, cutting into the men trapped on the outside of the openings. Bodies lay in piles and near to fifty men were dead or wounded.

'Bloody stupidity,' the engineer's Sergeant called out in a rage, not knowing Arc stood directly above him.

'Al-Din will now think he has foiled your attempt to build defences in the centre,' Enola said, as soon as she had calmed herself. 'But you hoped that would be the case, didn't you?'

'To arms!' Arc gave the order that saw the men down tools and run to their positions. 'Raise my colours and standard above the centre of the wall. Let him see who he is dealing with.'

The sound of hammering persisted from one part of the camp. Arc glanced in the direction of rhythmical percussion sounds of mallets on wood and saws cutting. 'Gavara,' he said to himself.

'What on earth is he building?' Enola asked, realising where her father was looking. 'It looks like the beams of a large hall roof.'

Gavara had built a frame overnight. Two parallel enormous A-frames aimed at the city gates. Large wicker panels protected the workers from bowmen on the city wall, and several Avolonian archers were returning fire. More men were constructing a new enclave to the palisade, closer to the city. For the moment they had protected it with a wall of jacks. Jacks were three wooden stakes that were fastened together in the middle to make a tripod cross. The ends were sharpened, and when several of them were locked together, they were a formidable defence and difficult to move or climb over.

Arc noticed the large ash trunks being dragged towards the construction by a team of horses. He wondered if Gavara was building some kind of giant ram to break down the gates, but he could see no wheels or sleds on the construction to transport it up the hill to the city gates.

'Ballista!' A cry rang out from further along the ramparts to Arc's right. Seconds later the first stone ball bounced off the turf in front of the palisades wall and thumped into the wooden poles.

Pompieum

When his trainer tapped his fetlock, Zanthus bowed his head and stretched his forelegs out to lower his body. General Pompieum stepped onto the block at the side of the magnificent white stallion and was helped up into the saddle. The General took the reins in his left hand and then brushed away his helpers with his gloved right hand. With a thrust of his hips, Pompieum urged Zanthus forward. The chalk-white beast sauntered towards the ridge where the Officers of the Imperial Army had gathered. The horse took its place in the centre of the group just in time for the General to witness the raiding party scattering the workers in front of the wall.

'So, he has not formed ranks outside of his defences to greet us?' Pompieum sounded disappointed.

'Now that he has seen the size of our force,' Captain Arinon spoke, 'the Lion cowers behind his walls.'

'Sire,' Pompieum spat back at the Captain.

Arinon's face was contorted with confusion. He suddenly gasped, realising his blunder. 'Sire, sorry sire. The magnitude of the moment scrambled my mind.'

Pompieum did not need to turn and frown at the man to let him know his career had just wandered into a downward slide. The disapproving expressions of the other officers made that clear.

'Lions don't cower,' the General replied. 'He is stalking us. He wants us straight down the centre so that he can wear us down and then thrust his blade into our flanks.'

There was a general mumbling of agreement from the gathering.

'But, sire' Arinon said, his confusion in the matter making him uncomfortable and hesitant, 'if you know that to be his intention, why are we readying to do exactly that? Why don't we just wear him down with raids and bombardments until he comes crawling out on his knees or starves.' After a brief pause he added, 'Sire,' just to make sure he had covered the protocol.

Pompieum smirked like a fox with a rabbit trapped beneath its paw. He was not here to show his military prudence, he was here for glory. Being given command of the Imperial army was an opportunity he would not squander. Destroying the Lion Crusade would be his springboard to power. He would not gain his place at the Emperor's side with weak tactics like a siege. Crushing his opponent in a display of military boldness was how he would showcase his greatness to the world and his master.

'We are not lambs come here to be herded by the hunter. We are the beast, and we are here to kill. He thinks by showing me his weakness that I will shy away from it, fearing a trap. Well, I see his trap, and I fear not.' Pompieum looked around at his officers, catching each man's eye, daring them to doubt his words. 'See, he invites me. He raises his colours in the centre, so let us accept his kind offer. Ballista!' The General smiled at his men so that they could admire his decisiveness while at the same time struggling to calm Zanthus, who had been startled by his shout. 'Smash down that wall.'

The group of officers applauded as the first stone thrown by the ballista pounded against the wall of palisades. They cheered the first time timber was shattered. Pompieum studied the construction of his opponent's defences. The large gates to the right and left of centre captured his interest.

'Gentlemen, he has built obstacles to the outsides of those gates. Ask yourself why he would need gates at all when surely his objective is to keep us out?'

'Sire, he intends to attack us on both sides,' General Darkwall gave as an answer. 'The defences are to give him time to retreat back behind the walls after decimating our men at the palisades.'

General Darkwall was famous throughout the Mander military. His horsemanship and skill with a blade while in the saddle had won him many victories and acclaim. But, it was his leadership of the cavalry to victory after victory that made him such a respected general, both with his Emperor and his men. He was a stern-faced man, with the narrow eyes of an inquisitive cat and a thick black beard that was crimped into waves and well oiled.

'Exactly, Darkwall.' Pompieum praised him as if he were a child being educated. 'We must make sure we have a surprise for him. Form your cavalry on either flank and cut down anything that comes out of those gates. Captain Arinon and Captain Nimitz.' Both men sat up tall in their high-pommelled saddles. 'When those walls break, march your infantry straight down the centre. Signal the city as soon as you intend to advance. Let this Lion feel the mighty jaws of Mander slamming shut on his hide. He will soon wish he had never set foot on our shores, now that he has made my acquaintance.' He looked at his two infantry captains. 'The first of you to break through and dominate inside the wall will be calling himself General by sunset.'

Both men's faces lit up with new eagerness. Arinon could not believe his luck. He had an opportunity, not only to redeem himself but also to further himself.

Pompieum drew his glittering curved blade and raised it above his head. 'Go!' he shouted,' startling Zanthus into raising his head, pink nostrils flaring and eyes bulging. 'Bring me the Lion's head.'

Arc

At the moment a battle begins, there is a kind of relief that spreads through the men and women who could die at any given moment. For some it is liberation from fear, the anxiety that haunts the dark shadows of the mind, a dread of the unknown, an anticipation of the horrors to come. Once that first spear is cast, or that first body drops dead to the ground, most are relieved that the terror is out in the open instead of lurking out of sight. It is an acceptance that there is nothing more they can do but play out the day and hope the gods have favoured them.

One of the Spartikens was struck down when a post was splintered in two by a shot from the ballista catapult. He died instantly as the wood crushed his helmet. It was as if a weight had been lifted off the shoulders of those around him. Yes, they were horrified and shocked, but they were also relieved, dying first was considered to be the worst fate of all.

The tree trunks that formed the palisades were pounded with stone after stone in a relentless bombardment. Individual posts cracked or were shattered, throwing splinters in all directions, but for the most part the wall held firm. One boulder spun high into the air in a ricochet off the posts. It landed between four Spartiken warriors standing with their shields held in front of them and their curved swords at the ready. Miraculously, none of the men were hit as the rock thudded into the ground, and they took it as a good omen. Many of the warriors waiting behind the wall had blood trickling down their face or the exposed flesh on their arms and legs, caused by splinters hurled from shattered posts.

'Are we just going to take this?' Eric called out, within earshot of the other Generals. 'The wall won't take much more of this. Send cavalry to destroy those catapults before they open a gap in the wall.'

Almost as if on cue, and to vindicate Eric's outburst, there was a thunderous crack, and a part of the palisade swung open like a gate. The dislodged section of about eight posts remained hinged at the bottom by the ropes securing the trunks together. The top and middle ropes snapped so that the panel fell at an angle, coming to rest against the surviving wall to the right. It left a triangular opening at the base of the wall about six paces wide.

Arc gave Enola a disapproving look, not about the wall, but about her officer's outburst.

'Hold your nerve, General,' Enola scalded her friend.

Another smaller section of the wall broke open to the right of the first breach. This left a significant part of the wall unsupported on either side and considerably weakened. The bombardment stopped, as suddenly as it had started. The Mander were obviously of the opinion that they had done enough damage to the barrier, and were eager to proceed.

'Shore up that section!' Arc roared. 'And bring the jacks.'

The three posts knocked out of the smaller breach were used to shore up the freestanding section of the wall that had survived the bombardment. On Arc's instructions, the jacks were placed in a semicircle encompassing both breaches. Hals was ordered to hold that position at all cost. Arc did not want the Mander held outside the wall, he wanted just enough of them getting in to form a killing ground between the wall and the line of jacks. It was a dangerous tactic. If too many broke through Hals and his troops would be overrun. A risk Arc was willing to take to anchor the Mander attack to the one spot. A breach in the Avolonian defences would be too great a temptation for the Mander to ignore. The offensive would place the smell of success in their nostrils, and they would blindly risk everything to gain such an advantage.

Arc, Enola, Cid and all the other Generals knew that now the bombardment had ceased, the offensive would begin. Arc led a procession of officers up a ladder and onto the ramparts. From there, they would be able to reconnoitre Mander positions. The main force of heavy infantry, to no one's surprise, was forming to attack the centre and the breaches in the wall. The usual banners and standards fluttered like bunting over their heads, with a large Mander flag in the centre. The pennants carried by the army were white with the crescent moon of Al-Din, embroidered in gold thread. The flag was two lateral red stripes separated by a white strip. In the centre, the Star of Kush was embroidered in golden braiding. So many people and lands had seen those emblems closing in on them in their last moments of freedom. Symbols of oppression and tyranny.

The Avolonian Generals remained stone-faced, while they watched the Mander Imperial Cavalry take up positions on either flank. The numbers were breathtaking. Row after row of armoured horsemen lined up to the east and the west. Their pennants were more numerous and flamboyant than those carried by the infantry. The front several rows had the slim triangular ensigns atop of their lances.

'More flags than your knights, Cid,' General Antona attempted to lighten the situation with some humour. No one laughed.

Arc stared out at the sea of enemies that flooded the lands around him. How many times had he stood and faced a tsunami of blades intent on his death? Only one thing had changed. The invaded have become the invaders, he now stood in another man's land, a man who, as he had done, would fight for his home.

'Flags and glory are not the prizes we seek here today.' Arc placed his hand on the hilt of the Lion Blade and held it tight. 'Nor is winning a city or defeating an army. There is a bigger picture, a loftier dream. Today's prize is just one more step to a better world. How we fight today is not what we will be remembered for. What we achieve later, because of how we fought on this day, is what the world will remember.' He gripped the hilt of Leovesica tighter to stop his hand shaking, his knuckles turning white. He grabbed Enola by the shoulder to prevent himself from grasping his temple to rub at the pain searing into his head. 'Do your jobs well, be patient. You will make your own luck today with hard work, which will bring opportunity.'

The air was suddenly filled with the beat of drums, and a moment later was joined by the sound of a multitude of feet tramping in unison. The Imperial Infantry was advancing.

'Cid,' Arc snapped. 'Take your Knights and keep whatever comes out of the city off our backs. Keep the bows and catapults aimed at the city gates. Go quickly, we have been distracted here longer than we should have been.'

Cid was gone in an instant.

'Would the artillery not be of better use aimed at the horde bearing down on our centre?' General Ioniedas asked.

Arc struggled to reply. The pain in his head was unbearable, and he felt the small tremor in his hands transcend into an uncontrollable shake. He was aware of the awkward silence as the others waited for his reply. Arc took a deep breath and managed to suppress the shakes enough to be able to speak. He could smell burning, but there were no fires.

'No. Keep the artillery trained on the city. We will have to make do with the artillery on the flanks. Have them converge their fire fifty strides in front of the wall,' Arc's words seemed strained, and a little slurred.

Enola stepped forward, concerned for her father. He waved her back and straightened himself up.

'Elektra and Ioniedas, form your Spartikens up against the wall to the right and left of the gates,' the Lion Lord said more assuredly. 'Elektra, the west gate. Ioniedas, the east gate. Watch the cavalry. React to nothing else with your reserves.'

The ascending volume of the approaching army was like an avalanche of sound, rumbling towards the Avolonians. Horns wailed and shrieked their message with a noise befitting the beasts lurking in the underworld. Warriors instinctively touched amulets hanging around their necks or mumbled a prayer to ward off evil. Moments later the gates of Calinkerbad opened like the jaws of a humongous monster and spewed out an army of Mander warriors.

Arc turned to leave the ramparts, calling out his final order as he descended the ladder. 'Enola and Antona, form up the Storm Legion's cavalry to face the west gate and wait for my order. I will lead the Lion Cavalry at the east gate.'

Arter & Hurcan

Gone were the days when before a battle officers passed out cups of ale or stronger spirits to give warriors the courage they needed. Training and more training were the beverage a professional army drank to make them brave. But that did not stop the more seasoned of the Spartikens from pulling a flask from their belts and taking a swig of some extra courage. Hurcan took a swallow from his own bottle and then handed it to Arter. He had to push him in the shoulder twice to get the boy to snap out of his trance.

'Oh, thanks,' Arter said, turning his gaze immediately back towards the gaps in the wall.

'Drink then,' Hurcan pushed his friend again in the shoulder.

Arter took a swig from the flask. His face immediately scrunched up into a grimace, and he smacked his lips like a dog trying to wipe a foul taste off its tongue.

'What the hell is that?' Arter handed the flask back. 'Are you trying to do the Mander's job for them, and kill me before they do?'

Hurcan laughed and took the flask. 'Put a fire in your belly though, hasn't it?'

'Arrows!' came a roar from the wall.

The Spartikens raised their shields over their heads. The sky darkened with ten thousand shafts, but Arter could not see them, his shield interwoven with those either side of him, leaving no gaps to see through or for arrows to enter. The rattle of arrowheads hitting shields rang out like a hailstorm on a barn roof. It suddenly made Arter think about the home he had left, and how his life on the farm did not seem so bad now. The loud clang of metal on metal rang out as an arrow hit his shield. The sound hurt his ears, but not nearly as much as the pain from the impact shooting through his arm.

'Hold steady!' an angry voice called out, as Arter allowed his shield to drop on one side. He further aggravated the man to his left when he tried to put his shield back up at the same time as everyone else was taking theirs down.

'Steady, lad,' Hurcan told his young friend, as they edged up to the jacks that were to be their only defence when the Mander came through the wall.

Arter watched the archers upon the ramparts of the palisade. They fired their deadly arrows individually, picking off targets as they saw opportunities. The sky darkened again, this time with Avolonian arrows shot by the bowmen of the Tornado Legion standing behind Arter. Less than several heartbeats later the call came from the wall again. 'Arrows!'

This time, the sky was already darkening before Arter had the chance to raise his shield. The hailstorm of shafts fell upon them once more. Screams pierced the cacophony of noise already assaulting Arter's ears. He went to lower his shield but had it jammed back into place by Hurcan's, who shook his head at his friend just as another wave of arrows slammed into the umbrella of metal shields. The Spartikens hid beneath their bronze covering for several more volleys. The arrows fell almost directly down from the sky, the enemy bowmen having to fire at a more acute angle as they drew closer to the wall.

The ballista catapults and the giant scorpion crossbows fired their missiles from the flanks. They cut bloody paths through the advancing troops, but the gaps opened up by the deadly bolts and stones were swallowed up by the Mander's vast numbers. The artillery brought a terrible wave of death and destruction but was no more trouble to the Imperial infantry than a few raindrops are to a swarm of ants. The Imperials held their line as they advanced on the wall.

Arter felt the trembling in the ground growing stronger. The enemy was almost at the wall. The sound suddenly changed from the rhythm of marching feet to the roar of several thousand battle cries. The trembling ground began to shake as the Imperials charged the final fifty paces to the wall.

'Here they come, lad!' Hurcan pushed his shield against the wooden posts of the jack in front of him and readied his kopis sword. 'At last we will see if these crimson tunics really hide our blood from the enemy.'

Arter saw an insane look in his friend's eyes that he had never seen before. His own eyes only showed the panic and fear he felt. 'Why do we have the jacks back here? Why are we not blocking the breaches with them?' Arter's questions went unheard, drowned out by battle cries and the boom of the first Imperials colliding with the wall. Warriors suddenly burst through the breaches in the wall, snarling and yelling as they exploded through the gaps. Archers took down the first brave Mander souls to penetrate the defences. But more came, clambering over their fallen countrymen, to get at the invaders.

It was all Arter could do to hang onto his shield and cower behind it as the enemy reached the spiked defences. He watched through terrified eyes as Hurcan slashed and chopped at the enemy. Blood sprayed from his friend's blade each time it was drawn back. Arter was paralysed with fear, trapped behind his shield, knowing that if he moved, he would be cut down in that instant. He felt the strength draining from his legs. 'Spears!' he heard Kurgin shout.

The second row of Spartikens jabbed their dory spear-tips through the gaps, adding more cries of pain to the deafening sound of battle. The spears stabbed into faces and necks, not looking for a killing blow, but to distract or disable a man so that he could be finished off by the curved blades of the Spartikens in the front rank. It was a tactic efficient in delivering death, Mander bodies piling up at the base of the jacks. Archers fired into the throng between the wall and the inner barricade, making it a killing ground. The archers on the ramparts fired down into those on the outside of the wall, every arrow finding its target in the cram of bodies. But the Mander kept on coming. They chopped at the wall to make the breaches wider, letting more significant numbers into the compound.

'Use your bloody sword!' Hurcan yelled at Arter, but he was terrified and remained behind his shield, hanging on for dear life.

The jacks suddenly moved, giving way under the force of the Mander attack. Arter's shield separated from Hurcan's. A snarling face, splattered in blood appeared in the gap. Arter screamed and rammed his sword at the face, closing his eyes at the same time. His shoulder jolted, and he heard the man cry out when the blade struck home. He snatched the sword back, not daring to open his eyes, sure he was about to be cut down at any moment, and even more sure he had just peed himself.

'Well done,' Hurcan called out, referring to the stabbing. 'Keep doing that.'

Arter opened his eyes to see his opponent on the ground, bleeding out. Instantly, another face filled the gap but was obscured by Hurcan's shield. Arter found enough courage to make a couple of chops over the top of the brass rim. Both times he felt the clash with solid steel and returned to hiding behind his shield and holding the line. The press of the Mander onslaught was becoming too great, and the line was starting to give. The Imperials had broken through in more than one place, and Arter could feel the panic in the other men around him.

Enola

Arrows thudded into the ground only a few strides away from where the Lioness sat on her mount, waiting for orders from her father. Archers of Elektra's Typhoon Legion raced to take up a position between the wall and their commander.

Antona raised an eyebrow. 'Do you think she would have sent those bowmen so quickly if you hadn't been here?'

Enola ignored the question. 'Why is he waiting so long?' The worry was evident in Enola's voice. She could see Mander warriors climbing over the top of the wall. They had brought ladders up to the palisades and were overwhelming the archers on the ramparts. On the ground, the Spartikens of Hals's Tornado Legion were under immense pressure. No matter how many Imperial warriors they killed, they were replaced twice over. The inner defensive line was breaking.

As if he understood Enola's worry, Antona pointed towards the city. The catapults and giant bows had done their job in breaking up the main Mander force as it charged out of the gates. The Jagger Knights were dealing with the enemy that had made it out of the city, fighting them in front of the ancient walls. But now the enemy was abseiling the walls on ropes, and coming out of every small door or opening they could find to attack. General Cid would have to retreat behind the inner palisades or risk being engulfed by the enemy.

Enola knew her father had a plan: he wanted to draw the enemy in close. But, surely this was too close? Every instinct she had told her to order more troops to defend the walls. She wanted to have confidence in her father's orders, but she didn't understand. She didn't need to understand. She had her orders, her job to do, as did every other General. Enola knew her duty, she just wanted to get on with it.

'At last,' Antona said when he saw the rider galloping towards them. 'Here come our orders.'

Enola's feeling of relief and excitement faded as she realised that something was not quite right. The expression on the messenger's face, as he reined in his mount, was clearly one of concern.

'It's the Lion Lord,' he said. You must come immediately.'

The messenger needed to say no more, Enola flicked her heels and Storm burst into a canter. Antona followed.

As Enola reached the east side of the compound, she headed for a crowd gathered around her father's warhorse. Armageddon was rearing up and pulling at his reins, it took two men to control the beast. The Lioness dismounted and pushed her way through the gathering. At the centre, she found her father on the floor. He was shaking violently in some kind of a fit. She rushed to take hold of him, but was restrained by Ioniedas.

'Leave him be. Let it finish. There is nothing you can do.' Ioniedas released his commander, as soon as she stopped struggling. 'I have seen this before. He has been struck by the Gods, it will pass.'

'I brought him the helmet, just as he asked me to,' Ethus started to explain, without being asked. He was holding the lion head war-helmet, its tangled mane hanging down to the ground. 'I cut the skin off, as I was told to.'

Enola could see that her father's fit was starting to subside, she turned to the boy. 'What happened?' she expected to hear that the Lion Lord had been knocked from his horse by an arrow or fragment of rock.

'He reached down for the helmet and just started to shake.' The boy was distressed. 'I couldn't stop him, he slipped from the horse. I tried to hold onto him, but he was too heavy, and he started to thrash about.'

'It's fine boy, you did well,' Ioniedas said, dropping to one knee.

Arc's fit had all but passed. Ioniedas cradled the Lord's head and shoulders. Enola felt so helpless but, before she could speak again, Hals burst through the crowd. He glanced at his Lord on the ground.

Holding back his concern for Arc and his desire to know what was going on, he said what he needed to. 'We can't hold out any longer. Give me reinforcements or attack, but do it now or we're finished.'

The urgency in the General's voice spoke louder than his words.

'You three, take the Lion Lord to his tent and send for Gavara,' Enola ordered.

'Shall we reinforce the walls?' Antona asked.

Ioniedas shook his head, and Enola responded. 'No, we must follow the Lion's orders.' Enola did not know if it was now too late to spring the surprise her father had planned, but what she did know was that if they survived by holding the Mander off now, it was a short-term solution that could only end in defeat further down the line. Her instinct was to defend and survive, her father's orders were to attack. 'Ioniedas,' he stood to attention, 'send what you can to help Hals. Antona, tell Elektra to do the same to help Cid, then lead the Storm Cavalry out. I will lead the Lion Cavalry.' There was a moment of hesitation and doubt. 'Now!' Enola bellowed to shock everyone into action. She mounted her white warhorse, Storm. 'Give me that,' she took the Lion helmet and put it on, adjusting the mane so that it hung down her back. The Lioness drew her golden sword and pointed the tip towards the sky. 'Seize the day, or die well trying!' She flicked her heels and Storm took off towards the east gate. 'Open the gate!' she called, 'Lions, on me!'

Storm bolted through the opening in the gate as soon as it was wide enough for him to pass. The day's brightness lit up Enola when she erupted out of the gate's shade, ten thousand Lion Cavalrymen behind her. The morning dew had already evaporated from the grass carpeting the ground beyond the wall. Clods of earth were thrown up by the horses' hooves in their eagerness to reach the enemy. Thousands of fearsome beasts were carrying their masters to war. Manes danced in the wind of speed, and tails flicked and swished as horses jostled for position. On bobbing heads, the beasts' eyes bulged and their nostrils flared in the effort to cross the open ground at their best speed.

The sheer size of the Mander force took Enola's breath away. It was like charging towards a vast river of humanity. She felt as though she were rushing towards a precipice, knowing she would be engulfed by a cavernous void, but unable to stop herself. She hoped that Antona had timed his charge from the west gate to match her own impetuous race into possible oblivion. It was too late to worry now; the play had been made and destiny was in motion. It seemed to take forever to cross the open ground to reach the enemy. Enola felt like she had been riding all morning by the time she swung her golden blade down on the first Mander head. Time slowed, her mind racing in the elation of the attack. But the advance was swift, quick enough to catch the enemy infantry unprepared. The Mander did not have time to loose arrows or to form a phalanx on their flanks. The Lioness and her cavalry ploughed into the infantry column like an axe into a straw bale, its tightly bound fibres splitting wide open.

A fox in a hencoop kills a hen and moves on to the next one. It does not eat or struggle with the more resilient birds. It snaps its jaws shut, tastes blood and moves onto the next victim, over and over until there are no victims left, and only the stillness of death remains. Cavalry without counter are akin to the fox, they kill and move on, slashing and chopping relentlessly, reacting instinctively and lashing out at anything that steps into their killing zone.

Antona timed his own charge perfectly. Driving the Storm Cavalry into the enemy like the woodman's axe into the base of the forest's largest tree. If the cavalry were the sharp blades that would cut wedges out of the enemy's trunk, the Storm Legion infantry were the saws that would cut through the hard wood of the tree's centre. Elektra and Ioniedas led the foot soldiers of the Typhoon and Cyclone legions through the gates to support the attack. Cavalry have a limited time of effectiveness against an infantry column before their momentum is slowed and they are engulfed by the mass. The supporting infantry would break up that mass and give the horsemen space to continue their frenzy of annihilation.

The Mander column was trapped, squeezed between their attackers, unable to pull back due to their own immense numbers, unable to move forward because of the wall's defences. The Lion Warriors and the Spartikens killed thousands, but tens of thousands more were ready to take the place of the fallen.

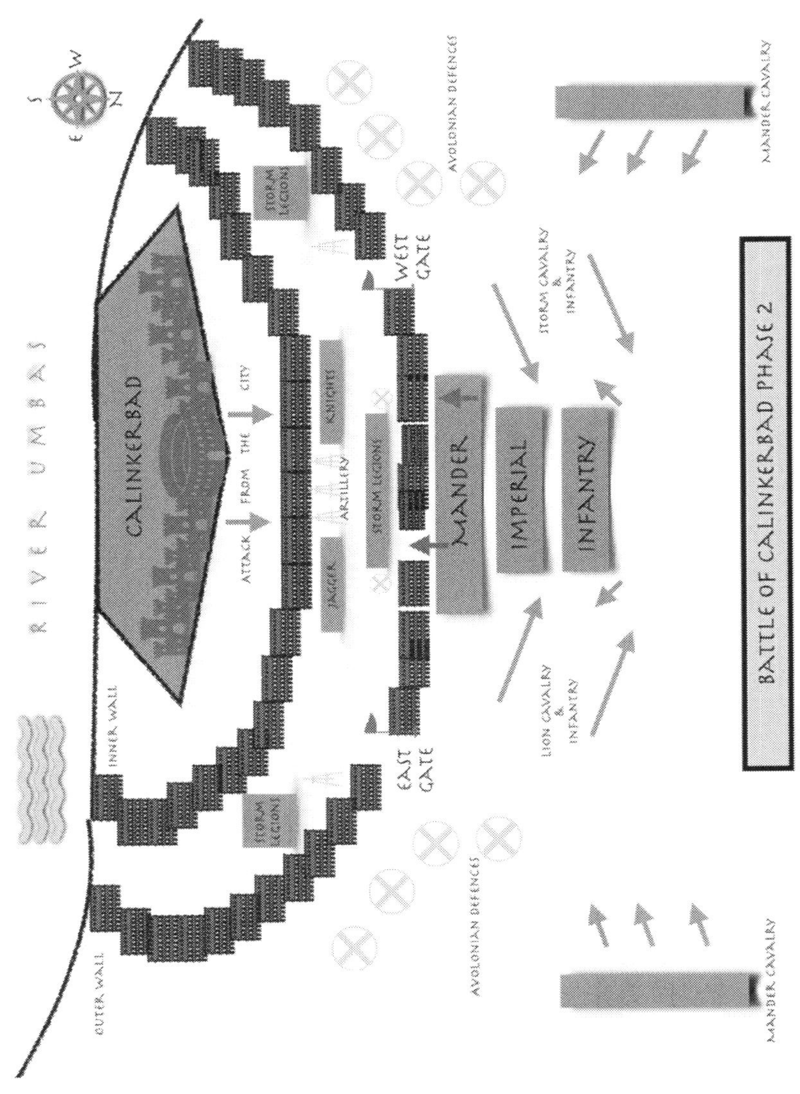

BATTLE OF CALINKERBAD PHASE 2
RIVER UMBAS
CALINKERBAD
ATTACK FROM THE CITY
INNER WALL
OUTER WALL
STORM LEGIONS
STORM LEGIONS
KNIGHTS
JAGGER
ARTILLERY
STORM LEGIONS
WEST GATE
EAST GATE
MANDER
IMPERIAL
INFANTRY
STORM CAVALRY & INFANTRY
LION CAVALRY & INFANTRY
AVOLONIAN DEFENCES
AVOLONIAN DEFENCES
MANDER CAVALRY
MANDER CAVALRY
W
S
E
N

Pompieum

Zanthus stamped impatiently at the ground, sensing the excitement in the air and eager to run with the herd. Pompieum patted his war stallion on the neck and ruffled his cotton-white mane in a vain attempt to calm the beast. Zanthus tossed his head and snorted as if to shrug off his master.

'Not long now, my impatient friend, not long,' the General said, watching the Lion Cavalry make its valiant charge towards his main force.

'You were correct, sire,' a staff officer called Lybian told Pompieum. 'As soon as their wall has started to give way, they are striking with their cavalry. They hope to force our troops away from the wall so that they can rebuild their defences. They are too late; their attack will be like throwing rocks at fish.'

Pompieum bathed in the younger officer's admiration. He had been angry at first when Atropolis had robbed him of the honour of leading the Mander army to Siena Mazda by suggesting that it should be the Emperor who should lead the main force against the Avolonians. He could see now that providence had steered his fate in this direction. He was in the right place at the right time. It would be he who destroyed the Lion Lord and saved the Empire from the crusading tyrant. He would be elevated to lead the armies of the Empire. The sons of Al-Din would bow to him, because he had been here when opportunity knocked, and he would seize the day.

'Look!' another of the officers called out, pointing towards the eastern gate in the Avolonian defences. 'The infantry is following. They intend to support the attack.'

'Then it's not just a lightning strike to pull us back from the wall,' Lybian laughed. 'He is actually going on the offensive. He actually expects to stand and fight. Why else would he bring the infantry to back him up?'

'Then we have him, Gentlemen.' Pompieum had to pause while he brought Zanthus under control. The beast had sensed the excitement in his master's voice and mistaken it for a command to move. 'Steady, boy. Wait until the foot soldiers are engaged in the fight and then give the signal to advance. Our cavalry will crush them against our infantry. Do not fear his boldness or admire his daring, I am not the son of an Emperor or soft aristocrat like the Mander Generals he has faced before. I am a leader who has earned his place at the head of an army and cannot be overcome by such tactics or forced into rash decisions. Success in battle is not about boldness or daring, it is about timing. We will wait for the exact moment when our counter-attack will be devastating.'

'He should have hit and run, that way he may have lasted at least half the day,' Lybian said.

'Even half a day would be no good to him,' one of the other officers said. 'The attack from the city must prevail sooner or later, then it's over for him.'

Lybian urged his mount into a better position to point something out to the Commander. 'I take it that is literally the head of a lion leading the charge,' he pointed towards Enola in the lion helmet. It was a long way to the top of the slope where he sat on his mount watching with the Commander, so he mistook Enola for her father. 'I thought he would be bigger.'

'I want his head on a pole, still wearing that ridiculous animal-head helmet, at the front of the Imperial army when we march to Sierra Mazda,' Pompieum said, and then added. 'Lybian, you will see to that.'

'I will,' the young officer replied, with too much enthusiasm in his voice, like a son keen to achieve his father's approval.

Pompieum and his officers watched in silence as the Avolonian cavalry smashed into their infantry from both sides. They were quietly impressed at how quickly the Avolonian infantry took to the field and formed into position.

'Their infantry is faster and better trained than we should like,' Pompieum spoke, breaking the silence. 'It is time to finish this.'

The Commander raised his hand high above his head, and the sound of horns filled the air. The melodic blasts set in motion ten of the twenty thousand horsemen and their mounts in what was to be a two-wave attack. The horn blast was echoed from across the plain, where it set in motion another ten thousand riders. Pompieum's eyes widened with the anticipation of his victory. There would be a swirling storm of blades and blood, and he would be in the eye of that storm commanding more than one hundred thousand warriors to glory. He sat high in his saddle, the sound of banners flapping all around him, and the mass of his invincible cavalry riding past him for as far as he could see to his right and left.

The advance had travelled only a short distance when the horns gave the signal to wheel the line left. Pompieum was furious, he had given no such order. He would have them ride directly into the rear of the Avolonian attack and smash it. He heard the horns on the far side of the battle signalling the same thing, only on that side it was the command for the cavalry to wheel right. It was then that the Commander saw the Avolonian reserves trotting out from the gates. He acknowledged that it was wise leadership to have kept troops back to be distributed where and when they were needed. But he knew it was too little too late for the Avolonians. When the storytellers spun their tales and sang their songs about the great battle, they would describe the Avolonian army as a wild best, cornered and fighting for its life. He knew this deployment of the reserves was a last desperate act of a trapped animal, swiping at the hunter with claws less than sufficient for the task at hand.

Elektra

Standing to the rear of the gate, Elektra watched as her sister led the Typhoon Legion to war. The General trusted Enyo to lead, she was a goddess of war and destruction who would follow the orders she had been given. Elektra had decided to stay with the reserves. She had a bad feeling about the Mander cavalry. She feared them more than any other element of the attacking army and wanted to lead any counter-attack against them. Her eyes narrowed when she looked to the horizon where the Mander cavalry stood waiting. She could see the enemy Commander, front and centre of his mounted troops. Elektra willed him to give the order to attack hastily and with confidence. She sighed, realising he was too smart to do anything other than wait for the right moment to strike.

When Elektra finally heard the horns signalling the enemy advance, she did not know if it had been a long wait or not. Time seemed to lose its relevance, whether it had speeded up or slowed down, she could not distinguish. The sound of the horns made her pulse quicken, and her heart was in her mouth when she saw the might of the Mander cavalry jolt forward.

'Warriors of the Typhoon,' she called out, 'advance!'

The Gods must have laughed at the absurdity of the scene, reserve foot soldiers running out to confront the might of the Imperial Cavalry. It would be like using a palm leaf to fend off a leopard. Elektra knew that, but she believed in tactics, training and resolve, and she had trained these warriors day in and day out for a moment like this: a moment that would change history or consign them to oblivion. The archers ran to the right and took up positions amongst the defences Ioniedas had built. The infantry ran straight ahead, in a long line that crossed the path of the enemy cavalry. Armour rattling was all Elektra could hear as she ran alongside her troops. The Spartiken Warriors of the Typhoon Legion carried their shields on their left arms, bronze discs with a large T and small Y painted in black on the front. Spears filled their other hand, dory-bladed tips jabbing at the sky as they ran. She took the warriors out until they stretched from the first defence to a slope that fell away to the south.

The front row of Spartikens dropped to one knee on Elektra's command. They locked shields and rested their spears on the cleft where their shields met, pointing their vicious blades at the approaching enemy. Each warrior took a metal jack from his belt and threw it out into the grass in front of him. The small metal objects were lethal to horses, though the ground would need to be flooded with the spikes to break a cavalry charge.

The enemy was getting dangerously close when the second row of infantry took their position. These men carried miniature wooden jacks out with them. These defences were a much smaller version of the ones being used to form a defensive cordon around the breaches in the wall. They were the brainchild of Ioniedas. He hoped these portable defences would be effective against the cavalry or at least cause enough of a problem to the horses' footing to slow any charge. The Spartikens threw the jacks over the heads of the kneeling front row. Then they took the small metal jack they had been issued, from their belts and threw them beyond where the wooden defences had landed. The ground was now shaking with the force of forty thousand hooves thudding into the dirt. The second row of Spartikens remained standing, and locked their shields together, on top of the shields of the first row. They held their spear above the double row of bronze shields, daring the enemy to run onto the points. The shield wall was like a thorn bush, a thousand paces long. Only, the thorns were as long as a man, with blades that were designed to open up extensive wounds in the flesh, causing any man or beast to bleed out quickly if they were unfortunate enough to be skewered.

Horns sounded, ordering the cavalry to charge, just as the third row of Spartikens arrived into position. They added their spears to the bristling defence by resting them on the shoulders of the second row. Elektra found herself wishing there was a fourth and even fifth line of defence to come, but three rows were what she had, and three rows were what she would have to make do with. She raised her officer's staff and hundreds of arrows arced into the sky. Many of the shafts were in flame and ignited the dry grass in front of the Avolonian phalanx. Fire, smoke, wooden jacks and metal ones separated the wall of bronze and blades from the advancing horsemen who were carried on a sea of armoured beasts. None of the Avolonian's efforts would stop this cavalry charge. It was a monster without compare. Elektra forgot to breathe, consumed by the sight rampaging towards her.

Horses don't appear to fall in a cavalry charge, they disappear, down in an instant and swallowed up by the mass before the beast hits the ground. The noise of the charge was deafening, but the screams of injured animals was a sound that could be heard over the thunder. From the corner of her eye, Elektra saw the first horse vanish; then a second and a third. A wave of arrows plunged from the sky into the seething mass of beasts. The shafts seemed to have no effect, but Elektra knew the silent devastation they were causing. Horses reared their heads at the sight of the brass pin cushion facing them. Many slowed or twisted to avoid running into the shafts. Some stumbled on the jacks and fell into the path of others. The once well-formed line of cavalry had become disjointed and confused. More arrows slammed into the Mander throng of horseflesh and riders as it collided with the shield wall.

The formation may have been slowed or fractured, but the force at which it hit the Avolonian line was ruinous. The collision between horses and shields was so powerful that Elektra felt the shock wave from behind the line. The clash was so loud that it made her stagger in a moment of disorientation. Spartikens were thrown back like sparks from a flint. Beasts screamed in pain as legs broke or chests were impaled on the dory spear tips. Elektra thought the line was destroyed by the impact until more and more of the front row made it to their feet and began slashing at the riders with their kopis blades. The charge had not been broken, but it had slowed enough and become so disjointed that the Spartikens were able to hold their ground.

The advantage now shifted to the men on foot. Terrified mounts were impossible to control, they just wanted to get away from the warriors hacking and jabbing at them with spears and swords. The beasts' eyes bulged, and lengthy tongues lolled out of mouths open in fear, lips curled, showing teeth and gums beneath flared nostrils. The riders were being dragged to the ground and butchered in their hundreds. It was not long before the horns sounded a recall. As the cavalry pulled back, Elektra realised her left flank had been compromised. The charge had managed to break through the line to the far left, and the Spartikens there had been slaughtered. The successful riders were now left behind when the rest of their force retreated. They made a hasty retreat rather than face the Spartikens' revenge. To the far right of the attack, some of the cavalrymen had ridden into the defences to chase down the archers. On that flank they had suffered the most from the bowmen's arrows and wanted revenge of their own. The obstacles did their job and stopped the horsemen attacking with any cohesive force. Separated and in the maze of defences, the Mander horsemen were soon cut down.

The first wave of cavalry reformed and made two more attempts at charging the Avolonian line to break it. The Spartikens held. It took a long time to rebuild the line after the third charge. Almost half the Spartikens were dead or wounded, so only the front row was complete, backed up by a second row with gaps and many of the less seriously injured trying to fill them. It was a sorry sight of blood-stained faces, battered shields and missing helmets, but it was a sight that filled Elektra's heart with pride. Horns sounded again, this time from up on the hill where the rest of the Imperial Cavalry waited. It was the order for the second wave to advance: ten thousand fresh horses, their riders full of energy and rage. Elektra looked around at her own warriors, they were exhausted and battered, there was no way they were going to survive the next assault.

The ground began to shake once more as the landslide of horse flesh rumbled down the slope. Elektra looked towards the defences: they had done their job stopping the riders from getting around their line, now she wondered if she could get her warriors behind them in time. She looked back at the advancing cavalry eating up the ground between them at a ferocious pace, and decided she could not. The was only one order left she could give, and if she timed it wrong it would cost the lives of every man left standing.

The cavalry charge picked up so much force that the Spartikens' armour was shaking when the advance was still a hundred paces away. Elektra waited until the horns sounded the final charge before giving her own order. The cavalry was at full flight and, now that they were committed, they would be unable to react to any changes.

'Squares!' she bellowed.

The line segmented in an instant. Four squares, bristling with spear points, formed in the time it took Electra to take several breaths. She found herself at the centre of one of the formations just before the charge reached them. Horses would choose a gap over a wall of spears any day, and that's what they did. The charging line divided into columns riding through the gaps and around the squares. Electra watched, dumbstruck as cavalry thundered by. It all happened so quickly that she did not think in time to order spears thrown. The cavalry was through, and now that they had the rear of the main Avolonian force in their sights, they were not turning around. Countering the Avolonian attack on their infantry was what would win them the day, and nothing was going to stop them now.

Elektra stood with her hands on her knees, panting. She suddenly realised that the loudest sound in her ears was the beat of her own heart, pumping blood around her body at a furious pace. The Spartikens were silent, looking to her for orders but she had none. They had survived and, in that instant, that was all she could think about. '*Enola*,' a new thought suddenly came to her. The point of stopping the cavalry was to keep them off her back. She had failed, and now they were through, attacking the Lioness. Elektra realised something. The Mander were now attacking the rear of the Avolonians because they had broken through her lines but, in doing so, they had left her behind. Instead of being crushed by the Mander charge, Elektra's last order had kept her force intact, all be it a reduced and battered one. She wasted no more time thinking about it and gave a command.

'Form up on me. Make an advancing phalanx. Uninjured men to the front.' Electra picked up a shield laying on the body of a fallen Spartiken, was handed a spear, and then lead the phalanx towards the rear of the Imperial Cavalry. 'Let's get the bastards.'

Electra did not know it at the time, but Ioniedas had much the same result fighting the cavalry in the west as she had in the east. He had broken the cavalry charge on his side and frustrated them with counter-measures. The Imperial Cavalry must have thought the gates of the underworld had opened up to release all its foul demons when Elektra led the Spartikens in an attack from the rear. Pompieum got his wish of being in the eye of the storm, but he did not command the winds. The hurricane of retribution was tearing Pompieum's army to shreds. The Mander commander's vision had been of standing like the

God of Storms in the centre of the battle, casting lightning bolts and whirlwinds at a terrified enemy. He had seen himself as a god and could not grasp the reality of the situation: he was nothing more than a leaf carried on the winds of an Avolonian storm.

Enola

Where there there had once been a field of baked grass and dusty soil, there now stood a swamp of Mander blood. The Imperial Infantry irrigated the land from the arteries of severed arms and sliced necks. Enola's stallion stamped through the flood of red ooze that would fertilise the ground for decades to come, plants always grew well where men perished. Storm tossed his head, startled by a swordsman lunging the point of a blade at his rider. The white horse was coated in a pink foam, a mix of blood and sweat that made the beast look translucent. More blood splattered across Storm's flank as Enola split her attacker's head in two with a slash of her golden sword.

The Lioness could see Antona fighting his way towards her from the west. She was instinctively battling her way towards him, and soon their two forces would meet in the middle. Such a meeting should never have come about. All the Mander had to do was stand their ground. They had such numbers that the horsemen of the Storm Legions and Lion Warriors should have been swallowed up and dragged down into oblivion. But the ferocity of the attacks led by Enola and General Antona had ripped the courage out of their enemy. Infantry feared an enemy at their back more than anything. Warriors who should have stood their ground favoured letting the mounted warriors pass in front of them, especially when they saw the violence inflicted on those with their backs to the horsemen. Too many of the Mander infantrymen backed off to one side or the other so they could use their shields to protect themselves.

Chaos swirled amongst the foot soldiers as men panicked in a scramble not to get trapped on the wrong side of the Avolonians. The chain of command broke down as Mander officers were targeted by the cavalry and cut down before they could organise any retaliation. Too few of the ordinary soldiers had sense enough to form a shield wall and push back against the riders. So the gap widened and the cavalry attack kept up the momentum. Two forces that should have floundered on a solid wall of resistance found an ally in the chaos that drove frightened men to prioritise self-preservation over orders and duty.

'Drive them back!' Enola shouted to Antona when they met in the middle. 'I see you left it to me to fight most of the way through to you,' she added in friendly banter. She was surrounded, outnumbered and fighting for her life, but she could still jest with a friend. Enola lived for this; she was actually enjoying the thrill of the fight. Where there should have been fear, there was only elation.

'Ha!' Antona responded. 'The Mander always were frightened of princesses on pink horses.'

The two said no more, the intensity of the fight demanding all their attention. The back half of the Mander infantry column was now cut off from the front. They tried to hold their own defensive line, but they were pushed back and the gap widened. Warriors, seeing the armoured cavalry hacking their way towards them, panicked and tried to flee. The line broke in place after place. Fear travelled through the ranks of infantry like vomit through fingers clasped over a mouth. Men at the back of the column were infected with the fear of those in the fight. Afraid they were exposed to an attack that could come at any time, the soldiers panicked and ran. It was a rout: tens of thousands of Mander warriors running for their lives. Fleeing troops are a gift to cavalry. Chasing down a running man on horseback is a sport, a sport the horsemen of Avolonia were well trained in.

Enola broke off from the chase, her sword arm was numb from the repetitive slashing and impact with armour, flesh and bones. She turned to assess the situation with the front half of the column. The infantry at the other side of the gap had formed a shield-wall as a rear guard. They were not attacking, just holding their position. Enola thought about rallying her troops and attacking the shield-wall. In less than a moment she dismissed that idea, deciding the frightened men at the rear-guard of the column were not her main threat. She had no idea if the warriors of the Tornado Legion, defending the wall, still fought or if they had been overrun. Neither did she know if Cid and his Jagger Knights had managed to hold off the attack from Calinkerbad. Hordes of Mander troops could come bursting through the palisades at any moment and turn the tide of the battle against her.

Enola wiped her face, leaving streaks of blood across her cheek. The lion's head helmet was incredibly hot, causing sweat to constantly pour down her face and the back of her neck. She had a thirst that would kill a camel. She switched her sword to her shield hand and grabbed a water skin from the saddle of one of her bodyguards. Enola drank deeply, and then poured some of the water into her hand and wiped her face with it. She wanted to take off her helmet and pour the cooling liquid over her head, but she saw the thirst in the men around her and handed the skin to the next man.

Enola ordered Antona to take control of this side of the wall and fight on. She would take the Lion Cavalry back behind the walls to reinforce Hals and Cid. If she was not too late, they might even live to fight another day. She expected to fight her way through the Imperial Cavalry, but what remained of them were already in retreat. Enola led her horsemen back towards the east gate. She passed Elektra who was standing over the body of a cavalryman, his blood dripping from the blade she held up in salute as her commander rode by. Enola returned the salute and rode on through the gate.

The chaos of the battlefield seemed almost orderly in comparison to the sight that met Enola behind the wall. Hals's Tornados were fighting for survival. The Mander had broken Hals's line in several areas and were in the process of rolling up the defences. Enola rode directly into that area of the fight. The enemy crumbled under the ferocity of the Lioness' charge. Renaldon, the most senior officer of the Lion Cavalry took control of dismounting the men at the back to join the fight on foot. They plugged the gaps, killing or driving back any Mander who had broken through.

Once she had broken the back of the most extensive Mander breakthrough, Enola rode on with the warriors who were still mounted, to help Cid at the inner wall. She left Renaldon to close the gaps and contain the Mander. Before Enola was halfway across the compound when she heard trumpets in the distance. There must have been dozens of horns, the sound carrying loud and far. She reined in Storm, who skidded to a halt. Enola squinted to better see the force that appeared on the horizon. At first her heart sank, thinking it was a well-timed Mander counter attack. Her spirits did not rise much when she realised it was the Corinthians arriving.

Enola had mixed emotions about the arrival of her new allies. She knew she should be happy to see them: she had broken the Mander attack, but they could rally at any moment and attack again. The Corinthians would help her pursue her fleeing enemy and prevent them from regrouping. Enola watched the Corinthian advance with suspicious eyes. *'What if there was treachery in their intentions?'* she asked herself. *'What if they were here on the side of the Mander, and attacked her?'* She decided there was nothing she could do about that now. Enola suspected the Corinthian Generals had waited to see which way the battle was going before showing themselves. She supposed that if the Mander had been successful, the Corinthians would have slipped away, leaving no one the wiser about their presence.

The Corinthians were an impressive sight as they marched down the slope towards Calinkerbad. Drums beat out an intense rhythm, and the whole army chanted in unison on every tenth step they took. The Mander attacking from the city were certainly not taking any chance about who the reinforcements were supporting. They began retreating back behind the city walls. Antona had forced the infantry outside the walls to surrender. They were trapped and could see the rest of their army running away, leaving them behind. Antona would tell later how he had only had to have his archers fire one volley of arrows into the densely packed infantry to jolt the white flags of surrender out of Mander tunics. But most suspected that the sight of the Corinthian army marching towards them may have contributed to the capitulation.

Word of what was happening outside the wall was passed to the Mander still fighting against Hals and Renaldon inside the compound. Despondent Imperial Infantrymen reluctantly stopped fighting and laid down their weapons. Exhausted Spartikens of the Tornado Legion staggered back from the barriers and slumped to the ground in groups leaning against posts, carts or anywhere they could rest. The Lion Warriors were better disciplined and had enough experience to deal with the newly surrendered men before seeking any rest. Weapons were collected and prisoners made to sit against the wall with their heads down, and their hands clasped on the back of their necks.

Enola wanted to secure the compound and close the gates as a precaution against the approaching Corinthians. Antona and more than half her force were still outside the walls, so she realised that some quick thinking was needed to bring the situation under control. There were still pockets of Mander resistance on several fronts. Enola knew she should pursue those that had fled the battlefield and prevent them from regrouping. But that would leave her at the mercy of the approaching Corinthians. She looked to the advancing army and then turned her gaze to look through the gates to where her Storm Legions were split into several factions, rounding up prisoners or fighting off any remaining resistance.

'Sargent Ukon!' Enola snapped, bringing the officer to attention in his saddle. 'Take two men and ride to the Corinthians. Demand they halt and hold their position.' Ukon took his two chosen men and led them through the west gate. Enola looked for another mounted officer. 'You!' she shouted at the closest man of rank she could see. 'Ride to General Antona, and tell him to bring his cavalry and join us to the west to form a line to block the

Corinthians. He's to leave the surrendering force in the hands of his infantry,' The officer found it hard to hide the confusion and irritation from his face. The confusion was over the question of whether or not they would fight the Corinthians, and the irritation that a man of his rank was being sent as a messenger. Enola sent several more of her horsemen out with the message for everyone to pull back to the compound. She felt her priority now was to regain control of the situation.

Enola was about to demand the Tornado Legion back onto their feet so that she could take Renaldon and the rest of the Lion Cavalry with her. She changed her mind when she saw how utterly exhausted they were.

'Victory is close at hand,' Enola called out to the tired men on the ground, her words feeling like a lie, as she did not honestly know if the enemy were in flight or about to counter-attack. 'But there is still work to be done. Can you brave men summon one last portion of resolve for me?' She looked at the blood-stained faces looking up at her sitting on her warhorse. General Hals stood in the background, allowing his commander to speak without interruption, knowing her kind words would have a better effect than his cold orders. 'I need you to take over from the Lion Warriors here so that they can ride out with me.'

The Spartiken Warriors of the Tornado Legion slowly rose to their feet. One man sitting close to Enola, remained on the ground. He hung his head, shaking uncontrollably.

'You, on the ground with the blade still in your hand. Can you rise?'

The man nodded and then vomited between his feet.

'Forgive him, Sir,' Hurcan spoke for his friend. 'He killed for the first time today.'

'We all killed many times today. That useless bastard did less than his fair share,' Erwin told everyone who could hear. 'Shit himself before the first spear was thrown.'

Enola looked at the stain down the front of the boy's leggings, a clear sign that fear had emptied his bladder. 'Did he hold the line?'

'He did, Sir.' Hurcan came to Arter's defence. 'Fought back when he could, too.'

'Then you did well. I vomited for a week after I killed my first man. All but two of the cadets I served with taunted me, just like that bastard.' She gave Erwin a frown. 'Now I lead armies into battle while they still serve in the ranks.'

Arter lifted his head for the first time to look Enola in the eyes. 'I thought General Antona and General Eric served as cadets with you?'

Enola smiled. I did say all but two bullied me. Now, can you get to your feet and show these smug bastards what you are made of, so I can get on my way?'

Arter jumped to his feet, a new enthusiasm giving him the resolve he needed.

Chapter 4

Enola

The Corinthians halted their advance. Enola did not know if it was because of the order she had sent or because she now blocked their way with her cavalry. The Corinthians marched in squares, their tear-shaped shields interlocked to form a barrier around them, and a forest of spears raised to create a crown of thorns above them. Only the officers were on horseback, and several of them broke ranks to ride to the front. The Corinthian officers converged on a rider with great white plumes rising from his helmet. The leader was flanked by two standard-bearers carrying the Corinthian's colours. They all rode to halfway between the two lines and stopped.

Enola kicked her heels, and Storm lurched forward towards the group. Antona and several other officers followed the Lioness. One of the Lion Warriors carrying a Lion banner at the top of his spear hurriedly rode to catch up with the Avolonian party. Antona looked back to one of his cavalrymen with the Storm Legion's colours flapping at the top of his spear and gave him an embarrassed jerk of the head. It took a moment for the horseman to realise he was being signalled to join his General, but as soon as he did, he flicked his heels and galloped his mount forward.

The Corinthian in the plumed helmet was Tyezore, Enola recognised him from the leopard skin cloak he wore. Her Lion helmet did not go unnoticed.

'Is that the Devil Beast on your head?' was the first thing Tyezore asked as the two groups came together. 'The one that murdered my brother?'

'It is,' Enola replied. 'The one my father hunted and killed with his own hands.'

'Then it is not yours to wear. It is disrespectful to my people and your father for a woman to wear such a symbol of power,' the Prince said, his tone laced with condescension.

'Look beyond us,' Antona interrupted. 'Do you think the thousands of dead Mander back there would agree with you?'

Tyezore sneered at the young General as if he were filth begging for scraps. He looked back to Enola. 'What is this? We come to your aid, and you stand in our way. Step aside, let us finish this for you.'

The rage of battle was still coursing through Enola's veins, and it was all she could do to stop herself drawing her sword and cutting down the arrogant Prince. She wanted to turn the Corinthians away, she did not trust them. Her thoughts and emotions wrestled around her mind. She did not want the Corinthians there, but the longer she spent brooding over that, the more of the Mander got away.

Antona saw the conflict in his friend. 'We did not know if you were friend or foe. All we saw was an unannounced force marching towards us. You could have sent messengers.'

'You wear the lion's spirit, but you have men speak for you.' Tyezore words were spoken as an insult.

Enola was angry at Antona for speaking for her, it made her look weak. But she was not going to reprimand him in front of the stuck-up Prince. Another rider from the Corinthian side was rushing to join the delegations. It was Sonaji.

'Where is the Lion Lord?' Sonaji asked with immense concern in her tone. 'Has he fallen in battle? Is he injured?' She stopped herself short of asking the next question.

'He was taken ill in the early stages of the battle.' Enola worried about her father's wellbeing for the first time since riding out of the gates to fight. 'You will find him in his tent being tended to. I do not know how he is, but no messenger has come with bad news.'

'I will go to him,' Sonaji announced.

She clicked her tongue twice and urged her mount forward, not waiting for permission. She rode straight at the cavalry lines which parted to let her through.

'Advance your army to the east,' Enola told Tyezore. 'The Mander infantry are retreating in that direction. Do not let them regroup, they are a formidable force and still greatly outnumber us. We will chase down their cavalry and then return to join you.'

In truth, Enola knew the Imperial Cavalry and their commander were well out of her reach by now, but she would give chase in the hope of keeping them away from their foot soldiers. She also did not want to leave the Corinthians in the camp while she was gone, so having them chase the infantry gave her some peace of mind.

General Pompieum escaped on the royal barge. An Avolonian squadron of cavalry almost caught up with him at the makeshift dock from which he was ferried out to the vessel. They missed the General but captured the white stallion, Zanthus, when the General's escort left him behind as they fled for their lives. The Imperial Infantry managed to regroup, despite the Corinthians efforts to keep them scattered and running. The Mander headed north-east and fought an excellent rear-guard action as they retreated. The Corinthians and Avolonian cavalry harassed them as long as they could. The Mander were still too large a force to stop, so they were left to get away.

By the time Enola had done all the damage she could to the retreating Mander army, and had managed to bring order back to the field, she still had thirty thousand prisoners to deal with, and a city to conquer. The sight that greeted the Lioness as she returned to Calinkerbad was the monstrous tower Gavara had built. She was informed that her father had recovered and was holding council in the operations' tent. She sent a message for her own officers to meet her there and then headed for the tent herself. Enola was keen to see her father, despite how exhausted she was.

'Wait for me,' a voice beckoned Enola, as she approached the tent. It was Gavara, who hurried to catch up with his prodigy, relying heavily on his staff to help move his ageing body so quickly.

'I see you have been inventing,' she said, nodding towards the ginormous construction, as her old friend caught up with her.

Gavara looked back towards his building site and shrugged. 'Take a moment to breathe and calm yourself before you enter,' the old man advised. Enola gave him a confused look. 'You are straight from the battlefield, and diplomacy is what you will require in that tent. These are difficult times for your father. He needs your compliance now, not the conflict I see in your eyes.'

Enola smiled. 'Nonsense, I'm just eager to see how my father is. I'm sure he will want to hear my account of the battle.'

Gavara followed Enola into the tent, worry written across his face.

Arc sat on the Ivory Throne. It was draped in wolf skins for comfort, and Arc had a bear skin around his shoulders. Sonaji stood by the throne, looking radiant and calm. She had an air of authority about her that with the exception of the Lion Lord, captivated the attention of the others there.

'Where have you been?' Arc demanded as soon as he saw his daughter.

Enola remembered Gavara's warning. 'I'm pleased to see you are recovering, father.' She could not help but notice the slur in her father's words and the sagging on the left side of his face. She carried the lion helmet forward and laid it at her father's feet. 'I have been chasing down Pompieum and his Imperials, lord.'

'And?' Arc asked, sounding cross.

Enola looked around at the officers in the room. Tyezore was there, with his plumed helmet tucked under his arm, its white feathers fanning out across his chest. Several other Corinthian officers stood behind their Prince. Cid was in the room, and Ioniedas and Eric with several other minor officers of the Storm Legions and Jagger Knights, but Antona, Electra and Hals were still to arrive.

'Has something happened in my absence to anger you?' Enola asked her father. Rather than waiting for an answer, she went on to point out, 'We have not only survived, we also have a great victory.'

'A great victory!' Arc bellowed, slamming a hand down on the arm of his throne. 'If the Corinthians had not arrived to take the day we would all be Mander prisoners by now.' Arc ignored his daughter's attempt to protest and continued his rant. 'What possessed you to make an all-out attack? Hit and run, conserve our forces, that was my plan.'

Enola felt Gavara's old bony fingers grasp her arm in the hope he could remind her to hold her temper. 'With all due respect, lord, your plans were not known to us.' She looked around the room for support. 'We won,' Enola stated. She was not expecting a hero's welcome on her return, but she did expect at least a little acknowledgement of her achievements. She saw Sonaji lean over and speak into her father's ear. A spark of suspicion flashed in her mind. *'Did this woman already have such a hold on the Lion Lord that he listened to her counsel over that of his daughter?'* Enola asked herself. In an attempt to suppress her feelings of jealousy and anger, she immediately reminded herself that she was a commander of legions first and the Lord's daughter second.

'Victory at too great a cost,' Arc snapped back at his daughter.

Enola glared into Sonaji's bright eyes, sure that she saw triumph reflected there. Her anger boiled. Gavara tightened his grip but knew he had lost her as she brushed him away. The room was silent, no one wanting to step into the fight that was brewing.

'Commander Enola made some prudent decisions in the circumstances,' Cid spoke up for the Lioness, attempting to prevent the eruption he knew would come. 'No one else could have handled the situation as well in your absence.'

Arc gave the Knight a dismissive look, but his words helped to defuse the situation. The remainder of Enola's Generals entered the tent, surprised that all eyes turned to look at them. It didn't take them long to realise that they had missed something significant.

Gavara had attended the Lion Lord directly after his seizure. He noted how grumpy and annoyed the episode had left his friend. He could now see that the anger still lingered and worried it would be a permanent part of Arc's demeanour. He decided it was time for an announcement of his own and banged his staff on a wooden board by his feet.

'The siege-breaker is ready,' he told the room. 'Have your troops assemble at dawn. I will open the gates for you.'

Tyezore huffed. 'Just like that. You think you can gain entry to a city with walls thicker than a house, and open gates built of iron and oak and defended from all angles?'

'I do,' Gavara answered simply, and with solid confidence.

Tyezore huffed again. 'The city is just logistics, it will wait. It would be a more prudent tactic to advance on the Emperor's forces gathering at Siena Mazda before they quash the other half of your army.'

Gavara attempted to give the Corinthian Prince his kindest smile, but it was as condescending as the words that followed. 'Tactics win battles, but logistics win wars.'

'We can't leave a garrisoned city between us and our lines of supply,' Cid said in support of the white-haired Pathfinder. 'It would be a very short-lived advance if we did.'

'Why not tonight?' The ivory creaked as Arc leaned forward on his throne.

Gavara smiled again, but this time it was genuine. 'The machine can throw rocks of such an immense size that we are having difficulty transporting them here. We will be ready by dawn.'

'Enola,' Arc snapped. 'You will form ranks at dawn. I want to see the Storm Legions in action. You will take the city.'

'The legions are exhausted,' Hals could not stop himself from pointing out. 'We need to tend to our wounded and give honour to the dead.'

'Silence!' Enola's rage boiled over. 'We have been given the honour of taking the city. Every Spartiken will be ready and do their duty.' She was not angry at Hals, but she knew her father would be. She protected her General with her harsh words. It was an honour to take the city, but it was also unfair to send in her battle-weary troops when there was a whole army of Corinthians rested and battle-ready. She assumed her father wanted to showcase the legions to his new-found friends, as well as test her. As if defeating the Imperial Army had not been test enough. 'Excuse me, Lord.' Enola bowed. 'I must take my leave and ready my warriors for the events of tomorrow.'

Arc flicked his wrist to dismiss his daughter. 'Go. Burn your dead and bandage the wounded. Tomorrow you fight.'

Enola gave Sonaji a threatening glare before leaving with her Generals. Sonaji responded with an insignificant huff of amusement at Enola's parting challenge, and affectionately stroked the back of the Lion Lord's head, flaunting her influence over the real power in the room.

'What was all that about?' Electra was the first to speak after leaving the tent.

'The Lion is not himself,' Ioniedas said in Arc's defence. 'That fit or whatever it was that struck him down has obviously taken a heavy toll on him. Did you notice how slurred his speech was?' He sniffed at the air. 'The dead are starting to smell already.'

'They will have to stink for at least another day if we are to fight in the morning. I'll not make my men spend the night piling up the bodies,' Hals told them as they walked.

'Have the prisoners do it,' Enola told him and then turned to Antona. 'You captured the Imperial's baggage, didn't you? Any ale?'

'A thousand barrels.'

A wicked grin stretched across Enola's face 'Give it to the Legions and butcher the lame horses. If my warriors are to face death again tomorrow, they can at least have their fill of meat and ale tonight.'

Many of the horses had gone lame after the battle, others had cuts and gashes too deep to heal. It was easier to slaughter them for food and replace them with captured stock. Every cavalryman feared to put down the friend that had carried him into battle. But every warrior felt it his or her duty to end the beast's life themselves. They would let others butcher the animal but, out of respect, a warrior would swing the hammer that put his crippled mount out of its misery.

'Talking about horses,' Antona sounded more cheerful, 'we captured that great white stallion the Mander Commander was riding. He's at least two hands taller than Storm and just as white. Bad tempered bastard though. Broke the leg of one of my men, and put two others on their backs trying to get him under control. Shall I have him sent to you? As commander on the day, spoils of war are yours by right.'

Enola shook her head. 'No, have him sent to my father as a gift from me. He likes bad-tempered horses, and it may go some way to thinning out the amount of anger he seems to feel towards me.' Enola felt threatened by Sonaji's apparent closeness to her father. She knew that protocol would dictate that such a momentous gift as the defeated commander's warhorse must be ridden on the next public occasion. Not only would her father have something to be grateful for, but they would also both be on matching mounts. Two leaders on white stallions, it would be a symbol of their bond and status to be seen by the whole army.

The night was full of sounds; drunken shouts from men who had faced death and survived, mixed with excited squeals from serving wenches and camp followers. The smell of roasting horse flesh masked the stench of death that surrounded the Avolonian camp. Enola surrounded herself with those she considered friends. She had drunk too much of the ale and wine from the captured supplies and encouraged others to do the same. Hals had passed out on one of the sofas, exhaustion making him more susceptible to the effects of alcohol. He had intentionally drunk too much too quickly, trying to wash the taste of blood out of his throat, and from his memory the twisted faces of the men put to death by his sword.

Antona was feeding more of the ale to the serving girls than he drank himself.

'Those two will be slipping away in a moment, mark my words,' Jenaliena whispered into Enola's ear as she topped up her cup with wine. She noticed the Commander was staring at the handsome General and the group of women, including her friend Plenty, swooning around him.

Four tents were linked together to make a kind of canvas hall. Enola made sure the atmosphere was hypnotic, with drummers pounding out a trance-like beat and pipe players weaving a melody into the air. The room pulsed with bodies swaying to the music, its gentler notes suffocated by laughter and raucous chit chat. The good humour was the result of Enola inviting only officers, and her good sense to have a balance of both sexes. Nevertheless, as it always did when warriors were mixed with drink, a fight broke out. Two men squabbling over a captured sword were clubbed over the head by the guards and unceremoniously dropped outside the tent to sleep it off.

Jenaliena took the wine over to Antona and his little group. The General gave her the usual greeting and took a handful of her bottom and squeezed. The young woman turned to look back at Enola, knowing she would be watching, and rolled her eyes. She gave Antona a disapproving smile and a curt tip of the head to show her disapproval of his familiarity. Enola saw the gesture, as Jenaliena had intended her to, but was disappointed when the girl chose to stay with the group, fitting in with the laughing and joking as if she had been with them the whole night. Enola had wanted Jenaliena to slap Antona across the face as soon as he touched her, and return to her annoyed and in a fluster. But girls like Jenaliena did not behave in that way, they could not afford to, depending as they did on the good will of the officers for their survival.

Elektra called out a drunken greeting to her Commander, passing by with a man tucked under her arm. She leaned on him as if he was there as a crutch to hold her up. He looked juvenile against the female General's massive frame.

'What, you looked shocked to see me with a man?' Elektra said, in response to the astonished expression on Enola's face. Enyo is the family dyke, not me. I like the sausage gang. Take this one, doesn't look much, but he's built like a tripod.' She lifted her cup in salute, spilling half of its contents over her captive. 'You should get yourself one,' Elektra suggested as parting advice.

Enola thought of Huwel, her huge and handsome pirate husband. She was missing him, and the friendship and intimacy they shared. They were destined to be apart, but the world had a way of throwing them together. Arc refused to acknowledge their marriage, and in honesty, neither Enola nor Huwel thought of themselves as man and wife. When they were together, they were together, and when they were apart, they were apart. Both lived for the moment and had no interest in how the other had passed the time between their meetings. Enola found the manly warriors surrounding her less than appealing when compared to Huwel. It had become even harder for her to make a connection now that she was the Commander of the Storm Legions. Even the men she trained with seemed cautious of her, afraid to say the wrong thing or to cause offence of any kind. The usual banter and flirting ended with Enola's elevation to commander. Power was making her lonely.

There was one who interested her, but Ioniedas had not taken up her invitation to join the party. He had chosen to celebrate with a group of his own in a smaller gathering. Enola felt strangely attracted to the man who had been forced onto her staff by her father. There was something that intrigued her about the aloof General. He carried himself differently from the usual brutes. He oozed sexuality, and there was just something about him Enola found desirable without knowing what it was. In her drunken state she decided, if he would not come to her, she would go to him.

Leaving the tent, Enola found the night air was too warm for her liking. She was in a continuous sweat, and her clothes felt uncomfortable. The smog from the campfires made the air taste acrid and it stuck to the back of her throat. Enola had taken too much of the white powder the Jagger officers had been handing around. They snorted a pinch of the stuff before riding into battle to heighten their senses. It had made Enola's heart beat rapidly, but instead of heightened senses, she had experienced nothing more than the room spinning. Now her sandals felt like lead, and she couldn't focus on one thing at a time. She swayed, then staggered into a stacked pile of spears. There was an almighty crash as the shafts fell onto shields. Enola looked back to try and see some reason for her stumble other than her own drunkenness.

Guards were standing either side of the closed entrance to Ioniedas' tent when Enola found it. The two men barred the way by crossing their spears as she approached. Both men gave each other a confused look when they saw who it was approaching. Enola stood with her hands on her hips, tilting her head in a way that questioned the guards' actions, and trying not to sway. Realising that whatever punishment Ioniedas would heap upon them for letting someone invade his privacy would be the lesser of two evils, they uncrossed their spears.

'I don't think you want to go in there, sir,' one of the men recommended, in a futile attempt to stop the Lioness entering and therefore saving his own hide.

Enola ignored him and pushed through the flap. Thick herbal smoke filled her lungs with her first breath.

Twisting lanterns projected shapes of light, tracing through the swirling mist to where they glided across the inner walls of the room. A piper sat in the far corner, playing a haunting melody that made the smoke dance and swirl. There was a couple naked amongst the cushions by the door, entangled in each other's limbs. Neither of them was Ioniedas, but they were both men. Enola stepped over them and made her way to the figure sitting at the centre of the tent.

Ioniedas was perched on one end of a sofa, the type you would expect to see in a brothel rather than a General's abode. She almost did not recognise him. His hair was unbound and hanging down over his shoulders. His eyes were darkened with black liner, his cheeks reddened with blusher, and his lips coloured with lush red. The painted face did not shock Enola, she had seen warriors before colouring their lips or darkening their eyes. What took Enola's breath away was the pretty smock Ioniedas wore. She had fantasised about this man's muscle-toned body pressing down onto her. She had imagined his hair-carpeted chest pressing against her breasts as she pulled him into her embrace. Seeing him sitting there, wearing women's clothes, another man's head in his lap, left her speechless.

Ioniedas was the personification of calmness. When faced by his Commander, his secret revealed, he placed the pipe of a bong between his lips and drew the cool heavy smoke into his lungs. He looked into Enola's eyes as he slowly blew a stream of grey smoke into the heady atmosphere. His gaze was cold and distant, knowing she judged him as others had done before her. He would make no apology for who he was. He remained silent, his hand, with its painted nails, stroking the head of his young companion.

Enola looked around the room to see several other warriors dressed as women, serving boys tending to their every need. She was confused and unable to focus, without a word she spun on her heels and stormed out. The hot night air actually felt cold in her lungs after the pungent smoke of the tent. The sudden change in climate and her own haste was too much, Enola bent double and vomited between her feet.

'Are you OK?' a voice called out from behind.

Enola stood up, unable to see who spoke to her because of her watery eyes. She stuck her head in the water trough standing a few steps from where she had vomited. The liquid was warm, but it cleared some of the fog from her mind and washed the taste of puke from her mouth.

'Jenaliena,' Enola said, with genuine surprise.

'Come on, let me take you back to your tent,' the young serving girl offered, lifting Enola's arm over her shoulder, and leading the taller woman in the direction of her sleeping quarters.

'No, no, let's go back to the party.'

'General Cid has called time on the drinking. He has sent everyone away to sleep and get ready for tomorrow.'

'Good old Cid,' Enola slurred. 'Cid's not his real name, you know,' she went on in a drunken conversation. 'He is El Cid, the Lord. It's a title, not a name, Cid means Lord. You see?'

Jenaliena helped her mistress to her tent. The two of them fell onto the sleeping mats, Enola giggling like a little girl, allowing herself to succumb to her drunkenness. Jenaliena started to get up but was pulled back.

'I've always wondered what it would be like to kiss a girl,' Enola said, through a grin almost wider than her face.

Jenaliena's eyes widened. 'Would you like to find out, now?'

Enola suddenly stopped grinning, and her face took on a severe look. Their noses were almost touching as they lay facing each other on the mats. For a moment they gazed into each other's eyes, and then it happened. Jenaliena closed her eyes and pressed her soft lips against Enola's dry, cracked lips. Enola became instantly lost in the kiss like she was in a fall without end. Both of them were drawn into an embrace that lasted the night.

Gavara

Gavara watched with little enthusiasm the light growing on the horizon. Working on his machine throughout the night, he had been fixing pulleys and aligning cogs. Both test firings had resulted in bits coming loose or cogs coming apart. A good artillery team could reload a catapult and have it ready to fire in a short time. The new and monstrously large weapon Gavara had built would do well to fire half a dozen times from sun up to sun down. The noise in the camp grew in time with the rising sun, as angry officers woke sleepy warriors still half-drunk from the previous night. Gavara knew he was out of time, and if his invention was to have any influence on the coming day's events, it would have to work now.

'Load the first rock!' Gavara called out the instant everything was in place. 'Not the big one, the smallest on first.'

Three men greased a track that led through the centre of the machine. Another two men fastened ropes around a block of stone that came up to their waists. The old man had called it the small stone, but it was at least eight times larger than the largest stones they used for the other catapults. A team of horses were hitched to the opposite end of the ropes. The whip cracked, and the timbers creaked as the block was dragged into the belly of the beast. Gavara measured the block's volume with his staff and had archers fire arrows towards the walls so that he could estimate the distance. Two wheels, one on each side of the machine and twice the height of a man, were being turned to pull down the mechanical monster's giant arm. Two men inside each wheel walked to keep it spinning. The beast groaned as the enormous counterweights rose, lifted by a complex array of pulleys and cogs. The throwing arm was constructed from the trunks of four trees encasing the lower half of one humongous beam.

The ordinary catapults were already in action, firing stones and fireballs at and over the walls of the city. They used either counterweights or torsion to propel their deadly projectiles. The gigantic contraption Gavara had built needed both methods of propulsion to lift the larger than average propellants. He had built this type of machine once before. It had not been successful at first because the throwing arm had always snapped once the stones reached a specific size. Several beams had been broken before Gavara fathomed that there needed to be tension in the beam before firing, otherwise the stress was too high at one single point, and the shaft fractured.

The men turned the wheels until the weights were as high as they would go, and the throwing arm was all the way back and locked into place. The sling holding the stone block was attached to the end of the beam, after it had been placed under tension by a chain fixed to a locking wheel.

'Not so much tension,' Gavara grumbled as two of his assistants grunted and heaved on the locking wheel with shafts. 'Less tension for the smaller blocks, more tension for the larger blocks.'

The two men gave each other a puzzled look, this was the most significant block they had ever loaded and the crazy old fool giving the orders called it small. The slack was taken up on the sling, and the machine was ready to fire.

The Storm Legions were already forming into ranks in front of Calinkerbad's walls when Arc turned up on Armageddon.

'Let's see what this monstrosity can do then.' The Lion Lord leaned forward to rest on the pommel of his saddle.

'Good morning to you too,' Gavara answered, without trying to hide his scorn of poor manners. 'She's called the Harpy, and we are lucky to still have the technology in my head, as you burned the plans along with the library in Lowground.'

'I have apologised for that more than once, old man. Now, let it go.'

'Thousands of years of wisdom, up in smoke. Ready to fire!'

Everyone stepped back from the machine, and the horses were tethered to a post in case the sound of the enormous weapon going off spooked them and they bolted.

Two men remained behind, one to release the weights and the other to release the beam.

'Two men to fire it?' Arc questioned.

'Both of them must fire at the exact same moment, or she will lose her power. I haven't had time to work out the details of that just yet. Fire!'

The two men responsible for the firing heaved back on their levers. There was an almighty whooshing sound as the weights dropped, and the beam creaked so loudly that the onlookers thought it must surely be splitting in two. Armageddon lifted his head and would have bolted if Arc had not steadied him. The Harpy's beam whistled as it swung through the air. There seemed to be a delay before the stone started to move, but once it did, it was a blur. Arc watched the huge stone glide through the sky. It cleared the wall, well left of the gates and must have devastated an area several streets in. It was like a small earthquake when the stone struck.

The men who had helped build the weapon and fire her cheered and whistled, obviously impressed with the distance achieved.

'She pulls to the left,' Arc observed while calming his warhorse with a pat on the neck.

'I know. I have eyes.' Gavara was disappointed.

'How long before you can throw one of those bigger stones at the gates?'

'It's not easy to say.' Gavara was now flustered. 'To aim, I have to move the whole contraption to the right and then load. It's never been done before, so I don't know how long.'

'Can you get the distance, right?'

'Yes, yes, it's all a matter of mathematics.'

'It throws well enough, so I suppose if you throw enough, one is bound to be on target.'

Gavara was offended that anyone would think he would leave anything to chance. He flapped his arms at Arc to leave and shouted instructions to his assistants.

Arc

Arc planted his banner on a small rise facing the city wall. Large sections of the wooden wall had been removed, it had done its job and was now in the way of the Avolonian Legions' advance. There was some discussion amongst the Generals as to what should be done with such an abundant supply of wood. Some wanted to build siege towers, not believing that Gavara's giant weapon was going to get them into the city. Others wanted to build ships to ferry the army east or to fetch provisions. Cid feared that there were so many dead that it would take all the wood they had to burn the bodies. Hals suggested throwing the Mander dead into the river.

'Let them float down to the sea,' he had said, 'and make a feast for the sharks and crabs and whatever other creatures can stomach their black souls.'

The red lion of Arc's banner danced on the yellow field, as the wind played with the cloth. Enola's new banner for the Storm Legions was placed beside her father's. It had the same red lion holding a lightning bolt, standing on a black field. The elaborate crest of the Jagger Knights was there, and beside it was the Corinthian war banner. Two black lions stood on their hind legs, back to back on a white background. One held a sword and the other a spear with a single shield, red with a white cross, standing between them.

Arc sat on Armageddon watching the Storm Legion's advance on his right and left. He was joined by Tyezore, Sonaji, Cid, and Jellicoe who was to be the new commander of the Lion Warriors. Arc had left Arcilus, the last commander, in Avolonia. It was a decision he regretted, but leaving his right-hand man eased his conscience about going. Arcilus was a military genius. Arc hoped that if anyone could keep his new nation safe in his absence, it would be him. Arc felt his hand tremble and looked to Jellicoe with hope-filled eyes, wondering if he would gain the men's respect in the same way Arcilus had. Arc felt his heart echo the beat of the drums as the legions advanced. He looked over at the Harpy, its giant beam was still not in the loaded position, and the legions would have to stand and wait. They had no ladders that were tall enough to reach the top of the wall, and it would take days to build siege towers.

Enola rode across the field from her legions on the east side, to her father's position. She was about to greet him by asking what he thought of the fine warhorse she had gifted him. Or, more to the point, why was he not riding the white stallion. In the end she gave no greeting, her words forced back into her throat when she saw that Sonaji was mounted on Zanthus. She could think of no greater insult than to have passed on her generous gift to his whore.

'The Storm Legions are in position and awaiting your orders, Lord,' Enola announced, unable to take her eyes off Sonaji on the chalk-white stallion.

The Lioness felt the rage pumping through her veins. She had cherished the thought of her and her father sitting on the white beasts for all to see: the strong bond of blood and loyalty between father and daughter evident and motivating. That vision of unity had been betrayed. Now, all would see two women on the same status symbols. The gesture had backfired on Enola; instead of it lifting her to her father's side in the eyes of the army, it had elevated

Sonaji instead. She wanted to scream out in protest at the injustice, but the foul bile of the betrayal burned her throat and silenced her voice.

‘Keep them out of arrow reach,’ Arc told Enola, and then looked over towards the Harpy. ‘Gavara is not ready.’

‘We could give them a chance to open the gates for us.’ Cid suggested. ‘Ships have been leaving the port all night. I would bet that most of the warriors and rich folk have left already.’

‘No more surrendering,’ Arc said, his voice as menacing as distant thunder. The hate he carried inside of him scraped its nails down the spine of his soul and its fangs bit into his heart. Whenever he tried to calm the beast within, it showed him visions of his daughter and wife murdered by his enemy, and the rage grew stronger. There would be no surrender, no mercy. He would wipe the foul stain of Mander from the earth, so future generations would never know it had existed.

‘Is it wise to take too much time over this?’ Sonaji asked. ‘We do not know what has become of your forces to the east. The Mander Northern Army could be closing in on us as we speak.’

‘She is right,’ Tyezore joined in. ‘I can make them open their gates without showing them the weakness that an offer to surrender would show.’

Jellicoe tutted. ‘You would torture and murder the Mander prisoners in full view of the city wall. That’s a Mander trait and not one we would dishonour ourselves with.’

Tyezore was quick to anger. ‘You will not think it so dishonourable when you are face down in the mud with a Mander blade in your back.’

‘Enough!’ Arc snapped. ‘We will see if Gavara is successful, and if he is not, then we will do what we must.’

Enola turned her mount to face the city. 'I will await your orders,' she called back as she urged Storm into a canter towards her legions. She could not believe what she had heard. Her father had been revered and respected for his compassion in victory. As a Mander General he had hanged his own men for raping and pillaging a defeated enemy city, and once free of his Mander masters he had banned slavery and torture of any kind. Now, he was considering such things. She would have no part in it.

Gavara

The Harpy groaned under tension, complaining about her restraints, grumbling to be released. A larger stone block than the previous had been hauled up the greased track and secured into the sling beneath the throwing arm. The whole structure had been moved to the right to aim its throw at the gates of Calinkerbad. All that remained now was to unleash the weapon's tremendous force. The Storm Legions watched with bated breath from their positions either side of the colossal gates. The Lion Warriors, Jagger Knights and Corinthians watched from a safe distance.

'Two more notches!' Gavara called out. Two men went to work levering the tension wheel with their staffs. After he heard two loud clunks of the wheels' ratchet, Gavara held up his hand. 'Ready.' His wispy white beard lifted on the breeze, and his deep blue eyes narrowed in concentration. His beard dropped, and so did his hand. 'Release!'

There was a thud followed by a whoosh. Everything creaked, and groaned as the Harpy's long beam was flung into the air by the falling weights. The mighty rock resisted for the blink of an eye, then the whole construction jolted as the stone was snatched from the ground and thrown skyward. Almost fifty thousand sets of eyes traced the stone's trajectory, heads turning in unison to converge on the mammoth doors which protected the city. Expectations were high, minds seeing the wooden gates splintering into a billion pieces, even before the stone had reached them. There was a colossal thud, and the land shook as an explosion of earth and sand burst into the air. As the dust settled a wave of groans washed over the legions. The gates were still intact. The stone had fallen short and was now an additional obstacle between the army and the gates.

The wind rolled in, and dark clouds raced across the sky, their shadows sailing through the Avolonian Army. It took far too long to load the next block of stone into the belly of the beast. Gavara knew that patience was wearing thin, but he would not be rushed with his calculations. He went back to the block twice, measuring it with his staff. Only when he was sure did he give the order to fire. This third stone to be cast by the Harpy spun in the air. It crashed into the turret to the left of the gates. The explosion of gravel and dust was flung out to rain down on the nearest Spartikens, who raised their shields to protect themselves. Again the earth shook, lasting longer this time as the top half of the turret and part of the adjacent wall disintegrated. Masonry crumbled to the ground, piling at the base of the wall. The devastation was immense, but the damage was too high from the ground to give any chance of troops entering. The thick beamed gates were still intact, but one more hit like that and they would not survive. The army cheered regardless, they had waited a while to see something happen, so any success was greeted with enthusiasm.

Arc

A messenger came running over to where Arc observed. The breathless man's message was not received very well. He told them how the beast had torn itself apart under the tension of the last throw.

'Gavara says he can fix her, but it will be noon before the Harpy is ready to fire again.'

Arc felt his disappointment sprint up the steps of his anger. 'Then get back there and help them, and tell Gavara, if the next one does not shatter those gates, I'll put him in that bastard sling.'

The man's eyes widened, shocked by the Lord's words, not knowing if it were a jest or a real threat. He ran back to the Harpy.

'That was an impressive strike. It would take the ordinary catapults days to have such an impact,' Cid pointed out, hoping to avoid what he suspected was coming. 'The next shot must surely throw the doors open.'

Arc had full faith that Gavara would eventually succeed, that was not the worry. It would take hours to repair the weapon. If his enemies from the east were closing in on them, every moment would be vital. The chaos that ensued when a city was captured could take hours, even days to subdue.

'Tyezore!' The Corinthian Prince straightened his back and sat up in his saddle, as Arc called out his name. 'You have until noon.'

A grin spread across the Prince's face, his white teeth a contrast to the grey light of a dull day. Cid's expression remained stern, knowing he had failed to prevent an act of cruelty that would trample on his core beliefs and chivalry.

'Jellicoe, Cid, have your troops take up defensive positions around the outer wall until the city is in our hands.' Both men gave Arc an enthusiastic salute. 'I will be in my tent; there are plans to be made.' His final statement was fooling no one.

Exhaustion showed plainly on the Lion Lord's face, but he did not want his weakness to show. Even he knew that if he did not rest when there was the opportunity, there could be another fit. Sonaji gave her lover an eager look, questioning if she should follow. Arc shook his head and turned Armageddon towards his tent. Two bodyguards followed their master down the hill, their mounts' hind quarters swaying in unison as they descended the slope.

Tyezore

Shields were stacked in rows so that they looked like slates waiting to be placed on the roof of a hall. Flies swarmed like smoke above the piles, feeding on the dried blood that coated the metal rims. Small mountains of swords were dotted around the pyramids of spears. The landscape where the captured weapons were being stored was a scene plucked out of a warrior's nightmare, a vision of the underworld, hell for the defeated.

Renaldon had been left in charge of the prisoners. He was surprised that the order had not come to start executions. There were too many of them. If an attack occurred, there would be a danger of an uprising. Renaldon had been a Lion Warrior since the days in Saxland when they were under the command of Mander officers. He knew what it was like to be captured in battle and forced to fight for your enemy. He had the good sense to form a wall of steel between the prisoners and the piles of captured weapons. He had also divided the prisoners up into pens, separating officers and those who were born Mander, from those who had been conscripted from the colonies. There was no food for them, but Renaldon had allowed them to fetch water from the river in return for killing their own wounded. It was a small mercy that worked for both sides. To be unable to fend for yourself because of a wound was no different from being slain in battle. It was one thing for a warrior to kill a man in the heat of battle, to end the life of another lying defencelessly at your feet was not an act of honour. The mercy for the Mander was that they could despatch friends and comrades in as humane a way as possible, and not having to watch the more sadistic of their enemies make a sport out of it.

When Tyezore came for the first thousand doomed men, Renaldon made sure he took only men born to Mander. The Corinthian singled out officers clinging to their own banners, knowing them to be high born from respected Mander families. The condemned prisoners were marched to the city wall, heads down and eyes that were so devoid of hope it was as if their souls had already left their earthly bodies. The prisoners lined up either side of the city gates, as close as they dared. The captives were forced to their knees, and a blade placed at their throats. Tyezore shouted his demands of surrender at the closed gates. No reply came. No counter threats or response of any kind. It was quiet, quieter than it should be. Traces of movement could be detected behind the thick doors and upon the ramparts, but they were fleeting and almost mouse-like.

Screams erupted, mixed in with the sound of hammering. Dozens of wooden panels were carried forward, each by four men and erected in front of the gates. Each panel had a Mander officer nailed to its boards. Hands and feet were spread to the four corners and nailed into place. Those who had clung to their own banners now had them displayed over their heads to show who they were.

'Come and claim your sons of Mander!' Tyezore called out. 'Open your gates or suffer their fate when we open them for you!'

Warriors with shields stood either side of the Corinthian Prince. He was now in arrow range of the wall, and they nervously stood ready to protect their leader. When no response came from the city, Tyezore walked over to the nailed prisoners at the centre of the display. He chose the one with the most prominent banner above him and proceeded to rip open his tunic. Once the man's upper body was exposed, Tyezore turned back towards the city.

'We have thirty thousand prisoners,' he paused. 'If I have to kill all of them, I will,' he paused again. 'If I kill all of them, then I will kill all of you. Open your gates now, and you live. If I have to break down your gates I will, and you will die like these men here. Your choice.'

Tyezore drew his sword and carefully slit the nailed man's belly open. The man screamed. His guts poked out, a mix of blood and steam smoking from the wound. The Prince stepped in closer and used his free hand to jiggle the flesh above the wound. Loops of the prisoner's intestines fell out and hung like a coil of rope. The man's scream was ear-splitting, but he managed to stop wailing long enough to spit. Tyezore ignored the futile gesture to step behind one of the shields. An arrow had struck the ground by the Prince's feet. Another struck the boards, and then another hit the shield Tyezore sheltered behind. It was like the start of a rainstorm, first a few drops, followed by an escalation and finally a hail. Arrows rained down from the city wall, anger and hatred in every shaft.

The Corinthian withdrew, giving an order to send a thousand souls to eternity with a simple nod of the head. The guard carrying the shield for Tyezore yelled out when an arrow struck him in the calf, but the Prince took little notice, enthralled by the vast numbers of Mander prisoners falling to the ground, throats cut or spines severed. The next thousand condemned men were already on their way before some of the first group were still. Mander arrows killed the men nailed to the boards in-range of their bows, a merciful death from brothers in arms. Tyezore had the remainder suffer the fate of his first victim, their bellies split and their guts displayed. He set fire to some of their limbs for good measure and to make sure the screams persisted. Three thousand prisoners died a horrible death without a single reply to any of the Corinthian's threats. He would have carried on all day if the word had not come that the Harpy was ready to be fired again.

Arter & Hurcan

The city wall looked like it reached all the way up into the Overworld of the Gods from where Arter stood with shield and spear in hand. He tried to keep his mind away from the butchery he'd just witnessed, sickened to the stomach by what he'd seen happen to the Mander prisoners. Arter imagined himself in their position, as if it was him on his knees with the blade at his throat. Death seemed inevitable in this war-ravaged place, it was only how and when that remained to be discovered. Arter did his best to stop his limbs from trembling. He was uncomfortable in his ill-fitting armour, it didn't feel like it belonged to him.

'Stop your fretting, lad,' Hurcan grumbled through the side of his mouth at Arter. 'They were dead men the moment they surrendered, and they knew it. Concentrate on staying alive instead of thinking about your death. Don't deny it, I know you too well.'

'You do,' Arter admitted. 'What will it be like in the city?'

'I don't know, it's always different. The only thing I'm sure of, is that it will be chaos. Stick with me. If we get separated, find your way back to the warriors you know.'

A sudden noise made both men flinch. It sounded like a mountain had split in two, the halves falling apart and crashing to the ground. The earth shook, and then there was a moment of silence. Arter instinctively looked towards the city gate. As if a god had struck the wall with a great hammer, shards of stone and clouds of dust flew outwards. The crash was so loud and the impact so immense that the hairs on Arter's arms stood up as he felt the shockwave. Rumbling, snapping and crashing sounds filled his ears as debris and the giant rock fired from the Harpy settled. Arter could not believe his eyes when one of the colossal doors to the city swung open and fell from its hinges. The loud bang as it hit the shattered stones strewn across the entrance was instantly followed by a cheer from the Storm Legions.

Enola appeared no more than thirty strides away from where Arter was standing in the front row of the Tornado Legion. The air smelled of stale ale and pungent body odour seasoned with the occasional whiff of flatulence. The Lioness steadied her rambunctious white stallion and pointed her famous golden sword at the legion.

'Warriors of the Tornado Legion, hear my words.' Enola's voice carried as if it came from a person three times her size and had wings to travel. 'You will be the first of us through the gates. Remember, you are Spartikens and Spartik will be watching over you. We are a liberating force, not a conquering one.' She paused just long enough to bring Storm under control, his enthusiasm for the day's excitement overflowing. 'Kill when you must, but accept surrender when it is offered. Any man who rapes or kills for trinkets will feel the hangman's rope around his neck before the sun goes down. Fight well, and show the world who we are. You never know, the Gods may be so impressed that they invite you to their feasting table to entertain them with stories of your brave deeds on this day.' She raised the tip of the golden blade to the sky. 'Warriors of the Tornado, I salute you!'

'Hurrah! Hurrah! Hurrah!' thousands of voices called out in unison, a great wave of sound crashing against the wall and echoing across the fields. The warriors of the

Tornado Legion stamped their feet, drummed their spears against their shields, and then advanced.

Enola was sickened by the slaughtering of prisoners. She had heard so many stories about her father taking cities and breaking armies without resorting to the type of terrorism she had just witnessed. Her warriors would regain Avolonia's honour, they would be fearsome and formidable, but compassionate when called for. She was determined to show her father and the Corinthians that there was a better way. She rode to the next legion, determined to make her point.

Arter's heart was galloping. His helmet shifted, limiting his vision, but he knew better than to try and adjust it. Keeping the line was all that mattered now. Protect the man to your right and trust the one to your left to do the same for you. Luckily, he had Hurcan on his left, the only man in the Tornado's he really trusted. To his right was a man called Hopper. When Arter first met the man he asked him if Hopper was a name or a description. The man was offended by the attempted jest, so the two of them did not get along.

'Arrows!'

Arter instinctively raised his shield in unison with Hurcan and Hopper at the sound of the warning. The rattle of steel points hitting the bronze shields rang out like the chime of a thousand bells. Muffled cries of men struck down by the shafts could be heard somewhere along the line, and men shuffled to close the gaps left by fallen comrades.

The sound of stamping feet and rattling armour filled Arter's ears, but he could still hear the roar of the monster as the Harpy let fly another enormous rock. This stone hit the arch above the surviving gate. The masonry exploded into a cloud of rubble and dust, obliterating the huge wooden door. There was a delay while men came to terms with their astonishment, but eventually another cheer went up from the Avolonian Army when they realised the way was now wide open.

Arter understood that both Hal's Tornados and Electra's Typhoons would converge on the breach at the same time. He also worked out he would be front and centre when the fighting started. Arter narrowed his eyes and put on his best war face, determined to show his resilience. But his legs felt weak and he hoped they would not let him down. Arrows were still bouncing off shields when the two legions collided. Occasionally the feathered shafts hit their mark through gaps caused by a stumble or obstacles. Debris littered the entrance and had to be climbed over. Arter could see arms and legs sticking out of the rubble, defenders killed by the falling masonry. What he could not see were any soldiers rushing to defend the breach. The arrow fire intensified but no shield wall formed inside the gates.

The front row of the Avolonian phalanx narrowed and segmented to pass through the ruined gateway, spreading out again as they entered the city. They were vulnerable to arrows shot from the wall until the second line came through to hold shields above their heads. Arter felt a shaft narrowly miss his head. He was wrenched to the right and turned to see Hopper grasping at an arrowhead protruding from the front of his throat. The arrow had entered through the back of his neck and gone all the way through. Blood sprayed between Hopper's fingers and flooded his tunic. Arter watched helplessly as the stricken man opened and closed his mouth in silent cries, his eyes wide with fear.

Arrows were now coming from the front, and Arter's shield protected Hurcan, so he dared not move to help the injured man. Hopper fell to the ground, his shield falling with him leaving Arter exposed to the archers in front. Shafts rattled off his shield and helmet as his vulnerability was noticed, but he stood his ground, his shield protecting Hurcan.

'Close!' Hurcan yelled when he realised what was happening. 'Close the gap!

Arter allowed himself to be shoved to the right by his bigger friend. An arrow sliced his cheek before the gap closed and he was safe once more behind the protection of a shield. He almost slipped in the pool of blood around Hopper's body and had to momentarily stand on the dying man's back to get into position. The warriors of the Storm Legions hoisted their spears above their shields and advanced. What little opposition there was melted away into the streets of Calinkerbad.

The phalanx had to break up to enter the streets. The Spartikens split into their divisions of two hundred and fifty warriors and then further divided into groups of fifty. A ring of resistance formed around the city's main square. The fighting was bloody and the Spartikens had to hack their way forward, paying for every step with blood and sweat. The resistance eventually collapsed and ended in a rout. The Spartikens chased their enemies through the streets, no longer an organised force but a rabble operating in small groups.

Arter was separated from his own division. He was fighting alongside Hurcan when they were ambushed from a side street. Hurcan and the others were swept down the road leaving Arter cut off. He had to run for his life. He survived by grouping together with a few others in the same situation. Now that most of the resistance was dead or on the run, Arter was trying to find his way back to his own division. He was told by some Spartikens from his legion that they thought his division were clearing out the narrow streets to the east of the square, so Arter headed in that direction.

The young Spartiken finally came across a familiar face. He recognised Hedrik standing in the doorway of what looked like a stable. His shield was propped against his legs, and he was casually leaning against the post, looking into the stable.

'Hedrik!' Arter called out.

The man spun around, visibly startled. When he saw it was Arter, he called something through the doorway and picked up his shield.

The next thing Arter heard was a woman's scream from inside the stable. He moved towards the door to confirm his suspicions.

'Get back!' Hedrik roared, pointing his short sword at Arter.

It was too late, he could already see inside.

'I see you in there!' Arter called through the doorway, ignoring Hedrik's threat. 'Is that you, Erwin? It is. You bastard, let her go.'

The woman screamed again, pleading for help. Erwin had ripped her bodice off and pushed her tattered skirts up so that she was naked except for her boots and the remnants of her skirt wrapped around her waist. He had the woman bent over a beam, pounding into her from behind, her arm twisted up her back and her pendulous breasts swinging with the rhythm of his thrusts.

'Bastard!' Arter called out, trying to push past Hedrik to stop the assault, but Hedrik trapped him against the doorway with his shield.

Erwin looked Arter in the eye but did not stop what he was doing. 'Kill the bastard,' he grunted through clenched teeth. 'No fucking witnesses.' He let out two more loud grunts as he brought himself to a climax. Holding the terrified woman in place over the beam, he reached down with his free hand and pulled up his leggings. He then let go of her arm and took a handful of her long brown curls to pull her head back. The woman fought and screamed. Erwin held her hair so tight that it caused her an unbearable amount of pain. She instinctively raised both hands to try to break his grip and free her hair. He drew his short sword from its scabbard on his back and stabbed her in the throat. Her screams were silenced.

'No!' Arter called out, the struggle between him and Hedrik escalating, but he could not get past to help the woman.

Erwin grinned at Arter as he pulled his blade free and thrust it again, this time plunging it into the young woman's heart. She dropped like a stone. He picked up his shield, which had been leaning against an old cartwheel, turned to spit on the woman's corpse and headed towards the exit.

Arter was forced back by the larger Hedrik, and he fell over a water trough just as Erwin reached them.

Hedrik looked into the stable and saw the woman's naked body lying in a pool of blood. 'What about me?' He asked, disappointed that he was not going to get his turn with their victim.

'You can have the next one,' Erwin told him as he made a move on Arter.

The two men battered on the younger man's shield until he could take no more and dropped it. Arter was battered but not beaten. He drew his kopis sword with his left hand so that he held a blade in both hands, and stood defiantly as the two men came at him again. He was a fury of sharp steel, raining blows on the two shields as if he was battering down the gates of hell. The rim of Hedrik's shield was driven into his throat, taking him out of the fight. He was out for only a few moments, coughing and spluttering until he recovered. He came back with a vengeance.

Arter had left it too late to run. His strength was gone. Erwin knocked him to the ground with his shield. Dazed and hurt, Arter dropped his kopis blade. The weapon clattered across the stony ground, leaving him only his short sword to fight off his attackers. Hedrik slammed the rim of his shield down onto Artur's arm and he dropped the second blade. He was defenceless. Erwin raised his sword to finish the boy but was stopped in his tracks by a shout.

'What's going on here?' Enola yelled. 'Spartiken fighting Spartiken.'

Erwin and Hedrik looked up to see their Commander reining in her mount, her bodyguards close behind.

'Caught the bastard raping, sir,' Erwin called out an explanation.

'That's not...' Arter was silenced by a boot in the face from Hedrik.

'It's true, sir,' Hedrik joined in on the lie. 'Poor thing's in there,' he flicked his head towards the barn. 'Had his way with her and then the bastard took a blade to her. Poor thing.'

Arter was too dazed to defend himself. He spat blood and bits of teeth from his rapidly swelling mouth, scarcely hanging onto consciousness. One of Enola's bodyguards dismounted and went across to the stable's doorway. He confirmed the crime, shocked by the grim sight that greeted him.

Enola was enraged. 'I recognise this one. A coward and a raping murderer it would seem. Take him to the square and string him up with the others where everyone can see.' She flicked her heels and Storm lurched forward.

Hurcan arrived just in time to see the Lioness leave and his beaten friend being lifted between two guards. He was told what had happened and he watched dumbfounded while Arter had his wrists bound by one end of a rope and the other end tied to the pommel of the guard's saddle.

'What happened?' Hurcan pleaded with Arter to tell him, but the boy was still too dazed to speak, his eyes glazed and expressionless. 'There must be some mistake. You can't hang this boy, he is a loyal soldier.'

'Can and will,' the guard answered as he rode away, Arter staggering along behind him. 'No amount of loyalty will save him now,' he called out over his shoulder.

'That boy would never do what they say he has done. There must be a mistake,' Hurcan looked at Erwin and Hedrik, his suspicion instantly raised. 'What have you two got to do with this?'

'He's a raping murdering bastard, that's all we know,' Erwin answered.

'No, not him. He wouldn't.'

'Well, he did,' Hedrik pointed at the stables. 'Proof's in there. Poor choice in friends,' he went on with a snigger. 'We'll not hold it against you, but there's many a man in the legion who will.'

The two men walked away, leaving Hurcan with his head in his hands, shocked and unwilling to believe this hideous crime could have been committed by his friend.

Enola

The fight for the city went on all day. It was more of a clean-up operation than a battle, as most of the Mander troops having left on ships before the assault. The soldiers left behind had orders to defend the city at any cost. Most had little stomach for the task, knowing they had been deserted. But some were fanatics who had stayed behind, determined to become martyrs for their God and earn themselves a place in paradise. The wealthy of the city had also left on those ships, taking with them their wealth, and leaving behind their slaves and anyone else without the funds to pay for passage. A small, and more resilient contingent of the defenders was holding out in the east side of the city. They had set fire to the shanty town which had been home to many of the slaves and poorer residents of the city. The flames spread rapidly through the clustered dwellings, and a black cloud of smoke hung over that section of the city.

Wide streets ran vertically and horizontally across Calinkerbad, dividing it up into large square blocks. Each block was a warren of narrow streets twisting chaotically in random layouts, a complete contrast to the well-planned main roads. The stone buildings were mostly two storeys high, some with wooden balconies or overhanging rooms added to the upper floors, giving the streets a cave-like atmosphere. They were easy places in which to hide or stage an ambush. Once all the main streets were under control. Enola ordered Antona and Ioniedas to advance their legions towards the dockland area of the city. Elektra and General Hal's were tasked with clearing the twisting backstreets of any danger. Once that was done, word would be sent to the Lion Lord that the city was his.

Most of the city's inhabitants had made their way to the docklands, hoping to find passage on a ship across the waters of the Umbas. Tens of thousands were left behind, crowding around the waterfront and calling out to the few boats anchored in the centre of the harbour. Some were slaves glad to be free of their Mander masters, but afraid they would face the same fate or worse from the invaders. Those ships' captains who had any sense had stopped returning to the port and remained on the far shore. Once the city had come under attack, the boats in the harbour had been swamped by panicking folk, desperate to make a getaway. The few boats that remained were greedy for coin, sending small craft to troll the banks for anyone with wealth who could be exploited. There were very few left with anything of value and, despite desperate pleas, the boats were now returning half empty to the far shore.

Enola was receiving reports all the time, but there were gaps in the information. She found it best just to go out into the city and find out for herself, rather than sending others who returned with half the story. Besides, she wanted to be seen galloping around the dangerous areas of the city. She had the heart and mind of a warrior, so hanging around in a command tent did not sit well with her. She longed to have the respect of her legions, and being seen in the thick of the action would enhance her reputation. So Enola raced through the streets with her bodyguards in tow, encouraging her troops, giving them orders, and inspiring them to greater deeds.

Twice the Commander came across fights raging between her Spartikens and the Mander resistance. Both times, to the dismay of her bodyguards, she showed little regard for her own safety and waded into the action, swinging her sword in swooping arcs and yelling her battle cry. The Lioness was a magnificent sight on her white war stallion. She wore a red cloak like the rest of her Spartikens, but her helmet was topped with a white brush instead of the red one worn by her Generals. Her silver breastplate shone, chains of authority hung from rings piercing the metal nipples. Enola had seen statues of Eridanus, Guardian of the Fifth Element with her nipples pierced in this way. Gavara had explained that it was a tradition of the Warrior Queens of old, who would fight bare-chested. Inspired by the women's determination to be seen as strong, Enola had fashioned her own armour in that way but had not yet found the resolve to pierce her own flesh. Her tunic, boots, and leather kilt were also as white as Storm's coat. Gavara designed the red cloaks and tunics to hide the blood, as did the brown leather kilts and sandals of the ordinary Spartikens. They also brought the men some team spirit, a sense of belonging that made them walk a little taller. Enola understood the psychological advantage this gave her army, but she had wanted something different for herself. She wanted the blood to show on her and her mount so that her warriors would know she had been in the thick of battle and not hiding at the rear.

After searching dozens of streets and finding no more excitement, Enola sent her bodyguards back to the square, promising to follow them as soon as she had spoken to some of the wounded men resting in one of the courtyards. The captain of the guard wasn't happy about leaving the Lioness alone, but he knew better than to argue. When Enola wanted some private time, she got some private time. She spoke with the wounded men and asked them how they had received their injuries and showed them the respect of listening to the tales of their personal battles.

After thanking each of the men personally, Enola headed back towards the square. She led Storm by the reins and sauntered down the wide main street. While passing one of the many darker, narrower lanes, she noticed movement in her peripheral vision. It was only the slightest twitch, but intuition made Enola stop and take a few steps back. Again, she just caught a fleeting hint of movement, a shape or a shadow gone behind a pillar before it could be distinguished as real. Enola tied Storm to an olive tree on the street's corner, drew her sword and cautiously made her way into the shadows of the narrow street.

'Show yourself!' she called out, leaning to one side to gain a better view around the stone column.

She held her breath, listening for any sign of movement. There was a faint click, like a stone being dropped or kicked, but it came from behind her. Enola looked over her shoulder to see the street still empty and Storm calmly nibbling on an olive branch. A bird flew between the rooftops, its shadow darting across the street. Enola sighed, realising that she was chasing shadows, and decided to break off her investigation of the street. She sighed again and allowed herself to relax, taking one last glance down the road before turning to leave.

Her mood changed in an instant. A chill shot down her spine, and her shoulders tensed. Standing in the middle of the street, in the shadow of the pillar, was a menacing figure. It was clearly a warrior, a Mander warrior, standing with his feet apart, arms by his side and a sword gripped in his right hand. The man did not move or even look at Enola, his lank hair mostly covering his eyes. He looked like he wanted to fight, and Enola enjoyed the excitement of the moment.

She had no shield, but neither did he. She heard the click again from behind and suddenly realised what was familiar about the sound. It was that half click, half scrape of a stone caught in the sole of a sandal or boot. She spun around and came face to face with two more Mander soldiers, no more than twenty paces away. One held a sword, the other a spear. She glanced back at the first man and let out a gasp, seeing that two more soldiers had joined him, both with spears.

Enola felt her blood turn cold with fear. She instantly reprimanded herself for allowing the emotion to take hold of her. She stilled her mind and focused on a way out. She was trapped, and the men were obviously intent on her death, their silence assuring her that they neither wanted to surrender nor escape. There could be no hesitation, she would have to make a break one way or another. She looked at a doorway to her left and darted towards it, crashing into the door with her shoulder. There was a loud thud, but the door was solid and did not burst open as Enola had hoped. One of the men let out a laugh as they all started to close in on her.

Stepping back into the centre of the cobbled street Enola thought quickly, searching her mind for a solution. She would run at the two men between her and her horse. If she could burst past them and reach Storm, she would be free. She was sure the other three warriors would reach her before she could break these two, but that was up to the Gods. It was decided, she would make it to Storm or die trying. Her heart sank when she glanced down the street, about to make her dash, the three men had become six or more as other soldiers stepped out of the shadows.

'Psst!' Enola heard from her left. 'Psst!' came the sound again, and Enola's eyes honed in on it.

Standing in the doorway was a young boy, about eleven or twelve, holding the door open. He flattened his back against the post to hide from the others so that only

Enola could see him. Dressed in a white linen tunic and pants, tied at the waist with a blue sash, he stared at Enola with puppy-like brown eyes in the centre of a mischievous face. He waved Enola towards him. She did not hesitate, without giving her assailants another glance, she bolted for the door.

'Get her!' Enola heard the cry from behind, accompanied by the tramp of heavy feet hurrying after her.

She carried the boy through the doorway and beyond with her momentum. He immediately took her by the hand and dragged her up a stone staircase. They hadn't reached the top when the first of the men came through the door and caught a glimpse of the two disappearing up the steps. The boy's eyes widened when he heard the men gaining on them. They burst through another doorway at the top of the steps and out onto the roof. The passage's acoustics made it sound like the soldiers chasing them where no more than a few steps behind when, in reality, they were much further back.

The boy pulled Enola towards the edge of the roof, but she broke free. He waved frantically for her to follow him but she responded by lifting a finger to her lips to silence him. Enola turned back towards the top of the staircase and pressed her back against the wall by the side of the opening. She listened to the men rushing up the steps and waited until the last moment before making her move. Enola timed it perfectly, swinging around just as the first of her pursuers reached the top. She lunged her sword into his stomach. He folded instantly, crumpling to the ground and tripping the man behind him. The off-balance man yelled as he realised he could not avoid the stab of Enola's blade. The gold sword's point entered the man's upper chest just below the clavicle. His own momentum pushed it deep. He flung himself back to be free of the weapon and crashed into his companions behind him.

Shouts and curses accompanied the sound of falling men from the staircase. Resisting the urge to look down the passageway, Enola ran to the boy. Taking her hand he led her up onto the lip at the edge of the roof. They both jumped to the next rooftop, still holding hands until they rolled to break their fall. They had no sooner come to their feet than the men chasing them appeared at the previous roof's edge. One of them threw his spear. His aim was true, but it passed through empty space, Enola agilely stepping out of its way. The boy turned and ran. Enola followed him away from the sound of the warriors jumping across in pursuit. The boy seemed to have a plan, so Enola chose to take a chance on him rather than turning to fight.

Another spear passed over the boy's shoulder and slammed into the side of a wooden building on the rooftop. It missed him by a hair's width, but he ignored it and darted around the building. Enola was tempted to retrieve the weapon and return it, but she did not want to lose sight of the boy. As she came around the hut's corner, he was waiting, holding a door open.

'In here,' he whispered.

She leapt through the opening and the boy slammed the door shut, and rushed to drop two locking planks into place. He then wedged a beam against the door and grinned as their pursuers slammed into the barricaded entrance. He led Enola down a ladder sticking up through a hole in the roof. The men's shouts and banging faded as the boy took Enola through a series of rooms, and then a doorway leading to a plank bridge across to another house. Once they were back to ground level, the boy took Enola by the hand again and led her through the narrow streets she hoped would lead to the main square. For a moment she thought they were home free, a thought that was dashed by the sound of nail booted footsteps hurrying towards them. A group of the soldiers had gone around the buildings, directed by those on the rooftop, and were now closing in on the pair.

'There she is!' a voice called out in a gruff Mander accent.

Six men or more came running around the corner, carrying spears and swords. They were hungry for blood, and hate and determination showed on their angry faces.

'This way,' the boy said, pulling on Enola's arm.

He led her out into a wider street, but the way was blocked by another group of men. Enola could see the main road beyond the gathering. Escape was so close, but denied at the last moment. She sighed and cursed her luck. Those giving chase burst onto the street behind Enola and the boy. They screeched to a halt when they saw their prey waiting for them. The group at the other end of the street started to advance, led by a large warrior. The rest of this group did not look like soldiers, some had blades and spears, but most were armed with knives or makeshift weapons made from tools or farming equipment. The one that looked like a warrior carried a cutlass, the broad blade catching the sun and reflecting a blast of light that blinded Enola for a split second. She drew her sword and readied herself for what was to come.

The huge warrior's strength and muscle tone became apparent as he approached. He was dressed for battle, unlike all but a few of those following him, who were dressed in anything from rags to fine cloth. The boy tightened his grip on Enola's arm, and she had to shake him free to advance on her attackers. She raised her golden blade, steeling herself for the attack. The massive warrior with the cutlass held up his free hand to stop Enola. He was looking at the Mander advancing from the other end of the street, and not at the Lioness. He let out a roar as he passed her by, running at the Mander, his ragged band of followers doing the same. The formidable warrior slapped the first Mander spear aside, shoulder charging the man while skewering the next with his cutlass. With a twist of his body and one sweep of the blade, the formidable warrior cut down the man with the spear. There was a scream from the next Mander in line as his severed arm, its hand still gripping the hilt of a blade, fell to the ground. The big warrior silenced his cry and finished off the man next to him.

Enola watched, astonished at the skill and ferocity of the strange-looking warrior who had come to her aid. He was overtaken by the mob following him, as they set about the Mander in a frenzied attack, screaming and hacking in a murderous venting of vengeance and hate. The fight continued on down the street, moving away from Enola and the boy, the Mander trying to flee for their lives. Enola grabbed the boy's hand intending to pull him towards the main street, seeing their chance to escape. The boy resisted, shaking his head and waving down the road at the warrior, now returning towards them.

'Zak!' The man's voice boomed out a friendly greeting. 'I see you have found yourself an Avolonian spear-maiden,' he whistled, 'and an important one at that.'

Enola tightened her grip on the hilt of her sword. 'Who is he?' she asked out of the corner of her mouth, realising the boy and their rescuer were acquainted.

'This is Jonotrix,' Zak said, with a formality that seemed strange in one so young. 'He fights for the people and freedom of slaves.' Zak spoke with admiration, and again in an unexpected formal way.

'And who might you be?' Jonotrix asked as he arrived, blood splattered on his face and still dripping from his blade.

Enola straightened her shoulders and raised herself to her full height. 'Enola of the house Saberlund, daughter of the Lion Lord and Commander of the Storm Legions.'

Jonotrix dropped to one knee, bowing his head. 'You are the Lioness, forgive me I did not know.'

Enola admired the well-developed muscles of the man's neck and shoulders. 'Nonsense, there is nothing to forgive. Stand, you just saved our lives. Where did you learn to fight like that? Your technique is not that of a regular soldier.'

Jonotrix lifted his head, a cheeky grin stretching across his face. 'I was trained as a gladiator before being taken by the Mander. I served as a bodyguard to the wealthy merchant who bought me. I escaped by jumping ship when they were fleeing your attack. I have tried to organise the slaves and street folk left behind. They know the city and can flush out the fanatics,' he gestured over his shoulder towards the fight, 'like that lot that came after you. Would have been a fine old feather in their cap to have killed the Lioness of Avolonia. What are you doing out here alone?'

Enola pursed her lips and arched an eyebrow. 'I'm asking myself the same question. I thought my troops had cleared these streets. I did not expect to come across so many. How are they eluding us, and how are you, for that matter?'

'If you don't mind me saying so,' Jonotrix spoke softly 'there are many places to hide in these streets and houses. Your men are moving too fast to do a thorough search. We use the large drains to move from street to street undetected, they probably did the same. They are looking for officers or even generals to assassinate or even capture. This fight is not over yet, and they are seeking an advantage. Beware, there are more fighters left in the city than they are letting be known. Me and my band of slaves and poor folk know where to look. We will clear this section for you. This lot,' he looked at the group returning from the fight, 'are thirsty for revenge against any Mander they can get hold of.'

Enola smiled her thanks at the offer. 'My men don't know you; they would misunderstand your intentions and attack you.'

'We can raise the cry, Avolonia.'

Enola shook her head. 'They would not believe you, thinking it trickery. No, bring as many of your followers as you can to the main square. I have use for them doing as you say, but let's get you recognised first. Zac, you come with me,' she looked back at Jonotrix, 'and thanks again.' She patted Zak on the back. 'You too, my young friend, you too.'

Jonotrix gestured down the street with a tilt of his broad chin. 'Your horse, I believe.

Enola turned to see a rugged looking man leading Storm. She climbed up on the stallion's back, held a hand out to Zak and pulled him up to sit behind her.

'Come to the square,' she called back to Jonotrix as she urged her mount into a trot towards the main street.

Jonotrix thought about shouting something after her, but before the words could form she was gone.

Arter & Hurcan

The small courtyard was suddenly silent. Hurcan was left stunned. He had watched his friend carted off for a crime he knew he was not capable of. He was sure he would be hanged, and he was helpless to stop it. He felt responsible.

'If only I had stayed with the lad,' he said out loud to no one else but himself and the sparrow that had landed on the edge of the drinking trough, dipping its beak in the cool water and fluttering its wings in delight. 'I should have had him on my left,' he told the sparrow. 'I could have pinned him in and defended him.'

The sparrow flew away when Hurcan leaned forward to scoop up some of the cool water in his spade-like hand and splashed it onto his face. He rubbed it in and took a deep breath, clearing his mind. One thought kept returning. There was a voice whispering to him from the shadows at the back of his mind. Those two in-breeds, Erwin and Hedrik, had something to do with this, he knew it. He suddenly realised that he wanted to be there for the boy when they hung him. If he could not save the boy, he could at least be a friendly face in the crowd. He rose from his seat with a groan and the sound of creaking from the leather straps on his armour. There was something else, another sound. Hurcan looked towards the dark entrance of the stable. He sighed, knowing his mind was playing tricks on him. He wanted more than anything to find some clue or proof that would free his friend. He laughed at himself, even if he could find the dripping blade that would prove his friend's innocence, it was too late. There would be no trial, no chance to appeal. In the field, battle-law applied, and Arter had been convicted, and may be already dead and hanging from a post.

Another sound came from within the darkness, the clatter of a falling rake or something similar. The hairs stood up on the back of Hurcan's neck. He approached the doorway and peered into the darkness. All was still inside. His heart sank when he saw the young woman's body. It would have looked like she was sleeping if it were not for the dark pool of blood she lay in. She was as white as candle wax, none of the horror she had endured showing on her silent features. Hurcan took a canvas sheet that was being used to cover a pile of hay and draped it over the body. 'Why?' he asked himself. He was about to leave, sickened to the stomach and anger growing in him, but something stopped him. He stood perfectly still, nothing more than an intuition holding him in place. The sound came to him, no louder than the footsteps of a mouse. It was almost not even a sound. It could have been a soft, tiny sound close by or a loud rumble so far in the distance it could hardly be heard. Hurcan tilted his head to hear better, standing perfectly still. He listened to the sound of sobbing, no louder than the flutter of a fly's wings. He turned his head slowly, attempting to discover where the faint sound came from. His eyes settled on an old door, lying on its side against a barrow full of straw.

He heard it again, and moved the door to one side, half expecting to see a cockroach or a barn mouse scratching at some scrap on the floor. Instead, two wide, frightened eyes stared back at him from under the barrow. A tiny girl, no more than four or five years old, was curled up, sobbing. Snot ran freely from the nose in the centre of her angelic but dirty face. Bits of straw were twisted into her long and tangled hair. She recoiled from the hand offered to her, fear shaking her body as if she was as cold as a hound left out in the snows of winter. As gently as he could, Hurcan pulled the child out of her hiding place. She resisted, kicking, slapping and letting out a terrifying hiss, like a cornered cat.

'Mummy!' she screamed, as Hurcan carefully prised her fingers loose from the barrow's handle.

He lifted the girl to his chest, trying to restrain her kicking and scratching without hurting her. She reached out over his shoulder towards the covered body. 'Mummy!' she screamed again, and dug her nails into Hurcan's cheek, leaving three bloody lines across his flesh. His heart swelled, and he was sure it would burst if she let out one more of her sorrowful screams. He suddenly realised that the girl must have seen everything. He rushed her out of the door, more to spare her from the pain of looking at her mother's body than any other reason or thought that had come to his mind. She kicked and screamed, reaching back towards where her mother lay.

'Mummy!' she called over and over while hitting Hurcan's head with her tiny fists, scratching his face like a wild cat and pulling his hair.

Hurcan felt the girl's pain in his own heart, but she was the key, he was sure of it. She could tell what happened to her mother in that dark place. He was convinced that whatever the girl said would clear his friend of guilt.

He tried to shush her, stroking her head in a vain attempt to calm her. 'Your mother is sleeping,' was all he could think to say. 'She sleeps now, she's at peace.'

Struck by panic, Hurcan rushed through the streets with the wailing child in his arms. As he came to the main square, he could see the body of an Avolonian soldier swinging by the neck from the limb of an olive tree. His heart sank, and he thought he was too late then realised it was not Arter. Relief flooded through him but was soon replaced by more panic. His head darted from side to side, attempting to see where his friend had been taken. He ignored all the shocked expressions and concerned frowns of men perplexed by the screams of a child carried against her will by a frantic man. He spotted a rope being slung over the bow of another olive tree in the square. Pushing his way through the press of legionnaires, Hurcan made his way towards the tree. He cursed when the rope that had resisted two or three attempts to wrap it over the bow, finally caught and was pulled taught.

'Sir!' Hurcan called out to the Captain in charge, his voice hoarse from his run through the streets. He cursed himself as he panted, trying to regain his breath. When he was younger he could have run twice as far, carrying twice the weight and still arrived able to speak without panting. At least the child was now silent, clinging to Hurcan in abject fear. 'Sir, I'm begging your pardon, but this little one can tell the truth of it. You have an innocent man there, I know it. Please, sir, wait to hear what the girl has to say.'

In truth, Hurcan did not know if the words from the girl would exonerate his friend or condemn both of them, but he had to try.

'Bugger off, sentence has already been passed on this one,' the Captain replied with a look that carried more of a warning than his words. 'Carry on,' he told the men tying the rope around Arter's neck. The boy's eyes were empty and forlorn. He did not look at his friend, he had been beaten half senseless, and allowed himself to be manhandled, seemingly accepting his fate.

'Please sir, before you make a mistake. At least let the girl speak. He's a good lad. She's the child of the dead woman,' Hurcan regretted his choice of words as the girl began to cry.

'Battle law applies here,' the Captain growled. 'There will be no trial. This one will hang as an example to any other murdering and robbing bastards. Now, step back or you will be dangling next to him.'

'Legion or Corum!'

'What?' the Captain asked, in response to the interruption from a new voice.

'Legion or Corum? It's a simple question with a big difference. If we were serving in the Corums of Avolonia, you would be right, and he should be swinging from that tree already. But we aren't, are we?' The Captain looked dumbstruck as the Veteran legionnaire stepped forward. 'We now serve in the Legions, which means a man must die for his crimes while still in the field...' he paused, . 'without the privilege of trial...' he paused again, 'unless someone comes forward to speak for him.'

'Well, what of it?' the Captain's cheeks flushed with anger.

'Well, what of it... what of it' he repeated. 'Someone has come forward to speak for him.'

The Captain laughed, his anger downsizing to irritation. 'The girl is terrified. She won't speak for anyone, I doubt she will ever speak again.'

'Ready sir,' said one of the two men hanging onto the rope, waiting to hoist up the condemned Arter, who was now standing on tiptoe, his head bent to one side where the rope tugged.

The Captain flapped his hand without looking at the men, and they relaxed the tension on the rope. Arter slumped into a seated position on the ground.

'So it's different in the Legions to the Corums?' asked the confused Captain.

The Veteran nodded his head. 'The child may be too frightened to talk now, but the man has the right to an abstention till sundown. If she has not exonerated or condemned him by then, he hangs anyway.'

Hurcan felt like the Veteran had just read his mind as he heard his thoughts coming out of the man's mouth.

The Captain pushed his helmet back and rubbed his face. 'This is above my pay grade. String him up I say, but I'll give you until the Lioness gets back, no longer. She expects to see him dead and swinging from a tree as a warning to others. If I get into trouble for this, you two will be swinging alongside him.'

The Veteran put a hand on Hurcan's shoulder. 'Josef,' he introduced himself. 'Let's take the girl somewhere quiet and let her calm down. Come, there is a woman friend of mine on the other side of the square.'

Hurcan looked at his friend, cross-legged on the ground with the rope still around his neck. He raised his gaze to the guards. 'Don't you two bastards go tugging on that rope before I get back, or …..' he held back from finishing the threat.

'Or what?' one of the guards called back.

'He's a good lad, so just don't' It was with great difficulty that Hurcan managed not to hiss a threat at the guards, and followed Josef through the square, the sobbing girl in his arms.

Enola

Storm ambled over the cobbles and into the square, Enola and Zac on his back. The sun still rode high in the sky but had begun descending. The crowds of exhausted warriors moved apart as if the warhorse were the prow of a boat parting the still water of a lake. Men sat on walls around the square, having their wounds tended or just resting their weary limbs. Most were too tired to raise a sound, but the square was still a hub of commotion: prisoners shouting in protest at being detained, and Spartikens hurrying in to rally more men to help them deal with a newly discovered pocket of resistance.

Enola saw two of her men hanging from a tree, their lifeless corpses swaying hypnotically in the afternoon's breeze. She felt a hint of regret creep into her thoughts and steeled herself against the emotion. Her father had made it clear to her that she would fail in her duties as a leader of armies if she shied away from the harsh punishments needed to control. *'It's a small step for men to take in battle,'* she remembered her father saying, *'from killing in the heat of a fight to rape and murder. A line must be drawn. There will always be those who are naturally the murderous type, but good men will follow the crowd in the madness and slaughter of battle, committing atrocities completely out of character and otherwise not in their nature. Hang them without reproach and let the good men see the line they mustn't cross.'*

The Lioness suddenly remembered she had given orders for three men to be hanged that day and wondered if one had escaped or was hanging in another place. Horns sounded to announce the Commander was in camp, and the Captain of the guard came trotting across the cobbled square, a dozen or more of Enola's bodyguards following dutifully behind. Enola's gaze turned to the sound of jangling armour. Warrik stopped a few paces short of his Commander. He was one of the older officers chosen to join the ranks of the Storm Legions, probably twice Enola's age, but he was still strong and had made a good account of himself in the contest Enola had won. He wore a constant frown as if he were in a perpetual state of anger. Enola couldn't ever remember the man smiling. There was no trace of light-heartedness in Warrik, which made him a good captain who received every word and action with a furrowed brow. He stood to attention, waiting for a sign that his Commander was ready to receive his news.

Enola remained on her horse and gazed across the thousands of Spartiken heads filling the square and the streets beyond. Warrik blinked in surprise when he saw Zak stick his head out from behind Enola's back. Enola followed her Captain's stare.

'That's another story,' Enola reached around and pushed the boy back behind her. 'Why are so many of our men held up here?

Warrik lowered his head so that his eyes were drawn into shadow. 'They have the way into the port blocked. Their archers are taking a fearful toll.'

'They have numbers enough to block us?'

Warrik looked uncomfortable. 'They have led us down a funnel. Our numbers mean nothing, where they have built their barricades they could hold out for weeks.' His face took on a new worry and looked as if he wanted to say more.

'Spit it out, man. You look like you have swallowed a bug.'

'It's your father, sir,' he blurted out, and then had to take a deep breath to steady himself.

Concern for Arc pushed Enola's irritation to one side. She hoped he had not had another fit. 'What of him? Is he well?'

Warrik's cheeks reddened, and a bead of perspiration appeared at his temple. He decided to get it over with and deliver the Lion Lords message. 'He is well, sir. Your father has sent a message expressing his disappointment and frustration that the city is not yet subdued in its entirety. He doesn't like being made to wait.'

Enola was outraged, 'What is wrong with that man? He had us waiting outside the walls half the day, he can blasted well wait a few more hours.'

'It will take more than a few hours to clear the barricades into the port.' Warrik saw the fury turning Enola's face crimson, and dreaded speaking the rest of his message. 'There is more, sir.'

'What more can there be?' the Lioness hissed. 'Don't tell me, he wants the streets painted white and the roads decked with flowers so that he can parade his Corinthian mistress through the town.'

The Captain was just about as uncomfortable as he could be. Arc may have been Enola's father but, during a battle, military law could not be ignored and Enola's words, even though they were spoken in anger, were treason. Warrik felt his own anger rising and used it to bolster his courage.

'Your father has sent an ultimatum. You are to deliver the city to him by sunset or...' his courage wavered, and he paused to gulp and clear the lump in his throat, 'or, he will have you removed from command and send in the Lion Warriors to finish the job.'

Enola was incensed. Taking the city was a chance for her to show she was worthy of her command. She and her troops were delivering in every way. Her blood boiled when she imagined Sonaji whispering unrest into her father's ear. She was about to order Warrik to take her to the barricades when she spotted Arter. He was leaning against a wall, his hands tied behind his back and the rope still around his neck. He had regained some of his composure and recovered somewhat from the beating he had taken.

Enola's fury overflowed at the sight of the condemned man still alive. She drew her golden blade. Warrik flinched, momentarily thinking the sword was being drawn in anger against him.

The blade was pointed at Arter. 'Why the hell is that murdering rapist bastard not swinging from that tree? String him up, now!'

The guards around Arter were startled into action by their Commander's rage. They faffed with the ropes, not sure if they should hoist him up or strangle him on the spot.

The Captain in charge came hurrying over to explain. On hearing the horns announcing the Commander's arrival, Hurcan and the veteran Josef had brought the girl over. Enola's eyes flicked between the Captain and the girl in Hurcan's arms. Warrik drew his sword and blocked the way to Enola.

'What is this?' Enola asked. She wanted to ignore the protest coming and ride off to inspect the barricades, but the girl caught her attention. She was gripped by a sudden intrigue and the need to know why she was being presented with a small child. 'I don't have time for this. Why have you brought a child here?'

'There is some doubt to the issue, sir,' the Captain spoke up, regretting he had allowed himself to get involved. 'There is a law...' he stuttered. '..a law in the field I'm told that gives this lad a chance if...' he was silenced by Enola's rage.

'I am the law here! He was to be hanged. Now, hang him.'

Josef stepped forward. 'Remember me, sir?'

A sudden calm came over Enola as if a gust of wind had brought a new mood with it.

'Josef, it's been a long time since Fwenga.' Enola's voice cracked, as she attempted to bridge her anger to the new calm.

'Not long enough for the scars to completely heal on one as old as I,' Josef replied.

'Nonsense, old campaigners like you heal twice as fast as a man half her age,' Enola now sounded calm, even jovial. 'Maybe you can shine some light on why my orders have not been obeyed. What's this girl got to do with anything?'

'A loyal friend of this man,' he jerked his head towards Arter, 'thinks this girl can speak for him. He thinks she saw her mother murdered and can point out the culprit. If she points out the boy, he hangs, if she points out another, he lives, that's the law the Captain spoke of.'

The Officer nodded. 'I've had the other two with him at the time brought here.'

'Very well, then. Ask the girl,' Enola ordered. 'Let's get this over with.'

Erwin and Hedrik were pushed forward, and Hurcan tried asking the child who had done the bad things to her mother. The girl took one look at the men around her and burst into tears. The more Hurcan tried to calm her down, the louder she wailed.

Erwin laughed. 'This is nonsense. We caught the bastard, holding a dripping blade over the woman's body, his leggings still around his ankles. Does our word count for nothing?'

Artur tried to protest. 'That's not...' his words were cut off by a blow from one of the guards.

'Looks like you'll be hanging after all,' the guard teased.

'Buttercup,' Zac said, climbing down from Storm's haunches.

Enola had forgotten the boy was behind her. She followed him and dismounted, handing Storm's reins to a warrior nearby.

'Buttercup, is that you?' The girl responded to Zac's question by stretching her arms out towards him. Zac took the child from Hurcan, and she wrapped herself about him. Her wailing gave way to a few stifled sobs, and she buried her face in his shoulder. All eyes were on the boy as he spoke to the girl. He got her to look at Arter and asked her something. She shook her head and then, without warning, she pointed at Erwin and Hedrik and started to cry again.

Erwin and Hedrik did not stick around to find out the outcome of the child's actions, they announced their guilt by bolting.

'After 'em!' the Captain roared.

The two men made it across the square, a path opening up for them by confused men thinking Erwin and Hedrik were rushing out on an urgent mission for the Legion. Warrik screeched in anger for someone to stop them, but confusion won, and the two men escaped the square.

All attention turned to Zac and little Buttercup.

'I know where she lives,' Zac told Enola. 'She has family, they will still be there, hiding.'

'Tell the guards where to take her,' Enola instructed, and then beckoned one of her guards closer. 'Go to the east of the square, there should be a group of local militia led by a huge warrior called Jonotrix. Bring him to me. If he is not there, leave instructions for him to be sent to me as soon as he arrives. Got it?' The guard nodded.

A short time later Warrik returned, red in the face and still panting. Following him were several of his men, dragging Hedrik with them.

'The other one got...' Warrik gasped for breath, 'away sir. Clean over a wall and was three hundred paces down a narrow strip of cultivated land before the first of my men could get over after him.' Regaining some of his composure, he went on. 'This one would have too if his pal had not pushed him off the wall to save himself.'

Hurcan let out a laugh, and called over to Hedrik, 'Now who made a poor choice in friends? I'll not hold it against you, but there's many a man here who will.' Hurcan noticed the brace of confused expressions around him. 'A private joke, he gets it.'

'Captain!' Warrik snapped his shoulders back at Enola's command. 'Do your duty.'

Warrik grabbed the dangling rope himself and went to placed it around Hedrik's neck. The prisoner tried to avoid the noose, but one of the three guards restraining him pushed his head forward so that the Captain could slip the loop over his head. The crowd went quiet, sensing the man's impending doom. Morbid curiosity drawing the mob in, until there was a tight circle of onlookers. Men and women further back than the first few rows stood on tiptoe or strained their necks to get a better view of the proceedings.

'It wasn't me!' Hedrik screamed, his eyes wide with terror. 'That bastard Erwin is the one that did her. I never touched her!'

Warrik looked at Enola, confused as to his course of action after the man's confession. He worried there would be some other battle-law calling for a stay of execution, and held out his hand to steady the two guards pulling the rope taught. Hedrik's hands were tied behind his back and his feet bound together. To keep himself from choking, he leaned his head against the rope to maintain balance.

The combination of Hedrik's confession and Warrik's indecision infuriated the Lioness. She pushed the Captain aside as if he were a small boy in her way, took the line from two startled looking guards, and heaved on it. Hedrik was stretched up so that his toes barely touched the ground, and he began to spin. Enola heaved again on the rope, dropping her hips so that Hedrik left the ground. He tried to cry out, but the sound was cut off, and he only managed a strained gurgle. The two guards jumped back to the line to assist their Commander, pulling the prisoner higher.

Hedrik pumped his legs back and forth, his body convulsed as it swung in a circle. The twine creaked as if it were about to snap, and one of his boots fell off, spinning into the mortified crowd. They had all seen much death and many horrors that day, but this was different, cold-blooded, one of their own. Arter stepped forward, reaching out for the man's bare foot, his intention to stop the wild swinging of his body.

'Let the bastard choke,' Warrik gave him a subtle warning, worried that the young Spartiken would swing on the hanging man's legs in an act of mercy to shorten his suffering.

Arter had no such intention. He stopped the swing by holding onto the foot, contorting his face in disgust as Hedrik's piss poured over his hand. He watched the choking man kick a few more times before hocking up some phlegm and spitting on him. Arter then turned away, leaving everyone else to watch the man's face bulge and grotesquely disfigure, his kicks weakening as death seeped its way in.

Enola waited until Hedrik's convulsions slowed to little more than a series of twitches before walking over to the trunk of the olive tree. Giving the rope one more firm tug, she tied it off. The Commander climbed back onto her horse.

'We are not murdering rapists!' Enola called from the saddle. 'We are an army, warriors of honour. Take a good look, this is what awaits the dishonourable amongst you!' The crowd listened, though many of them still gawped at the morbid sight of Hedrik's body as the last trickle of life dribbled out of it like the piss dripping from his feet. 'Josef, join my guard, and bring your two new friends with you,' she meant Arter and Hurcan. 'Zac, with me. We have barricades to break.' It was then that she noticed Jonotrix towering over the guard she had sent to find him. When their eyes met, he arched an eyebrow as a comment on what he had just witnessed. Enola was not in the mood for greetings or explanations. 'Jonotrix, bring your followers to the port district. We will talk there. Captain Warrik, see to it that our newest recruits are recognised as friends and not enemies.'

Zac jumped up behind Enola and pulled his blue sash from where it had become trapped under him before wrapping his arms around Enola's waist. She kicked her heels. Storm raised his head in protest but obeyed. He took his master and the small boy out of the square, heading for the harbour.

Arc

Sonaji watched the Lion Lord shift and turn on his throne of ivory. He was impatient and unable to relax. She watched his mood swing from pride for his daughter leading an army to conquer a city, to anger that she did not do it the way he thought best. Sonaji nurtured the latter mood, seeing Enola as a threat to her plans. Arc was having difficulty focusing. At moments his mind was as sharp as the edge on the Lion Blade, but then drifted into episodes when he could not remember if he had just said something or only thought it.

The noise of battle sounded distant from outside the walls of the city. Reports were brought to Arc twice an hour, telling him of progress or the lack of it. He listened to complication after complication, and excuse after excuse, as to why the day was coming to an end but the city was not yet won. He had tens of thousands of warriors waiting outside the walls, but he knew it would do no good to send them into the city. They would only add to the chaos and confusion, so for now they waited.

'There is another messenger,' the officer in attendance informed the Lion Lord.

'Already?' Sonaji asked in response. 'It was only moments ago that the last one delivered Enola's latest excuses.'

The officer tried not to look offended, but Sonaji's critical words felt like a slight against him personally. 'This messenger is from Edius-Max and our absent forces.'

Arc's eyes widened. He leaned forward, and eagerly ordered for the messenger to be sent in.

A young officer in Lion Cavalry armour entered the room, half jogging, half staggering. He was covered in dust, looking like he had been out in the desert for days. Dropping to one knee, the young man bowed his head and banged his right fist against the left pectoral of his breastplate in salute.

'Tell us of the situation in Siena Mazda,' Gavara invited the officer to speak.

The man croaked a few words that were inaudible, so water was called for. After he had drunk sufficient amounts of the cool liquid to clear his throat, he spoke again.

'Lord, I have instructions to speak the words of General Edius-Max as he told them to me, and not to try and interpret any of it myself.'

Arc smiled, thinking it very typical of his most experienced officer. Edius-Max had been the most senior officer in the Saxish army before they were conquered by Mander. He had then served in the Mander Auxiliaries, joining Arc's crusade at the head of the auxiliaries after the defeat of Atropolis at the battle of Caputhora.

'Tell us, has my resourceful General defeated the Emperor's army without us, or is he in need of my assistance?'

The young officer looked up at the Lion Lord, his bemused expression clear for all to see. He had not expected humour, being only accustomed to Edius-Max's serious nature. He decided the best response was to speak the words he had been so careful to learn and remember.

'Lord, the situation is dire and needs your careful consideration, therefore I am to give you the details and then return with your answer.' He paused until Arc waved a hand for him to continue. 'We came across the forces of Prince Xarius at the Barbican River. We followed them on the opposite bank before gaining an advantage when the river turned south and we were able to get ahead and block their path, just east of the Ibres Hills. Both forces camped opposite each other but no hostilities were engaged in. On the third day the Mander Army, led by the Emperor Al-Din began to arrive and set up camp to the south. This second force kept on arriving for the next two days.' The young man paused to check his memory. 'Three days,' he corrected himself. 'We were then faced by a force estimated to be around one hundred and fifty thousand strong. On the fifth day they started to advance on our position. We withdrew to the north, but it soon became apparent that they had a force waiting there, intending to trap us against them. We turned west and had to fight a rolling retreat to the Ibres Hills, where we could not be flanked by the greater numbers.' The room was silent with those present hanging on every word the messenger uttered. 'The Mander intention was to finish us off in the hills. Our rear was safe from attack due to the steep nature of the terrain, but the same terrain prevented our escape. The Emperor and his army waited overnight to advance on our hillside defences. This was a mistake on their part, as the wind blew strong the next day into their face. When they attacked, we were able to fire arrows well beyond their range, as the wind carried our arrows and blew back their shafts. We were able to advance, collect their arrows and fire a storm of death onto them, and then draw back into the hills before they could retaliate. This happened three times before the Mander gave up. Their losses were horrendous, with our losses being minimal, losing less than a hundred warriors in skirmishes with those who tried to break our lines on foot,' The boy paused to gather his thoughts before delivering his conclusion. His eyes rolled as he recounted what he had said, checking he had left nothing out. The room remained silent as the officers present, Sonaji and Arc all waited. 'Since their retreat, the Mander have not attacked again, but are camped on three sides. They are being reinforced all the time by the Imperial Army returning from here. Edius-Max assumes you have had some success due to the disarray these troops are in when they arrive. My General therefore wishes to know the Lion Lord's orders. Hold or retreat? He says he can hold, but there is nothing stopping the Mander circling around the hills and advancing on Calinkerbad. I personally would not like to have to fight my way out of that place. They are surrounded and they would have to pass in range of a forest of artillery in all directions.' The messenger looked sheepish as he stopped speaking, realising he had spoken out of turn by offering his opinion.

Arc stared at the messenger, silent in his thoughts. Half of his army was trapped in the Ibres Hills. It was not news he wanted to hear, but it was an outcome he had feared ever since he heard that the army had been split. For all Arc knew, the armies of Al-Din may have already crushed Edius-Max. Wars were not won or lost in one battle, but this was a crusade. Arc had built momentum since leaving the coast to march on Mander-Kush. The Jagger Knights had joined him, the Corinthians, Simterians and Arians all followed his banner along with tens of thousands of common folk who had swapped their ploughs and shovels for a blade to free themselves of oppression. How many of those would still be standing in the ranks of his army if he could not stop a slaughter in the hills of Ibres.

Arc turned to Gavara. 'What news of the Pirate fleet?'

The old man frowned and stroked his wispy white beard, running it between two fingers and his thumb. 'They are trapped at Ratlarbig. The Mander have built a stone pier under half the width of the river, opposite the stone fort on the peninsular. Small boats can sail right over it, but ships have to go around, forcing them to pass under the walls of Fort Ratlarbig where they can be shattered by the catapults on the ramparts. Huwel must find a way through, but if you are thinking we have time to wait for him to reach here with supplies, think again. Time is not on our side. Edius-Max and half your army will be bones in the dust by the time pirate ships reach these shores.'

Arc knew the old man well and his tendencies for the dramatic, but this time the drama was real. Al-Din would know to act fast. Why wouldn't he? He had half the crusading army trapped, he only had to clench his fist to crush them.

General Eric coughed to draw attention to himself before speaking. 'From the reports I have, the Mander have stripped the city of anything that might have been of use to us. We captured some supplies from the Imperial Army, but after last night's feast there is not much left. It will mean rationing.'

'No army ever won on half rations,' Tyezore cut in.

Arc watched the Corinthian Commander, narrowing his eyes as if it helped him see into the man's mind before asking, 'And you, what is your situation?'

'We have enough for now.'

Arc turned back towards the messenger who was now paying all his attention to the bowl of broth and a brick of bread he had been given. 'You crossed a desert to get here from Ibres?'

The young man chewed quickly, struggling to swallow the bread he had rushed into his mouth before he realised he was being spoken to again. He nodded. 'Two days on a fast horse. The dust was unbearable.' He wiped away the dribble from the side of his mouth and continued. 'It's more of a dusty plain than a desert, but I came across no water or forests of any kind.'

Arc watched the boy continue to shovel in his food, unable to decide if he liked him or not. 'It must have been hell to force yourself on through such a place.' The young man nodded, continuing to chew another piece of broth-soaked bread. 'You must cross it again with all haste, and take my reply to your brave Commander.' The boy's pleading expression gave away his worry about returning before he had a chance to recover. 'You will have a fresh horse, and I will send two good riders, extra rations and water with you. Get back there quicker than you came and I will reward you with a gold coin.'

'If I live to collect it,' the messenger mumbled to himself, instantly racked with the worry that someone may have heard him.

'Speak up, boy,' Tyezore roared at him.

'I said, with all the speed I can,' the boy lied. 'As soon as I have your reply.'

'We need to be done with the city,' Arc announced, slapping the ivory arm of his throne before standing up. 'Enola's advance has faltered at the edge of the harbour area. If we are to help Edius-Max, the cavalry will need to be ready to leave at first light. No,' he changed his mind, 'they must leave tonight, and ride all night and day to get there. Send a message to my daughter, "The city must fall before sunset." Send her Hellfire and catapults. Burn the bastards out. If she fails, I will send in the Lion Warriors to relieve her and her legions.' Arc walked down the few steps to where the young man knelt and lifted him to his feet. 'Tell my old friend we are coming. He is to attack the Mander force to the north of his position. He will know when the time is right, so be ready. If he breaks through, and he should, he is to fight a rolling retreat to here, through the dust plain.' He pushed the boy to send him on his way. 'Tell the old fox to bring water, lots of it, and not to stop his retreat for anything.'

Enola

It was as Enola had feared. The way into the harbour side of the city was a bottleneck where numbers counted for nothing. There were already Spartiken bodies littering the ground in front of the barricades, arrows sticking out of their lifeless corpses like bristles. There were three main streets into this section of the city, and all three were protected by numerous archers. There were no other ways in due to the back to back buildings. The Spartikens had died trying to pull down the barricades, archers picking them off as they dragged away a table from the top of an upturned cart, or a beam entangled in other obstacles. Their efforts and sacrifice were to no avail. Every piece they had removed was replaced just as quickly.

Spartiken archers were shooting across the rooftops in a deadly game against the defenders. Each man would pop up or lean out to fire an arrow, but had no time to aim for risk of being shot himself. The action did little more than reduce the Mander hit rate and create a stalemate. The defending archers were numerous enough to make it very costly in lives for each attack on the barricades, even if a higher number of shafts went harmlessly skittering off the cobbles.

In the time Enola had been watching, she had seen four of the Mander archers killed by her bowmen as they leaned out from their hiding places to shoot. It was little consolation as in the same time over a dozen of her own warriors had fallen prey to enemy shafts. She thought of ordering her troops to rush the barricades but realised the futility of such an order. If they did break down the deadly obstacle, there would be another waiting for them, fifty paces down the street. There were more than enough defenders to hold this position for days. They had led the Legions on a merry goose chase around the city all day, making them believe their numbers were few, while they fortified this location.

Enola knew that with time she could break down the defences, but time was something she did not have. The sun was already sitting low in a red sky, hiding beneath a veranda of rain-threatening clouds. Once that sun set, she would have failed, and she would lose the control she had worked so hard to achieve. She could not let that power fall into the hands of Tyezore or the likes of Sonaji; she would not allow it. Enola thinned her lips and narrowed her eyes, steeling herself for what had to be done.

Antona and Ioniedas had their legions spread along the length of the port district. The buildings were higher on the port side, so the Mander had a good vantage point to watch over the attackers. The two Avolonian Generals were unable to make use of any attack in large numbers. Out of frustration, they had ordered one full-frontal attack on the buildings and walls that made up the boundary of the port area. The Generals led from the front, charging into the blocked streets to assault the barricades. Most of the attackers came to a halt up against the walls, unable to access the crowded streets. Mander archers took a vicious toll on those men. Too many Spartikens fell, trapped against the stone with nowhere to hide from arrows.

Bodies piled up in the entrance to the narrow alleyways running between some of the houses. These small openings that were usually barred by nothing more than a wooden gate or a few metal bars had looked like a weak spot and possible access to the port. It was a false hope, they were a killing ground. The warriors who, full of hope and dreams of heroism, made it into the narrow channels between buildings, were slaughtered like fish in a bucket. Spears, arrows and even stones rained down onto men too tightly packed to avoid them. Anyone who entered the narrow alleys did not return, their blood-drenched corpses stacked on top of each other like rabbits for sale in a market.

Time and again Antona and Ioniedas were forced to retreat. The cost was unthinkable and the damage done to the barricades repaired long before another attack could be mounted. Enola watched on as her legions threw themselves at the walls with little more effect than the waves lapping against the harbour's stone piers. The sun was sinking and Enola felt the burden of command pressing down so hard on her young shoulders that her back was physically bending. This was the reason her father had not wanted her to enter the competition to be Commander of the Legions. He knew the burden of responsibility that came with it. Yet it was her father's threats that heaped this burden onto her. His words and tenacity weighed heaviest and she feared the consequences of failure.

Antona, Hals, Warrik and several other officers joined Enola on the rooftop. At the Commander's invitation, Jonotrix was also up there with a few of his followers. Ioniedas remained in charge of the Spartikens attacking the barricades, and Elektra had control of the Spartikens in the rest of the city.

'Your father is sending carts with catapults and Hellfire,' Warrik told them, feeling like he had been nothing but the bearer of bad news all day.

Hellfire was a despicable mix of burned lime and sulphur blended with naphtha, which Gavara had made to fuel the army's lamps. The final ingredients Gavara kept secret, he called it nitre, and no one was allowed its recipe. The crafty old Pathfinder developed the fearsome substance to burn ships. Once Hellfire had ignited the timbers of a ship its fate was sealed. Water would not put out the flames. Ships' hulls burned below the waterline. Men unfortunate enough to be set ablaze by the substance would jump into the sea, attempting to douse the flames. It did them no good, they could be seen burning as they sank, the flames as bright under the water as they had been above. Despite its effectiveness it was not a widely used weapon at sea; captains feared having the clay pots full of the liquid on board. One accident would send any vessel down into the dark depths with every soul aboard.

'He wants us to burn them,' Hals pointed out the obvious. He gave Jonotrix a nervous glance and then went on, 'The whole district is full of refugees, they'll burn or drown if we throw Hellfire into the streets.'

Enola turned to Jonotrix. 'You have heard the situation. For whatever reason the Lion Lord has decreed the city must be taken before nightfall. I assume your followers have friends, even family in the port. If you do not want them burned alive along with the Mander, give me solutions.'

Jonotrix shook his head. 'There are no quick solutions. Those barricades will hold until you can walk over them on the piles of your own dead. Your warriors' bodies are already blocking the alleyways.' His face morphed into a pleading expression, which looked out of character on such a fierce man. 'Even if you do burn them out, it will be a day or so before you can enter the fire-scorched streets.' He hoped that in some way his words would give Enola pause for thought and prevent her using the incendiary weapon.

'They watch our every move.' Exhaustion showed on Antona's face as he spoke. Dried blood matted the young General's hair on one side of his head and encrusted that side of his face. His helmet was tucked under his arm, but the divot where he'd taken a blow was clear for all to see. 'They are well co-ordinated. We can see some kind of tented structure at the far end of the centre road. I assume it is a command tent.' His voice was full of emotion. 'Every time we hit them, they are ready for us. We are washing their streets with the blood of our warriors, turning men into memories, for little or no gain.' Antona looked towards the white structure in the distance. 'They have a leader, and he is pulling the strings from that tent.'

'Shulz is his name,' Jonotrix's face hardened, and he tightened his grip on the hilt of his sword at the thought of the man. 'He is more mercenary than Mander. He's the City Council's attack dog. They have used him to control the streets of Calinkerbad for years. He is a vicious hound who knows what he is doing. Kill him, and you will have cut the head off the serpent, but you'll never get close to him, he's too clever for that.'

The oldest looking man amongst Jonotrix's followers stepped forward. 'Begging your pardon, madam.' Enola let the incorrect title pass without comment, guessing the man did not have a military background. 'I am from that district. It is a warren of narrow streets around the outskirts, but once you are a short way in, the roads widen. The slums have been cleared and replaced with large houses for the merchants. The streets are wide, and I would imagine tough to defend.'

Hals laughed. 'That much we know. The problem is we can't get to those open streets.'

Enola saw that the man was offended. 'What's your name?'

'Geramain,' he replied, a smile spreading across his face.

Enola returned his smile. 'I am sure you would not be telling us this if you did not have an idea about how it could be done.'

Geramain's smile widened. 'I have, madam,' he paused and looked a little perplexed. 'Is that the correct term for a warrior like yourself, madam?'

'It is not,' Enola told him. 'But you are welcome to use it, if you wish, or you can call me sir like everyone else.'

'Well, sir, there are ways in, but not for great numbers. You will need ladders, and there will be no space for shields.'

'Go on, you have our attention.' Enola spoke softly, trying not to become agitated by the man's slow progress in getting to the point.

Geramain pointed towards and area of the wall to the west and began to speak, but before he could utter a word, he was silenced by Warrik.

'Put your arm down, you fool.' Warrik's tact gone with his patience. 'They are watching every move we make. Don't give them any indication of our intentions.'

'Sorry, I wasn't thinking.' Geramain brushed off any offence and continued. 'Those of us living in the desolate streets of Poorside, grow as much food as we can for ourselves. We have strips of land between the houses that we call allotments.'

'Yes, I have seen one,' Warrik cut in. 'That bastard rapist legged it over melons and cabbages to get clean away from us.'

'Well,' Geramain went on with more confidence, 'my allotment is on the west side. It runs from the wall to halfway through Poorside. At the far end it is only separated from the merchants' yards by one wall and some wooden fences. Knock those down, and you have a clear run through to the open streets of the harbour area.'

'You'll be behind the barricades,' Jonotrix added when he noticed the stunned and confused expressions on the Avolonians' faces.

'But, how do we get into the allotment without being turned into Mander pin cushions?' Antona asked. 'Their archers will fill us full of arrows before we can get over the wall.'

'None of the drainage tunnels cross from this side of the city to the port area.' Geramain attempted to answer the question. 'We have been using those all day to get around groups of Mander defenders. I, myself used them to escape the family that owned me.'

'Yes, yes, well done. Now, can you get to the point?' asked Warrik, eager for the man to get on with it.

Geramain furrowed his brow, giving Warrik a piercing stare. 'No tunnels that I know of, except one. We had to link up with one of the drainage systems to stop the allotment flooding when the river was high, so we built a drain that links up with the system of tunnels on this side of the city. You can get into the other side that way. It's only a small tunnel, it won't fit many at a time, but it will get you in unseen.'

Enola grabbed Geramain by the shoulder. 'I could kiss you, little man. You may have just saved your kinfolk, or at least given them a chance.'

'It's a bit of a long shot,' Hals pointed out.

'We'll need archers and men with hammers in the front ranks,' Enola told everyone. Nobody point or look to the west, surprise is vital. We need to be in before they know it. Jonotrix and Geramain, bring me a dozen men or women who can move fast and know those streets. Where shall we meet?'

'The entrance to the drain is at the back of the two long storehouses, they should hide us from view,' Geramain told the Lioness, and then was disturbed by a sudden thought. 'There will be water in the tunnel.'

'Let's hope it's not so deep as to block our way,' Enola responded. 'Hals, get me three hundred archers there, and have the rest of your legion ready to follow us.'

'Through the tunnel?' the General asked.

'Through the openings we make in the wall, if all goes well,' Enola answered him. 'Get in fast, and hit them hard. Warrik, bring my guards. Find as many hammers, axes and grappling hooks as you can. General Antona, you keep the Mander busy at the barricades. Now go, you two first.'

Hals and Warrik nodded and then left casually, so as not to draw attention from Mander eyes. The others waited a few moments, then they all left in different directions.

Geramain's heart pounded. In his earlier years, he had been brave and strong, but his fortitude and strength had dwindled in his time serving as a slave to the Hoppet family. He had not been born to slavery, growing up as a street urchin in Poorside. He was a merchant's debt collector for many years, but when he fell on hard times he sold himself into slavery to save his family. His wife had married another since then and, as far as he knew, she and his two daughters lived with the merchant in his large house to the affluent west side of the port. He heard rumours that his eldest had married a merchant's son and lived on an estate across the Umbas. He hoped that was true, as it would mean she was out of danger.

Enola splashed her way towards where Geramain stood, his back pressed against the damp wall of the drain. Light from the exit reached down onto their faces, shadows from the metal bars of the cover laying dark lines across their upturned expressions.

'So, there is just one wall between the road and the allotment?'

Geramain nodded in reply to Enola's question.

'And how far to the yard?'

'Not all the way to the far side, there's a fence and then a wall.'

'Follow me over there and make sure we get to the right spot,' Enola told Geramain without taking her eyes off the exit. 'Let's go.'

Enola was first out into the open, followed by Geramain and a stream of archers. The open ground stretched for two or three hundred paces deeper into the city, closed in on both sides by buildings. Rickety wooden gates covered the few gaps between the structures, blocking the way into narrow alleyways. The ground looked to be mostly dry and hard. A young crop could be seen growing out of a few patches of ploughed land, its greenery adding colour to an otherwise drab field.

The fields and the rooftops were deserted, the sound of Antona's diversion attack on the main barricades echoed off the walls surrounding the allotments. The shouts of men and the metallic clash of weapons hovered in the air like a memory. There was a bitter smell of animal faeces coming from the cultivated ground. It was more offensive to the senses than fields in the open country where the smell of muck seemed healthy and synonymous with the countryside. This smell was sour, almost sewer-like.

Enola saw that some of the first men out of the tunnel were Josef and the two men who seemed to keep crossing her path.

'So, are you a rapist and a murderer?' The question was aimed at Arter, but Enola asked it for the benefit of anyone who overheard.

Arter shook his head. 'I think if you truly thought that, I would not be here.'

'He's a good man, sir,' Hurcan assured the Commander. 'You won't regret saving him from the rope.'

Enola looked at Josef expecting him to say something in defence of his new friends, but he was a veteran and knew better. 'Time will tell on that. I'll make my own judgement on whether or not any of you are good men.'

The was something about this frightened young man and his loyal companion that had gained Enola's interest. Gavara taught her never to ignore opportunities or people thrown into her path by fate. She was intrigued to see if destiny would show its hand if she kept these two close. At the very least, she would measure their worth in the fighting to come Then she would decide.

When enough archers had emerged from the drain, and men with hammers started to appear, Enola signalled the advance. A brace of the bowmen followed closely behind the Lioness, their bows half drawn and their heads jerking around, looking for defenders on the rooftops. It was deserted. Men stumbled and cursed as they crossed the furrowed land, mud and muck sticking to their feet. The crash of hammers on the stone wall made Enola cringe, they were surely too loud and would soon bring unwanted attention. She glanced over her shoulder and saw that holes were already appearing in the wall, more warriors and bowmen pushing their way through the gaps as soon as they were big enough.

When Enola reached a fence at the far left of the area she stopped, pressing her back against the wooden posts. She looked back for Geramain, who was rubbing his hands together, attempting to remove the sticky dirt from a fall.

'Is this the place?' Enola spoke in a loud whisper, gesturing for Geramain to hurry. 'You,' she pointed at one of the bowmen. 'Put your hands together and lift me up.'

The fence was too high to see over, so Enola stepped into the bowman's cupped hands and allowed herself to be heaved up, being careful to remain bent so that her head didn't suddenly pop up and catch the attention of anyone on the other side, or even worse, become a target. The man kept his back against the fence, his face not showing the disgust he felt at having the muck-covered boot in his well-kept archer's hands. Enola slowly raised her head to look over the fence into the merchant's yard. There was no one in there. The yard was littered with discarded crates and upturned barrels. The goods that had been stored there were obviously cleared out with some haste.

'Axes!' Enola called, as she jumped down.

With great arcing swings, the men set about the fence. They used the curved back of their axes to rip out planks cracked by the blade, opening up man-sized gaps in an instant. Enola was the first through, her archers streaming through the gaps in their determination to keep up with their Commander. The group raced down the yard and over to its open gates, like a line of ants. Enola could not believe her luck. They had penetrated deep into the city without being detected. She was looking down a wide street directly at the command tent they had spotted earlier. If they could make it down this road, they would be behind the barricades. Speed was everything now. Too many defenders were mulling about between the yard and the tent for them to reach that point undetected. They would have to sprint down the road, firing arrows as they went. It would be a desperate dash, but what other choice did they have?

Two of the Commander's largest bodyguards arrived, panting from the effort to catch up with Enola, obviously ordered by Warrik to stick with their Leader. She was also surprised to see Geramain still with them, a short sword tightly gripped in his hand. She grinned as Arter and Hurcan scrambled across the yard, their eagerness to impress obvious. Joseph followed the two Spartikens, stepping across the yard like a cat following its prey. He was in no hurry and had nothing to prove. His focus was on staying alive by outwitting the enemy, his experience showed in his calmness and deliberate actions. Enola hoped there were many more like him with her. She waited again until there were enough archers with her and she could see sword and pike-men coming through the fence to join them.

'The cry is Spartikens. Don't stop until we reach that tent, then turn on the barricades. Kill anything in our way.'

Enola knew they would be fighting as a rabble, but she wanted chaos and confusion. All they had to do was cause enough panic and distraction for Antona to overcome the defences, and they would be in. She cursed the fact that she had brought so few in her caution not to be discovered. If she had known they would get this far, she would have brought heavy infantry better suited for the fighting that was to come. More would follow, so for now she would have to make do with what she had. Speed would be her best weapon.

The charge did not start with an order or even a battle cry, Enola simply unslung her curved bow from her back, nocked an arrow, and ran out into the street. The rattle of a hundred feet skittering over the cobbles followed the Lioness. She had gone less than thirty paces when she saw the first of the enemy turn towards her. The archer's eyes were wide with surprise, and he lifted his bow to shoot from his rooftop position. He had neither time to draw the string of his bow or call the alarm before Enola's arrow took him through the throat. She was an excellent shot and could easily take a bird in flight, so even while running it was an easy shot for her.

Several more figures appeared at the edges of the rooftops, men come to see what had happened to their comrade. A hail of arrows flew past Enola from behind, some sparking as they ricocheted off the stone lips of the rooves, others hitting their mark and killing defenders. Bodies tumbled to the street below. The alarm was raised and shots returned. Arrows flew at Enola, whizzing past her. She wished they had shields as men hit by arrows cried out. More Mander defenders ran out into the street, the first of them struck to the ground by shafts already flying down the road. The Avolonians were closing in on the tent, their arrows disappearing through its canvas panels.

'Spartikens!' Enola cried as she let another arrow fly at a man who had stepped into her path.

'Spartikens!' the street echoed with the cry shouted by the attackers, stabbing fear into the hearts of the defenders. A firestorm of arrows flew in both directions, men screaming and falling on both sides.

Enola slung her bow and drew her golden sword as she reached the tent. Two burly men with drawn swords came rushing out of the front of the marquee. Enola's bodyguards stepped around her and made short work of the two defenders. Avolonian archers scurried around the corner and let their arrows fly at the backs of those defending the barricades. Spartikens spilled into the streets behind the defences, shouting their war cry, as they went. It turned into bloody hand to hand combat as the Mander resistance panicked and rushed back to aid their Commander.

Three more warriors wearing armour and well-armed, came rushing out of the tent, setting about Enola's two guards with a fury. At the same time a group of Mander defenders with a mix of pikes, swords and axes came running around from the back of the marquee, instantly heading for Enola. Josef snatched up a shield from a pile stacked against the side of the tent. He flung it into Hurcan's arms, then passed another to Arter, and kept the third for himself. The three men rushed to put themselves between the advancing men and their Commander.

'Cover her!' Josef suddenly called, halting the two others as he reversed direction.

Josef raised his shield in front of Enola, shouting at the others to do the same. Arrows instantly rattled against the three raised shields. Both Arter and Hurcan saw the danger in time. A gaggle of archers had formed on the corner of a rooftop, aiming their bows at Enola. A second wave of arrows drilled into the three shields but the Lioness was unhurt. A spear hit the shields next, and the arrows stopped as the group of Mander foot soldiers reached Enola's position. The three men stood their ground to defend their Leader. Arter was stuck through with an arrow in his shoulder, and Hurcan had a shaft through his calf but they fought on regardless. Josef was in the centre of the three, a rock holding them in place.

Enola was about to join the fight when she was overtaken by her own warriors with swords and axes. The three men with shields, and the battle, were carried away from Enola and the tent. Her two guards returned to her side, one of them with a deep gash in his sword arm, the other with a cut to his cheek, both of them panting like overheated dogs. All around them warriors fought face to face, and chaos reigned.

Enola could not tell if they had the upper hand or if they were about to be stopped in their tracks. She remembered Shulz, the serpent's head. She led her two bodyguards and a few others into the tent. Her head darted from side to side as she took in the scene. Several men were on the ground, arrows standing proud from their still bodies. One man was sitting against a post, an arrow skewering his face from one side to the other. He pulled feebly at one end of the shaft, trying to work it free. Another man stood with his sword drawn, an arrow shaft sticking out of the base of his neck where it met with his shoulder.

'Shulz,' Enola stated, knowing him to be the Leader because of the general's breastplate he was wearing.

He snarled at the Lioness and lunged his blade. Enola, surprised at his speed, was forced to dance out of the way to avoid the strike. The General was seriously injured but his strength had not yet left him.

'Call off your dogs,' Enola commanded. 'It's over. More need not die.'

Shulz gave his answer with another lunge. 'Never!'

Enola patted the blade away and reversed her thrust. The point of her sword entered at the base of Shulz's breastplate, Enola dropping to one knee so that it went up at an angle through the General's stomach and behind his ribs. Shulz vomited blood, spraying it across the room as he forced himself to curse his killer with his final breath.

'The Almighty will smite you...' Shulz managed to say before his legs gave way and the life left his eyes.

Enola retrieved her blade, wiping it on her victim's cloak. 'He may very well do that, but you won't be around to see it. Take his head. Let's put a stop to this madness.'

Enola emerged from the tent to see Antona's warriors flooding through the barricades and down the street towards her.

'Sound your horns!' she called out to the Mander fighting within earshot. 'Your General is dead, it is over.' Enola held up General Shulz's severed head by a plait of hair at the back. Shulz's lifeless face tilted down and blood dribbled from the dead lips.

Those Mander close by recognised their Leader and backed away from the fight. One had the good sense to raise a horn to his lips and blow the signal to stop. He blew it twice more before others joined in to blow the order on their horns. The fighting stopped, and there was an eerie quiet as men stepped apart, not yet trusting that the fight was over. Then the clatter of swords and spears being dropped on the cobbles rang out, and warriors knew it really was.

Enola looked around her. Arter and Hurcan sat on the ground to her right, bodies all around. Both men pressed against the arrows sticking out of them, but they were superficial wounds that would heal quickly enough. Sorrow poked an icy finger into Enola's heart when she saw Josef on his back. The veteran's eyes were open, lifelessly staring at the sky, a spear standing like a flagpole from his gut.

'We would have been minced meat without him,' Arter called over to Enola, seeing where she looked.

'He was a good man and a brave warrior,' she replied. 'You are good men too. You have my thanks.'

Arter smiled at that and watched his Commander turn and walk further down the street. He realised that this time he had not been so afraid during the fight. For once the spinners of fate had chosen to be kind to him. He laughed at himself, he had an arrow through his shoulder and strangely thought that was kindness. He reached over and slapped Hurcan on the back.

'He took that spear in the belly saving my sorry ass,' Hurcan said softly to his friend.

Enola looked around, sickened by the brutality of the fighting that had gone on. Two women lay dead on the ground, stuck together, each holding a blade that pierced the other as if they had both won and lost the fight at the same time.

'Geramain!' Enola suddenly called out, seeing the recently freed slave slumped against a wall, an arrow sticking out of his chest and blood dribbling from the corner of his mouth. She handed Shulz's head to another and rushed to Geramain's side.

He sat against the wall, his short sword coated in blood still in his grip. 'I got one of the vermin,' he said, nodding towards the blooded blade in his hand.

'Don't speak,' she told him. 'We will get this arrow free before you bleed to death.'

He shook his head. 'I can feel the shaft against my heart, I am done for.'

'Nonsense, old man.' She looked around and saw a warrior with a field bag and waved him over. The man took a heavy-looking set of clippers out of the bag. The old man groaned as he was eased forward and the arrowhead was clipped off. The warrior laid him back against the wall and turned his attention to the portion of the arrow protruding from his chest.

Geramain stopped him from taking the arrow out. 'One moment,' he said politely and looked up at Enola. 'I would like very much to have seen my daughters one more time, but it is an honour to die a free man, no longer living on my knees.'

He closed his eyes to brace himself.

Enola took his hand in hers. 'You will live to see those girls again. Imagine how proud they will be when you walk up to them, a free man and a hero of Calinkerbad.'

Geramain smiled. The warrior waiting to pull out the shaft looked to Enola. She nodded, and he pulled the shaft free. Geramain's head fell forward. Everything was still for a moment. Enola and the warrior were stunned, he was dead.

'The old guy was right. The shaft was too close to his heart or something.' The warrior put the clippers back in the bag and left.

Enola felt a tear stinging the corner of her eye. She had only known this man a short time but he had symbolised why they fought the Mander. He could have hidden away and let others fight for his freedom, but he chose to be in the front line. She tightened her grip on his hand.

'Sir!' A voice called out.

Enola looked over her shoulder to see Warrik on his mount, Invincible, holding Storm's reins. She glanced at the twilight sky. 'See to it this one is honoured,' she shouted over to Arter and Hurcan, who were both having arrows removed. 'Let's take this head to my father before the sun is gone,' she said, striding towards Warrik.

Enola rode like the wind through the streets of Calinkerbad, carrying Shulz's head. The men and women of the legions cheered as she rode by, Warrik, Elektra and a handful of her guards riding after her. She was heading for the main gate. She had done the impossible and would deliver the news herself just to see the look on her father's face.

Chapter 5

Arc

Servants hurried around the tent lighting lamps as the last of the day's glow vanished and the sun disappeared below the horizon. More wood was added to braziers around the room. Smoke from the new wood lingered, seeping into everything it touched, and irritating throats and eyes. Food and watered wine were laid out on a side table close to a larger one that had been carried in and surrounded by high-backed chairs from the city.

Razor, Grand Master of the Jagger Knights was the first to return to Arc's command tent. He was followed by Cid, his second in command, and the two men took their place at the table. General Eric of the Storm Legions, General Renaldon of the Lion Cavalry and Commander Jellicoe of the Lion Army all walked in together. Commander Tyezore came in soon after with an entourage of his generals dressed in an array of feathers and animal skins.

'Your officers can stay, but there is no place at the table for them,' Arc told Tyezore, as he and his generals started to take seats.

The Corinthian did not look pleased, but he did not take offence and nodded towards the food, which his officers descended upon. The fare was mostly leftovers that Sonaji's servants had scrambled together, but there were one or two delicacies that the Corinthian Officers did not hesitate to snatch at. The first thing Sonaji did on entering the tent was to scatter the Corinthians and banish them from the food table to the far side of the room. Tyezore gave his cousin an indignant stare which was returned with interest. Sonaji's expression spoke volumes about her displeasure.

'Keep your jackals on a tighter leash, dear cousin,' Sonaji said as she took her place at the table.

Tyezore was about to retaliate to the indignant treatment of his bondsmen, but was prevented by Enola's boisterous arrival. The Lioness marched over to the table closely followed by Warrik and Electra, looking more as if they were trying to catch her, rather than keep up with her. All eyes were on the cranium she carried by its hair, and all mouths were open in astonishment. Enola slammed the severed head onto the table.

'The city is yours,' Arc was told in a discourteous and provocative manner by his daughter.

Enola stood defiant, her arms folded and her gaze fixed on her father, expecting and willing his wrath to explode at the affront he had just been subjected to.

Arc raised an eyebrow. 'Shulz?'

The head sat awkwardly in the centre of the table, its eyes half-open in a dumb stare and its tongue protruding between blood-splattered rows of teeth.

Enola was surprised that her father knew who it was. She let out a spontaneous laugh that eased the tension in the room.

'Why am I not surprised that you know who that is. I'll wager you have spies in every division of my legions.'

'Or your messengers told us about all your developments during your valiant acquisition of the city,' Gavara suggested. 'Well done, Commander. Only a Saberlund could have achieved such a feat in such a short time. Well done.'

Gavara pulled a seat out for the Lioness and she sat. Enola tried to remember if she had mentioned the Mander resistance leader's name in dispatches as the head was removed from the table.

'Put that on a spike for all to see,' she ordered, dismissing her thoughts about how her father knew who the head belonged to, assuming if she had not told him then it was highly likely that the information had come in dispatches from one of her Generals. 'That trophy cost the lives of too many of my Spartikens. Make it a long pole.' Enola was still unnerved by her father's calmness. She had expected him to be quick to anger, which would have given her the opportunity to challenge his threats that clearly showed his doubt in her abilities. His sudden tolerance of her insolence had thrown her off balance, it was more like his old self, the leader and father she knew him to be.

Arc brought everyone at the table up to speed with Edius-Max's situation.

'Cid, you will lead your Knights in an attack against the Mander to the south of the Ibres Hills.' Arc was interrupted by coughing from Grand Master Razor. 'Is that not to your agreement, Grand Master?'

Razor gave Arc a curious smile. 'I am fit and well again, my lord. I will ride at the head of the Holy Knights, as it is my place to do so.'

The Lion Lord gave General Cid a worried glance, but the Knight had nothing to offer about the matter. They both knew this was a task suited to the younger Generals, but they were also aware of the Grand Master's right to lead his own Knights into battle.

Enola said what the others were thinking. 'Are you sure you are well enough for this mission, Grand Master. I don't mean to offend, but it will be a hard ride over unforgiving terrain, and then a hard battle at the end of it.'

Razor remained silent while he waited for any traces of his anger to melt away. He would probably have exploded in a rage if anyone else in the room had suggested such a thing. Luckily it had been Enola. Even though she was perhaps the most fearsome warrior in the room, other than her father, she was still a woman. Razor's Knight's code of chivalry would not let him be anything but tolerant of the fairer sex.

'Thank you for your concern, but I am well enough, and my place is at the head of my Knights.'

No more was said about the matter, and Arc explained his plans to the Grand Master.

'Are we to hold the position to the south until you arrive with the rest of the army?'

'Strike and retreat.' Arc slammed his fist down on the table to give his point emphasis. 'Remember, you are a diversion from the action to the north. Do not get drawn in by your successes. Retreat behind the hills and link up with the main force to the north. Help form a rear-guard for their escape.' Arc turned to Renaldon. 'Take the Lion Cavalry to the north of the hills. Attack there. If Edius is in any fit state he will join you, and our army will retreat behind you.'

Jellicoe seemed worried by the plan. 'They will have a mass of reserves to the centre. What will stop them from countering our every move and overwhelming us with numbers?'

Arc shrugged. 'Al-Din is commanding his army in the south. Any reinforcements will be reluctant to be led away from their Emperor fearing a trap. Enola's cavalry will follow you. Use them to counter any Mander reinforcements or manoeuvres. Where is Antona?' Arc asked his daughter.

'He's securing the Dockland area.'

'Get him back here. He's to lead the Storm Cavalry, all of them. I want you here to lead the Legions.'

Enola felt outraged, she wanted to lead her cavalry, but she knew that any protest from her would just make her look like an obstinate child.

'Not wanting to labour the point the Grand Master brought up earlier,' Renaldon said. 'but if we get Edius-Max and his troops out of the hills, do we form defences until the rest of the army can reach us on foot?'

Arc took a deep breath. He could not be sure of the outcome. He was experienced enough to know there could be no expected result from such a venture, there were far too many variables.

'If you can, keep retreating. Draw Al-Din away from his supply lines.' Arc stretched his arms, pushing himself back from the table.

'And if we can't retreat?' Cid asked.

'Then you must hold until we arrive.' Arc rose from his seat, and everyone else responded instantly to do the same. 'Use windriders between our two positions. I must know of your successes and failures.' Arc paused. 'Gentlemen, our survival depends on it.'

Razor and Cid left to prepare their Knights for the ride. Renaldon went to organise the Lion Cavalry, and Elektra left to ready the horsemen of the Storm Legions for Antona to lead. The others took the opportunity to take some food before returning to the table. Enola drained a mug of wine, and then refilled it with water and did the same again, attempting to quench her thirst.

'I have lost many warriors, and many others are wounded,' Enola told everyone. 'If we are to march at dawn, I will need to reinforce with the best of the prisoners.'

Arc shook his head. 'They are men of the Mander Imperial Army, their loyalty is too strong to expect them to switch sides to save their skin. This is the first time they have known defeat. Atropolis paid the price for relying on auxiliary troops at Caputhora. Men forced to fight turned on him. Edius-Max cost him that fight with the desertion of the Saxish Auxiliaries. No, legions weakened by battle will serve our cause far better than legions of men forced to fight. The fate of the prisoners is sealed. We can't feed them, and we can't leave good men behind to guard them.' He turned to Jellicoe. 'Have your men put them to the sword before we leave.'

Jellicoe's expression was a mix of sadness and horror. 'Men of the Lion Warriors were all prisoners at one time or another, it will not sit well with them to kill in this way. Give me two thousand of them to integrate. I will only take those willing to slit the throats of the Mander True Bloods.'

Gavara joined the debate. 'I need a workforce to rebuild the city's defences. There are many wounded from the legions who are not fit to make the march you are proposing, but they will be fit enough to hold a spear to the backs of working prisoners. Calinkerbad is of great strategic importance to you. It is a foothold in the heart of Mander, a bastion from which to strike. Do not abandon it unless there is no other way.'

Arc could see the logic in Jellicoe's argument. The Lion Warriors were just that, warriors, not murderers. Arc was in a dilemma: his army needed replacements, and a workforce would be necessary to rebuild the city and its defences. It was a bold and desperate action to attempt to save Edius-Max and half of the Avolonian army trapped in the hills. There was little chance of any decisive victory, it was more likely that they would need to retreat and the port city would be their only sanctuary in a hostile land. Arc's fears ran deep, with only wounded men to watch over the prisoners there could easily be an uprising. There was a danger the Mander could regain control of the city in his absence.

'Very well. Take your two thousand, Jellicoe. Enola, take one thousand for each of the legions, and leave your wounded behind to guard the four thousand I'm granting to Gavara. All of you, choose wisely, only those of non-Mander origin and willing to save their skins by joining us. Their first act as an Avolonian will be to blood their blades on the throats of those prisoners left. Kill any man who comes to you with a clean blade, for he will be a viper in your midst.'

The old man's mouth opened about to protest, closing again without uttering a word as he thought better of it. This would mean the death of more than half of the prisoners. The thought sickened him to the stomach.

'There is a price for all this mercy,' Arc added. 'I want all our artillery mobile and moving with us. Gavara, I want the Harpy on wheels and following us. We will need every advantage we can get.'

'Impossible!' Gavara exclaimed, flapping his arms about.

'Nevertheless, making the impossible possible is what you do.' Arc rose from his seat. 'We march at dawn.'

Enola

Enola's bones were damp with exhaustion. Her footsteps were heavy as she made her way to her tent, the thought of sleep almost overcoming her before she got there. As she pushed the flap to one side to enter her tent, she was surprised. Jenaliena was stood by a tub made of oak planking and filled with steaming water. The servant girl immediately got to removing the Commanders armour and clothing.

Enola had neither the energy nor the will to protest. Once naked, she simply stepped into the heated water and lay still with her eyes closed as Jenaliena washed and rubbed her entire body. She was asleep in less than a moment. Jenaliena only awakened her mistress once the water had cooled and Enola's fingers had wrinkled like dried figs. She lovingly dried off the body of her mistress and then helped her into the bed she had made earlier. Jenaliena laid down beside Enola and softly stroked her skin until the two of them fell into a deep sleep.

Dawn arrived like a bold thief, stealing the darkness along with any chance to sleep longer. Enola stealthily left the bed, intending not to wake Jenaliena. Her body had only partially recovered from the aches and pains of battle, and she could not remember ever feeling the limitations of her strength in such a way before.

'Must you go so early?' a sleepy voice called out from beneath the furs on the bed. 'And without so much as a kiss?'

Enola smiled and finished strapping her breastplate on before returning to the bed. She sat on the edge running her hand through the soft furs, and then through Jenaliena's hair, pushing it from her face. She leaned in, kissing the young woman on her trembling lips, breathing in the warm smell of sleep and the sweet scent of womanhood as she did.

'I will leave word that you are to tend to my baggage while I'm gone. You are to attend to no one else from now on and have no other duties but mine. Understand? I will inform the guards.' Enola held Jenaliena's hand, pondering if they were lovers or just very good friends. 'A boy is coming from the city. His name is Zac. Put him to work, but look after him.'

Jenaliena simply nodded, though her eyes were bright with gratitude, joy and a hint of mischief.

From outside the commotion of an army readying itself to march was already loud and chaotic. Enola reluctantly rose, strapped on Leo-fang and began to leave.

'Come back safe,' Jenaliena called after her, sitting up in the bed and ensuring her breasts were exposed.

Enola paused to answer but just smiled instead at the brazenness of her new friend. Saving to memory the vision of Jenaliena's womanliness and the touch of her soft lips, she left.

The Jagger Knights

Cid rode night and day by the Grand Master's side. The older man had almost fallen from his saddle more than once. His determination to show resolve and ability to hold onto his command of the Knights could quite possibly kill him before any Mander Warrior had a chance to. Like every other Knight, Razor's eyes had been left red and swollen by the race across the sandy plains. He wheezed, and his lungs burned after two days of breathing in the choking dust through a scarf tied over his nose and mouth. Cid was in a similar state, but the younger man endured it as if he were dealing with no more than a minor irritation.

Several Knights fell from the saddle while riding through the dark. They were men who had hidden their wounds, thinking themselves capable of making the arduous ride with their injuries. Some had not been missed until the morning when their mounts appeared with empty saddles. Others who could not continue were more fortunate and were left a skin of water and their horses. Most would not recover in the dusty lands, but the advance could not be slowed to care for them, they would have to take their chances alone.

When the Ibres Hills came into sight, it was a vision that brought both relief and joy. The Knights had endured the wind and dust of the plains, and their spirits lifted on seeing the green meadows and streams rolling down from the hills. The Ibres Hills ran as far as the eye could see to the north and south. Lonely clouds sat on the highest peaks, looking like the hats worn by farmers to protect them from the sun. Large birds could be seen circling on the warm air rising from the dark granite outcrops. The sweet smell of damp grass and hillside flowers was overwhelming after days of nostril-clogging dust. Pulling down the scarves that covered their faces, the Knights gulped in lungfuls of fragrant air.

Razor rested his Knights by a narrow lake. He let the men wash and drink their fill of the clear water, but he allowed no fires to be set to cook rations. Three patrols were sent out to scout the area and ascertain the enemy's position and numbers, they returned with grave news.

'Honourable gentlemen, it seems that the Mander are camped in great numbers to the south of the hills,' the Grand Master told the gathering of his most senior officers. 'Many of the Imperial Army, whom we have already fought against at Calinkerbad, have escaped to join their Emperor here. We cannot let this deter us. We must take their attention away from the Avolonian attack to the north and, God willing, give General Edius-Max the time and opportunity he needs to retreat. Based on...' Razor was hit by a sudden bout of coughing. Cid handed the Grand Master a cup of water and helped him sit against a large boulder while he regained his breath and composure. 'Sorry, gentlemen, that blasted dust gets to the bottom of your lungs. We can make little impact on the numbers we face, but we can cause a barrel load of confusion. Surprise and manoeuvrability will be our strengths. Strike hard while they are still encamped, and be out of there before they have a chance to respond.'

Cid and several other of the Holy Order's most senior Knights stood around their seated leader, towering over him. These were men of honour and brave protectors of their faith, but none among them would willingly step into Razor's shoes should he be unable to lead. To a man, they also knew how the Knights were in awe of their Grand Master and the example he was setting for them. This was a man they respected and would die for. Those same Knights, who coveted the Grand Master's title, understood the commitment needed to lead. It would take them years of dedicated service to gain one morsel of the admiration the men had for Fastidious Razorback, Grand Master of the Holy Knights of Jagger's 11th order.

'We shall divide our force. The Cid will lead one of four squadrons of Knights.' Razor used the Vice Master's title inherited from the days when his great grandfather was the Grand Master. Cid was the old Jagger word for lord, and his great grandfather had been known as El Cid, The Lord. In the years since Cid inherited the title, old and knew had been mixed up. The men now called him The Cid. His real name was Martin Antolinez the 4th. He still carried his great grandfather's sword, the Blessed Blade, Colada. 'Sir Malcon and Sir Rasputer, you shall both lead a squadron, and I shall lead the fourth.' The Grand Master looked to the other Knights in the room. 'Gentlemen, you shall organise the knights into four squadrons. Take the names of men who have sworn oaths to the four of us. Instruct them about their duties in accordance with my orders.' The Knights waited patiently, their left hands on sword hilts, ready and obedient. 'They are to protect their leaders at all cost; they are to ensure we retreat at the proper time and are not drawn back into the fight for any reason. The fire in a man's blood during battle can easily melt the ice needed to freeze his heart into ignoring the peril of others, and steel his nerve into following orders. Now, leave us and make it so.'

The three Knights remaining with Razor thought the orders were strange and hoped for an explanation, none of them wanting to question the Grand Master just to settle their own curiosity.

'Do we attack this evening?' Cid asked. 'It is already late in the day, and the light will not last. Riding across the plains in the dark is one thing, but fighting on horseback after sundown is another matter entirely.'

Razor placed a reassuring hand on his nephew's shoulder. 'If all has gone well, the Avolonians will attack at dawn. We will do the same. While there is light enough we will take up positions ready to attack at first light. I am afraid I must ask you to endure a cold night without fires. Have your men rest and sleep in shifts. Cid, you will take the younger Knights to the south, where courage and youthful enthusiasm will be needed over experience. You two will take the centre, left and right. I expect the Emperor's camp to be in that vicinity. There will be strong resistance, so do not hang around long enough for them to organise. Give them hell and get out of there,' Razor paused to give his next words intensity. 'You are not to be drawn into returning to the fight for any reason. Is that clear?' All three Knights nodded. 'Each squadron is responsible for its own destiny.'

'If half the army are already here, why don't we just stand and fight when Arc arrives?' Sir Malcon asked, thinking it to be a logical question. 'We have a chance to defeat the Mander in one place.'

Razor frowned. 'They would counter us on all fronts, it would never be more than a desperate attempt to push them back and would leave us in a weak position to defend. We must draw him away from his advantage and supplies. God willing, we will all retreat to join the Lion Crusade and face the enemy again. Remember we are not here to win. We are here to blind the enemy from what is really going on. Give the flock time to sneak by the wolves. Now, let us pray.'

All four men dropped to one knee and bowed their heads in prayer.

The sun crept over a distant hill, bleeding an amber hue across the horizon. A cold wind blowing through the night had made sleep difficult, not that any man had slept well knowing the dawn would see him riding into battle. Cid walked his horse down the grassy slope made slippery by the morning dew. He yawned elaborately, stretched his free arm, and looked back at the column of Knights following him.

Cid gazed jealously at the fires in the distant Mander camp. 'I think I'll take more pleasure this morning from stealing Mander breakfasts than I'll get from slitting their throats.'

Cid's acting squire, Ruffas, let out a subdued laugh. 'Didn't save any of your rations for the morning then?'

'You're my squire, so you should have saved some for me.'

'Acting squire and I ate what I had. No point in saving food you might not live to eat. Die on a full belly, that's what I say.'

Cid chuckled at Ruffus' comments, enjoying his twisted philosophy. 'Is that what I think it is?'

Ruffus looked at the dead tree Cid was pointing at. The dark and twisted silhouette stood alone on a hillock, looming over the landscape like a sentinel.

'It's a lightning tree, an oak if I'm not mistaken. I've only ever seen one before, on the edge of the Jagger desert.

My grandmother calls it the Spirit Tree. She says it was once part of a great forest where the ghosts of those turned away from death's paradise roamed. She believes a tree so old is struck by lightning on God's command, to be a portal for ghosts between the underworld and ours.'

Cid usually had no interest in superstitions or omens, but he found Ruffus' chatter relaxing, so he encouraged him to carry on by asking a question. 'Why would such a great tree grow here, where no other trees grow?'

'I imagine it was much the same as in our own lands,' Ruffus began answering. 'It would have been hundreds of years old when lightning struck. These lands have been cleared of forests for agriculture. Maybe superstition prevented them from felling a Spirit Tree.' He shivered as he felt a chill run down his spine. 'I don't blame them. I can sense the spirits in this place. Gives me the heebee jeebees.'

'Or you sense your own death,' Cid mumbled.

'What's that you say?'

Cid did not answer, relieved that Ruffus hadn't heard him.

The column had been walking just over the far side of a ridge, keeping themselves out of sight from the Mander camp. As Cid crossed the ridge, he gave the order to mount up. The Knights strapped their kite-shaped shields to their arms and put on their helmets. Cid's family banner was hoisted aloft, and the Jagger Knights wasted no time in cantering down the hill.

Cid looked to his left and could see the columns of Sir Malcon and Sir Rasputer descending from the hills. Razor's force was too far to the north for him to see. He was sure that the alarm would soon be raised in the Mander camp, but he had sense enough not to increase the pace. It was too far to gallop the horses all the way, they would arrive at the fight blown. A spent horse was a death trap for a knight, so they cantered on at a leisurely pace, hoping the Mander were more complacent than diligent.

Fortune shined on the Jagger Knights that morning. The alarm was raised just as the mounted warriors came into close enough range to charge. The camp was slow to awaken, and the Knights were deep amongst the shelters and panicking residents before they met the first resistance. Tents were burned. Fleeing men were cut down by a blade strike to the back of the head, or a lance in the back. It was a stampede of humanity. It was as if the Knights had overturned a giant rock to reveal an ants' nest, but it was men, not ants, running in all directions, gathering belongings and looking for safety.

Stallions trained for battle trampled those too slow to get out of their way. With ears pricked back and eyes bulging, steeds snapped at frantic Mander warriors who could do nothing more than throw their hands up to protect themselves from the beasts' teeth. Screams and yells bounced around the air like echoes in a forest. Not all of the shouts came from the panicking, some came from Mander officers trying desperately to gather men around then to form pockets of resistance. They knew that deeper in the camp their own warriors would be organising and horsemen would be mounting up. They just had to stay alive long enough for their fellow Mander to reach them.

Cid saw one such group rallying around a large Imperial officer, a banner flapping above them, attracting all who could see it. Cid called out to Ruffus and others close to him. They rode at the defiant group as its numbers swelled. Just as he reached the resistance, Cid's path was blocked by a warrior with a pike. The man aimed the weapon directly at the Knight's head. That was a mistake, he should have targeted the horse. Cid deflected the pike with his shield, which he twisted so that the blade slid by without any danger. The man was quick enough to step out of the way of the horse, but not Cid's boot. The Knight kicked his attacker in the face, his steel boot stripping the skin from his chin to his forehead. Cid rode past the fallen man, leaving him to be finished off by a Knight with a lance.

Cid raised Colada and brought her down in a chop aimed at the Officer's head. The Imperial Warrior blocked the blow with his own blade, shouting angry defiance at his attacker. Cid was oblivious to the man's words and swung his sword down on him again and again. The clang of metal on metal sounded like a smithy hammering on his anvil. There was more power and rage than Cid knew himself to be capable of in every blow.

The Officer's eyes widened as he realised his strength was failing. He tried to pull back, and that was his mistake. Cid changed the angle of his stroke, catching his opponent off guard. The Officer saw the blow coming but was unable to block it. Colada bit into the Imperial Officer's neck, half severing his head before stopping at the spine. The man dropped to his knees, his face turning grey as the blood drained from his head. More blood overflowed from his neck and flooded down his body. Cid swung again, leaning over to reach the kneeling man. This time bone did not stop the blade, and the Officer's head tumbled to the ground.

Ruffus killed the man holding the banner, snatching up the colours and throwing them like a spear into a burning tent.

'That would have made a good souvenir,' Cid told him.

'Never thought of that,' came the reply.

'Call the retreat,' Cid ordered. 'We've done what we can here.' He could see organised ranks advancing on their position. 'Let's get out of here before we are trapped.'

It was a strange feeling for Cid to be running from a foe with his troops unbeaten. It was an orderly retreat towards the hills, the air crammed with the rumble of horses' hooves. The beasts' ironclad feet threw up great clods of earth as they raced across the meadows and up the hill. Cid used the lightning tree as a marker and felt a chill as he passed under its twisting and leafless branches. Before reaching the top, Cid held up a hand to slow everyone down. They were being pursued, but the enemy was far enough back that the Knights could afford the time to ease off on their mounts. The last thing they wanted was to have blown horses at the top of the hill. It was hard enough on the beasts having to carry a knight in armour on the flat, cantering up the long hill could ruin the lungs of any steed.

Cid let the Mander horsemen giving chase get close. They were not in proper formation, and in their eagerness to catch the Knights and avenge their dead comrades they were exhausting their mounts.

'Wheel!' Cid called out.

It was instinct for the Knights to obey, and they turned instantly, forming a tight level line several horses deep.

'You remember your orders were to retreat?' Ruffus reminded his commander.

'We are retreating,' Cid smiled. 'It will be harder for the enemy to catch us with the bloody nose we are about to give them.' Cid took a deep breath, then yelled. 'Charge!'

The Knights flowed down the hill like floodwater breaking the banks of a river. The Mander had no time to organise their line, and the Jagger Knights shattered their formation and sent them scattering. Some stood and fought, cut down in moments. Others fled back down the hill, realising they were done for.

'Call the retreat again,' Cid ordered.

Every instinct the Vice Master had, wanted to chase down a fleeing enemy, but he had his orders. 'Sting and retreat.'

The Mander did not make the same mistake again. Instead of chasing down the Knights, the Mander strengthened their positions and kept their cavalry at the ready.

'They are not buying it,' Ruffus said, looking down from the ridge. 'If we disappear now they will be free to march north against Edius-Max.'

Cid let out a sigh. He knew Ruffus was right, but they had to regroup with the others at the meeting point.

'Stay here and stay visible,' Cid told Ruffus. 'If they attack, you retreat. I'll take my Oath Knights and meet the others. Razor will have the same grasp of the situation as we do, he won't want to retreat either.'

The others were already gathering as Cid galloped down the grassy slope. He could see dozens of Jagger banners, Sir Malcon's and Sir Rasputer's amongst them. He could not see the Grand Master's colours and wondered if he was still engaged with the enemy. The other two senior Knights rode out to greet Cid.

'What happened?' Sir Malcon asked, looking at the thirty or so Oath Knights following the Cid. 'Are these all that survived?'

'The Mander are not pursuing us. I've left my Knights where they can be seen to keep the Mander on their toes. Any news from the Grand Master?'

Before either of the Knights could answer, a ragged column came bolting over the hills. No banners were flying, and the riders seemed to be in a panic.

'Mount up!' Sir Rasputer called, in case the enemy was right behind the approaching Knights.

All had gone well for the squadrons led by Cid, Malcon and Rasputer. They had all had similar experiences and lost very few. Their men were in an excellent mental and physical state. The approaching Knights did not look as if they had been as fortunate. As they came close, one of the Knights peeled off from the rest and headed for the three senior Knights.

'Sir Peregrine!' Malcon called out to him, shocked at the state of the man.

Sir Peregrine was splattered from head to foot in blood. Most of it was not his, but a cut on his forehead had left the right side of his face encrusted with his own dried blood. He had sharp features and a thick black moustache that curled up at the ends.

'Razor,' he gasped. 'He is captured, along with half of our squadron. We rode into a force that was ready for us. Their mounted cavalry split us in two. We fought like dervishes to get through to him, but there were just too many of them.'

'Captured, not slain, you say?' Cid asked as the man took a water-skin offered him by Sir Malcon, and took two great gulps from it.

'Grand Master Razor ordered us to retreat,' Sir Peregrine told them without being asked. They fought on when the retreat sounded, but it was hopeless. They were surrounded and trapped. From a position on the hill I saw, with my own eyes, the Grand Master pulled from his horse and led away.'

‘And then you left in such a disorderly panic?’ Sir Rasputer asked in a disapproving tone.

‘They rode up the hill after us in great numbers, taking their time, so we stood our ground and let them tire their horses on the climb. What we did not realise was that they had warriors in the hills. We had been flanked by more of their cavalry. They seemed to come out of nowhere, and arrows rained down on us from the rocks above. We barely made it out with our lives. Many good Knights are lying dead in our wake.’

‘How far behind are they now?’ Cid asked. ‘Is an attack imminent?’

Sir Peregrine shook his head. ‘I heard them sound the recall as we came through the pass up there.’ He shook his head despairingly. ‘They seemed to be expecting us.’

‘It’s more likely that their scouts got wind of our forces to the north. None of us three met with any resistance. They were probably readying to march north and reinforce their army there. But they did not break camp to chase us, so they must now be wise to our plan. We have to stay and harass their southern flank to give Edius a chance to fight his way out.’

Harass the Mander is what they did for as long as they could. Eventually the Imperial archers and infantry took up positions in the foothills, blocking that line of retreat. The Mander Cavalry were in a position to counter any of the Knights’ advances long before they could be of any effect. Cid and the Jagger Knights were eventually forced back behind the hills. With no other options open to them, they headed north, hoping to aid the Avolonian escape. A day that had started so well ended with the loss of their Grand Master and far too many Knights. As they left the southern hills of Ibres, Cid looked back at the lightning tree, and uncharacteristically questioned his own disbelief in the spirits.

Edius-Max

Fighting a retreat in an orderly fashion is something every commander prepared for, but never actually wanted to do. In truth, Edius-Max had done it several times before. He had retreated from the Mander as a Saxish General; fled from the Avolonians as a Mander officer, and now he retreated from the Mander as an Avolonian Commander. If he had been a humorous man, he would have chuckled to himself about his irony laced military career. He saw nothing funny about the twisting path the weavers of his fate were leading him along. He had seen too many atrocities; lost too many good friends, and his current situation was tenuous, at best.

Leading warriors in a retreat is one thing, having the camp followers retreat with them is another thing entirely. Many of the wives, children and traders following the army had been cut down by Mander blades as they ran to the military for protection. The Mander had come thick and fast, catching out the followers more readily than the army. Those who survived ran to the hills with tales of a vicious slaughter.

The Mander soldiers captured anyone of a good slaving age, along with trade goods and food. They butchered anyone else unfortunate enough to fall into their hands. Avolonian Warriors wept when they found out their wives had been taken. Their grief was not so much for the captured women, but for their babies and small children who would have been put to the sword. The young and the old were valueless in the slave markets, so suffered the most in such raids.

The surviving followers were getting under the feet of the Warriors, hampering their ability to fight as they retreated.

'Get these blasted civilians ahead of us, and keep them moving,' General Memfis bellowed at his men while trying to organise them against an imminent attack.

The Avolonian Cavalry attacked at dawn. It came as no surprise to the Mander, their scouts reported seeing the columns of horsemen arriving the night before. The attack was still a big enough distraction to give Edius-Max time to bring his troops down from the hills. Memfis formed a rear-guard with his heavy infantry to the south. Edius-Max led the light infantry to support the Lion and Storm Cavalry attack. The manoeuvre worked for as long as it needed to.

Now they fought a rolling retreat with the cavalry sweeping the flanks to stop any lightning attacks. Edius-Max and the other officers had been relieved when the Jagger Knights arrived. There were not as many of them as expected, but their arrival meant that both flanks had enough cavalry to protect them at all times.

The Mander followed, continually probing for weaknesses in the Avolonian formation. The Avolonian defence was sturdy, but the retreat was slow due to the camp followers staggering and stumbling ahead of the warriors. They had to be kept moving, or enemy archers would have time to form up and rain arrows down on them. The men at the back were taking enough fire as it was. Shields needed to remain interlocked and held high to protect the rear-guard from the archers.

Several Mander riders at a time would charge in and launch their spears at the shield-wall. Avolonian archers did not let them get away with such bold tactics. They limited the attackers' effectiveness by keeping them under intense fire. The attackers let fly their spears with little time to aim before making a hasty retreat. Many of the missiles fell short or were blocked by shields. More of the horsemen went down from arrow hits than Avolonians struck by spears. A bodkin arrow hitting armour or the scream of a horse hit in the chest by one were horrible sounds, but both were sounds that the warriors in the shield-wall of the Avolonian retreat learned to enjoy.

Edius-Max had a clear view of the Mander army, its lines growing deeper as he watched. They would be ready to attack as soon as the retreat faltered. An obstacle such as a river or hill would bring the withdrawal to a halt. Arc had given him orders to keep retreating across the dust lands, so that is what he would do, for as long as he could. They were just reaching the dust lands, and already most of the Mander army had caught up with them. Memfis pointed out the Emperor's banner at the centre. If Al-Din was there, a major attack would come soon.

The Generals were relieved that no attack came before nightfall. Darkness did not stop the retreat; the Avolonians kept moving. No one knew when arrows would fall out of the night sky, bringing death and terror. Children cried, and women screamed, but the warriors had to force them onward. Morale was low, and even the returning light at dawn didn't lift spirits, and the retreating mass trundled forward at a snail's pace.

Edius-Max was in two minds, his military experience telling him he couldn't save both the camp followers and his warriors. The logical thing to do was to abandon the civilians and march at full pace to join up with the Storm Legions. At least that way they stood a chance of fighting off Al-Din's army. The General shook off such thoughts, logic did not rule this day. He was marching into the dust lands. He had a good supply of water, but even early in the day he could tell it was going to be a scorcher.

The sun joined forces with the Mander, adding its heat to the list of threats the Avolonians must endure. By the end of the day, most of the water had gone. The Mander had launched two offensives, the Lion Cavalry and Jagger Knights seeing them off with well-timed counter-attacks. It would be wise to continue marching through the night. Edius-Max laughed at himself for thinking about what was rational, he gave up on that idea long ago. They could not advance through a second night, it would be the death of them. They would have to stop and rest as best they could.

The Lion Army formed a defensive line, shoulder to shoulder with shields locked together. It was the most dangerous time; if the enemy attacked in numbers now, they may well succeed in annihilating the rear-guard. The civilians fell to the ground and slept where they lay, huddled together in groups. The warriors took it in turn to grab two hours sleep. Many of the men and women were too tired to fall asleep, so they rested with their eyes closed, a multitude of thoughts tumbling through their minds. Arrows pummelling into shields filled the night air with metallic clangs. The cries of those hit by a shaft flying out of the darkness plucked at everyone's nerves. No one knew if the next arrow had their name on it; they could only hope that the next cry everyone heard was not theirs.

Dust rose around the tramp of tired feet long before the sun had risen. The retreat must continue for there to be any hope of survival. Edius-Max was sure the Mander would attack today. He was almost out of water and assumed it to be the same for Al-Din's army, but he did not know for sure. The Mander Army seemed resilient and determined. The General could only hope the enemy was as exhausted and thirsty as his troops, but he doubted it.

By midday the sun was blisteringly hot. Dust rose from the dry land, swirling around the retreating army like shoals of fish, flitting and weaving to avoid the fishermen's nets. The Avolonians were out of food and down to the last dregs of their water. The ground turned to sand, making the going more difficult. Edius-Max had just about reached the decision to halt and make a stand, deciding it better to die facing an enemy with a sword in hand than face down in the dust. Whatever the Lion Lord planned, Edius was sure it hadn't taken into account the army making such slow progress. The Mander had time to gather their forces; just by counting the banners, the General could tell the enemy was at full strength. Edius-Max hung his head, covering his eyes with his hand to give them a small respite from the stinging dust.

'General Sir!' a voice called out over the wind and clatter of an army on the move.

Edius moved his hand to see an officer on horseback with two scouts behind him.

'The scouts have returned to report, Sir.'

Edius sighed, then pulled the scarf off his nose and mouth to allow him to speak. 'Don't tell me, there's a river coming up. If it is, it will be the end of us. We need to turn and fight here. I'll give the order.'

'No sir,' the officer looked a little confused. 'It's the Lion Lord, Sir. His army awaits us only three or four leagues from here. We are saved.'

The General frowned. 'There are a hundred thousand heavily armed Mander right behind us. I wouldn't exactly say we are saved.' Edius welcomed the news, it just felt to him a little like he was jumping out of the frying pan and into the fire. 'Does he intend to advance to our position?'

One scout answered, 'No, sir, you are to keep moving at all cost until you reach them.'

Edius flushed red with anger. 'Does he not know our situation? Very well, give the order for the archers to lay down cover fire, while the rest of us pick up the pace.'

'But Sir,' the officer's voice quivered. 'I thought you knew. There are no arrows left. We've even shot back the ones we collected from the Mander.'

'Blast!' Edius thought for a moment. 'Order the Lion Warriors to form a shield-wall with the Lion Cavalry and Jagger Knights on each flank. Let's make it look like we mean to stand. That should give everyone else time to reach the Storm Legions. The order is to hold until an attack is imminent and then break. The infantry can hitch a ride with the cavalry. They won't like it, but it will get them out of there sharpish.'

'Let's hope those Mander bastards are the hesitant type, or else the blasted camp followers will be less than halfway to safety when they feel a blade at the back of their necks.' Antona joined in the conversation, arriving in time to catch the General's orders.

Edius-Max's lips curled into a mischievous grin. 'That's why your Storm Cavalry will be giving the slower ones a ride. Get as many of them as you can out of here as fast as you can and then come back for more.'

Antona considered protesting, thinking his cavalry better used to engage in the fight, when the Cid, General Memfis and General Renaldon turned up at the same time to receive their orders.

'Very well,' Antona capitulated, and set off to do his duty.

Arc

Chaos is a subjective state. There was order in the ranks, four Storm Legions and the Corinthians formed into rows of interlocked shields, bristling with spears. The Storm Cavalry was a complete contrast to their foot-soldier comrades. They galloped in and out of the Avolonian lines, women and children draped across riders' laps or seated behind them. Arc watched as the surviving camp followers were unceremoniously dropped at the feet of the army. Through squinting eyes he saw the cavalry unload their human cargo, then instantly turn around and head back out to fetch more. From time to time clouds of dust obscured the Lion Lord's view. The wind was annoying, and he longed to be inside.

As Enola made her way over to her father, the wind tugged at her cloak, lifting it up and flapping it around her body.

'General Antona reports that Edius-Max is making a stand to give . . .' Enola had to turn her head away from the wind and shut her eyes tight to protect them from the sand in the air. She waited for a gap in the gale before continuing, 'To give the civilians a chance to escape.'

Arc decided against struggling to be heard over the squall. He flicked his head towards the tent positioned a hundred paces behind the lines of warriors. A humongous structure approached the camp from the other side of the shelter, drifting through the swirling clouds of grit. Gavara had arrived with the Harpy. The great beast of a machine could be heard over the windstorm, creaking and groaning on the axle the old pathfinder had designed and built for her. Two teams of horses were pulling the monster weapon, whips cracking over their backs to keep them moving.

Gavara appeared out of the dust, a fragile figure wrapped from head to foot in canvas. He was being pushed from side to side by whirling gusts as he walked ahead of the Harpy. Gavara saw Arc and his daughter through a narrow slit in his wrappings. He followed them to the tent, almost tripping in his hurry to be out of the wind. The three of them converged on the shelter at the same time and entered together.

'What a terrible temperament this place has,' Gavara said, unrolling the cloth from his head. 'It's been like walking through hell on earth for the past day and a half.'

Sonaji was already in the shelter, clean and in a gown more suitable for palace life than a combat tent.

'It's a ridiculous place!' exclaimed Sonaji. 'No more than a day's ride from here we crossed meadows and travelled through forests. I have to say, it's not a pleasant experience crossing fields burned to destroy their crops, but how does it turn into a desert so quickly?'

'That's what happens when all the trees are cut down. Or when the land is over-farmed,' Gavara started to answer her question. Sonaji picked up a goblet, more interested in its contents than the old man's explanation. She swirled the wine and then took a gulp. Gavara continued, 'this was all once thick forest, full of life. They hunted animals, cut down trees and grew crops until they drained the ground of everything it had. Then they left.

When are folk going to understand that the natural world is self-sustaining, if left alone? We have to work with nature, not against her.'

Enola and Arc finished taking off their cloaks and used the water bowl provided to clean the grime from their faces before taking wine to wash the dust from their throats. Gavara did the same.

'Edius will have to retreat fast,' Arc continued the conversation Enola had started earlier, when they were out in the wind. 'We are not advancing to help him, we will hold our ground. If they chase him all the way to our lines, they will run into a shield wall and a hail of arrows and spears.'

'Good luck with the arrows in this wind,' Enola commented, refilling her goblet at the same time. 'I've already ordered the catapults and giant bows to the front. If they dip so much as a toe into our killing zone, we will greet them with a volley of pain and destruction.'

'Very wise, very wise,' Gavara repeated himself. 'Make them come to you, fight on your terms. I haven't been able to see much of this place, Arc, but I assume you have chosen well. You have always been talented at choosing the place of battle. I assume there's high ground to the south that will protect the flank?'

'There are also dunes to the north to help protect the other flank.' Arc gave his answer as if he was trying to impress his old mentor. 'It's not the terrain that attracts me to fight here. The nearest water is behind us, so Al-Din is far from his supplies and any freshwater. That will make his superior numbers work against him. We will let him come to us, but I can't allow him to make a standoff. We need to persuade him to bring the fight to us.'

'Oh, he will fight,' Gavara slumped into a seat. 'But, he will wait as long as he can. There are rumours that they have sent for the southern army. It can't possibly be the full might of Xarius' command, but they could well tip the balance.'

'Balance,' Enola scoffed. 'We are already outnumbered three to two. I think the balance is well and truly tipped.'

'That's nothing but hearsay,' Sonaji sprung to her feet and had to steady herself on the tent's centre pole. 'None of our scouts have seen this mythical army. Hold and defend that is your plan, and it's a good one.'

Arc raised an eyebrow. 'And I think you may have had enough wine for one night.'

'Darling, one can never have too much wine when stuck in a dust-scoured nowhere like this.' Sonaji sat again before she fell.

Enola huffed, but yells from outside prevented her from making any comment. Sonaji was the only one not to respond to the alarm being raised, as the other three grabbed their cloaks and rushed out of the tent.

The sound of horses' hooves drowned out the noise of the blustering wind. All three factions of the Avolonian Cavalry thundered across the dusty plain towards Arc's camp. A high cloud of sand and dust followed in their wake. Infantrymen clung to horses' bridles or to the pommel of a saddle, their legs bouncing wildly as they tried to run alongside the beasts. Lucky ones were seated behind riders, holding onto their waists. Arc knew those men well and was sure that they were more afraid to be on a horse than remaining behind to fight the enemy. Infantrymen did not appreciate horses. They were pleased enough to follow them while charging at the enemy, but they hated the thought of ever having to ride one.

Arc could not see if the enemy were in pursuit or not. The dust and the chaos obscured his view, but he did not hesitate to give the order. 'Artillery!' he called out, his voice cutting through the noise of wind and hooves just enough to reach the sergeants on either side of where he stood.

The catapults creaked as the cogwheels used to draw back their beams were levered over the last few notches into firing position. They had been loaded and drawn back earlier, to prepare for this moment, never more than two-thirds cocked so as not to damage them with prolonged tension. Arc waited until he thought the retreating troops were inside the range of his artillery before giving the order to fire. He had no way of knowing if more of his own warriors were behind the cloud of dust and sand, but to delay would be to invite disaster.

The air fizzled with the sound of boulders arcing through the sky. Men watched as the projectiles flew over the returning army and disappeared into the clouds of dust. Second and third volleys were ordered. Artillerymen worked frantically with levers to reload the war machines and fire again. Most of the returning warriors did not hesitate to take up positions on either flank. The Lion Warriors formed a phalanx on the right, and the Jagger Knights and Storm Cavalry dismounted and formed a shield wall on the left.

The People's Army, under the command of General Memfis, did not understand what they should do. Too many of them impeded the professional warriors. Fearsome sergeants bellowed at them to get out of the way and form up at the rear. Some did, but many others with too little experience just barged into positions where they could.

No attack came as the dust started to clear. The wind dropped to little more than a breeze, the occasional gust blowing as a reminder of its power. The Avolonian line was so still and quiet, it was as if it had been frozen in time, waiting for the enemy. Spears were lowered in the direction they expected the enemy to advance from, and swords drawn in readiness for the attack. Warriors listened to their own rapid heartbeats pounding in their ears. The air crackled with anticipation as the army waited with bated breath, shields tightly locked together.

The dust clouds parted to reveal horses lying on the ground. Some lay still, others kicked their legs as if trying to run. One or two struggled to get up without success. The dust cleared, and they could see the bodies of men scattered between fallen mounts. One of the enemy held on to his head and staggered. He fell to his knees and vomited. As the clouds of dust settled into no more than a grimy haze, the Mander army could be seen fleeing back to whence they came.

A loud cry rose from the full length of the Avolonian line. It was more cheering from relief than triumph, as they had not won the battle just turned back the cavalry giving chase to Edius-Max and his troops.

'I want prisoners!' Arc yelled.

Dozens of Avolonian riders sprang forward and were soon amongst the fallen Mander. The injured beasts were quickly euthanised, their meat a welcome addition to the army's meagre rations. Few of the felled warriors would live long enough to be of any use. Not many men hit by artillery fire lived to tell the tale. The majority never knew what happened to them before it snuffed out their life in an instant. Most of the injured who clung to life could not speak, or refused to talk knowing their survival to be unlikely.

Arc greeted Edius-Max with an uncharacteristic bear hug, neither man being known to have an affectionate nature.

'You look exhausted, man,' Arc held the General at arm's length. 'You led the bastards right to us.'

'I'm not sure I have done you any favours,' Edius responded.

Cid arrived and Arc turned to him, placing a hand on his shoulder. 'I'm deeply sorry to hear about the Grand Master.'

Cid bowed his head, and simply said, 'He's a brave Knight and a good friend.'

'You men need to rest,' Arc told them. 'See to your men, then come back to my tent. We will have a short briefing, then I insist you get some sleep.'

The vomiting man turned out to be the most likely to survive interrogation, so they took him back to camp with two others who could just about speak. The rest of the mortally wounded had their last flicker of life extinguished with a spike through the eye or a blade across their throat.

'It is as we feared,' Arc told the others who had returned with him to the shelter. 'Another army is travelling north to this position.'

'They already outnumber us. How far away is this army?' Enola asked. 'We need to attack and then turn to face the new threat.'

Arc scratched his chin, remembering what they had told him, then rubbed at the pain in his temple before replying. 'Three days march, four at most, the interrogated men seemed to think. I've sent scouts out to ascertain the accuracy of this intelligence. If the information is true, then Mander-Kush is practically wide open to attack. If we hadn't split the army, we could have changed tack and taken the capital.' Several in the room unconsciously lowered their eyes, knowing they were partly responsible for the decision to split the army. 'Then again, if we hadn't achieved such a convincing victory at Calinkerbad, these reinforcements would not be in such a hurry to get here, and Mander-Kush would still be well defended. The wise thing to do when outnumbered is to choose the right location to make a stand. I have chosen this place because it's as good as any to defend, and if we have to attack, the conditions will make it difficult for both sides. We have the advantage of water nearby, they don't, but we are starving, and they are not.' The Lion Lord saw that some of his Generals were eager to add comments to his words, but they had the good sense to wait for an invitation to speak. 'We must stand our ground and hope the Emperor is foolhardy enough to advance. If not, they will force us to advance on them before their reinforcements arrive.'

'Attack tomorrow,' Enola blurted out. Arc raised an eyebrow but did not prevent her from continuing. 'Scatter them to the winds before they can swell their numbers. From what I've seen, they are disorganised and have no heart for a real fight. We cut them in two at Calinkerbad. We can do it again here.'

There was a murmuring of agreement and lots of nodding heads around the room. Sonaji silenced them with a hiss.

'Nonsense, we are at our strongest when we stand and defend. The Mander losses will be great. The reinforcements will be as useless as pouring buckets of sand into a river, hoping to stem its flow.' Sonaji seemed to have recovered from the effects of the wine, speaking clearly again. 'It will wash away their lives like sand grains in the current.'

Arc considered both points. Turning to Edius-Max he asked, 'What did you observe, chaos or order?'

Edius-Max's expression was more grim than usual. Dark circles hung beneath his eyes as evidence of the ordeal he had just endured. He rubbed at several days-worth of stubble on his face. His once raven black beard was now completely grey. 'We caused chaos, but they regrouped well and gave an orderly pursuit. I cannot say the same for our auxiliary troops. They were ill-disciplined and easily broken. Hard to blame, their arms and armour are massively inferior to those of the enemy.'

'We can do something about that,' Gavara told them. 'There is a line of carts following the Harpy. They're full of the swords, shields and spears captured at Calinkerbad. I filled many of the carts with armour and boots. If they don't mind a little blood, the auxiliaries can have them.'

'Blood will wash off,' General Memfis gave a sullen reply. 'We will gratefully accept them. I can't guarantee it will make them better warriors, but a farmer with a good sword and shield is less likely to run away when the enemy come.' The quality of his troops was a great source of embarrassment to Memfis. He did everything in his power to train them and get them ready for battle. It seemed that no matter how often he drilled them, they were still farmers and traders at heart, ill-disciplined and clumsy in the battle lines. 'They will stand their ground,' Memfis added, seeing that he had lost the Lion Lords attention.

Arc's hands started to shake. The pain in his head intensified, and he found it hard to focus. He lifted his hand intending to rub at the pain, but the room suddenly went black.

Arc fell to the floor, shaking uncontrollably. The room was stunned, only Enola and Sonaji reacted, each letting out an involuntary shriek.

'Put a pillow under his head!' Electra called out. 'He's having a devil fit, my brother had them all the time.

Give him room and get a bloody cushion under his head, now!'

Electra barged through and had to place the cushion herself. Enola supported her father on one side and Sonaji supported him on the other.

'What must we do?' Enola looked up at Gavara, her eyes anxiously wide.

'Nothing we can do. It must pass naturally.' Gavara pushed the others further back to make more room. 'Give him space to breathe.'

'It will pass. My brother did this all the time as a child. He was always fine the next day,' Electra said to comfort Enola.

'Did your brother's fits last so long or have this level of intensity?' The worry made Sonaji's voice sound angry.

Electra shook her head.

Enola thought her father's fit would never stop. When it finally did, they lifted him onto a sofa. He lay there in a deep sleep.

Sonaji took control. 'As you know, officers of the Lion's army, I speak for the Lord when he is incapacitated. I say the discussions are over for one night. Return to your troops and prepare to defend our position.'

Enola rose from her place at her father's side intending to confront Sonaji. Gavara lowered his staff to block Enola's way and shook his head when she gave him a challenging glance.

The interaction between the two did not escape Sonaji's notice. 'Enola, your Storm Legions will dig in and defend. See to it.'

Enola became a seething volcano of anger, her lips clenched and her eyes bulging. Gavara looked to General Antona and General Electra for aid, and they coaxed their Commander out of the room.

Once out of the tent, Enola let out a scream. 'That blasted woman. Who does she think she is?'

Antona shushed her. 'Don't give her the satisfaction.'

Enola shook free of Antona's grip and headed towards her shelter. 'She poisons my father's ear,' she told her Generals as they followed. 'My father is sick, and she sends me away when I should be by his side. I see through her, she's nothing more than a power-hungry bitch.'

Enola ripped the flap of her tent open and stormed inside. Elektra and Antona gave each other a concerned look. They did not follow their Commander into the shelter, deciding it would be better to let her cool down in private. The two called a goodnight and headed back to their legions.

In the tent's dim light, Enola stripped off her armour along with every other stitch of clothing covered in irritating amounts of dust and sand. She brushed sand from her naked body with the flat of her hands, then crossed over to the small fire that had been set. She suddenly felt cold and threw another log into the burning bowl suspended by chains from a tri-pod. Enola reached for the jug of wine on a table next to the fire, filled a cup, drank it and then filled the cup again. It was then that she realised that something was not quite right.

There weren't any servants in camp, they had all been left behind in Calinkerbad. Enola was so accustomed to being tended to that she thought nothing of the luxuries awaiting her until now. She was suspicious, and looked around the tent, her eyes widening when she saw a figure step out of the shadows.

Jenaliena stood there, grinning, the light from the flickering flames making her shadow dance on the canvas wall. She took two steps towards Enola and then pushed the straps of her dress off her shoulders. Enola watched the gown float to the floor, gulped down the wine, and threw the empty cup into the fire. The two women stepped into each other's embrace and kissed passionately. No words came from either of them, only the pursuit of their lust until both women were satisfied.

'What are you doing here?' Enola tried to sound displeased.

Jenaliena laughed and pulled a fur cover over them. 'You can't say you are disappointed to see me after a greeting like that' Her mood darkened. 'I didn't tell you at the time, but the night you left, I had a dream.'

'You were so bothered by a dream that you came rushing out to a war zone?'

'It was no ordinary dream. I saw myself kneeling on top of you in bed.'

'Sounds more like wishful thinking than a nightmare to me,' Enola interrupted, a wry smile on her face.

'I was franticly trying to wake you, shaking and shaking you, but you would not wake up. It seemed so urgent, and I looked so afraid. I asked Gavara to bring me here, on the carts.'

'And he let you come? It doesn't seem like anything out of the ordinary to me.'

Jenaliena gave an over-exaggerated frown. 'I told Gavara about the dream, he was concerned. He said,' she thought for a moment, 'that to see yourself in a dream was to have met your own ghost. He thought it serious enough to let me come along.'

'That's just typical Gavara, always looking for omens and signs from the spirit world.'

'He said our subconscious minds see and understand so much more than we know. He thinks I have subconsciously seen something coming, an evil stalking you or harm that will happen to you. I don't know what yet but, at least if I'm here, I may be able to recognise it or stop it before it happens.'

Enola shrugged, and tried to not let Jenaliena's concern affect her, 'What of Zac? Did you find him?'

'He's safe, with the big guy, Jonotrix.'

Enola rolled over onto her back, pulling Jenaliena over to rest her head on her chest.

'I need to sleep,' Enola mumbled, seconds before she started to snore.

The shaking fit left Arc exhausted. He slept deeply, his dreams all blood and blades as he fought his way through battle after battle. The faces of men he had slain on the blood-drenched fields of combat returned to haunt him, forcing him to fight them once more. Voices of friends long-dead called out to him in the heat of the fight, but no matter how hard he tried, he failed to save them from their lethal fate.

Amongst the chaos and destruction, one voice sounded calm, kind words drifting out of the mist of battle. Arc recognised the gentle tones of the voice, but unable to find a face to go with it amongst the dead and the dying. The Lion Lord pushed the cries of men and the din of war out of his mind, attempting to find the owner of the soothing voice. A face began to form in the fog that rolled over the lands of Arc's nightmares.

'Jem.' The name tasted like warm honey on Arc's lips. His wife's ghost smiled and lifted a hand to his cheek. All else was silent as he sank into the calmness that arrived with Jem's spirit. Arc drank in the vision of his departed soulmate. She wore his favourite dress made from powder blue chiffon, its folds pressed against the curves of her body by the slightest of breezes. Jem's stare was every bit as penetrating as it had been in life; he desired once more to be drawn in by her blue eyes. Her silken auburn hair lifted as the air weaved through its tresses. Jem had a kind face, slim but round, her full lips matching the colour of the terracotta tiles that lined the roofs of Highground, not too red with just the right amount of brown.

Guilt prodded Arc, threatening to spoil his newfound calmness. He remembered the rope placed around her neck by the Mander. Never would he forget the look of love she gave him, a parting gift, as she fell from the wall. Arc recalled the sense of hopelessness as he watched his tormentors end the love of his life's existence. His heart tightened as he again pictured her final tear drop falling from her eye as she dropped from the wall. Jem recognised the pain in her husband and took his hand.

They both sat and gazed into each other's eyes. Arc tried to say he was sorry for not protecting her from evil, but she raised a finger to his lips to silence him before he uttered his first syllable.

'Do not worry about me,' she told him. 'You have two daughters who depend on you. Tend to their needs, don't allow others to distract you or squander the love that is rightfully Fawn's and Cubb's.'

A sadness pressed down on Arc's shoulders to hear his wife talk about their children. When she had passed, the girls were so young. Both Cubb and her grandmother, Chick, had perished at the hands of the Mander.

'Fawn has taken her confirmation name. Now, she is Enola, and Commands a great army,' Arc whispered the words with pride.

'You are too hard on her,' Jem scalded him. 'She cannot be the boy you always wanted. Hers is only half a heart without her sister. They must find each other to be whole again.'

Jem's words confused him, but Arc felt himself awakening before he could reply. He heard her voice again, but now it was entangled with sounds from the real world, and the fog swirled in again, hiding Jem from him.

'Don't be the tyrant, search your heart and save your daughters.' The last words faded into the mist as Arc began to awake.

Gavara's stick-like figure, fiddling with bottles and vials from his wooden medical chest, was the first thing Arc saw as he awoke. The old man must have sensed Arc's eyes burning into the back of his head because he spun around and crossed the room to greet him.

Gavara stood by the couch, leaning over Arc. 'Welcome back. Drink this, it will calm the sweats.' He handed him a cup.

'How long have I …?' Arc cut his question short, the pain in his head screwing up his face.

'Been out?' Gavara finished the question for him. 'For a night and a morning. It is only to be expected, I fear it will only get worse.'

Arc tried to get up, but Gavara placed a bony hand on his shoulder to stop him.

'Drink the potion fist, it will give you strength and take some of the pain from your head. When that's working, I'll give you another for the dizziness. And, before you ask, all is in hand with the army. Sonaji ordered that we hold our position. The Mander are doing the same. So, it's a standoff, and it won't make one jot of difference if you rush out there now or take an hour to strengthen yourself for the task first.'

Arc sighed, he knew his old friend was right. He drank the potion and scraped his tongue with his teeth several times to remove the disgusting aftertaste.

Gavara recognised sadness in his friend's eyes. 'These fits take too much from you. You have lived longer than I ever hoped for when I nursed you back to life from that terrible head wound. I fear the fits will only worsen.' He clasped his hand to his chest as if clutching at his heart, struggling to find his next words and unable to hide the pity in his eyes.

'If you're going to tell me these fits will kill me, don't bother. I get it, I never planned to reach old age. Looking at your creaky old body makes me think it nothing but a blessing. But, I want to see this crusade through to the end. If we win here, Mander-Kush is ours, and the Empire will fade into memory.'

'Then you must keep up your strength and maintain a sharp mind.'

Arc laughed. 'It will be easier to be strong than to be sharp. I'm sleeping too little, with the obvious exception, and when I do, my nightmares haunt me for days. It makes me forget too many things. I can't recall the names of officers I promoted only days ago.'

'Yet you remember names and events from your childhood as if they were yesterday,' Gavara interrupted.

The sorrow flooded back into Arc's eyes. 'Jem, my wife came to me while I slept. I remember her last moments as if they were happening now. The Mander tore half my heart from my chest that day. The giant bastard, Garlion ripping the other half out when he plunged his blade into my darling Cubb. His bones may be rotting in the fields of Caputhora, but I carry the consequences of that day wherever I go.'

Gavara felt a lump in his throat and sat on a stool next to Arc. He had played his part in creating the feared warrior that was the Lion Lord by allowing him to believe his youngest daughter had perished, when in truth, she was safe in the mountains of the Frozen Kingdom. The girl Arc had seen the monstrous General cut in two, was a child so alike Cubb that both the Mander and Arc were fooled into believing it was her.

The old man's conscience plucked at his heartstrings, it was time to confess. He had watched for too long as hatred and loathing tore at the flesh of his friend's soul.

'There is something I must tell you before it is too late,' Gavara stuttered.

He did not get the chance to complete his confession. Horns sounded the alarm; Arc jumped from the sofa, grabbed Leovesica, his trusted blade, and his lion's head helmet, and was out of the tent before Gavara stuttered another word.

Chapter 6

Arc

Banners flapping in the wind filled the horizon. It was a bright day, even hotter than the previous one. Arc rode Armageddon to where he could see his own colours flying.

'Make way for the Lord!' a diligent officer called out, and a path opened through the ranks of warriors. Men cheered to see their leader well and in the saddle of his warhorse. Dark rumours circulated about the Lion Lord's wellbeing, and the army was pleased to see them untrue. The cheers muffled by the scarves tied around mouths to keep out the dust. Arc had no scarf and looked as if he defied the wind and the dust. Defiance was not his intention; he had simply forgotten his scarf, and he found it difficult to breathe. He would cover his nose and mouth against the irritation at the next opportunity.

'What's happening?' Arc asked, pulling Armageddon to a halt in front of the gathered Generals. Sonaji sat confidently on the great white stallion Arc had received from Enola. She was not a warrior, but dressed in an overly ornate set of armour specially made for her. Arc thought about sending her back to the camp and reprimanding his staff for allowing her near the front line. He decided against it. He'd been incapacitated overnight, and they had done what they thought was best in the circumstances.

'Sir, should you be out here? Are you recovered?' Memfis asked what everyone else was thinking.

A stern look from Arc was enough to make Memfis realise his mistake. He had asked the questions out of genuine concern, but would receive no thanks from his commander for pointing out his weakness.

'I'm fine,' Arc snapped. 'Now, do I have to ask again?'

Edius-Max spoke for the group. 'We have taken up defensive positions, as per your wishes and the instructions of Lady Sonaji.'

'And the alarm?'

'We thought the Mander were advancing, but they were only wheeling out that huge contraption.'

'Is that what I think it is?' Arc threw the question out to anyone.

'The Queen of Death,' Memfis answered. 'I watched them throw my father down that diabolical thing, along with two hundred of his men at the siege of Arndalin.'

'I'm sorry,' Arc told him. 'My stepbrother, Davos, spoke of this abomination. The Mander used it in the mountains above Highground to terrorise our warriors.'

'It's a usual Mander tactic we have seen too often before,' Enola cut in. 'They mean to provoke an attack from us by committing atrocities. We did the same to them with no success at Calinkerbad,' Enola felt compelled to point out, if only to prick Tyezore's conscience for the cruelty he'd shown the prisoners he'd tortured and executed. 'Do you not think we should deny them the pleasure of torturing us and attack now? We are only delaying the inevitable.'

'Hold your nerve!' Sonaji screeched at Enola. 'We stand our ground, make them advance. Let this Empire die on the spears of our phalanx.'

Arc could see the two women in his life locked in a hateful stare. He realised he had better do something before Enola's temper snapped, he feared for Sonaji's safety.

'Lincon!' Arc barked at the captain of his guards. 'Escort the Lady Sonaji back to the safety of my quarters. Ensure she is comfortable and well protected before returning here.'

Sonaji's cheeks flushed red with anger, she wanted to disagree so strongly that it tasted like bile in the back of her throat. She knew it was pointless to say anything, to challenge the Lion Lord on the battlefield would be a mistake that would threaten to destroy the core of their relationship. The bedchamber was where she was at her strongest, so she would save this fight for there.

Lincon tried to take hold of Zanthus' reins, but Sonaji snatched them out of his reach and flicked her heels so that the white stallion lurched towards Arc. She leaned over and whispered into the Lion Lord's ear and then rode off towards the camp with Lincon in pursuit. A look of shock lingered for a moment on Arc's face, fading instantly when he heard trumpets sounding from the Mander contraption. The blast on the horns was obviously to attract the Avolonians' attention.

The Queen of Death is a killing machine about four men high. They wheeled the tower forward on a wooden chassis and had steps leading up to an elaborate platform. A slide of shining metal dropped steeply from the front of the deck, curving outwards about halfway down, and then rapidly falling away again at the end. The slide started as a smooth and wide shoot, but as it began to curve, the metal folded away into a blade. Sand, carried on the breeze, rattled against the blade, playing a metallic tune that made hairs stand on end.

Arc and his officers watched as a prisoner was forced up the steps and out onto the platform. The man was a Jagger Knight, his hands tied behind his back. He stood at the edge of the podium, trying to appear defiant with two spears lowered towards his back. Flags positioned all over the tower excitedly snapped and twisted in the wind. The Emperor and his entire entourage moved forward of their own defences to take up a position with a better view of events to come.

'What's he doing?' Antona asked, pointing out a lone figure walking ahead of Al-Din's party.

A single warrior advanced, dressed in more armour than any of the Avolonians had ever seen a man wear. He carried a long sword over his shoulder. It was a huge weapon that looked like it had been taken from a colossal statue. He stopped in the open ground about midway between the two opposing lines. Placing the tip of the sword in the sand and clasping both hands around the hilt, at chest height, he just stood there.

The horns sounded again, just to make sure they had our attention. A long silence followed that even the wind seemed to obey. Avolonian eyes fixed on the man standing at the top of the tower, their guts churning with anxious anticipation. The man twisted, prodded in the shoulder with a spear. Then his feet were kicked out from under him, and he dropped onto the slide.

It happened in a blink of an eye, but the speed did not hide the horror from vision. Crimson wings of blood opened up on each side of the blade, as the prisoner's body sliced in two. The pieces of the man's body thudded to the ground on either side of the Death Slide, like half carcases of a butchered pig thrown from a cart. Blood splatter painted two outstretched arms in the dusty ground. The entire Avolonian line gasped in horror.

Arc looked towards the Cid, the Knight's face frozen with anguish. There was another short blast on the horns, and a lone rider galloped out from Al-Din's advanced party. The Mander herald carried a banner which seemed out-of-place. The messenger came to a halt a cautious distance from the Avolonian line and in front of Arc's banner.

'That's Razor's family crest,' Cid growled through gritted teeth.

The herald threw the banner into the dust at the Avolonians' feet. 'That belongs to him,' he twisted in his saddle to glance back at the Death Slide.

Most concentrated on the rider, so no one noticed another figure ascending the scaffold. Their eyes widened when they saw the Grand Master standing at the edge of the slide.

Cid could not contain himself and shook with anger. Arc moved to the Knight's side and placed a hand on his shoulder to steady him.

'As you see,' the herald called out. 'Your Grand Master is about to be welcomed by the Queen of Death. The most exulted Al-Din, light of the world and ruler of all that is earthly, is a most merciful ruler. He offers you the opportunity to win back the life of your precious Master of Knights.'

'It's a trap,' Arc spoke from the side of his mouth. 'They will never let Razor live. They are toying with us for their amusement.'

'All you have to do,' the messenger continued, 'is to send a champion to fight our champion. The Granite Knight, there,' he glanced over his shoulder, 'is a new breed of warrior, an Ephielite from the far-east. Our exulted leader has a desire to see how you fare against him in combat. Beat him and your Grand Master goes free.' The herald held up a timing glass. 'But, you must do it in one turn of this glass or the contest is forfeit, and your Grand Master slides.'

Arc took a tight grip of Cid's shoulder. 'This is a trap. I forbid you to fight. Razor is condemned whether or not you fight.'

The Avolonian front ranks cheered. Sir Peregrine rode out towards the Granite Knight.

'Blast, damn him!' Arc yelled, realising it was too late to call him back.

Cid grinned. 'Sir Peregrine is a good Knight. He holds himself responsible for the loss of the Grand Master. His soul would never find peace in this life or the next if he did not take this chance to save Razor and redeem himself.'

'He's a bloody fool who will die for nothing,' Memfis grumbled. 'No disrespect meant.'

'He is right to obey what his heart commands,' Cid defended his comrade.

The herald rode off to join the two warriors at the centre of the field. Sir Peregrine dismounted, fixed his arm into his shield's straps, and drew his sword. The Granite Knight took his mighty sword in both hands and turned the point skyward. Sir Peregrine circled, but his opponent followed his movements without leaving the spot.

'Let the contest begin!' the herald called out from the saddle, turning the sand-filled glass to start the time.

Sir Peregrine lunged forward and began a savage attack on the Knight. He repeatedly struck left and right with lightning speed. He failed to drive his rival back, and his blade did little more than scratch the Knight's granite coloured armour. Sir Peregrine was shocked by the power that came with the Knight's first sword swing. He was sent reeling backwards by the strike, his shield buckled by the impact. As Sir Peregrine staggered back, dust rose from his steps, caught on the wind and was carried away like smoke.

The Jagger Knight knew in an instant that he could not overpower his adversary, he would need to wear him down or catch him off balance. He looked to the timing glass, his eyes widening when he realised it was almost half empty. There was no time for his strategy, he would have to attack like a mongoose on a cobra, dancing and twisting to avoid the serpent's strike until it made a mistake.

A sound of metal on metal rang out like an alarm bell, as Sir Peregrine unleashed a tempest of blows at the Granite Knight. The Ephielite skilfully used his giant blade to block the well-aimed blows. On the few occasions the Granite Knight countered with blows of his own, they came close to knocking Sir Peregrine off his feet.

The Jagger Knight was running out of time and desperate to strike a killing blow. He risked everything to get close enough to slip his blade between any of the narrow gaps in the joints of the Knight's armour. Sir Peregrine waited until his opponent made a mighty swing and then, ducked under the huge blade and thrust his own sword up at a gap in the Granite Knight's armpit. The blade hit chain-mail, and Sir Peregrine's heart leapt in his chest when he felt the metal tunic give way to his thrust.

Sir Peregrine's joy was short-lived as his rival closed the gap by switching the direction of his swing. The blade had not penetrated deep enough into the armpit to do any severe damage, and the blade was now trapped in the folds of the granite armour. Sir Peregrine was too focused on retrieving his blade to see the danger posed by the Granite Knight's reverse swing. The mighty sword hit the upper part of the Jagger Knight's shield arm, cutting through metal, flesh and bone as if they were rope. The blade sliced entirely through the arm and almost its full width into Sir Peregrine's breastplate.

The Jagger Knight went rigid, his shield falling to the dusty ground, his severed arm still in the holding straps. A growl of triumph came from the Granite Knight as he stepped back, pulling his sword free of the breastplate. Sir Peregrine felt the warm blood flowing down his side. He was surprised to feel nothing from the stump of his severed arm. His body was racked with pain, but he could not pinpoint it to his wounds. He tried to swing his sword one more time, but it was knocked easily from his grip by his foe.

The Granite Knight lifted his fearsome sword to make the killing blow but hesitated as he watched his challenger sway. Sir Peregrine felt his strength drain away and fell to his knees. He looked up, not at the great Knight about to take his life, but at his Grand Master, standing on the platform. He had failed his leader again, and imagined Razor looking down on him, disappointed. Sir Peregrine's heart wrenched in two at the thought of spending an eternity in his Grand Master's disapproval.

The Granite Knight put an end to his rival's anxieties when he cleft the Knight's head in two with one mighty downward swing.

Cheering came from the Mander lines. Arc watched as his enemy waved their banners, enjoying the spectacle of death.

'It has begun,' Arc said into the wind. 'We are playing their game now, and it will not end until one of us breaks.'

All eyes were on Razor, still standing on the edge of the platform, waiting to die. Moments of expectation passed, but the Grand Master was not pushed from the platform. Instead, the herald rode back to the Avolonian lines.

Memfis huffed. 'He must have a pair on him to come back here, after that.' He turned in his saddle to the foot soldiers. 'Give me a feckin' spear, I'll stick the bastard.'

No one took the General seriously and continued to watch the herald's approach.

'I have been instructed to make you a gift of another chance to save the leader of the Jagger Knights.' The herald searched amongst the gathering of officers until his eyes met with Arc's. 'My exulted Emperor, the all-wise and all-knowing Al-Din, will give the Grand Master a stay of execution. The conditions are that a Lord challenges the Granite Knight, and, as before, if he defeats the Ephielite, Grand Master Razor will go free.'

'I am a Lord,' Cid called out. 'I will fight your champion.'

Cid started to ride forward.

Arc blocked his way by putting Armageddon in front of him. 'Mourn Razor, he is already dead, there is nothing you can do.'

The Cid was not a man who could let this go. He had been weaned on breastmilk laced with generations of Jagger honour. Arc also knew that the Mander toyed with them, dangling the prize close enough to give hope but never close enough to take. The Mander were famous for their psychological warfare, experts at finding that one thing that would feel like a dagger through the heart and destroy their fortitude.

'Sorry,' the herald suddenly called out. 'I may have used the wrong expression when I said, "A Lord." What I meant to say was "The Lord," the Lion Lord.'

Arc spat to the side in a superstitious gesture to avert evil. He did not look towards the herald, keeping his eyes firmly fixed on the Cid. The Lion Lord could clearly see his own dilemma in the Knight's expression; it would now be seen as his fault when Razor was pushed down the Death Slide. Arc racked his mind to find a smart way out of the situation, he even looked around for Gavara, but his old friend was busy with other things.

'A man cannot be afraid to die for his desires or his responsibilities,' Arc said, with no confirmation of whether or not that meant he would fight.

Cid cleared his throat, attempting to hide the emotion he knew would show in his voice. 'You are right,' he took a deep breath. 'I see it now, they will resort to any measure they can to torment us. We cannot pander to their games and allow them to use the hostages against us. I would do anything to save the Grand Master or any of the captured Knights from the monstrous fate awaiting them. But, I know in my heart, that given a choice, Razor would order us not to let them use him in this way.'

Arc shook his head. 'No, they have been too clever. I see hope in the eyes of your Knights. Not until they have seen for themselves the evil we face, will they understand.' He turned to the herald. 'I will fight your champion!' The Avolonian Generals groaned, as the herald rode off with the news.

Arc turned back to his warriors. 'Mark my words, this will be the last challenge we accept. No matter the outcome, or whatever follows, no soldier is to leave the line. Send the archers forward. Anyone taking more than three steps forward from our lines is to be shot. Give the order along the line.'

Arc took off his helmet. 'Fetch me the lion's head.' He studied the helmet in his hands. The sides and the nosepiece had scratches and dints from other battles mixed in with ornamental engravings. The mantel was a small head of a lion raised on a plinth topped with a brush imitating a mane. Fondness was not the reason he took time to view the helmet in detail, he was trying to gauge the steadiness of his hands without anyone noticing. He saw the slightest tremble in his fingers and sighed. A doubt crept into Arc's mind. He was not afraid to die or worried that his courage would not hold up, but he worried that his body would let him down.

An aid came running with the lion helmet, its mane tangling in his legs as he ran. 'Here you are, Sir.'

Arc swapped the helmets and placed the beast's head onto his own. A cheer came from the warriors around the Lion Lord.

'Give me your shield,' Arc told one of the infantry warriors close by, as he unfastened his own from his back. 'My cavalry shield will be no use against that oversized blade, and Cid, give me that massive club you keep strapped to your horse.'

Cid looked down to where the weapon was fastened. 'You mean the mace?'

Arc nodded and held out his hand so that the Knight could pass it to him.

'You don't have to do this.' Cid held onto the mace while he spoke to Arc.

'Yes, I do.'

Arc knew the futility of what he did. He had been drawn out of his lines to fight a Mander champion once before. The demon left behind in his head after that encounter was still stalking the shadows of his mind. He had killed the giant, Garlion, on the battlefield of Caputhora, but failed to save his daughter. He suddenly remembered that it was Enola's intervention that probably saved him on that day.

'You stay out of this,' Arc told Enola, pointing the mace at her.

The Lion Lord rode Armageddon towards the Granite Knight, his ears filled with the cheering and banging of shields from the Avolonians. On hearing the Lion Lord would fight, the Emperor's chariot drove closer to the action, surrounded by his entourage of champions, Generals and guards. Arc glanced back at his own lines and gave them a stern look to ensure they did not advance. The archers were already in position, so no one was going to disobey Arc's order to stay put.

Arc pulled up Armageddon thirty paces short of the Granite Knight, close to the herald.

'What, no banners or squires for the great Lion Lord?' the herald asked, his confidence every bit as cynical as his words.

Arc curled his lips into a snarl. He had no need for banners; the enemy knew who he was, and his army certainly did. The lion head helmet, visible from a distance, no one was going to be in any doubt who they faced when they fought Arc. He lowered his head, fixing a determined stare on the Knight, pulled his shield tight into his chest and took a firm grip of the mace.

The Granite Knight did nothing, said nothing, just stood there in silence, gripping the hilt of the giant sword with both hands, its tip resting in the sand between his feet. Armageddon snorted and stamped at the ground with a foreleg as if he was readying for battle.

'Not this time, old friend, this is my fight, and mine alone.' Arc gave the warhorse a nudge with his shoulder before setting off towards the Knight.

The herald tried to give a pompous speech about the timing glass and the rules, but Arc was too focused on his rival to take any notice. Every step the Lion Lord took was filled with determination. He did not hesitate or wait for the herald to start the contest, Arc walked straight into combat. The Knight, momentarily startled by Arc's directness, fumbled to raise his sword in time to meet Arc's advance.

The two warriors clashed with some force. Arc rammed his shield into his enemy's chest and face, already too close for the huge sword to stop him. The Knight had power enough to swing Arc around and away from him, precisely what the Lion Lord wanted him to do. Arc struck his opponent on the back of the head with the mace. The blow caused the Knight to stagger forward, but he quickly recovered and swung the oversized blade as if he had never lost his footing.

Arc moved like greased lightning to get back close to the Knight, taking the sword blow on his shield. He was so close that the Knight could not bring the swing's full force to bear, but the impact still had enough power to deaden Arc's shield arm. The Lion Lord used the force to roll him past the Knight for a second time, again he struck the back of his rival's head with the mace. There was a clang that sounded like a gong strike. This time the spiked club crushed in part of the Knight's helmet, causing him to stagger several steps forward.

Arc rushed in to strike the opponent twice more before the Knight swung his sword again. The blow struck Arc's shield with enough force to crush the centre of the metal disc, sending an excruciating pain through Arc's arm.

His teeth slammed together, dazing him and blood sprang from his nose.

The Granite Knight sensed his moment had come when Arc slumped to one knee, dropping his shield. Raising his sword, the metal-clad Warrior pointed it down at Arc's back and thrust with all his might. The blade struck the ground with force, but Arc had already rolled to the side. He leapt up high, using the elevation to slam the mace down onto the Knight's helmet, crushing it enough to make him stagger.

Arc had dropped his shield intentionally, placing it between his enemy's legs. The Knight tripped on it, and before he could recover, Arc launched himself onto his foe's back. The Knight fell forward, forced to drop his sword and put out his hands to break his fall. There was a mighty crash as all that armour hit the ground. Arc rose to his feet, dazed and staggering to find his balance. The Knight started to rise, pushing himself up onto all fours.

Arc reacted quickly, pounding the back of his rival's head with the mace, and using his foot to push the Knight down again. The Lion Lord hooked the mace onto his belt and drew Breath Taker, his sword, before jumping onto the pile of armour. The Knight bucked and struggled with fury to try to dislodge his enemy. Arc balanced as if he stood on a raft in the rapids, placing the point of the sword on his foe's neck to steady himself. He worked the blade under the lip of the armoured neck guard until he found the aventail, a curtain of mail that hung from the helmet.

As the Granite Knight felt the point of the sword touch the base of his neck, he attempted to roll. Arc pressed a foot against his opponent's shoulder and wasted no time in forcing the blade through the aventail and into the Knight's neck. The point stopped when it hit the bone, but it did not stop the Knight from bucking with everything he had. Arc unhooked the mace from his belt and used it to hammer the sword through his enemy's spine. Under the force of the blows, the bone gave way, and the Knight went still.

Arc looked towards the timing glass, relieved to see it not yet empty. The herald's eyes bulged with surprise, his mouth wide open.

'Release him to me,' Arc pointed up at Razor.

Cheering came from the Avolonian lines, but the Grand Master did not appear jubilant. He had told his captors he would jump rather than be used against his friends, so they tied his hands behind his back and put a chain around his neck, the other end held by a guard to prevent him committing any noble acts. Razor jerked his head towards the Mander line, trying to draw the Lion Lord's attention to something.

Arc looked towards the Emperor's location and saw another Knight on horseback riding in his direction. This warrior carried a lance and a cavalry shield, shaped like a kite. This warrior was armoured more conventionally, with light plates not too heavy for his grey mount, and loose white robes that lifted and swirled as he rode.

'Get out of here!' Razor shouted from the platform. 'They will never let...' his words cut off by a tug of the chain.

'What treachery is this?' Arc hissed at the herald.

'My exulted Emp... Emperor has many cham... champions,' the herald stuttered, worried that the Avolonian was coming for him. 'He answers to no one, so if he changes the rules, we obey. I assume he intends you to fight them all.'

'Or two or three at a time when that fails,' Arc said under his breath, no longer paying any attention to the herald.

The Lion Lord sheathed Breath Taker, and picked up the dead Knight's humongous sword, before mounting Armageddon. His next challenger was almost upon him, quickening the pace of his mount and lowering his lance when he saw Arc climb on his horse. Armageddon was elated to be in the fight, racing towards their challenger like a giddy pony, only three times as big. Arc held the long sword like a lance. The new contender must have been grinning widely when he saw his lion-headed adversary attacking without a shield. He leaned into his lance and braced for the impact, his own shield covering his neck and torso, aiming the tip of the weapon at Arc's chest.

The Lion Lord waited until the last second to drop back in his saddle, lifting his legs high to balance and guide the blade with his foot towards his enemy. Arc felt the point of the javelin scrape over the rim of the lion helmet a split second before he was almost jolted off the horse's back when his sword struck the Knight. The blade was wrenched from his grip, and he instantly righted himself in the saddle. He pulled on the reins to bring Armageddon to a halt, turning in time to see his rival fall from the saddle. The huge sword had gone through the Knight's shield, breastplate and out of his back. The man was dead before he hit the ground.

A short blast on a horn came from the direction of the Mander and two more riders raced out towards Arc.

'Save yourself Arc, I'm a dead man!' Razor called from the high deck. 'You know it. I will not let them have you too!'

The Grand Master did not fear death; he had lived a life as bright as the summer sun, filled with honour and heroic deeds. The humiliation of his enemy using him against the Knights he loved so dearly clawed at his soul. The desire for an honourable end to his life was overwhelming, and he would not tolerate his leader sacrificing himself for the slightest hope of saving an old man.

Arc had always known it was folly for him to accept the challenge. He knew the Mander only kept Razor alive as leverage against him. Arc sure, as was Razor, that the moment they had no more use for him, they would push the Grand Master down the Death Slide. Razor tried to jump, but the Mander holding the chain anticipated the move and firmly pulled him back. The guard did not expect the Grand Master to switch direction to fly at him. Razor twisted around his guard, entangling him in the chain. The man yelled to his companion for help, but he was too slow to react. Razor dropped low, using the power in his legs to hurl them both off the platform, bound together by the links.

The two men crashed against the slide, landing just above the blade, their shackles ringing like a bell as metal struck metal. In the blink of an eye, both men were cleaved in two, top from bottom, their body parts falling to the ground like an overhang of snow dropping from a roof. Razor had his wish, and the Mander would have no further sport at his expense. Arc's stomach churned at witnessing such a cruel end to his friend, but his thoughts soon turned to his own survival. He would not run, instead, drawing the Lion Blade, Breath Taker as he called her.

Arrows suddenly flew over Arc's head, he turned to see Avolonian archers running towards him, and Enola riding in his direction, her bow at full stretch. Mander archers soon joined the two new challengers, running out to meet the Avolonian threat. Mander Cavalry were racing towards the Death Slide, and Arc realised the danger. He turned Armageddon and headed back to his own lines, careful not to make it seem like he fled. Arc, concerned that his own troops would be panicked into an attack wanted to calm them and quash any advance before it started.

The herald must have thought his number was up as the Lion Lord rode in his direction, but instead of drawing his sword against the quaking messenger, Arc gave him a message.

'Tell your exulted Emperor, I'm coming for him.'

Blue skies persisted over the desolate ground between the two armies. Strong winds came and went, and then came again, blowing the sand from one side of the plain before changing direction to return the grains whence they came. The Mander held about forty Jagger Knights captive. For the rest of the day, those poor souls were marched out one by one and dispatched by the Death Slide. The great tongue of steel reached down into a small lake of blood. The slide was flanked on either side by piles of indistinguishable flesh, body parts jumbled together to appear like a monster climbing out of a child's nightmare. A multitude of carrion-eating birds squabbled and fought over the bounty of flesh. All-day long Mander riders jeered, shouting insults and challenges at the Avolonians, hoping to badger them into a fight.

Arc had his archers' fire upon any Mander heralds or challengers who dared approach, preventing them from tormenting his army or luring any of them out of the lines. He sent for Gavara and asked if he thought the Harpy could take out the Death Slide. The vile contraption was out of the range of conventional artillery, but Arc hoped it was within range of the colossal catapult. A shake of

Gavara's head gave the answer. He worked frantically to put back inline the pulleys and gears of the monstrous artillery piece; all its workings having been knocked out of alignment on the bumpy journey from Calinkerbad.

With the Harpy option off the table, Arc ordered the whole army to draw back several hundred paces to where they did not have to witness the demise of their comrades. To anyone with eyes, the Jagger Knights' anguish was apparent and heart-wrenching. Men of their order, friends, even lifelong companions, died in the most horrendous fashion.

The Cid had the Knights dismount, and their horses taken out to graze, not that there was any grass in this dust-choked place, where life lay dormant deep beneath the parched earth waiting for a rare deluge to awaken growth. The horses would have to make do with the dried husks of desert grass that clung to existence in that desolate place. Cid feared that many of the Knights would be unable to restrain themselves from making a dash to save a friend. It would not help to get themselves killed in a valiant act, or worse, cause the deaths of many others who may follow them. Cid led his Knights in prayer for the condemned men. Hundreds of Jagger Knights knelt with their hands clasped and their heads bowed.

Arc had initially moved the army back so they did not have to witness Mander cruelty in detail. It only dawned on him later that the withdrawal was more to his advantage than he first thought. It would worry the Mander that the Avolonians were thinking of escaping. Even if they were not fooled into an attack, it would force them into overstretching themselves to stay close to their enemy.

The Lion Lord gathered his officers in a Council of War. He gave them the news that Mander reinforcements were no more than two days' march away. It was already late in the day and evident that their enemy would not attack.

'If we wait any longer, we will miss the opportunity to smash the Emperor's army before it is swollen by a river of soldiers flowing down from Mander-Kush,' Arc told the room full of officers. 'Break him now, and it will be too late for the reinforcements; we can turn on an unprotected Mander capital, sweeping them out of the way as we go.'

The decision was made, the Avolonians would attack the next day. Scouts ran in and out of the war tent with intelligence on Mander positions, their strengths and weaknesses. By the time night fell, the War Council had committed to a plan. Now, all they needed was for the daylight to return. Arc dismissed his officers with the insistence that they took some rest.

'Excuse me, Lord,' Gavara took a hold of Arc's arm. 'There is one more thing I think you should consider.'

'Lord? You never call me, Lord, Gavara. It must be something serious.'

The old man led his friends away from the others, not wishing to be overheard. 'I know the Emperor well from my time at his court. There will be a turning point in the battle. Al-Din has his veterans, he saves them as a last resort. He has never had to deploy them since the great Madesimo, Davos' father, pushed him to the brink of defeat, many years ago.'

'We can handle his old guard,' Arc said.

Gavara nodded. 'I believe you can, but I'm not being very clear. The veterans are not the danger. Al-Din has an attack weapon that is a danger to your success. As he has taken a defensive stance, he won't use it unless he is losing.'

Arc huffed. 'If he is losing, then we are amongst them, and he can't use any great weapon against us without killing his own men.'

'Not a weapon as such. Elephants, you have seen the beasts, you know what they can do. If he is fearful of losing, Al-Din will send in his war beasts.'

'I've seen them, but I've never had to fight them. Is there such a thing as an elephant spear or some vicious weapon we can use against them?'

'You don't defeat elephants with weapons. You defeat elephants with elephants.'

'But, we don't have elephants.'

'No, but we are clever enough to use their own strength against them,' a sly grin spread across Gavara's face.

Arc rolled his eyes. 'You're going to go on about water, again aren't you? Telling me to be like water and move with the forces.'

'Trumpets,' Gavara smiled. 'Trumpets and horns, that's how you defeat elephants. You'll understand when it happens. Overcome the elephants, and the day is yours.'

Arc could not hide his confusion. 'Find me some trumpets then and tell my men what to do with them. I'll leave that up to you.' He placed an arm around his old friend, feeling nothing but bones in his grip. 'There is something else you can do for me. I may have need of your services in the morning. Be ready, I'll send for you, and bring a ring.'

'A ring?' Gavara chirped. 'Where am I going to find a ring before tomorrow?'

Arc was amused at his friend's fluster. 'Same place you're going to find all these trumpets.'

The wind calmed at night, allowing the warriors of the Lion Crusade to gather around small fires. The order had gone out informing the army that battle would come with the first light of day. There was enough of a breeze to clear the air of smoke from the campfires, and some men just sat staring in contemplation at the multitude of stars. The night sky was crammed with an array of celestial lights, almost as if the Gods gathered to take their seats around the arena of war, hoping to see: valiant deeds; courageous acts; drama and death. The Gods adored the spectacle of war, and many of the warriors prayed that night, hoping their favourite deity would watch over them.

The veterans gathered others around the fires and told tales about the heroes in battles past. They hoped to alleviate the fears of those less experienced, though there were not many unbloodied swords left amongst the crusaders. Some younger men told stories too. Their intention to brag about their own virtues in the hope a spear-maiden would take a liking to them and be impressed enough to bed them. Sexual companionship with a spear-maiden was every new male recruit's fantasy. The sex workers amongst the camp followers only needed a coin or two to lie back for a horny soldier; whereas, a warrior had to work hard to stand out from the pack, or even fight, for just one night with a spear-maiden.

Sexual tensions and frustrations ran high in the camp because of the scarcity of the contraceptive used by the camp followers and spear-maidens. Silphium supplies were low, and the giant fennel introduced by Gavara had become exorbitantly expensive. Silphium seeds were now being used as currency and were more valuable than silver. Without silphium, the women had to resort to the foul-tasting Vulpecula's Lace, a wild carrot, an effective morning-after contraceptive which had unpleasant side effects. Spear-maidens did not want to put themselves through the discomfort of Vulpecula's Lace for any man, so a kind of sexual standoff had developed in the legions.

Sergeants were happy about the lack of interaction between the men and women of their divisions. No one wanted a pregnant spear-maiden marching into battle. They had all heard the stories about groups of female warriors ignoring the discipline of the battle line to gather around and protect a spear-maiden with a swollen belly. The story was a myth, probably spread by the less liberal officers in the legions, but it still caused some concern. Those same backward-thinking leaders would rather their warriors returned to the old ways of finding their gratification amongst their own kind when on a campaign.

Arc gave orders for anyone not involved in the fighting to return to Calinkerbad at first light. He did not want the worry on his mind of what would happen to them should his army suffer a defeat. He certainly did not want them hindering a retreat in the way Edius-Max had been encumbered.

The Lion Lord returned to his quarters to find Sonaji waiting for him. She lay seductively on the bed, wine and fruit on a small table to one side.

'You are to leave for Calinkerbad with the civilians in the morning,' Arc firmly informed Sonaji.

She pouted and tapped a hand on the bed's coverings for him to join her. 'Are you displeased at my news? I have brought wine for us to celebrate.'

'It was a wicked manipulation to whisper news of that kind into my ear at such a time.' Arc unfastened his sword belt and hung Breath Taker on the tent's centre post.

'Nonsense, I was just overjoyed and unable to contain myself. I just did not want you going into battle and getting yourself killed without knowing I carried your child.' Sonaji poured herself a cup of wine. 'I heard about the duel with the Granite Knight, and you accepted that challenge despite knowing about my condition. Are you not happy? Do you want me to swallow a dose of Vulpecula's Lace?'

Arc shook his head, disgusted at the mention of the vile vegetable. 'No, I am pleased about your condition, just not as pleased about the timing. You will leave with the camp followers in the morning, for the safety of you and the child. I will hear no more about it. Guard!' A guard came running into the tent and stood to attention. He looked awkward and tried to evert his eyes from the alluring Sonaji. 'Sharpen my sword, that bastard Knight's armour has put a ding or two in her blade.'

The guard snatched the weapon belt containing Breath Taker, and left in a hurry, almost tripping over a rug in his efforts not to glance at Sonaji.

The Corinthian Princess laughed as the guard stumbled out of the tent. She patted the bed again, and this time Arc joined her. Sonaji wasted no time in taking her lover in hand. If she must leave in the morning, she had urgent business to attend to before dawn.

Sonaji rode a black mare through the darker sections of the camp. Her beautiful white stallion was too conspicuous for her intentions. She had left Arc's side as soon as she had satisfied his lust and plied him with enough wine for him to lose the fight against his need to sleep. She made her way over to where the Corinthians had set up their camp and rode directly to Tyezore's grand tent.

The King's Son sat in a throne-like chair at the head of a table. The rest of the camp was starving, but this table was filled with the remnants of a feast. Tyezore's bondsmen and highest-ranking officers occupied the other seats around the feasting board. Young women scantily dressed in colourful Corinthian silks were draped over some of the men's laps while others danced frantically to the beat of a drum. The woman sitting across Tyezore's lap purred like a kitten as she stroked the head of the leopard skin the Commander wore over his shoulder. The girl smirked with blatant pride in the knowledge that she had lured the most powerful man in the room to her embrace.

Tyezore acknowledged his cousin entering the room by raising his goblet. His eyes were red, so bloodshot that Sonaji could not see where they ended, and his ebony eyelids began. A couple of the men watched the Princess walk over to her cousin, contempt in their eyes. It sickened Sonaji that there was not a single Corinthian woman allowed to carry arms in their army, while the Avolonians filled their ranks with spear-maidens. Her own people still saw the woman's role as domestic. Yes, they respected the female voice in their society as long as they raised the children, cooked the meals and danced for their pleasure. She would change all that when she ruled her nation.

'I must speak with you alone,' Sonaji told her cousin.

Tyezore stared at the Princess with the same contempt as his men, but his father had insisted he pay her respect while she was their connection to the Lion Lord's power. He clapped his hands, and the drumming stopped. The dancers froze like statues, and all eyes turned to Tyezore.

'Leave us,' the Warrior Prince ignored the protests from his men and whispered something in the girl's ear.

She giggled, then rose to toddle off in the direction of his sleeping chamber. 'We fight in the morn!' he shouted after his men, his goblet raised high in a toast. His men responded with a cheer, patting each other on the back before disappearing with the women in tow.

As soon as they were alone, Sonaji handed her cousin a parchment. Tyezore took it, saw that the royal seal was broken, and raised a questioning eyebrow.

'I'm sorry,' Sonaji uttered with false humility. 'I believed the message to be from your father to me. I would have sent the messenger on to you, but after reading the contents, I decided it was too dangerous to do anything other than bring it myself. I'm being sent away in the morning.'

Tyezore read the contents of the parchment, his brow furrowing as he took in the gravity of his father's instructions. 'This could get us all killed.' He rolled up the message and dropped it into the brazier burning by the side of his chair. 'Have you any idea why my father has so radically shifted his policy?'

Sonaji shook her head. She had learned to imitate the written hand of her uncle years before. The document was a fake, and the instructions hers and not those of the King. She was not worried about any consequences of the deceitful act; by the time she was discovered it would not matter. There was a coup planned in Corinth, and it would be Sonaji's brother on the throne once he had killed the ageing Odexsius. She was weaving her own web of intrigue to ensure he kept that throne, and that she rose to power at his side.

'Your father must have his reasons for the shift, but it is above me to know or ask why.' The deceit was hidden in Sonaji's voice, but if Tyezore had looked closer, he would have seen it in her eyes. 'Should things not go to plan, I will use my influence with the Lion Lord to assure him it has all been a misunderstanding. You have nothing to lose by following your father's orders.'

'If this goes wrong, the Lion Lord will have separated every Corinthian head from its shoulders before you have a chance to whisper your poison into his ear.' Tyezore calmed his anger. 'Your influence has faded, I saw that today when the Lion sent you away. He favours his daughter's counsel over yours these days, and it seems he is sending you away again in the morning. If the Lord falls prey to another fit and you are not here to take command, it will be that scar-faced pup of his. She has no love or trust for us Corinthians, you have seen to that.'

It was Sonaji's turn to frown. 'I still hold sway over the Lion Lord. He only sends me away because he thinks I carry his child, he wants me safe.'

'And do you?' Tyezore's expression could not make up its mind whether to be suspicious or shocked.

'Don't worry about the Lion's whelp. I have plans for her.' She avoided answering his question.

Tyezore huffed. 'Like the last time, you promised to rid us of the Lion? He made short work of your assassins out in the bush. You will get us all killed with your scheming and lies.'

'Don't be so dramatic, cousin. It does not become you; you're a great warrior, a leader of men, act like one. For our plan to work, I will need your fastest and most trusted scouts. Send them to me as quickly as possible.'

'Our plan?' Tyezore narrowed his eyes. 'Don't you mean my father's plan.'

Sonaji's chest heaved with a dramatic sigh. 'Of course, I mean your father's plan.' A thought suddenly crossed her mind. 'Are any of the Assegai with you?' Tyezore gave a cautious nod. 'Just the one.'

'Then send the assassin to me. I have need of his services before dawn snatches away the chance to strike.'

Tyezore fathomed what she had in mind and shook his head. 'No, I have someone who will better suit your purpose. There is one of their own, an outcast, a distasteful man who spies for me. He is..., was a legionary, he can pass through the camp like a ghost. His name is Erwin, I will send him to you. I knew he would be of use one day.'

'How do I know I can trust him?' It was a sensible question for Sonaji to ask.

Tyezore laughed. 'The Avolonians want to hang him. He's on the run, wanted for rape and murder. Should suit what you have in mind perfectly. Am I right?'

Sonaji smirked. 'As always cousin, you know me well. Send him to me.'

Enola

Enola flopped onto the soft bed and allowed Jenaliena to pull her boots off and unclip her armour. The inside of the tent glowed with a warm amber light radiating from two dozen candles. Shadows hopped from one space to another as the wind bullied the tent, snapping at its folds like an angry dog.

'You were a long-time returning here from the war tent,' Jenaliena probed her companion, wondering what she had been doing. 'I saw all the Generals leaving the tent quite a while ago. I was out gathering wood, there is so little in this barren place. I was lucky to find some of your legionnaires breaking up a cart. I just had to mention your name, and they were more than obliging. At least they will have a warm fire in their tent tonight.'

'They don't have a tent,' Enola mumbled. 'They will try to find a dry spot, build a fire, and sleep close enough to the flames so that later the embers will afford them a little respite from the cold.'

Enola sounded drowsy, the warmth of the tent and Jenaliena's dulcet tones were like a sleeping potion to her weary mind, the bed sucking her in as if it was made of the thickest honey, clinging to her limbs and making it impossible to lift them.

'Poor souls,' Jenaliena referred to the men who had helped her carry wood to the tent earlier, and now braved the cold night and bitter wind with no more than a blanket and their shield as protection. 'I heard that the army will attack at dawn.'

'At last.' Enola's voice so heavy with fatigue that her words were almost lost in the wind's increasing bluster. The heat from a blazing fire in the brazier adding to her drowsiness, it seemed that wood from carts burned well.

'Will we win?' The girl's question received no more than a shrug as an answer. She was afraid, and hated the feeling of helplessness battle forced upon her. She was no warrior, even though she wanted to pick up a shield and a sword and march by her lover's side. A sudden warmth came over Jenaliena; this was the first time she had thought of Enola as her lover. A smile beamed across her face. For once she felt like she belonged. She was more than just the serving wench, the plaything of whichever officer she'd been sent to attend. Finally, she belonged somewhere, and it made her heart flutter. 'I met my own ghost again last night, in the same dream that brought me here. I could clearly see myself kneeling over your chest, shaking your shoulders, trying to wake you. I kept shouting Attika, listen to Attika.'

'Attika?' Enola whispered the question.

'That was the name of my dog as a child. He was a big lad, followed me everywhere. He died saving me from a pack of wolves, held them off until my father and several hunters arrived. The pack tore chunks out of poor old Attika, but he stood his ground between those vicious beasts and me. My father always said if it had not been for Attika's distinctive husky bark being different from the other hounds, they never would have found me in time.'

Enola made a faint mumble to acknowledge the story, then was quiet for a moment before starting to snore gently.

Jenaliena stroked the back of her hand softly over Enola's cheek and watched her sleep. With her heart glowing in the warmth of the affection she harboured, and her back warmed by the blazing fire, Jenaliena lay down next to Enola, snuggled into her and drifted off into a contented sleep.

The fire was little more than a few smoking embers when Enola awoke. She could hear dogs barking somewhere in the camp, and half-remembered the story about Attika. She was aware of Jenaliena sleeping next to her and felt some small regret that she had dedicated the whole evening to her legions rather than the young woman's company. It was still dark outside, but Enola instinctively knew that dawn could not be far away, and she still had so much to do in preparation for the coming battle. Enola gently lifted Jenaliena's arm off her chest and raised herself up slowly, so as not to wake the girl. She blew out the few candles still burning and used a lamp to guide her way to the exit. Turning the light as low as it would go without extinguishing the flame, Enola left the lamp on the floor so it would be conveniently placed when she returned.

The night air was cold, and the wind continued to bluster. Enola had never known a place like this one; it was home to the wind. She strapped on her belt, the familiar feel of her golden sword in its scabbard slapping against the side of her leg. The sky was still in a glove of darkness, not yet tainted with an inkling of dawn, nevertheless, the camp was full of the sounds of warriors readying themselves for war. Enola cursed under her breath. Foolishness could lose a battle just as easily as surprise could win one. There would be no surprise with all this noise going on, the Mander would know something was afoot and would be making their own preparations.

Enola saw General Antona standing by a fire, laughing and joking with a couple of his officers. Two guards were startled into attention as the Lioness passed them on her way over to Antona.

'You look very jolly for a man about to go to war,' Enola bent to warm her hands on the fire.

'As should you,' Antona replied, with more glee than any man should be capable of at that ungodly hour. 'We are young, battle brings that excitement we crave. Valour and glory on the field are what we live for.'

'Or die for,' Enola grumbled, rubbing her hands vigorously next to the flames. 'You have been in enough battles to know that blood, fear and horror rule the day. Valour and glory come later in the stories and poems.'

The two officers excused themselves, seeing this was not a conversation they would be wise to participate in.

'You're in a sombre mood for one who has just spent the night with the second most beautiful woman in camp.' Antona nodded towards the tent Enola had emerged from.

'Do you have any objection to a little girl on girl action?' Enola took on a challenging tone. 'The heavens only know how you men can't wait to ride each other whenever the opportunity presents itself.'

Antona threw his head back and laughed. 'I think that is a fantasy of yours. I, for one, have never tapped another bloke, and know few who have.'

'You know Ioniedas, he even wears women's clothes. I'll bet he is back there in Calinkerbad, breaking in every handsome slave he can gather.'

'There you go again, fantasising.' Antona was smirking. 'Ioniedas is different. It's who he is. He has shown his great courage on the field of combat, and the men show him the respect of not judging him.' He let out a short sharp laugh. 'He won't be breaking any slaves in, he prefers to be broken rather than break. Anyway, he has a husband.'

'A husband,' Enola was shocked. 'How can he have a husband? Men can't have husbands, no more than women can have wives.'

'Oh, you have led a sheltered life. These are modern times.'

A smile finally appeared on Enola's face along with her agreement of her friend's perspective. 'Come, walk with me. I must inspect the hills beyond the right flank before the legions gather there.' They walked towards the black silhouette of hills sitting beneath a sky rich with stars. 'Who is the first?' Enola suddenly asked. Antona could do nothing more than show a blank expression. 'You said I spent the night with the second most beautiful woman in the camp. Who then, in your opinion, is the first?'

Antona could not help laughing again. 'Without a doubt, Plenty is the first. She came from Calinkerbad with Jenaliena. Why do you think there is such a big smile on my face and a lightness in my step? She's tucked up safe and warm in my bed, as is Jenaliena in yours.'

'Oh,' Enola's response making her seem in some way disappointed.

Antona's grin widened. 'You didn't think I meant you, did you? I'd rank you third or fourth. Mind you, there are those twin sisters that came in with Edius-Max,' he teased. 'That would make you only about the fifth or sixth in line for the camp's most desirable maiden.'

Enola punched her friend in the shoulder. 'There was a time when you thought me the fairest maiden of all.'

Antona gave a half-hearted chuckle that faded. 'You toyed with my young heart. Plenty tells me Jenaliena is falling for you, will you break her heart like you broke mine?'

The dark figure moved between the tents like a shadow following the moon. He found his target and used the shadows to conceal himself from the guards as he approached. Pressing his slender frame against the canvas, he watched two guards at the far side of the tent, wearily leaning on their spears. Erwin placed the edge of his blade against the tight twine holding a panel to the post. There was the faintest sound, a twang disappearing on the wind like a whisper lost amongst a hall's rafters. The second and third string made the same barely audible noise as the assassin's blade relieved them of their tension. There was no sound as the shadowy figure slid through the gap in the canvas

The tent's interior was almost as light-starved as the night outside. One small lamp sat on the ground by the exit, casting its feeble glow no further than the nearest wall. Erwin melted from one shadow to the next, like a phantom, silently approaching the bed in the centre of the room. A nest of tangled locks protruding from the wolf fur blanket was all that could be seen of the sleeping figure. The wind shook the shelter as if it were trying to warn the victim of approaching danger.

Erwin slithered to the edge of the bed on his stomach, a murderously sharp dagger clenched between his teeth. The whites of the man's eyes grew larger, focusing his insane stare on the head. He took the knife from his mouth and slid it under the blanket behind the mass of hair. The assassin waited, enjoying the moment, the brief time when he held the fate of another in his deadly grasp. He could choose not to take her life, stealing away into the night, confident in his abilities, but he wouldn't. An evil smile stretched across his face, the life was his to take, and the sweet taste of that power made him salivate, wetting his lips with anticipation.

It had been impossible for Erwin to hide the grin on his face when he heard who he was to kill. Revenge would be a sweet reward for all the cold nights he had spent in hiding from the Lioness' justice. He blamed her, and her stupid rules, for his change in fortune. Now, he would be paid well for doing what he would have happily done for free. It had been a lucky twist of fate that Erwin's and Tyezore's paths had crossed. In exchange for spying on the Avolonians, Erwin was given a safe place to hide, free to roam the camp as long as he stayed away from his old legion, where he would be recognised.

Erwin's free hand hovered over the head, ready to press down should his victim suddenly awake, he slid the knife into position at the woman's throat. He froze, footsteps approached the tent's entrance, voices sudden and loud directly outside. The dark figure held his breath, his eyes fixed on the door flap, narrowing with determination. He waited, motionless, poised like a cat about to pounce. His heart pounded with excitement, willing to be discovered, daring an intrusion. It would be one more life for him to steal before he was lost amongst the shadows. The voices trailed off into silence as the guards left with the man who came to speak with them.

Letting out a silent sigh, Erwin turned his attention back to his victim. He lowered his head and breathed in her scent. He smelt the vanilla in her hair, closing his eyes to heighten his senses. He savoured the moment; his head giddy with excitement. These split seconds before he took a life, were the essence of his existence. Power coursed through his veins, and he lavished in the arousal it brought him. In one swift movement, he pressed the side of the head into the pillow and drew the razor-sharp blade across her throat.

The victim stiffened, awakening to find her face forced into the pillow and a burning pain in her neck she could not comprehend. Panic swept through her convulsing body when she felt the warm blood gushing over her chest. She tried to scream, instead, choking on the blood her attempted breath drew through the gaping wound in her throat. She frantically slapped at the hands restraining her. All attempts to struggle quickly faded as her life drained away. The slaps diminished into feeble strokes, and then all was still.

Erwin's heart pounded as he sensed death approaching his victim. He felt her go limp in his grip, revelling in the bittersweet satisfaction of his work. He wiped the blood from his hands on the wolf fur, then bent to lay a gentle kiss on the dead woman's head. Engorged with the power murder had brought him, he evaporated into the night's shadows.

A plethora of horns being blown all over the Avolonian camp greeted the new day. Captains barked orders at men half dazed by sleep, instilling them with the sense of urgency needed to get them into ranks. The sun had barely stuck its head above the horizon, but the heat of the day was already showing itself in beads of sweat pouring from men's heads. Gavara pushed his way through the frantic crowds of warriors and spear-maidens readying for war. He had heard the news; half the camp had heard the news about Enola returning to her tent to find her servant girl murdered in her bed.

The old Pathfinder felt his heart tightening as he approached the young woman he had known for so long and was fond of. Several of the Lioness' personal guards milled around the open flap of her tent. Angry words and gestures were being exchanged, no doubt blame was being apportioned and rebuked. Enola sat on a pile of stones, gathered for catapults which at present were being wheeled towards the enemy. Her shoulders drooped and her head hung so that the old man could not see her face as he approached. Gavara sat beside Enola, he would have placed an arm around any ordinary woman to comfort her, but this was no ordinary woman, this was Enola Saberlund, daughter of the great Lion Lord, Commander of the Storm Legions.

'Is it true that it was an assassin?' Gavara placed a sympathetic hand on Enola's shoulder. She nodded. 'Poor girl, in the wrong place at the wrong time. You were obviously the intended victim,' he squeezed her shoulder. 'I know she was someone to you. Her dreams were filled with visions of you, and I brought her here knowing she would fill some grim purpose.'

'She was a friend,' Enola sniffed. 'A very good friend, if you know what I mean. I was not in love with her, but she was someone I cared very much about.' Enola lifted her gaze to the fire, the last of the wood burning brightly. In those flames Enola remembered Jenaliena's warm smile and cheerful laugh. On the breeze she could smell the spiced oils the young woman used to soften her skin, even the vanilla she loved to comb through her hair. Enola felt her sorrow turning to anger. 'Who? Who would do such a thing? There is a traitor among us.' A sudden look of concern flashed onto her face. The thought occurred to her that if it were Mander assassins sent in the night, they had most likely targeted her father. She stiffened. 'My father.'

Gavara held her in place, realising she was about to bolt off on a false errand. 'He is safe. I doubt this is the work of a Mander infiltrator. You were the only one targeted, and they knew where to find you.' The old man sighed. 'Your father is briefing his Generals. The business of war waits for no man or tragedy.' His worry for the young woman he'd watched grow was bubbling to the surface. The day would be full of death for her and she would need the rage battle brought to see her through. A sorrow disposition would not serve her well. He need not have worried, she was a warrior, tempered on the battlefields on the Lion Crusade.

'I will kill a hundred of the Mander bastards, for Jenaliena. Another hundred each for my mother and sister. Today is their day of reckoning and I will be the weapon that cuts the sin out of them.' Enola stood up, assuming Gavara would follow her to find her father, her rage impatient to be released on the enemy. 'Are you coming, old man?'

The Pathfinder shook his head. 'I am to return to Calinkerbad with the rest of those who are of no value in battle.'

'But you are the greatest military mind amongst us. My father will need your counsel, you can't leave now.'

Gavara was genuinely flattered that the Commander of the Storm Legions gave such value to his knowledge. It showed him she had come of age and that all the time spent tutoring her was not wasted. 'It is your father's order that I go. Win or lose this battle, he will not be hindered by hangers-on or those too slow in retreating or advancing. If the day goes well, the army will have to move quickly to counter the smaller force marching in from the south, and then to Mander-Kush with all haste. Should events not go to plan, he wants the option of a retreat to Calinkerbad to regroup. Either way, the army will move too fast for the camp followers to keep up, so we must leave. Your father has made his mind up. I fear his ears are too open to his new wife's opinions.'

'Wife!' Enola screeched. 'When? How?'

'It seems there is to be a child. They sent for me to make a legal union before your father went to join his Generals.'

Enola's cheeks reddened with new anger. 'She already had too much sway on his decisions. Now she will be unbearable. It is not a good thing that a great man is led by the nose. She rules him with her thighs.'

'Your father was sure you would feel that way. He didn't want the child born a bastard should he fall on the field today. I'm sure the bride will arrange a wedding with all the pomp and ceremony that entails just as soon as possible. But, for now, she returns to Calinkerbad with me.'

Horns sounded to gather any remaining warriors to the battle lines. Enola's troop of bodyguards stood waiting for their Commander, they fidgeted with impatience. A young lad came racing towards Enola, she held out a hand with her fingers spread to stop the boy before he started blurting out his message. She knew he brought word to summon her to the Lion Lord, but she had one last thing to say to her old friend and tutor before he left.

'Take the girl's body with you to the city, and pay a few coins to have her placed in the ground by the river, and a few words said over her. She would like that. I don't want her dropped in the pits with the dead from today's battle. She had a gentle soul and deserves better. Will you do that for me, old friend?'

Gavara stood and embraced the Lioness. A feeling of worry, that most have when seeing friends or a loved one leave for battle, prickled his skin. He wondered if he would ever see her again. Quietly, he sniffed back a tear threatening to reveal his emotions. 'I will say the words over her myself.' Gavara had tried for days to confess to Arc that his youngest daughter still lived, never finding the right moment. He pondered telling Enola, deciding the revelation would need to wait, the young woman had enough emotional turmoil to deal with for one day.

'Sir,' a worried-looking Warrik stood in front of his Commander, nervously rubbing the palm of his hand over the hilt of his sword. 'We must go.'

Chapter 7

Arc

Tumbleweeds skipped across the barren surface of the plain, like frightened goats running from a wolf. The northerly wind played in the dust, dragging its clawed fingers through the sand, and casting handfuls into the air to be scattered like the foam of a wave crashing over rocks standing fast in a turbulent sea. The sun rose in the east so that the Mander Army was nothing more than featureless silhouettes on the horizon.

It was still early in the morning, yet the sun was already making life uncomfortable for those wearing armour. The heat by midday would be unbearable, constricting throats with a debilitating thirst. Arc's Avolonian Army faced the sun in silence, eyes squinting to keep out the sand and bright light. They tied rags around their faces, covering nose and mouth as a protection against the choking dust.

Arc climbed onto Armageddon's back. The great warhorse showed his usual irritation at being mounted. The stallion kicked at the ground and flicked his tail to make sure his displeasure did not go unnoticed. But his ears pricked up, revealing how delighted he was to have his master back in the saddle. Armageddon hated everyone and everything, forever angry and menacing, but that's what made him an excellent warhorse. The only thing that conquered his anger was his loyalty to Arc.

The Lion Warrior reached forward and slapped the huge beast's neck a couple of times to calm him. Arc then reached for his lion's head helmet and put it on. It was instantly hot in the morning sun, but the head and mane of the fearsome creature slain by his own hand, was now his trademark. The beast's deadly fangs lined the rim of the helmet, while its terrifying eyes stared out from the crown. The lion's magnificent mane reached more than halfway down Arc's back.

When Gavara had presented the Lion Lord with the lion's head stretched over a metal war helmet, he had said, 'It reflects the soul inside. Men will quiver with fear at seeing the nature of the beast that roams in the warrior's essence.'

Arc cared little for the symbolism of the helmet, he knew his men liked it and so did he. A cheer went up as the Avolonians saw their hero mount the famous warhorse. To some he was a great leader, to others he was a God of War, but there was not a man, woman nor child in the Avolonian camp that did not revere the Lion Lord. They believed in him and would follow him into the flames of hell if they must, trusting he would guide them to victory.

Warriors sat around campfires listening to the legends that were Arc's chronicle. Storytellers enthralled their audience with tales of the Lion Warrior, how he had charged alone into thousands of Mander troops, driving them back so far, and so fast that they had fallen over each other to escape the Lion's blade and the wrath of his demon mount, Shadin. He had challenged the Gods that day on the fields of Caputhora, and won. Warriors wanted to be him, women wanted to be with him, children prayed at night for him to keep them safe, but few really knew the man behind the legends.

Arc felt neither like a god nor a hero. He knew the reality of those victories that were now legends. He was haunted by what the cost had been in lives and suffering. There was no defence for the embellishments and flattery added over time. The Lion Lord was grounded in facts. The most prominent of which, was that he faced an army of trained warriors with an army composed of too many farmers and tradesmen.

Dust blew in Arc's face as he rode into the wind, along the Avolonian line. Men and women cheered and waved their flags as he rode by. The stream of dust and sand being blown against him gave the illusion that he travelled faster than in reality. He sat tall in the saddle, a vision of strength and confidence, but the man inside felt neither of those things. His old wound clamped his head in pain. He rarely managed more than a couple of hours sleep these days, and his memory regularly failed him. He had recently suffered another fit, and now his hands trembled and he feared he could lose control at any moment.

Armageddon slid to a halt, his feet ploughing through the sand like the bow of a boat through the mirror-calm water of a lake. Arc had reined the beast in at the centre of his army. Behind him, his own banner fluttered in the wind: the red lion on its hind legs, clawing at an invisible enemy; the yellow background, usually bright, dull against the background of sandy hills. He narrowed his eyes to peer across the expanse to where his foe stood silent, waiting, unmoving.

'So, he will stand at the centre,' Arc said to the wind when he saw the banners of Al-Din fluttering in the middle of the Mander line.

He had met the Emperor once before, in the Jade Palace of Mander-Kush. On that occasion, his life had been in the balance. He was a prisoner: a man with no memory of his past; a broken man who depended on a prince who believed their fates were intertwined. Gavara instigated that belief, filling Prince Atropolis' head with stories of destiny.

Pathfinders like Gavara, shape the world with the text from a prophesy. Bringing those two men together had set off a chain of events that changed the world, as he had intended it to. That destiny was still playing out, here on the plains of Mander, in Avolonia and in the frozen lands to the south. That broken man of many years ago, now returned to challenge the Emperor who once held Arc's life so precariously between his fingers. Hatred, anger and the lust for vengeance fuelled the Lion's heart, raising him from the ashes of his broken life. A life that had been torn to shreds by Mander cruelty and oppression.

Al-Din gathered his strongest forces around his banner. The centre of the Mander line heaved with elite warriors, led by powerful Generals, veterans with battle experience coursing through their veins. They would hold, and Arc's army would crumple against them like clay forced into a brick mould. That is why Arc split his own elite warriors between the centre and the flanks. It was a dangerous tactic, a necessary risk to solve an unfathomable problem.

The Lion's army would be forced to advance. They had no choice. They were out of provisions, another hostile army approached from the south and Al-Din would never be fooled into making the mistake of attacking when he knew full well that time was on his side. So, Arc would attack, but not in a conventional way. Armageddon snorted, the dust irritating his flared nostrils and stinging his bright eyes. Arc looked to the horizon. There was not a single bird in the sky, he wondered where they had all gone to avoid the dust. Squinting to peer through the haze, he thought he could just about make out the worshipping towers of Siena Mazda in the distance. That city was Al-Din's last bastion of defence between the Avolonian Army, and the prize of Mander-Kush. He was wrong, that city was thirty leagues to the east, and it was a trick of the light that made distant rock formations seem like buildings.

It had been one battle after another to reach this point. The roads from the coast were littered with bodies, victims of both conflict and disease. Arc had brought the people some hope with his crusade to destroy the Empire. Tens of thousands flocked to the Avolonian banner, hoping to free themselves and their lands from Mander oppression. But this had been more of a hindrance than a blessing. Too few were warriors, and too many needed to be fed. The too young and the too old alike drained provisions faster than they could be gathered.

Diseases the Avolonians had never seen before, culled great swathes of the camp followers in the early part of the crusade. The army was halted for months by the bowel sickness that killed both weak and strong. At times the stench of death had hung over the camp like a dark cloud of doom. Arc was forced to demand that everyone who could walk, start marching. On the move, and away from the foul contagions of lousy sanitation, most recovered. Few who were left behind were so lucky.

One year and several moons had passed since the Lion Lord landed on the northern coast of Mander. The victories at Fwenga and Tibuzar that had inspired so many to join the Lion's crusade now seemed a long time ago. Arc thought his troubles over when he captured the port city of Calinkerbad. Such a citadel would be full of the provisions they needed and Huwel's pirate ships could bring supplies up the river.

Al-Din proved to be no fool. He sacrificed Calinkerbad to lure the Avolonians into his trap. He made Arc's army fight a bloody battle to gain the city, but once they were inside its high walls, they found deserted empty warehouses. The Mander had abandoned the city and fled upriver to Mander-Kush. Some fled downriver to the town of Ratlarbig, which was on the opposite bank of the river from Calinkerbad and out of reach of Arc's troops. From there they could blockade the river to prevent the pirate leader from sailing supplies to Calinkerbad.

Arc won himself an empty city, at a hefty price. Now his supply lines had been cut, and Al-Din had placed his army between Calinkerbad and Mander-Kush, so Arc had to fight or starve.

Al-Din did not have it all his own way. He hoped reinforcements from his Southern Army would return in time to trap the Avolonians at this remote place. He was deprived of the superior numbers the Southern Army would have brought him, but his army was well fed, well-armed and had the defensive advantage. Arc would have to attack or face greater numbers later.

Arc watched as the scouts rode towards him, each man reining his mount to a halt, before banging his chest in salute. The riders were caked in dust. They removed the rags from their faces, revealing clean skin below. The first scout tried to speak but had to gulp water from a skin before he could make himself understood.

'No change, sir. They are holding their position.'

Arc sighed and looked to the distant pile of flesh in front of the Mander line. He remembered the horrors of the previous day and the reason he gave the Jagger Knights the honour of holding the centre. He would not need to invoke the killing spirit in men who had witnessed an enemy butchering their comrades. To add insult to injury, Mander pike-men had collected the dead Knights' heads, spiking them atop of their pikes. These men stood in the Mander front line, jeering and jostling the gruesome poles to taunt Knights already sickened with grief and coveting retribution. Grand Master Razor would be avenged, the Knights of the Holy Jagger Order would see to that.

Arc turned to the rest of the scouts, each in turn nodded his agreement with the first man's statement. Arc rubbed at his temple, stroking the indentation that caused him so much pain and discomfort. The scouts waited while their leader mulled over his thoughts.

'My order is to close and stand,' Arc eventually said.

The scouts scattered to the far ends of the line, carrying the Lion Lord's command. Arc drew the Lion Blade, Leovesica, and pointed to the sky. He said nothing more. No great shout to advance. No great speech to lift the hearts of his troops. He just jolted Armageddon into motion with a flick of his heels, and his army followed.

The Mander army watched as the Avolonians advanced. A great cloud ascended into the morning sky to blot out the vista of distant hills. Ninety thousand pairs of sandaled feet churned the sand into a billowing avalanche of dust. The ground shook, but the wind softened the sound. Heat haze rose from the baking ground, distorting the view of the approaching menace. Banners appeared and disappeared as they dipped in and out of waves of heat. The advancing line seemed disjointed, as if viewed through broken glass.

The Mander had confidence in their numbers and superior armaments, but as the banners of the Lion Warriors, Jagger Knights, and Storm Legions came into view, that confidence slithered away into the darkest corners of fear. They too had heard the legends. Tales of fearsome warriors in red cloaks, led by a God of War with a Lion's head, were all they talked about since marching out of the gates of Mander-Kush.

Mander officers judged the mood of their troops and called out reassurances.

'Remember, we have the one true God on our side,' they shouted into the wind. 'We have the divine Al-Din with us, father of the world and destroyer of non-believers.'

It was not their faith that sent an uneasy shiver down the spine of the Empire's army, but the almost unfathomable reality that they were facing an enemy, so deep in their own lands. Never did they think that any foe could cut so deep into their homeland. Mandorians were shaken to the core, threatened by a mighty army, one step away from the heart of their own country.

It is new for the Mander to call themselves Mandorians. Atropolis coined the name to represent the true-bloods, the faithful, born of pure Mander bloodlines, the superior race. Mander is now only the name of the Empire and those inducted into it. There is a new order in the Empire, the chosen ones, they are the lords and officers. Safe to say, every warrior standing on that plain, in the Mander army, thought themselves to be Mandorians, but only those born to a true bloodline would ascend to any position of influence.

Fear writhed in the stomachs of men, but they had faith, they believed that followers of the Questerus would be eternally victorious over faithless heathens. They would successfully defend their homeland, and if they died doing so, they would be rewarded for all eternity in the afterlife.

Arc pulled on the reins to bring Armageddon to a halt. The trained warriors behind him stopped instantly. The wings of the line, filled with soldiers who until recently were farmers, traders or craftsmen, took a little longer to come to a halt. They scurried back to line up with the centre, throwing up dust that rolled over their leader in a twisting cloud. The rags tied around their faces hid their embarrassed expressions.

As the dust cleared, Arc made no attempt to hide his displeasure. He wiped the grime from around his eyes and his mouth before signalling to archers, who were waiting and ready for the Lion's command. Two bowmen pushed their way through shields and stood either side of Arc. They trapped one end of the longbows against the ground, with their foot, and bent the other end until it was low enough to notch the string.

It took great strength to brandish such a formidable weapon, and many years of practice to even fire one of its double-length arrows. The archers loaded arrows with a white cloth tied around their shafts. Their bows creaked as they drew back the strings until puckered lips could kiss them. The bowmen released in unison, without any order being needed, as if their thoughts were connected. The arrows flew in a long arc, drifting only marginally southward on the wind. They slammed into the ground, twenty paces short of the Mander line.

The white cloths on the arrows twitched in the breeze, close to the ground, unlike Al-Dins banners beyond them, flapping and flailing high in the wind. The Mander cheered, for no reason other than the arrows appeared to have fallen short.

Arc grinned to hear the misguided joy of his enemy. 'Bring up the Harpy.'

He could see artillery all along the Mander line, but he had stopped his army short of their deadly range, the archers' shots had confirmed this. No traditional bow, a giant crossbow or catapult had the range of a longbow when fired by an adept bowman. No catapult that is, except one.

Behind Arc the lines of troops parted. A loud groaning from greased axles bearing a great weight carried on the wind. Sandy dust blasting against wooden panels hissed, as if someone had poked a nest of angry vipers with a stick. The monstrous war machine, known as the Harpy, swayed and lurched as it made its way to the front.

Arc had seen the plans, watched it being built, but still he was in awe as they brought the monster to bear. Gavara designed the machine to break down the gates of Calinkerbad. A system of counterweights rapidly levered forward the Harpy's great throwing arm. The monster could launch three times the weight a standard catapult could throw, and reach just as far. Loaded with normal sized ammunition, it could throw it almost twice as far.

Dust rode on the wind like smoke from burning crops, obscuring Arc's view of his adversary. He knew there was nothing he could do to tempt Al-Din into giving up his advantage and attacking, but he could make him pay a heavy price for standing his ground. If his plan worked, Arc hoped to dramatically reduce his enemy's advantage.

'Feed the Harpy,' the wind delivered Arc's order.

A whip cracked, and a team of horses dragged a colossal stone up a greased ramp leading into the belly of the beast. Ropes creaked as they levered the mighty throwing arm into position. Suspense momentarily tamed the wind. Arc watched the Mander's centre, where Al-Din's banner dominated a flotilla of lesser regal pennants sailing over the heads of his enemy. He imagined their apoplexy and scorn as they watched the futility of loading a war machine such a long distance from its target.

A loud crack unleashed the Harpy's mighty throwing arm, followed by the whirring of cogs. The enormous chunk of stone arced across the sky, crashing back to earth far to the right of the Mander centre. It extinguished a huge swathe of souls in an instant. An exasperated gasp came from the Mander; a mass expulsion of air, as if the whole of the army were one creature winded by the blow. Men had stood and watched the missile hurtling towards them in disbelief, not thinking to move out of its way. Warriors died where they stood, unable to move, turned into red smears on a dry earth in the blink of an eye.

Arc listened to the sustained cheers of his army until another crack rang out from the Harpy. Artillery men adjusted the machine's aim, and the Lion Lord felt his excitement rise, hoping to win the day with one blow, a direct hit on the Emperor. The enormous projectile screamed through the air, causing panic in the Mander ranks. The rock smashed into the enemy, reducing them to a smear of torn flesh and shattered bones. Arc saw the devastation caused by the impact but bit back his frustration when it struck far to the left of centre. He regretted sending Gavara off to safety, he was obviously the only man who could aim the super weapon.

Recovering from their shock, the Mander lines responded by dropping back a few paces and spreading out. Their reaction was a well-used tactic against enemy artillery fire, they were simply giving themselves room to move out of the way. Men would still die, but in smaller numbers. Arc ordered the rest of his artillery forward and began the bombardment that was a prelude to his advance.

Next, Arc sent the archers forward. He knew their value; the enemy would have to endure a tempest of shafts. He noticed that many of them had trumpets hanging from their backs or horns hanging from their belts. *'Gavara,'* he thought. Arc watched the first volley darken the sky, great looping shots to spear down on an enemy. A second volley screeched into the air before the first reached its target. The wind took some of the sting out of the shafts, but they fell on the Mander horde as numerous as rain drops in a summer shower. Archers took arrows from the quiver, nocked them, drew, and let fly in no more than two breaths, arrow after arrow, until eager fingers grabbed at an empty quiver.

Hidden behind shields, the Mander endured a hail of barbed shafts, unable to look up to see if an artillery shot headed their way. Not knowing but expecting was the most effective psychological warfare, even short-lived it shattered the confidence of an army. The instant arrows stopped rattling on shields, Mander archers stepped forward to return fire, collecting undamaged arrows from the soft ground, and sending them back down the throats of Avolonian bowmen. At that same moment, Mander catapults awoke, unleashing death into the sky. Arc watched his archers scrambling back to their own lines. He questioned the wisdom of sending them out without shields. It confirmed his fears when he saw the bodies left strewn on the ground in greater numbers than he would expect if they had shields.

It was time to advance. There were no more big stones for the Harpy. She had caused untold damage to the Mander line and morale, only disappointing in her failure to hit a bull's eye anywhere close to the Emperor. Arc drew the Lion Blade and pointed it at the enemy. The ground shook with the first steps of the Avolonian advance. Only Arc and his Generals were on horseback, the elevation enabling them to command, knowing it made them an easy target for arrows and spears.

An advance of this size needed to be on foot. The sheer width of the line made a cavalry charge unthinkable. There were cavalry protecting both flanks, and at the rear, to counter any incursions from Mander horsemen. But rivals would fight this battle toe to toe, shield to shield, killing with the smell of an adversary's foul breath in their nostrils. The Lion Lord roared in defiance, his voice like a blow to those close by. He sat high in the saddle, his hawkish stare fixed on the enemy like a man looking into his future.

Armageddon carried his master into battle, the heart and violence of the beast showing in his wide eyes and angry mouth. The beast was oblivious to artillery fire fizzing overhead, and arrows slamming into the surrounding ground. He had the smell of blood in his flaring nostrils dragging him towards the enemy. He tossed his head as a feathered shaft skittered across the armour plate protecting his neck. Arc reached forward and reassured his mount with forceful pats, dust rising from each blow.

The advance gained momentum, swallowing up the ground between the two enemies. At fifty paces, Arc wanted to charge. Instead, he let the Jagger Knights flow around him so they would not trap him between the two lines as they clashed. Mander catapults, giant bows and archers had taken their toll on the Avolonians, but the advance did not falter. Even the auxiliaries made up of farmers, merchants and outcasts maintained some semblance of discipline.

'Spears!' came the cry from dry-throated sergeants.

Warriors from both sides hurled long shafts across the narrow gap between the two forces. They grunted with the effort of throwing a spear, and men screamed as steel punched into their bodies.

The lines came together like a ferocious beast snapping its jaws shut. The noise was brutal as shield hit shield and terrified men yelled their war cries in search of the courage they needed. Arc, elevated on his stallion, made a fine target, his lion helmet more visible than the banners catching the breeze over his head. He fended off a spear and swung Breath Taker downward to cleave a Mander head in two. Enemy warriors on horseback angled their way towards the Lion Warrior, dreams of glory turned into nightmares as they fell to the mighty Lion Blade. Arc was splattered with the blood of his victims; the wind playing in the folds of his cloak, fluttering it like a banner; his heart and confidence driving forward those warriors closest to him.

Gavara

Clean winds swept over the ridges of the hills with greater haste than those in the valley where they were laden with dust. Gavara reached the top of the ridge just in time to see the Harpy hurl destruction towards the Mander and wished he had not. 'Fools, incompetent ninnies,' he thought as he watched the colossal projectiles strike wide of their mark. *'They are over compensating. Half a notch each throw, I've told them a thousand times.'*

From his elevated position, Gavara could clearly see the formations of both armies. The scale of it all filled him with awe. The Mander lines were deep, divided into cohorts. Arc had been right to divide his line into three. His plan was to smash the Mander's centre, or at least make Al-Din think that was his objective. It would be almost impossible to break down a defensive line of such length and breadth as the Mander had brought to bear. Arc needed a new type of war craft to overcome the odds facing him.

Gavara's heart swelled with pride when his searching gaze picked out Enola at the head of the Storm Legions on the right flank. She was to draw the enemy flank away from their centre. Once that was achieved, Tyezore would lead the Corinthians into the fight. With the help of the Avolonian cavalry, the Mander left flank would be overwhelmed and rolled in on its own centre. With Al-Din committed against Arc's force, there would be nothing he could do without dramatically weakening his own position.

Gavara had witnessed the fire of vengeance in Arc's eyes. He recalled the words Arc had growled at him when he had tried to warn Arc of the dangers such a bold strategy would hold. *'I hope he tries to shift against the Storm Legions. I will cut through his line until I find him and rip him apart with my own hands'.* The sound of horns carried up to the ridge. Gavara narrowed his eyes to thin lines

to watch the advance. He saw Arc sitting high on Armageddon's back. His mind was cast back to the day he watched from the hills as Arc rode out of Jomora. Back then, Arc was a man who wanted nothing more than to find his two daughters and live in peace. Gavara's heart tightened when he thought about how destiny had treated that man. He kept those memories like coins in a purse, knowing that one day there would be a price to pay for his part in Arc's turbulent fate.

A warm wind buffeted his old bones, but Gavara felt a chill as he watched the Storm Legions angle towards the right. It was dangerous to open up a gap against such a dominant force. The one saving grace was that the enemy could not be expecting it, so they would not know immediately how to react. The Avolonian left flank made the same manoeuvre, forcing the Mander to an angle to face them. There were not enough Avolonian reserves to reinforce General Hal's legions if they were successful in drawing the enemy wider and separating them from their main force. The cavalry would protect the rear, but it was doubtful that they would break through the Mander right flank. All the eggs were in Enola's basket.

A timely gust of wind hit Gavara just as the two lines crashed against each other, and it was as if he felt the force of the collision. Even seen from a distance, the fighting was brash and wild. The old man's eyes fell upon the multitude of banners entangling with those of their enemy as the two lines became that one seething, slithering monster that is the battle.

Gavara strained his old eyes to see behind the enemy lines. Like grey ships on a river of sand, he saw what he was looking for.

'Elephants,' he said to the wind. 'So, I was right. He has brought his giant beasts of war to trample us under foot.'

It was then that a sensation like dread gripped the Pathfinder: starting in the pit of his stomach, like the first hint of indigestion, it grew until it pushed like a boulder inside his ribs. He looked to the southern hills over the battle's right flank. A sullen light ripple in the day's heat, turned the horizon into a liquid haze. He did not know the origins of this trepidation, only that he sensed danger lurking in the distance. He knew better than to ignore the anxiety; it was not born of any supernatural talent, just decades of experiences waving warning flags at his intuition.

'We have to go,' a voice called from behind.

Gavara turned to be confronted by the two guards responsible for escorting him to Calinkerbad. The old man flapped his hands as if a swarm of bees had suddenly attacked him.

'No, no, no. We must go back. I must warn the Lion Lord.' Gavara was now hopping from foot to foot in desperation.

The guards gave each other a discerning look. 'My Lord said you would be like this when the fighting started. I'm to disregard any cleverness that comes out of your mouth and take you to Calinkerbad, no matter what.'

'Yes, yes, but first we must return and warn our Lord.'

'Warn him of what?'

'I don't know yet, but I sense a danger.'

The guards laughed. 'We've got to warn them, but we don't know what of. What do you make of that, Perry?'

'It looks to me more like he's desperate to pee, dancing about like that. Come on, we've got to get moving,' Perry told them. 'There's more than his bony ass at stake here.'

'Begging your pardon Sir, but there is nothing you can say that will persuade us to take you back. Orders are orders. Please don't force us to treat you rough, Sir. Be reasonable.'

Gavara stormed towards the guards, and when Perry went to stop him, the stick thin, white-haired old man struck him with his staff, and bolted past. The other guard could not help but laugh.

'We had better get after him,' Perry said, rubbing his head where the staff had struck him.

Enola

The Avolonian right flank

Hatred gripped Enola by the throat. She did not see the enemy for what they were, an impenetrable wall spreading as wide as the eye could see. The Lioness paid no attention to the cliff face of shields spiked with spears, swords, and axes. She was devoid of fear for the seething mass of warriors who were inpatient to kill and humiliate invaders they despised. In

Mander eyes, the warriors of the Lion Crusade were life that did not deserve to live.

Anger, not worry, burned bright in Enola's eyes. Vengeance, not fear, filled her heart. Sorrow and self-pity were banished to the back of her mind. Today would be about revenge, and the Storm Legions would be the stick Enola used to punish Mander: for Jenaliena, for her mother, her sister. Her mouth salivated with the taste of retribution.

The Lioness dismounted, sending Storm to the back of the lines. Sitting in the saddle made her an easy target for archers, and she wanted to be in the thick of the fight, toe to toe with her enemy. Enola angled her legions towards the southern hills, the Mander line stretching to follow her. Antona had the right flank and Enola the left. She strode towards a gathering of banners, knowing she would find great lords and princes with their bravest warriors gathered around their colours.

'Shields!' the cry went up as Mander arrows darkened the sky, the order echoed along the Avolonian line.

Enola did not miss a step as a hail of shafts thumped into bodies and punched through shields and armour. A split second before arrows pounded them like drums, Arter and Hurcan raised their shields either side of their Commander. Several more volleys of feather-flighted death rained down on the advancing army, taking a devastating toll. Enola saw one of her captains spitted through his neck, the arrow's grey feathers brushing against his face as he continued to march. He tried to clear his throat by spitting a black gobbet of blood into the sand, determined to reach the Mander line and make them pay for inflicting a mortal wound upon him. He staggered and managed only a dozen more steps before dropping to his knees and vomiting blood. He tugged hopelessly at the shaft, but fell face down into the dust, never to rise again. Men of the legion with whom he had shared his life, marched over him.

The enemy were close now. Enola drew her golden sword, raised it above her head, and began to trot.

'Spears!'

Every Spartiken heard the cry, knowing it signalled the real start of the battle, the dash across the remaining divide to strike the first blows. The Avolonian ranks broke into a trot, those with spears drawing their arms back in readiness to throw. The pace of the charge increased with every step, the army trying to keep up with Enola. Every confident stride she took towards their foe filled those around her with courage and resolve.

The ground rumbled, as thousands of spear shafts were launched with a cry that would shake the heavens. The Mander retaliated both with spears and voice. Enola's mind was drowning in the din of battle as she braced herself for the impact. The Mander shield wall gave way under the force of the collision. Enola found herself in the second, then third row of the enemy's ranks, hacking and slashing at soldiers stunned by her sudden appearance. Mander warriors who expected their shield-wall to protect them were now falling to Avolonian blades like grass to the scythe.

Warrik yelled at his men to stay with Enola. 'On me!' he called to urge the Commander's bodyguards on. 'We must not lose the momentum. Don't get bogged down in individual fights.' He caught his breath. 'On me! Hack at them, then move on!'

Enola fought her way towards the banners of a Mander prince; all who dared to stand in her way were cut down by the ferocity of her blows, powered by anger and hatred. Arter and Hurcan swept away any threat from the sides. Hurcan struck one man so hard in the neck that his mail shattered, sending metal rings raining to the ground. The Lioness was drenched in the blood of her foes. To the Spartikens around her she seemed invincible.

'Keep moving!' Enola shouted at Hurcan, who had stopped to fight a group of men determined to reach her.

Hurcan moved on, leaving other bodyguards to take his place holding the attackers back.

A giant Mander captain with a huge war-axe stepped in front of Enola. The man's beard sprouted from the opening in his helmet, leaving no room for any other features. He swung the axe at Enola's head. She dropped to one knee, feeling the weight of the weapon's head sweep through the brush on her helmet. Thrusting her blade upward with her whole body, Enola struck. The golden blade went into the bushy whiskers and through the giant's throat. In the same instant, Arter's sword took him in the chest and Hurcan's blade pierced his stomach. Together, the three of them pushed over the tree trunk of a man, retrieved their blades and carried on.

An evil grin crossed Enola's face when she saw the Prince's eyebrows raised in surprise. He was not expecting the attack to penetrate so deeply, so soon. The young royal was about the same age as Enola. He stood on a chariot, which put him a head above the seasoned-looking warriors around him. The large curved sword he held looked out of place in his small hand. He was not a warrior, his fearful expression gave that away. What he was, Enola realised, was an opportunity to strike a blow that would rock the Mander to the core.

The chariot's horses were absent, probably sent to the rear when the Avolonian advance started. In their place were a multitude of banners, white silk with golden stars and the crescent moon of Mander snapping and flapping in the sand-filled gusts.

'The Prince, rally to Prince Haslan!'

Enola heard the call for help. Seeing Mander warriors surge forward to protect the young man, she glanced to see if her own elite troops were with her. Deciding there were enough to do the job, she roared the order to attack. The Prince's bodyguards stood their ground; they would fight to the death to protect their master.

The fighting was bloody and ruthless, two groups of worthy opponents locked together in mortal combat. Enola found herself pressed against a warrior twice her width, neither of them able to angle their blades at each other. The man's breath reeked of his breakfast, fish and stale ale. He clubbed Enola's helmet with the hilt of his sword. Her ears rang, and she saw a bolt of lightning flash across her eyes with each blow. When she did not go down, the man used the hand guard of his weapon to lever off her helmet. The headgear would not come off, its straps holding fast, but it slipped back enough for Enola to feel vulnerable. Steam rose from her exposed brow, where her opponent aimed his next blow.

Enola instinctively closed her eyes in anticipation of the pain. Instead of the blow, her face was splattered in hot blood. Her eyes were only closed for a split second, but in that time a spear-maiden thrust her spear at the man's head, slicing his cheek open like a second mouth in the side of his face. The Mander warrior reeled backwards, opening up enough space for Enola to lower her sword. The tip of Leo-Fang rested against the man's chest, the hilt against her own. The Mandorian had nowhere to go; he was trapped against the blade, and it started to sink in. First, Enola felt the blade slice through the leather breast-plate, then the sensation of his mail giving way. The tip hit bone and went in no deeper.

The man was frantic, the spear-maiden was now latched onto his sword arm, forcing it upward. In a desperate attempt to save himself, he slid his other arm out of the shield straps and grabbed at the blade in his chest. As blood oozed between his fingers, he realised he would not shift the blade that way. He reached for his dagger with his bloody hand and slammed it into the neck of the spear-maiden. She screeched, releasing her killer's arm as she dropped to the sandy ground. He never managed to swing his sword which dropped from his hand as Leo-Fang sank into his chest, slicing his heart in two.

The Avolonians began to gain the upper hand. The Prince's bodyguards were being cut down, but none of them ran, they died where they stood. To Enola's surprise, the young Prince had not fled. He was hacking at his attackers over the side of the chariot's rail, missing everyone and hurting no one.

'He should run,' Enola thought. 'All his fine armour and royal blood won't save him now.' She pushed her way through to the chariot.

The Prince was swinging his weapon wildly, panic and fear ruling his actions. His guards were dropping all around him; no one could find the correct angle to strike up into the chariot. The Prince got lucky, his blade slammed into the helmet of a spear-maiden just as Enola reached the chariot. The spear-maiden's companions were infuriated to see their friend take the blow. It was a false bit of luck for the Prince; the blade stuck in the side of the woman's head, trapping him against the chariot's rail. It was all the advantage the livid spear-maidens needed to get at the boy. First, one spear punched into the Prince's side.

Then a second punctured his armour, broke ribs and entered his lung.

The boy froze, his eyes wide and pleading. Enola climbed onto the chariot's axle to face the Prince. While she stood there gazing into his wide, tear-filled eyes a third spear ripped into his stomach. The young man coughed up blood. He opened his mouth to speak and then, for reasons only known to him, he thought better of it. Enola wondered if he was going to beg for mercy, which was pointless as his wounds were fatal, or if his last words would have been defiant.

'You should have run.'

Enola gripped her sword in both hands in a backswing, grunting as she heaved it at the boy's neck. The Prince's head tumbled through the air, the spear-maidens letting out a cheer, their fallen comrades avenged.

'Spike his head atop his own banner,' Enola ordered. 'So that his troops can see he's dead, and his father will get the news like a dagger in his belly.'

After the death of the Prince, the battle ebbed and flowed, neither side making any significant losses or gains. The Spartikens slaughtered the Mander in their thousands, but for each one they cut down, two more took their place. The ground was a sticky paste of blood and sand, slick in parts. Warriors would die if they slipped, pierced by a sword through the back or a dagger to the throat while they lay on the ground. Order deteriorated, men and spear-maidens no longer fought for a side, they fought for themselves and the warriors by their side.

Generals Hals & Elektra

The Avolonian left flank

Gusts pushed and pulled at Avolonian shields, twisting the bronze discs so that shards of light flashed into the enemy's eyes. Dust devils crashed in and out of the ranks like children running through a crowd. The wind whistled through the forest of spears crowning the advancing line. General Hals and General Elektra rode together at the head of their legions. Ten thousand warriors of the Tornado and Typhoon legions followed their lead.

The Spartikens sang their hymn of death as they marched, the tramp of their boots in time with their words. The last verse ended with a cheer. The singing stopped, but the sound of twenty thousand feet stamping in unison went on.

'Is it true?' Hals called out to get Elektra's attention.

She suspected that she was being baited, but decided to play along. 'Is what true?'

A smile sprang to Hals' face. 'Is it true that before a battle you rub your tits in nettle paste? Makes you spear-maidens even more vicious, I'm told.'

Elektra narrowed her eyes; the jibe angered her, but she did not want to give Hals the satisfaction of knowing he needled her. 'True of some spear-maidens, but I don't have any tits. I do have balls bigger than yours, though.'

Hals laughed. 'I don't doubt it. The Mander will get more sport hanging them from the top of a spear than they will from spiking your head.'

Elektra tried not to be offended. She was always trying not to be offended in the male-dominated career she had chosen. In his own clumsy way, General Hals was trying to treat her as an equal. She relented that it must have been hard for him, not only to accept her as an equal, but also to have the Lioness as his commander. He was old-school, an officer even before women were allowed in the ranks. Not that that ever prevented a spear-maiden from pretending to be a man and joining a shield-wall. Times had moved on, and thousands of men like Hals were still learning how to deal with it.

'Looks like they spiked the heads of every one of the Jagger they butchered on that bastard slide of theirs.' Elektra nodded towards the centre where the heads were atop of spears, being jostled around to taunt the advancing Avolonians.

'Poor sods.' Hals started to rein in his mount. 'We'd better...'

'Shields!' a captain called out, the warning echoed along the line.

Hals cursed as he raised his shield, knowing he had left it late to dismount. Arrows thumped into his shield, and he cursed again as he felt his mount go tense and then skitter sideways. The General dismounted before the second volley of shafts rained down, thudding into the ground around him.

'Archers!' Hals yelled the order, and was crossed a moment later by the shadow of thousands of arrows, answering his call.

The army flowed around the two Generals.

Elektra handed the reins of her mount to an aid. 'Are you alright?'

'Shit, no!' Hals eyed the feathered shafts sticking out of his horse. 'I knew we had come too close, should have dismounted fifty paces back. Sorry, old pal.' He patted the beast's neck to calm him. 'He's done, a dead horse walking. There's blood in his breath.' The beast snorted a crimson mist out of its nostrils as his reins were handed to the aid. 'Bye, old chap. You were a good one.'

Surprised at the sentiment shown by the tough warrior, Elektra waited a moment before speaking, 'Come on,' she drew her sword. 'We need to catch up.'

The two Generals rushed to join the front line, braving arrows and then spears until the two armies were locked together in deadly combat, shield against shield. The Mander shield-wall held. It became a contest of strength, warriors pushing their shoulders hard into the back of their shields, trying to gain an advantage. The Avolonian third row thrust their dory spears over the rims of Mander shields. Other spears probed under the lower rims, hoping to find a gap or tip a shield forward so a warrior in the second row could hack their curved kopis blade into the gap.

Hals heaved on his shield, giving way every so often in the hope of opening a gap for him to dart his blade through. Every time he did, his arm came back with a new cut. He could hear the screams and grunts of Elektra next to him. He could tell from the sound of her when she would push. He timed his own efforts to match hers, that way they opened bigger gaps. He had an idea, and he changed shoulder to face Elektra.

'You men,' Hals pointed at two warriors using spears. 'Put your shoulders to the shields, over there, behind the General.' He turned to two others. 'You, shoulders against here, behind me.'

An arm came over the top of Hals shield, slashing a blade down on him. It glanced off his helmet, and a spearman jabbed the dory point of his lance at the hand, there was a scream and the arm disappeared, back from where it came.

'What's the plan?' Elektra grunted between shoves.

'Keep the rhythm and wait for my signal.'

With all of them pushing, more gaps appeared. The spearmen took the opportunity, thrusting their shafts through, fishing for a neck, a face or a chest to stab. There was a scream as one of the spear tips found its mark, and the line broke. The Avolonians felt the resistance against their shields give way.

'Now!' Hals roared.

Suddenly they were chasing Mander warriors, who were trying to get out of their way. A Spartiken fell backwards as the pressure vanished from his shield, but the others rushed past him, screaming their war cry.

Elektra slashed one man across the back of the legs. He fell, to be finished by a spear thrust between his shoulder blades. Hals split a warrior's helmet in two, the man running into his fellow warriors who stood their ground. Blood flowed down Hals' blade until the man dropped away from it. Then he thrust it into the startled man left facing him. The Mander recovered from their initial panic, but their line was broken, and they were falling victim to Avolonian blades and spears.

Arc

Centre of the battle

No distinguishable line marked where the Mander started and the Avolonians ended. The centre of the battlefield broke down into a chaotic, free-flowing mass of warriors attacking, screaming and killing, or screaming and dying. In places, Avolonians hacked at short shield walls, no more than six or seven shields wide, the Mander on the edges dying first. Mostly, it was warriors going hammer and tongue against each other in small groups. Men would win one micro battle, then immediately rush to another, hoping to gain an advantage for their side.

The ground was thick with blood, turning sand into sludge that sucked at Arc's feet. The Lion Blade collected Mander souls, as Arc fought his way towards the Emperor's banner. His heart pounded at the thought of winning the day by taking Al-Din's head. Arc did not know if his army was winning the day, or if it was just him and the Lion Warriors with him that were advancing.

A Mander Knight ran at Arc, his spear aimed at the Lion Lord's throat. Arc knocked the shaft to one side with Breath-Taker, and cut across the attacker's face with a backswing. The Knight screamed and stumbled blindly into a pack of Lion Warriors, their blades cutting the life out of him in the blink of an eye.

'Are we winning the day or am I about to be engulfed by an enemy I have wandered too deeply amongst?' Arc asked himself,

not knowing if he was winning or losing. His question was answered in a way that made him rub his eyes in disbelief.

Directly in front, giant grey figures swayed above the enemy. There was a sound like a horn, but so loud and so alien that it struck fear into the bravest of hearts. The ground under Arc's feet shook, and the trumpeting sounded from a hundred beasts. Al-Din was sending in his elephants.

'Gavara was right, the Emperor has brought the beasts of war. If he is sending them against us, then we must be winning the day. Has Enola broken the flank?' Arc stopped his advance and turned to see if Tyezore had advanced to support his daughter and the Storm legions. He frowned when he saw the Corinthians still waiting in reserve. *'Advance, you fool. Now is the time. Strike while we have momentum.'*

Arc had no more time for thought, the first elephant was upon him. The beast seemed bigger than Arc had thought possible. A metal armour plate protected the creature's forehead, and a breastplate hung from chains around its neck. Circlets of razor-sharp blades crowned each of the beast's long tusks, to be swept from side to side by the juggernaut's head, ripping to shreds any unfortunate warrior in their way. Those who avoided the blades would be trampled under feet the size of tree stumps.

Archers in turrets strapped to the elephants' backs, rained arrows down on anyone who slipped past the beasts. Mander warriors backed away from the stunned Avolonians and disappeared behind the beasts.

'Archers!' Arc yelled, more in panic than reason.

The beasts were bearing down on the Avolonians as archers rushed forward. The first volley of shafts thumped into the grey beasts. The arrows had little effect, just making the giants trumpet with anger. Arc suddenly realised the significance of Gavara's advice.

'Horns! Sound the horns!'

Rather by luck than intention, the archers called up had brought horns and trumpets with them. Hundreds of instruments were unslung and raised to trembling lips. A deafening noise was blasted at the elephants. Several of the creatures charged, but most of the beasts stopped in their tracks, their minuscule eyes widening with fear.

One charging animal tore through the warriors blocking its path, like the prow of a boat shattering water into white foam. Men were flung, broken and dying, like leaves on the wind. Another beast came straight at Arc. He rolled out of its way, but slower men were crushed to a pulp. The Lion Lord's rage took control, and he slashed at the colossal beast. Arc's blade cut deep wounds in the elephant's flesh, but seemed to have no effect. An arrow glanced off his helmet, and another snagged in the lion's head mane. Then the beast was past him.

Then Arc saw it. The hunter in him recognised the tendon at the back of the animal's leg. He chased after the beast and slashed Breath-Taker at the hamstring. It was like chopping at a taut rope holding a ship to shore in a strong current. The creature trumpeted in pain, throwing the archers from its back in a frantic attempt to get at its attacker. The beast limped after Arc, only to have its remaining hamstring cut by the warriors it turned its back on.

Avolonian archers persisted with the infernal noise that sent the beasts into a terrified panic. Archers without horns to blow fired arrows by the hundreds into the elephants' thick grey hides. In their need to escape the cacophony of blasting horns and trumpets, the animals turned on their own men, trampling and crushing as they fled. They caused havoc in their own ranks. Many of the beasts picked up their own warriors with their trunks and flung them over their shoulders at the men making the noise.

Avolonians were crushed in their dozens by the panicking beasts. But, as the elephants turned and fled from the maddening sound and painful arrows, they left hundreds of Mander warriors dead in their wake. Arc could not believe his eyes; the terrified beasts had cleared the way to the Emperor.

'Lions, on me!' he called, rushing forward.

If he could take the Emperor, he would take the day.

The Mander royal bodyguards scrambled into position to block the attack, but they were too few. Men who only moments before had been scared witless by marauding elephants were now hastily trying to form a shield-wall around their Emperor. One brave Mander officer called for archers and the survivors of the stampede to gather themselves.

Al-Din was sitting astride his jet black Axonian stallion, the finest horse of the best of breeds. He was flanked to his right by Xarius, his third son, and on the left by General Nimitz. Arc could see Al-Din's eyebrows raised in surprise as he watched the Avolonians charging towards him.

Arc thought the Emperor would turn and flee before he could reach him, but he stood his ground. Xarius and Nimitz raised their shields to protect their leader, blocking two or three arrows that were on target. As the two forces clashed, Arc launched his spear at Al-Din. The shaft flew true, parting the shields protecting the Emperor and sticking him in the shoulder. Al-Din bellowed with the pain of the impact, but the spear did not penetrate his armour. Colliding with the shields had robbed the shaft of its power, nevertheless it broke away several plates of the

Emperor's armour. Arc cursed as he watched the shaft clatter to the ground.

'Get him out of here!' Nimitz roared, putting himself between the enemy and his master.

Xarius grabbed the reins of his father's mount and hastily led him away. As the Prince turned his back on the Avolonians to ride off, Arc saw an arrow slam into his hip. Xarius arched in pain, pulling his mount's head back. The beast reared up and collided with Al-Din's horse, causing the Emperor to fall from the saddle. A second later, more Mander troops arrived to defend their Emperor, and both Al-Din and Xarius were obscured from Arc's view.

The sound of horns filled the air. Arc's heartbeat quickened, hoping the horn blasts signalled panic in the Mander troops, caused by their ruler fleeing the field. He soon realised that the horns were signalling the retreat of his own troops. The Avolonians disengaged and backed away in an orderly fashion, their discipline holding, despite their confusion.

The Mander were not following, their own horns howling on the wind demanding their obedience. Arc looked around for any clue to explain what was happening. He called for his banner so that his Generals could find him and report. Arc kept one eye on the enemy and one eye on the horizon beyond them. There was a large cloud of dust in the distance. Arc's heart sank, only an army on the move would send so much dust into the sky. The Mander reinforcements had arrived.

'Sir!' Commander Jellicoe had followed the banner to find his leader. He was riding Warspite and leading Armageddon by the reins. 'Mount up, you'll see more from up here.'

As soon as the Lion Lord was in the saddle, he saw Tyezore leading his Corinthians away to the south. 'Treacherous bastard.'

'The coward has ignored my orders to advance several times.' Jellicoe spat as if he needed to get the bitter taste of the Corinthian's treachery out of his mouth. 'Enola was crushing the enemy's flank. The battle was ours, but the coward stayed put.'

Arc was no longer listening to Jellicoe, he was transfixed on what he saw behind the fleeing traitors. There was another huge cloud of dust rising in the west. This cloud was even bigger than the one in the east.

Arc nodded towards the second cloud. 'Have we been flanked?'

Jellicoe didn't need to turn, he had seen the cloud. 'That's Atropolis in the east. He must have ridden all night to get his troops here so soon. He must have spies in our camp, how else could he have known to hurry? Shields.' The last word was a warning of incoming arrows. 'As for the cloud behind us, our scouts say there are no Mander troops within a hundred leagues to the south or west, it's clear to the Umbas river.'

Arc pushed back the lion helmet and scratched the front of his head. 'That's too big a cloud to be our troops from Calinkerbad. Who the hell is it?'

'We'll find out soon enough. Whoever it is, the Mander seem as nervous about them as we do. I think that's what's holding them back.'

'We can't take the chance,' Arc frowned. 'They are a hostile force until we can confirm otherwise. Order the retreat back to the river, that way we will have the water protecting our backs.'

Generals Hals & Elektra

The Avolonian Left Flank

General Hals listened in disbelief to what the horns sounded. He echoed the order to retreat, not believing his own words. 'We are winning, why retreat now.' Hals suddenly began to worry. 'It mustn't have gone well on the other flank. Damn, we were winning our fight here.'

It was a bloody retreat. The Spartikens were amongst the Mander and had to fight every step of the way. They were vulnerable until they got back to some semblance of a line. Warriors died in the retreat, but not one woman or man panicked or ran. It was only when the Storm Legions broke free of the Mander to form an orderly line that Hals became aware that some Spartikens had been cut off.

A group of about fifty warriors were deeper into the Mander than the rest of the legions when the retreat sounded. They could not get back as quickly as the others and were trapped. Hals' heart skipped a beat when he saw Elektra's banner in the middle of the surrounded force.

'Call the cavalry. Assemble on my banner.'

The retreating line opened like two veils being drawn apart. Warriors pushed away from the advancing horsemen, or were pushed aside by angry sergeants, intolerant of those too slow to move. When the cavalry reached him, Hals wasted no time. He took the mount of a disgruntled-looking horseman and then pointed his blade towards their trapped warriors.

Hals flicked his heels and his mount rode out into the empty space that had opened up between the two forces. He was a fine horseman, leading the cavalry, arcing the charge to where the Mander defences were thinnest. The enemy had little time to react. The last thing they expected was a cavalry charge to save fifty warriors, half of which were already dead or dying. General Hals took off a Mander head with the first swipe of his sword. It tumbled through the air, a shocked expression frozen on its face.

The Mander defensive line had hurriedly formed and was in no position to withstand a cavalry charge. The cavalry smashed through the line, slashing blades and thrusting lances. Hals fought his way towards Electra's banner. The General stood beneath her colours, hacking chunks out of the press of Mander warriors trying to kill her. She was a vision of rage and retribution, her blade defying the enemy their prize.

The cavalry charge had now lost all its impetus, and was in danger of becoming ensnared. Avolonian swords rose and fell, horsemen hacking at anyone or anything that dared to step into their killing zone. Each of the surviving Avolonian infantry was hauled up behind a rider, as the cavalry began to back out of the tightening snare of Mander warriors.

Hals forced his mount between Elektra and the enemy horsemen either side of him slashing at the enemy. He was not sure if he was rescuing her from them or them from her. She looked up at him, eyes filled with rage, baring her teeth, and frothing at the mouth like a wild animal. He held out his arm and pulled her up to sit behind him.

It was at the moment he turned his horse to leave that it happened. At first it felt like he had been hit in the side by a blunt object, then he felt the metal rings of his mail give way. His gut boiled with pain, only his anger keeping him in the saddle. Red faced, and eyes bulging, he turned and bellowed at his assassin.

A Mander warrior looked up at Hals, both his hands firmly gripping the spear embedded in the General's side. He was trying to pull it out, that was a mistake, he should have let go. Hals had enough life in him to bring his blade down onto the man's helmet, splitting it from brim to stern. Blood poured over the warrior's lifeless eyes as he crumpled to his knees, still gripping the spear.

Hals roared with pain, the weapon levering upwards in his gut.

Elektra hacked at the dying man holding the spear shaft, slashing her blade until he let go and fell to one side. She thrust her arms around the wounded general and grabbed the reins. The horse was panicking and needed little encouragement to flee from the throng of swords and spears. One of the two cavalrymen with Hals was dragged from his horse, a dozen blades rising and falling above him in a killing frenzy. The other rider followed Elektra and his wounded general, protecting their flank.

The spear fell from the General's side as Elektra galloped the mount across the gap to the Avolonian army. She felt hot blood and other liquids wash over her legs. Hals went limp in her arms, falling forward onto the horse's neck.

'Stretcher!' Elektra yelled, pulling up her mount as soon as she was amongst the Avolonians. 'Fetch the sawbones, your General is badly wounded.' Two warriors lowered Hals from the horse, both gagging at the mess spewing from his side. Two spear-maidens threaded their spears through the handles of their shields, linking them to make a stretcher, and General Hals was laid upon it.

'Where's that damn sawbones, doesn't he know his General needs him?'

One of the shield-maidens looked up at Elektra, shaking her head. The General flew into a rage, cursing and yelling at the sky.

A sergeant of the Typhoon Legion took Elektra by the arm. 'We must go. We are withdrawing.'

Elektra came to her senses. She gazed at the dead General lying on the shields. He was the last person she expected to owe her life to, or to mourn for.

'Bring the General, he's a brave soul and he will pass over with the honour he deserves.'

Arc

The wind mocked the retreating Avolonians. Arc watched the columns of smoke rising from the artillery he had ordered burned. He could see flames engulfing the Harpy, her giant throwing arm standing straight up like a flagpole, defiantly refusing to burn. The cloud of dust to the east was almost at the Mander camp, proof that Atropolis had arrived. Arc had sent scouts out to discover who the army to the south was.

'They are not following us,' Jellicoe told his Commander. 'May be we shouldn't have burned the catapults?'

Arc shook his head. 'They wouldn't have saved us, and they would have slowed us down. It's more important that we get to the river.' He looked towards the cloud of dust approaching from the west.

'That's a large force,' Jellicoe followed Arc's gaze. 'From the size of that dust cloud I'd expect twenty, if not thirty thousand.'

'Where the devil are those scouts? Have Lincon take the Lion Infantry to form a rear guard so that Enola can take her legions across the river.'

Jellicoe let a reluctant sigh escape. 'Lincon didn't make it. Torn apart by an elephant.'

'Then you go,' Arc said, as if he were unaffected by the terrible news about Captain Lincon. 'And send the scouts to me as soon as they are back.'

Jellicoe nodded towards two riders approaching fast. 'Looks like I won't have to.'

The horses skidded to a halt, sending up their own dust cloud. One rider leapt from the saddle, threw his reins to the other, dropped to one knee in front of Arc, saluted with a bang on his chest and bowed his head.

'Well, whose army is that?' Arc asked.

'Ours Sir. I mean sort of. It's not...'

Arc's patience was non-existent. There was no place for dithering on a day full of fear and death like this one. 'Spit it out!' he yelled. 'Who are they?'

The scout took a deep breath. 'There's no army Sir, just pack animals led by two dozen of our men. They are dragging bundles of branches and bushes along the dusty ground. The size of the cloud makes it look like there're thousands of them, but I doubt there's more than a hundred. They said that Gavara sent them.'

Jellicoe laughed. 'The old fox has bought us some time with his trickery. The Mander will think we have reinforcements.'

Arc gave Jellicoe a stern look. 'It only delays the inevitable. We failed today, so now we will have to face them again. Their reinforcements are real. And ours are just an illusion. You can't beat your enemy with a fantasy. Delay crossing the river until nightfall. Arrange the troops as if we mean to make our stand here. If illusion is all I have, then let's make it a good one.'

Darkness is a good friend to a magician, and when darkness fell, it wrapped its cloak of concealment around the Avolonian camp. The moon was nothing more than a thin crescent, its light paled by the dusty air. Arc stood with his back to his own camp fires, watching the numerous specks of light in the Mander camp. They were as many as the stars in the sky on a clear night.

'Now I see why you ordered so many fires lit when there is so little here to burn. At least we have food to cook, thanks to Gavara.' Enola came to stand by her father's shoulder.

'Deception and illusion are powerful weapons when the enemy has a superior force. That little illusion of Gavara's earlier gave the Mander reason to pause, and us time to gather what little we had from our camp.' Arc gave his daughter a smile. 'All those fires will make them think our army is greater than it is. Cooking some of Gavara's animals will add to the illusion, but don't slaughter too many, you'll need them to carry the wounded and your baggage.'

'And the line of fires in front of the camp?' Enola asked.

'To blind them. They can't see beyond the light, so they will not know you have taken your legions back to Calinkerbad.' Arc paused, recalling a memory. 'I witnessed the Nomad Chief, Saluke, lure the Mander General, Rhakitha into a trap by setting his fires away from his camp. The fool Rhakitha marched straight into an ambush. That's Saluke's golden sword you carry. If I hadn't killed him, he would have been a good ally on this crusade.'

'I won't leave without you. I'd rather die by your side, here on the battlefield, than starve to death in that blasted city port.' Enola spat to ward off the bad luck in her words. 'I hate that city. We should take a leaf out of the Nomad's book and lead the Mander into a trap. We hurt them today. We would have won if that traitor Tyezore had attacked when he was supposed to. Do you think he has joined the Empire?'

'I'm sure of it. Your legions fought well today, but we are finished here. No point in forcing a bad situation; we have overstretched ourselves. We won't be riding into Mander-Kush this winter, but we can pull back, regroup and come back stronger next year. The Emperor will want to destroy us here and now, let's not give him the chance.'

'I'm sorry,' Enola looked into her father's eyes. 'If we had listened to you and not split the army, we would not be in this situation.'

Arc put his arm around his daughter's shoulder. 'You won your command; now prove you are worthy of it by learning from your bad decisions and moving on.'

'We could all leave. We would have a good head start by dawn.'

Arc shook his head. 'No, we will lose too many. They will ride us down, even encircle us. You need to go, get behind the walls of the city and wait for me. I suspect that Al-Din is wounded, or at the very least he's in shock. I almost got him with a spear, but those hags who weave our fate saw fit to deny me. They dangled the carrot of victory and snatched it away before I tasted it. But the Mander will be hesitant, and the arrival of Atropolis will cause no end of confusion.' Arc laughed. 'He could upset any apple cart. I will strike them again and again with the Lion Cavalry. They will be chasing their tails for days before they realise you are gone.'

A thought suddenly dawned on Enola. 'Oh no, don't tell me this is about revenge? Atropolis is here, and you think there may be a chance to kill him.'

Arc threw his head back and laughed. 'That would truly pull a nail out of my heart, but I want to see the end of his father's empire more. I will have my day with that demon for slaughtering your sister, but I can wait.'

Enola changed the subject. 'Why did you marry Sonaji in secret?'

'It wasn't in secret. It was as public as I could make it.'

'It was secret from me. I had to find out from Gavara.'

Arc frowned. 'I sent for you, but you were nowhere to be found. Sonaji is pregnant with your brother or sister. I wanted them protected if anything happened to me. Marriage seemed the best way. Her cousin, Tyezore, seems to object to the arrangement, she warned me he would. Though we didn't think he would go against his father's orders and desert us.'

'And if anything does happen to you?'

'Then you will protect them.'

Enola opened her mouth to speak, but thought better of it.

Arc was aware of the rivalry between his new wife and his daughter, and didn't question Enola's silence, thinking it better to leave some things unsaid.

Arc suddenly did something he had not done for a long time, he hugged his daughter. To the world she was the commander of legions and a famed warrior, but to Arc she was still his little girl.

'You need to get going.' He held her at arm's length and looked into her eyes. 'Edius-Max and Jellicoe and all our remaining cavalry will stay here with me. Memfis and his army will come with you. They didn't run today, but their spirit is broken. They have been pushed across this unforgiving land from the Ibres Hills to Calinkerbad. Many of them will desert before you get to the city. Don't waste your time chasing them. Get to Calinkerbad with those that still have some resemblance of spirit.'

As Enola walked past the flames to disappear into the darkness beyond, Arc felt the cold touch of the spirits on his heart, and tried to ignore the fear that he would never see his daughter again.

The thin light of dawn made a silhouette of the Lion Cavalry, standing on the ridge about five hundred paces back from the river. The rest of the army were long gone, but Arc was hoping the Mander would think they were hidden behind the hills. Al-Din's scouts would eventually discover the truth, but that would take time, and time was what Arc needed. A relentless wind howled across the plain, tugging at banners, and loose clothing.

The enemy did not come rushing with the first slivers of light. Arc watched from his saddle as Mander scouts patrolled the far bank of the river. Jagged stumps littered the water's edge where resilient trees had clung to existence in this harsh land, before being cut down for firewood. The air had a metallic smell, which combined with the smoky aroma impregnated into clothing by camp fires.

The Cid pointed to scouts on the southern horizon. The Jagger Commander had insisted on staying. He would not order his Knights to stay, but every one of them volunteered. This was now a crusade of honour and revenge for the Knights of the Jagger Order. The Mander had cut them deep, and there was a black cloud over their Order that could only be lifted by a torrent of Mander blood.

'Only a matter of time now.' Cid raised his chin and looked down his nose at the distant scouts, his eyes smouldering with hate. 'They will send their cavalry north and south to flank us and come directly at us with their infantry.'

'I hope they do,' Arc replied. 'Wait until they are passing us on either flank. Then, we advance across the river and form into four squadrons.'

Edius-Max leaned forward in his saddle. 'You intend to trap us, with the river at our backs?'

'The river will protect us from the cavalry to the rear. If we advance, they will be forced to form their defences or risk us riding through broken ranks on a rampage of slaughter.' Armageddon sensed the malice in his master's voice and began stamping at the ground and flicking his tail. Arc reached out and patted his neck. 'It will take them all morning to form ranks. That's a whole morning of extra time our army will have to reach Calinkerbad.'

'There will be no escape from the other side of the river when they attack,' Jellicoe pointed out. 'If we cross the river it will be suicide.'

Arc swallowed the anger rising in him. 'You can take your men and leave, if you don't have the stomach for this.'

Commander Jellicoe laughed at the suggestion. 'Arcilus would run me through with that golden blade you gave him, if he found out I left you out here. No, I know as well as you that this is our army's only chance.'

'I'd rather face death head on than be cut down running for safety,' Edius joined the debate. 'If we don't stand here, they will catch us before we reach the safety of the city. A rear guard will be useless against a force this size. We escaped once because they were hesitant. They won't hesitate again. They've tasted our blood, and will pull us down like a pack of wolves on an injured elk.'

'I just want to kill the bastards,' Cid snarled.

The others chuckled at the forthrightness of their friend's hate.

'Take your Knights and chase the scouts away from the river,' Arc ordered Cid. 'Hold the crossing. We'll follow when the time is right.'

Crows filled the sky above the advancing Mander army. The creatures squawked, angry at being forced to take to the air when there was a feast of carrion littering the previous day's battleground. The Mander marched over the bodies of the previous battle to take up positions on a new field of war.

As Arc predicted, thousands of Mander horsemen rode along the Avolonian flanks. The Lion Lord simply allowed them to pass and form a barrier across his line of retreat. But Arc had no intention of retreating. He ordered his eight thousand mounted warriors to advance across the river where they formed into four squadrons.

Arc, Edius-Max, Jellicoe and The Cid knew what was expected of them, and took the lead of a squadron each. The Avolonians carried no banners, were not announced by drummers, and there were no foot soldiers to follow them into battle. In complete contrast, the advancing Mander army was an ocean of coloured flags and pennants. Drums beat a threatening pulse, as if a giant heart in the beast of war was pumping the scarlet blood of destruction through the veins of an army.

The Mander came to the field in an unexpected formation, three rectangles made up of hundreds of squares.

'I should have known,' Arc told himself when he saw Atropolis' banner in the centre of the middle rectangle. Gavara had taught the Prince how to deal with cavalry at the battle of the desert crossroads. They had defeated the Nomad horsemen on that day when Arc had formed his men into squares, thinned the horsemen as they rode through and then trapped them with his own cavalry. Atropolis was about to do the same to him.

The drums' beat changed, and the centre formation advanced while the two rectangles on either side held their position. Atropolis was setting his trap. All Arc could do was watch as the snare tightened, quietly pleased at the complexity of his adversary's manoeuvring. The more elaborate the trap, the longer it would take to spring.

The four Avolonian squadrons barely stretched the width of the Mander's forward formation. They looked like foothills at the base of a colossal mountain, dwarfed in stature. There was something strange about how the Mander were advancing; it was clumsy and slow. Three groups of densely gathered banners looked like sails on ships sailing through a sea of warriors, each vessel anchoring opposite an Avolonian squadron.

Arc thought he could see horses, but the banners obscured his view. 'Chariots,' he thought. Atropolis' colours fluttered amongst the middle cluster. The clusters on either side also had an elaborate banner at their centre, but Arc did not recognise which general or prince they belonged to.

'This day will have its rewards to match the sacrifices if we can cut deep enough into our enemy to rid us of those three lords. They have come here to cut my flesh and shatter my bones. Let's see if I can disappoint them.' Arc's eyes narrowed, his hate focused on Atropolis' colours snapping in the wind. 'They will have their moment of glory, but it will cost them more dearly than they could ever have imagined. This day will haunt their nightmares for as long as they draw breath, if they survive.'

Arc looked over his shoulder to see the Mander cavalry advancing towards the river. The trap was closing. He sensed it was time to make his move. Once he ordered the attack, there would be no turning back. The Mander cavalry would cross the river and they would flank him. Chaos was the order of the day. Chaos and as much destruction as was humanly possible.

'Riders!' Arc called out, and two men urged their mounts forward. 'Tell General Edius and General Jellicoe it is to be the Orion's Arrow formation. Aim for those banners and kill whichever Lord is hiding behind them. The Cid is to stick to the plan and flank the bastards on the left.' Arc paused, searching for his next words. 'Beyond that, I have no orders. Keep moving, strike, and survive. The Gods willing, some of us may make it back to

Calinkerbad.' He took his lion's head war helmet from its hook on his saddle and put it on.

Arc advanced, the Lion Warriors forming behind him into the wedge shape of Orion's Arrow. Many of the warriors had been with Arc when he led them in the arrowhead formation against Salamanca at Fwenga. Just as many had followed Arc's insane charge that defeated Atropolis at Caputhora. Some had even been with him when he rode Shadin in an arrow-headed charge against the Merron horde at Ribbelstead.

The Lion Lord looked to his right and left to see that his generals had done the same as he and were ready. 'Now, they will reap the hurricane of retribution.' Arc raised his hand, and horns blasted the order to advance. Armageddon strained to get ahead of the formation, Arc keeping the thunderous beast in check by pulling his head down. 'Patience, my boy, not yet.'

Three arrowheads of cavalry advanced on the Mander squares, while Cid led his squadron in an arc around the left flank. The Avolonian horsemen held perfect formations in all three arrows. Arc waited until he was in arrow range of the Mander line before releasing Armageddon from his restraint. The angry beast opened his stride, keen to be at the enemy. He was an evil beast, trained for war and hungry for violence.

The charge crossed the open ground to their enemy. Eight thousand mounts urged on by their riders, hooves casting up clods of earth and a trail of dust that rose into the wind. But no arrows came. The Mander parted, co-ordinated by blasting horns. The three Arrows of Orion were drawn in with nothing to crash against, passing through the squares.

Arc saw the way open as far in as the clustered banners, his Lion Blade drawn and pointing at his goal. The mane of his lion's head helmet trailing in the wind. The pennants parted to reveal a great black mouth. Instinct made Arc's next move for him. With all the force he had, he swerved Armageddon to the right. The next thing the Lion Lord knew was a terrible noise and heat, his mount vanished from beneath him. It was as if the earth opened up and the fires of hell were erupting. He hit the ground hard, his sword torn from his grip, and all went momentarily black.

Arc gasped for breath, his face in the dirt. His ears rang, and his head felt like it was held in a vice. Dust swirled around the Lion Lord as he struggled to rise to his feet. He could see little and hear less. He staggered around looking for his sword, but it was gone. He found the lion's head and put it on. As the dust began to clear he saw men, his men, staggering around, some screaming, some with limbs missing or hanging torn and mangled, all blooded, but he could hear nothing but the ringing in his ears. 'What kind of monstrous weapon had caused such destruction?' An unfamiliar smell filed Arc's nostrils, bitter smoke that hung at the back of his throat.

The next sight froze Arc to the spot. Armageddon was down, kicking his legs and trying to lift his head. Dark blood thickened by the dust trailed from horrific wounds. A gash starting at the beast's chest ran a third the length of its body. Both front legs were broken, but still kicking at the air. Arc saw the mace he had taken from Cid days before, still strapped to his saddle. He untied it, hindered by a broken finger.

Arc stood by the beast's head, reached down and patted its blood-stained neck. A moment of tenderness amongst the chaos and death. The Lion Lord took a deep breath, then struck a powerful blow to Armageddon's forehead with the mace. The beast went limp, shuddered, and then was still.

Arc turned in time to see Mander warriors bearing down on him. He snatched up his shield and clubbed the first man to reach him. The heavy metal mace crushed the Mander's helmet. He dropped to the ground, tripping those following him.

Arc beat two more attackers to the ground before yelling, 'On me!'

It surprised him he could hear again. More Lion Warriors joined their Lord. Mander warriors backed away from Arc's fury. Surrounded and outnumbered, the red mist of battle possessed him, and he killed in abundance.

Arc was standing over a man he had beaten to the ground, his victim's face smashed to a pulp. The Lion Lord felt his strength suddenly leave him. His hands began to shake, and he dropped the mace.

'No, not now,' was his last thought, falling to his knees, his body violently shaking as the fit took control, and he lost consciousness.

The acrid smoke was the first thing Arc noticed as he started to wake. Voices with Mander accents shouted orders, incoherent to Arc's confused hearing. He fluttered his eyelids attempting to open them.

'He's awake,' a gruff voice announced, and they dragged Arc to his knees by hands made strong by years of weapons training. 'Fetch the master.'

With blurred vision, the Lion Lord saw Lion Warriors he knew well, on their knees and lined up in rows. They were bloody and beaten, their heads hanging in shame.

'Lift your chins, men,' Arc called out. 'Don't give them the satisfaction of...'

A blow from the back of a gloved hand silenced Arc. He shook it off and watched an elaborately armoured man stroll towards him.

'It's been so long,' a familiar voice said, with a calmness out of place on a battlefield.

Arc looked up, squinting to focus his vision. The man looked vaguely familiar. He was tall, wide at the shoulder and thick in his arms. He was clean shaven, unusual for a Mander Lord or General. His war helmet had cheek pieces that hid most of his features but extenuated his noble nose. Arc noticed his eyes, dark and snake-like with a piercing stare. His heart began to quicken. Only one man had eyes like that, Atropolis.

The Priest General threw his head back and laughed. 'He recognises me. I can see the hate in his eyes.'

This was not the Atropolis Arc remembered. He had been of lighter frame, bearded, even not as tall, if that was possible. Arc had known a prince who needed champions to fight for him. This Atropolis was an imposing figure, a formidable warrior who looked capable of fighting his own battles.

Arc was on his knees, his hands tied, but he looked around for any opportunity to snatch a weapon and strike at his enemy. There was nothing. The Mander army surrounded him, squares of warriors standing to attention as if they were still waiting for the battle to start. The noise of fighting could still be heard, but it seemed distant. Arc hoped his warriors fought on. 'Keep the bastards here,' he thought.

Arc's eyes fixed on a huge black object resting on a chassis of thick wooden beams with wheels the size of a horse. Half a dozen guards stood around the monster holding objects Arc did not recognise, but assumed they were for the servicing of the beast. One man held a long pole, another a rope smouldering at one end. Arc realised that this is what the banners had been hiding, the giant mouth that had exploded in his face. His eyes flicked to the captured Lion Warriors kneeling in rows in front of the intimidating black cylinder.

Atropolis laughed again. 'We have been waiting for you to wake up. You have felt the breath of my dragon on your face. Now you will have the chance to see her feed.' He nodded to the guards.

The soldier with the long pole lowered it towards the man with the smouldering rope. He blew on the hemp until it glowed red and then tied it to the pole. Arc's heart was pounding. He felt an impending doom, but could not foresee what horror awaited his men. The pole was lowered so that the rope hovered above the rear of the metal dragon. The way the man holding the pole cringed, baffled Arc, and the Mander guards covered their ears.

The rope was lowered, there was a puff of smoke, and for one moment there was a silence as if time had stopped. It hadn't. In the next instant, Arc's world was rocked in an avalanche of noise and confusion. He saw flames erupt from the mouth of the beast, and the kneeling men disappear in thick black smoke belched from the belly of the monster.

Arc's eyes were forced shut by the blast, his ears hammered by the noise. He forced his eyes open, watching as the smoke cleared. The acrid smell made him want to gag, as he hoped to see his Lion Warriors still kneeling in front of the beast. Several bodies faded into view, mangled lumps of flesh to the right and left of the cylinder. Arc's eyes bulged when the smoke cleared enough for him to take in the full scene. The men had vanished. There was nothing but scorched ground directly in front of the beast.

Atropolis watched Arc intently, enjoying the horror on the face of his nemesis. 'The world has changed from this day onward. War has changed. No cavalry, infantry or city wall can resist the fiery breath of my dragons. Today, just three of them destroyed the famous Lion Cavalry. Soon I will have a hundred, then a thousand. The time of armies is over, this is the time of the dragon, and they serve the Lord Kush.'

'New weapons won't convert the world to your cruel God,' Arc snarled. 'What is made by men can be defeated by men.'

Atropolis drew his sword and rested the tip of its blade on Arc's throat. 'Oh, the world will bow to Kush, but first my dragons will destroy the rest of your army hiding in Calinkerbad. Your sacrifice here won't help them. They are trapped. Your Pirate fleet cannot pass Ratlarbig's defences, and Corinth is again a hostile land to you. I will blast down the walls your army hides behind and feed every last one of your crusaders to my dragons. Give him his sword.'

A warrior carrying the Lion Blade and Arc's lion helmet stepped forward. He jammed the point of Breath-Taker into the ground and forced the helmet onto Arc's bleeding skull. Then he took out his dagger and cut the ropes binding the Lion Lord's wrists.

Arc rose slowly, trying not to reveal how weak he felt. The Mander guard's eyes flicked between Arc and the Lion Blade, and Arc knew what he must do. While Atropolis took off his cumbersome general's coat, the guard announced the contest.

'You have witnessed the destruction of the Lion Cavalry by the seventh son of our exalted ruler, Al-Din!'

the guard shouted. 'Now see justice served by Atropolis, the servant of Kush and conqueror of the Lion Crusade!'

Atropolis slashed at the air to warm up his sword arm while he waited for Arc to stagger towards him. The Priest had trained every day since his defeat at Caputhora, hardening his mind and body, honing his skills, motivated by his humiliation. The last time he had met Arc, he was a prince with all the weaknesses a royal life brought, but now he was a hardened killer. Executing this heathen was the work of Kush, and he would enjoy it.

Arc's legs were weak and his hands still trembled, not yet fully recovered from the fit. He pulled his sword from the ground, the hilt familiar in his grip. He knew this was all for show. Atropolis wanted the glory that killing the Lion Lord would bring. He thought about refusing to fight, but he would probably end up in a cage, paraded around the streets of Mander-Kush, humiliated and disgraced.

Arc let his hatred bring him strength. The man who murdered his daughter faced him with a blade. He had a chance to kill him, and nothing else mattered for now. Arc clenched his teeth and swung Breath-Taker. Atropolis parried the blow, sidestepped, and then knocked the blade down. The Lion Lord's hands were numb, his grip weak, and he had to let the blade's tip rest on the ground. He leaned on the sword's hilt, panting.

'Pick it up,' Atropolis snarled, disappointed at how weak the fit had left his adversary. 'I'll not be cheated out of my satisfaction. When I have cut your body into chunks and fired you from the mouth of the dragon, I will drag your last child from her hiding place in Calinkerbad and have a hundred of my Immortals rape her for a year before I gut her and hang her naked body over the gates of Mander-Kush.'

Arc used the threats to fuel his anger. He felt the fire of revenge racing through his veins. Arc pushed the heavy lion helmet from his head, letting it drop to the ground. Steam rose from his matted hair, and it relieved him to be free of the cumbersome object. Lifting the blade, he stepped closer to Atropolis. He lunged again, this time when his blade was parried, he rolled with the force and struck again. Atropolis was caught off guard, having to move quickly to avoid the strike aimed at his neck.

As Arc's strength flowed back into him, the contest became more even. Atropolis was accustomed to dominating the best of warriors with a sword, but even an under-strength Lion Lord was a worthy adversary. Arc grew in strength as the duel went on. Atropolis found himself more and more on the back foot, defending himself from blows that became faster and more powerful with every strike.

Rage filled Arc's head as he battered his opponent backward with a tornado of blows. Revenge burned in his eyes. Death meant nothing to him, the lust for retribution consuming him as he witnessed fear in the eyes of the snake that had murdered his daughter. Atropolis was driven back until he fell to one knee, his blade held over his head in the hope it would save him.

Arc raised Breath-Taker for the killing blow. Hate, revenge and fury powering the strike that would rid the world of the Warrior Priest. Atropolis closed his eyes and cowered in expectation of the blow, but it never came. He looked up to see Arc frozen to the spot, his sword raised, and the point of a spear sticking out from his stomach.

The pain of a spear thrust through Arc's back sent his body into spasm. He hung onto his sword until a second spear plunged into his chest, then Breath-Taker fell from his grip. The two guards holding the shafts piercing the Lion Lord's body used them to force him to the ground.

Arc dropped to his knees. He looked down to see the tip of a spear protruding from his middle, his guts visible and bulging through the mouth of the wound. He took short sharp breaths, every one of them agonising, the second shaft piercing his lung. Hot fluid flowed over Arc's folded legs, and he did not know or care if it was blood or his bladder releasing. He used the last of his strength to lift his head and watch Atropolis rise to his feet.

The two guards held Arc upright with their spears, the shafts penetrating him from front to back and back to front. Atropolis towered over the kneeling Lion Lord, his sword poised to strike.

'The time of lions is over,' Atropolis spat on Arc's upturned face. 'Your crusade is a failure and will die with you. Your death will mark my victory.'

Arc smiled, dark blood overflowing from the corner of his mouth. 'My death will not bring you victory.' He had to force a mouth-full of blood through his lips. 'It will only unleash my daughter's wrath.'

Atropolis howled with laughter, and the surrounding warriors echoed its scorn with laughter of their own. 'Now you will die, and tomorrow the same blade that severs your head will gut the last of your spawn.'

'I'm already dead.' Arc hissed through blood-stained teeth. He was cold and knew his life's blood had drained away into the sand around his feet.

The hairs on Arc's neck stood up, as if a warm breath was coaxing them to life. He felt a presence, a gentle spirit drawing his thoughts away from the pain. 'Enough,' a voice no louder than the beat of a butterfly's wing whispered. 'You have done enough. It's time to come with me.' He felt the soft words breathed into his ear.

'Jem,' Arc mumbled to himself. 'After all these years, you have finally come for me.' He felt her gentle touch take his hand. He saw Atropolis draw back his sword. He lifted his head to expose his throat and closed his eyes. Arc did not see the blade swinging at his neck. He took a last breath and allowed his soul to drift away on the scent of Jem's perfume.

Atropolis grunted with the effort of the swing, and Arc's head tumbled through the air, thudded into the dust, and was still. The Lion Lord was dead.

Chapter 8

Atropolis

The night of a thousand knives

Thousands of Avolonian cavalry lay dead in the field, those who survived were in disarray. Man and horse lay side by side, the Dragon Cannons indiscriminate in their decimation of the Lion troops. The Lion Lord's head was spiked on a pole between the heads of his two Generals, Edius-Max and Jellicoe. Atropolis had any surviving officers hung, and their stomachs slashed so that their innards fell out.

Captured Avolonians and Jagger Knights were forced to kneel and watch their officers be executed. The lucky ones were beheaded, while the less fortunate were made to stand in front of the Dragons and were blown to smithereens so that Atropolis could display his new weapons to the wider Mander army.

Atropolis wanted to chase down the fleeing cavalry and Avolonian Army, but his brothers thought otherwise, and they still commanded the army. Al-Din was injured, he had broken limbs and ribs in a fall from his horse during the battle. The Emperor lay in his bed, gripped by a fever and consumed with grief for the death of his youngest warrior son. Prince Haslan's was the only body so far to be retrieved from the battlefield and given funeral rights.

Xarius and Apollis would not advance their armies until their father was out of danger. They ordered the bodies of Mander officers fallen in battle to be collected from the killing grounds. Common soldiers would be stacked into piles and burned close to where they lay. Atropolis was furious. He wanted the dead left where they were, their bodies to rot and their bones to bleach. He wanted future generations to cross a desert of bones, a warning to all who would dare strike at the heart of Mander.

Emperor Al-Din lay still in his sickbed, drifting in and out of consciousness. Atropolis was at his father's side, so was the Emperor's chief cleric. Mesteroph had found two new allies in Xarius and Apollis. The two Princes preferred his counsel to that of their fanatical brother. Atropolis felt the balance of power tipping away from him. He commanded a force of Immortals, and while his father was incapacitated, he was acting commander of the Imperial army. Xarius led the Northern Army and Apollis the Southern army. Combined, they far outnumbered Atropolis, meaning he could not act without their agreement.

Two physicians fussed around the Emperor. One mopped the sweat from Al-Din's face and tried to administer a tonic. The second physician tended to leeches sucking at the Emperor's newly set arm. Atropolis shooed away the medical men as soon as his brothers entered the room. The Emperor's tent was palatial, huge and furnished to the highest standards. Xarius and Apollis crossed the room. Xarius limping, the wound to his hip making every step painful. They passed the physicians on the way to their father's side.

'Leeches?' Xarius questioned, having seen the physician's blood splattered bowl as he passed. 'Has our father not lost enough blood already?'

'How is he?' Apollis asked Mesteroph, seeming to ignore his priest brother on purpose.

'He had a turbulent night. No doubt troubled by the loss of your younger brother, but the news of today's victory has lifted his spirits.'

Al-Din was sleeping, unaware his sons were gathered around him. The room smelt sour, a cocktail of oils and potions plastered on the Emperor's injuries, and the heady stench of urine in pots by the bed. The darkness of night was creeping in like a thief to steal what little daylight remained. Several fires around the sides and a large chandelier hanging in a canvas dome at the centre kept the room bright.

'According to Haslan's guards, it was the Lion's bitch pup who took our brother's head,' Apollis told them.

'I will cut her heart out and feed it to the crows to avenge our brother.' Xarius narrowed his eyes. 'Did you execute the guards for their failure?'

'I made them fall on their own swords. There will be no paradise for them. They will walk the underworld for all eternity, blinded and speechless.'

Xarius let out a rumble of satisfaction. 'You cut out their eyes and tongues, good.'

Atropolis gestured towards a seating area. 'If it is revenge we want, then we must advance on Calinkerbad, without delay.' His words sounded like an order instead of the diplomacy he had intended. 'We must crush the remnants of the Lion Crusade, burn it to ash and scatter it to the winds.'

'They're trapped,' Apollis barked. 'Their Pirate fleet can't pass the defences at Ratlarbig. They have nowhere to go. We will stay here until our father recovers. They will wait.'

Xarius filled a cup with wine from a jug, drank it in three gulps, and slammed the cup back onto the table. 'For a man of God, you're a ruthless bastard, Atropolis. Where did those dragon weapons come from? I've never seen a cavalry charge stopped in its tracks like that.'

Atropolis smiled, his disdain for his brother well hidden. 'One must understand the past to see into the future.'

Apollis laughed, spraying wine as he did so. 'What's that supposed to mean? You got lucky today. Surprise was the real weapon. If the Lion Lord had seen the new-fangled artillery, he would have easily ridden around it. Then what would you have done. No, it was trickery won this day.'

Atropolis did not answer. He poured more wine for his brothers and sat back to scrutinise the two Generals.

'Are your officers gathering for our blessing?' Mesteroph asked.

'All of mine from captain and above are kneeling out there waiting for you,' Xarius finished his third cup of wine. 'At least they are out of the wind.' He wiped his lips with the back of his hand. His stomach rumbled loudly. 'I need to eat. Only you, Atropolis, would build a chapel out of canvas in the desert.'

Atropolis leaned forward. 'You can thank Mesteroph for the chapel. I'd have been happy for them to kneel out in the wind.'

'A holy place for holy work,' Mesteroph cut in. 'Have your men left their weapons outside?'

'My brother's bastard Immortals saw to that,' Apollis turned to Atropolis. 'You need to teach those thugs some decorum, treated my officers like shit. There'll be bad blood between them. There'll be fights later, mark my words. Good men will end up with their throats slit or a knife in the back, you'll see. At least the bastards know their place and waited outside the chapel.' His stomach rumbled too, as if in sympathy with his brother's hunger. 'Let's get this done. I have other things to attend to.'

'One moment,' Atropolis held up his hand to prevent anyone getting up. 'I will have the men sing a hymn while we finish here. I have something important to tell you.' He got up and crossed to the tent's entrance, where he spoke to the guards.

Moments later, the sound of singing came from the canvas chapel, Muffled and out of tune, but enthusiastic enough.

'Thank you for your patience,' Atropolis told his brothers as he returned to his seat, his sword trapping against the arm as he sat. He noticed sweat on Xarius' brow. 'It is possible that our father will not last the night.'

'Nonsense!' Apollis blurted out. 'He is as strong as a bull. It will take more than broken bones to finish him.'

Apollis had no sooner finished speaking than he doubled over in pain. Xarius tried to sit up, but found he was too weak and could do little more than hang onto the arms of his chair. The singing in the chapel stopped, replaced by shouts and the sound of panic.

'What you are hearing brothers is a change of command,' Atropolis said, seeming uninterested in his siblings' sudden debilitating condition. 'I may have been misleading when I said it is possible that our father may not last the night. The Emperor has consumed the same poison that is draining the life out of you both. He will definitely not last the night.'

'Bastard,' Xarius groaned, trying to rise and unsheathe his sword, the pain slamming him back down before he could.

Apollis was silent, both hands white at the knuckles as he gripped the arms of his chair, his body shaking. Turning to Mesteroph, Atropolis could see the shock in the cleric's wide eyes. He was not a man who was easily frightened, but this was a scene of madness, a dance of insanity.

'You're insane. The Council of Als will hang you for this,' Mesteroph screeched, anger seasoning his words. 'No, not just the Als,' he was now trembling with rage. 'God himself will condemn you for this blasphemy.'

A smile crept onto Atropolis' face. 'The twelve Als have voted a successor, and that successor is me. Your old ways die here with the Emperor. I will lead Mander into a new era. No more empire building and tolerance of other cultures and false religions. The world will bow to Kush, no exceptions and no tolerance. The Questerus demands obedience. I demand obedience, and I shall have it, by devotion or by the sword, it doesn't matter to me.'

Horror twisted Mesteroph's face. 'You're mad, your brothers' armies will rise up and cut you to pieces.'

Atropolis shook his head. 'Those screams you hear are the last sounds of resistance. Officers loyal to my brothers are being put to the sword in the chapel and all over the camp. Men loyal to me will replace them, leading the great North and South armies into my New Order.'

'Madness, utter madness,' Mesteroph babbled as he rose from his seat and headed for the exit. 'I will put a stop to this.'

Watching the cleric leave, Atropolis seemed unconcerned. He sighed. Two guards entered the room.

'Thank goodness,' Mesteroph said, waving his hands at the men.

Both guards looked to Atropolis. He gave a curt nod. The guards drew their blades, and a moment later Mesteroph was lying in a spreading pool of his own blood.

Rising from his seat, Atropolis studied his brothers' faces. The Princes' features were twisted, made unrecognisable by the pain they had endured. He drew his dagger, thinking to slit their throats and spare them further suffering. It was too late for Apollis, his wide still eyes confirming he had already succumbed to the darkness. Xarius was in the last throes of death, so Atropolis returned his dagger to his belt.

He watched as the brother who had dominated him as a child slipped from the mortal world. The great General he had heard so much about from a bragging father was gone. All but one of the exulted Al-Din's powerful sons were gone. Only Atropolis remained: Emperor Atropolis, once he had been ordained, crowned, and taken the sceptres of Kush.

Atropolis held a military funeral for his father. Al-Din's body burned on a funeral pyre five men high. Prince Xarius and Apollis burned on pyres either side of him, watched by the whole army. The next day Atropolis was crowned to the cheering of a hundred thousand warriors. Word was sent out all over the land that there was a new Emperor, a New Order. This was the time of Atropolis, servant of Kush.

The Emperor's first order was to form a column and march on Calinkerbad. They advanced under one banner, Atropolis' crescent moon. Officers newly promoted had the crescent moon embroidered on their tunics. Warriors painted it on their shields. Every man in the newly unified Army of Kush was proud to wear the half-moon badge, to be led by the hero who slew the Lion Lord, and who had turned back the crusade that had dared to invade their homeland.

The army in its entirety thought Al-Din's death was a consequence of his injuries, so the murder of his sons and a thousand officers was overlooked as if it had never happened, or had merely been the outcome of a power struggle. The Council of Als had sanctioned Atropolis' succession, and that was not for the common folk to question.

Enola

Banners silhouetted by a sinking sun filled the horizon. Enola watched from the ramparts as the Mander Army formed up around Calinkerbad. It was a ravenous beast cornering its prey. Strong, vibrant, and infused with new life, the Mander warriors poured over the landscape. Enola's own troops were exhausted and starving. They had felt the bitter sting of defeat, leaving their hearts heavy and their spirit drained.

Cid, and what remained of his Knights survived to return with news. The Lion Lord was gone, his cavalry annihilated. There was nowhere left to run. No fight that could be won. The city's stone walls only bought the Avolonians a little time, a delaying of the inevitable. Enola's blood boiled with rage. She imagined charging out of the city gates, her army at her back, and smashing the Mander lines. She would find her father's murderer, squeeze the life out of him and take his head to hang over the gates.

'I thought I would find you here.' Gavara joined Enola on the rampart. 'I don't need my spies to tell me what my eyes can see. Atropolis has ascended to Emperor. His father must have perished in the battle, and the strongest son has seized control.' Gavara sighed and placed a hand on Enola's shoulder. 'I have done your father a great injustice,' he sighed again. 'I will not let another moment pass without telling you what I should have told him.'

Enola shrugged the bony fingers from her shoulder. 'My father is dead.' Her expression remained sullen. 'I sensed it. I felt the blade that struck him from this world as if it struck my own flesh. He is gone, and the world has changed.'

'I felt it too, even before the scouts brought news of the head and the lion helmet, carried on pikes in front of the Mander column.'

Enola's knuckles turned white, ferociously gripping the wall to contain her anger. Her father, the greatest leader of her time, would be denied a warrior's right of burial. He would suffer indignity in death. His head carried as a trophy by his sworn enemy.

The moment Enola had dreaded came all too soon. The Lion Lord's head, and what Enola assumed were the heads of Edius-Max and Jellicoe, where brought forward. Riders placed them where they could be seen from the city. Three heads, and the lion helmet atop of pikes were rammed into the ground, flanked by Atropolis' banners.

Anger echoed from the walls as Enola screamed with rage. 'I will cut that devil's heart out for this! We will not wait behind these walls to die in shame. I will wound them grievously before they finish us, and I shall see that bastard's head on a spike before I take my last breath.'

Gavara waited a moment to let Enola calm down, and then he could contain himself no longer. 'Cubb lives.'

Enola took no notice of the old man's words. She glared at the enemy, her face almost purple with rage.

'Cubb is alive,' he said louder. 'Your sister is alive.'

There was a sudden silence, Enola's eyes flicking between the enemy and Gavara. Realisation suddenly drained the colour from Enola's face.

'What are you talking about, old man? Have you finally lost your marbles? I saw her run through with a sword.'

Gavara shook his head. 'No. You saw the young girl I sacrificed to save your sister. Cubb is alive and well in the Ice Kingdom, where I left her.' There was a long moment of silence. 'I suspected what Atropolis would do to Cubb if he found and confronted your father. I found a companion for Cubb, a child so alike that only I could tell the difference between them. I have done many things I regret in my duty as a Pathfinder, but sending that child to her death is the worst of them.'

'You let my father go to his death not knowing his daughter lived? Knowing the pain he carried? Knowing how it tortured him?'

Gavara did not answer. He just looked at the ground and nodded.

There was a clatter of armour as Cid came up the stone steps leading to the ramparts. He approached Enola, bowed his head, and pointed over the wall.

'Those are the monstrous beasts I told you about. I watched with my own eyes as they ripped swathes of men and horses to ribbons. The Mander scouts we captured called them the Dragons, but they could tell us nothing about their workings.'

Enola looked to where Cid pointed. It looked as if three ships were sailing across the fields in front of the city. Each cart rolled steadily forward, covered in banners that flapped in the wind like sails. Huge teams of horses pulled the vehicles towards Calinkerbad.

'Lightning seeds,' Gavara mumbled.

Enola frowned. 'Lightning seeds?'

'He has discovered the power of the black powder. The ancients called it lightening seeds. One touch of a flame and you have instant lightning. Oh, it's harmless enough in the open, used for tricks or display, but you can't contain it. They used it in fire sticks made of bamboo wrapped with cord that fired stone balls. They'd kill a man at fifty paces.'

Enola watched the Dragons sail across the battle-damaged fields into positions facing the city wall. 'What happens if you contain it?'

'You can't, that's the point.' Gavara waved his hands around. 'One touch of a flame and it breaks out of any container, shatters any wall. It explodes.'

'If it's so powerful and you know about it, why haven't we used it?' Enola asked.

Gavara let out a sigh, as if a child had asked him why the sun went down in the evenings. 'The knowledge has been hidden for millennia for good reason. Our ancestors saw the lightning seeds' destructive power. They feared that in the hands of a tyrant it would be devastating. They hid all knowledge of it, fearing the end of the world. Atropolis has not only discovered the secret of the black powder, he has learned how to channel its destructive properties in these Dragons of his.'

'Can you make some of this... black powder?' Cid asked.

Gavara shook his head. 'The ingredients are very specific. I doubt we could find any of them in any quantity. I'd need at least a hundred pigeons.'

'I will ride out with what is left of my Knights and destroy these Dragons.' Cid turned as if to leave.

'No!' Enola snapped. 'That's just what he wants. These walls are thick, and the gates are protected by the new wall Gavara had Ioniedas build. Let's gauge the bite of these Dragons before we throw our dice.'

The answer came sooner than expected. The metal cylinders spat fire, and a moment later, thunder sounded on a cloudless day. Smoke belched from the Dragons' mouths. A half of a moment later there was an impact against the wall that sent Gavara, Enola, and Cid crashing to the ground. Dust filled the air, and small shards of rock rained down.

Enola forced herself to her feet, coughing and dazed; her senses muffled, her ears filled with a whistling noise. She waved her hand in front of her face to clear the dust. Her eyes focused on the centre of the blast, a little further down the wall from where she had been standing. There was a pile of rubble and the dismembered body of a guard who had been standing there.

Cid's face was coated in dust, and blood dripped from his nose. 'We must leave, they will fire again soon.' He took Enola's arm and tried to lead her away.

She was in shock and pulled free of his grip to run to the wall and peer over the side. One shot had hit lower down the wall, doing little damage. Another had passed over the wall to drop through a roof, leaving no more than a barrel-sized hole in the tiles. But the third had struck near the top of the wall, shattering and loosening stones. It would not take too many strikes like that to undermine the wall's stability.

'That is not new technology,' Gavara said, approaching the wall. 'It would have taken decades to perfect such destructive weapons. Only the Merovingians in the east had such knowledge, and they haven't been seen for hundreds of years. So, where in God's name did he get those weapons?'

'I don't care where they came from, he has them,' Enola snarled. 'Summon what's left of our Council. We must decide our next move. I'll not hide from that bastard behind these walls.'

Sonaji

The blast from the first Dragon shots echoed through the city's narrow streets. The only civilians left in Calinkerbad were the camp followers and the slaves left behind by the Mander. Mothers covered the ears of frightened children. The alleyways came alive with folk rushing to find their loved ones or returning to their lodgings. The air reeked of fear, filled with the sound of war-weary people.

From where Sonaji sat in City Hall, it sounded like a storm was approaching, thunder rumbling in the distance. She smiled when her advisors told her the attack had begun. It was time for her to make her move and secure her ascension to the Corinthian throne.

The Lion Lord's widow wasted no time in taking control of the city on her arrival. Arc gave her guards orders to take her there, but now he was dead, she was free to give her own orders. Her marriage to the Lord gave her the natural succession of rule on his death. She had his seal, and no one would question her authority when she carried the Lord's child in her womb.

True, she had faked the pregnancy to trick Arc into marrying her, but by the time anyone would find out, it would be too late to spoil her plans. By then, the Avolonians would be Atropolis' slaves, and she would sit on the Corinthian throne.

Thunder rumbled again as the Dragons roared for a second time. It had been a long time between shots, but the initial fear had not faded. Among the frightened people scurrying around the hall, Sonaji spotted her guards escorting a rough-looking man towards her. It was Erwin. The assassin dropped to one knee when he reached where Sonaji sat on the Ivory Throne.

One guard stepped forward and saluted. 'Your Highness. This man says he has a message for your ears only. We searched and disarmed him,' the guard added, to ensure she would not reprimand him for endangering her by bringing a stranger into her presence.

'Leave us. I will hear what he has to say in private.'

The guard hesitated to obey his mistress' command, worried to leave her unprotected. Sonaji waved her hand, irritated at the delay, so the guard saluted, turned and ushered the others away.

'Your Highness. I bring news from the Emperor,' Erwin said, when he was sure no one other than Sonaji could hear.

'Al-Din?'

Erwin shook his head. 'Atropolis is now the ruler of Mander. His father and closest brothers are dead.'

'Then he has been true to his word, and Kush truly favours him. How did you get into the city?'

'I sailed a felucca into the harbour under cover of darkness. I let your guards capture me. It was the quickest way to find you. Your Highness, I am your man now. The Corinthian troops are under Mander command awaiting your return. Atropolis has arrested Tyezore. The Emperor thanks you for sending word to him. It was most useful, and he was able to use your intelligence to great effect.'

Sonaji stroked the smooth ivory tusk forming one arm of the throne. It felt cold to the touch, matching her mood.

'I'm surprised to see you after you failed me. You were supposed to put an end to that Lioness bitch. Instead, you slit the throat of her slut lover.' Sonaji looked at the lion brooch. 'Is that where you got that trinket from?'

Erwin nodded, his cheeks flushed with embarrassment. 'It was, Your Highness.'

He raised a hand to the silver circle that fastened his cloak. The metal was cold to the touch, his fingers tracing the outline of the prancing lioness design. Sonaji saw a spark in his eye and suspected he was remembering the killing stroke that had won him his trophy.

'What does Atropolis want of me?'

Erwin raised himself. 'If you are in command, you are to have the Avolonians surrender to him. Your reward will be as agreed, the throne of Corinth. I have a blank parchment with his seal. He says you can write whatever promise you need to get them to open the gates. It does not matter to him; he will make slaves of them all. But you can tell them if he has to fight his way into the city he will kill every living thing in here. And he will get in, the Dragons will see to that.'

Sonaji enjoyed the sense of achievement she was feeling. Her heart pounded. All her ambitions were coming true. She would sit on the throne of Corinth, not her cousin, or her brothers, but her, the first woman to rule her nation.

Sonaji could see the assassin was holding something back. 'What else do you have to tell me?'

'There is another I must find in the city. I have a message for the leader of the slave resistance. A man called Jonotrix. But there is one other thing,' a smile spread across Erwin's face. 'Atropolis requests a gift from you, a gesture of loyalty. He wants the Lioness' head, and the satisfaction of knowing it was taken by her father's lover.'

'From your smile, I assume you see a way of redeeming yourself for past failures.'

Erwin bowed deeply. 'I do, Your Highness. I do.'

Enola

The few surviving Avolonian leaders met at City Hall. Enola brought her generals, Elektra, Antona, Ioniedas, and Eric, who was to take over from the deceased General Hals. The Cid and Gavara entered behind this group. Jonotrix, and the young boy, Zac, followed close behind. Zac had been on Enola's tail ever since her return, never letting her out of his sight. He objected when Jonotrix made him wait at the entrance, but capitulated when the slave leader told him they needed him to keep watch.

The first thing Enola noticed as she walked into the hall was that Sonaji had her own guards stationed around the room's perimeter.

Sonaji sat on the Ivory Throne, flanked by several of the surviving generals and a few new ones she had appointed.

'Looks like us against them,' Antona mumbled through the side of his mouth.

High-backed chairs were set out in a circle with the Ivory Throne included like a jewel on a ring. Everyone took their seats, except Enola. She walked to the centre of the circle. Her eyes were glazed with emotion, her face still smudged with dust from the blast on the wall. The Lioness took a deep breath, while turning in a full circle to look into the eyes of each and every person gathered in the hall.

'The Lion Lord is dead.' Enola had to close her eyes and gather herself before she could continue. 'My father is dead, and our world will not be the same from this point onwards.' She trembled inside. Seeing her father's head on a spike had shaken her to the core. She was hardened by battle, had grown up with war, but her soul was still that of the little girl who longed for her father's embrace. Enola hid her grief behind her anger. 'The Mander fleet is at Ratlarbig. Our own ships can't pass that bottleneck, so we will be trapped by them here in the city. To all accounts it looks like Mander has a new Emperor. When he orders his fleet here, and he will, we will have to fight on two fronts. That will be the end of us. I, for one, will not be taken alive. I will not see my legions enslaved. I know they would rather die on their feet than live on their knees. No one is coming to our aid, but we have enough warriors to see this task through. We will show the world what determined people can do, or leave this earth with a legacy of bravery and defiance. The Lion Crusade will go on in the hearts and minds of others, who one day will dare to stand against tyranny and oppression.'

The room cheered Enola's words, but the cheers soon died down when Sonaji had her new chancellor bang his staff on the ground. All eyes turned to the Ivory Throne.

'The Lion Lord, my new husband taken from me.' She wiped a tear from the corner of her eye. 'It was by his wish and the law of our land that command of the army falls to me. They are fine words you speak, Enola; your father would be proud. Nevertheless, the new Emperor has sent a peace offering. If we open our gates, he swears that we can join his Empire as free citizens. I guarantee our safety.'

Enola's face reddened; she had to grit her teeth to stop herself shouting a reply. 'Our safety guaranteed? By that same man who, at this very moment, is firing the severed heads of the Lion Cavalry over our walls?'

'Such atrocities will stop as soon as we are no longer enemies.' Sonaji straightened her back and narrowed her eyes. 'It is now time for you to take your seat, Commander Enola. Whether or not you approve, I will broker a peace, and you will obey my authority. Your father gave his seal to me, and his authority with it.'

Enola laughed. 'You think a hurried marriage makes you fit to command our army? It does not. I assume command and there will be no peace.'

Leonardo had only that morning been appointed as the chancellor and saw his opportunity to shine. He stepped forward.

'There can be no contesting command of the army. The Lion Lord left clear orders that in his absence, Sonaji was to take command. I have the papers, and she has the seal of command.'

The Chancellor grinned like the cat that got the cream, bowed to Sonaji, then returned to his seat.

It was Gavara's turn to stand. 'Not entirely true. The orders you have are for command in absence. Not command in death. The succession is to the next highest commander, and that is Enola.'

'Nonsense!' Sonaji screeched. 'Absence, death, it's the same thing.'

Gavara shook his head. 'No, you can contest the succession only by fighting a duel with Enola, and I am sure you do not want to do that. Or, if it will help everyone agree, we can take a vote. If Enola loses the vote and you have the support of this Council, she may choose to hand over her power to you.'

Sonaji looked around the room, confident she had the numbers needed. 'Very well then, a vote. I have the Lion Lord's seal, and you all know that supersedes any tradition of succession. Raise a hand to vote my immediate and uncontested ascension to Commander of the Lion Crusade.'

Several hands went up immediately. A couple more followed hesitantly. There were twelve seats in the circle, and there were six raised hands, including Sonaji's.

'Those for Enola,' Gavara called out.

Six hands went up.

'It is a draw,' the Chancellor announced. 'So, Arc's orders stand.'

'No,' Gavara challenged. 'In the event of a draw in military matters, we revert to the rule of combat.'

'Enough!' Sonaji bellowed. 'I will command. Do you think I did not anticipate your annoying attempt at a coup?' She clapped her hands. 'Guards!'

The tramp of a hundred feet stamping in unison, combined with the clatter of armour and weapons, filled the room. The noise echoed in the rafters, as fifty soldiers surrounded the circle of chairs. The warriors lowered their spears, a threat to anyone who dared move.

Sonaji stood up, her expression smug, and her head held high. 'You will bow to my command. Those who voted against me will be relieved of theirs.'

Enola slowly drew her sword, its golden blade rasping against the mouth of its scabbard. None of her generals showed any concern or moved to join her.

'Take her away!' Sonaji shouted to the guards. 'Before she does something stupid with that weapon.'

None of the guards responded, and there was an uncomfortable silence. There was a sudden clatter of armour, as Captain Warrik pushed his way through the guards to enter the circle.

'Madam Sonaji, I beg your pardon, but it is you we have come for.'

Sonaji stood there, trying to look defiant, not knowing what to say. She suddenly realised these where not her men, they were Enola's Spartikens.

'Do you think your scheming had gone unnoticed?' Enola asked. 'You carry my father's seed in your womb. For that reason alone I will not put you to the sword as traitors should be. Your Corinthians plunged the knife deep into our back when Tyezore deserted the field.' Enola's eyes widened, her hatred bubbling to the surface. 'Corinthian treachery cost us the battle. I'll not have that same treachery leading us into slavery. Warrik!' The Captain stood to attention. 'Take the lady Sonaji to her quarters; she is no further threat to us now.'

Warrik led Sonaji away. She did not resist, looking straight ahead as the guards parted to let her through. Her new Chancellor followed.

Enola turned her blade towards the generals who had voted for Sonaji. 'The enemy is literally at our gates. Do you all swear to obey me?' There was unsure nodding, but no one objected. 'Then listen closely. I will not be trapped in this city to rot. Great warriors like my father, Edius-Max, and Razor did not give their lives so that we could be enslaved. We will let our enemy weaken themselves against these walls until it is inevitable they will gain entry. Then, we will ride out, attack, and win the day or die with honour.'

There were mumbles of discontent that faded when one of the Council plucked up the courage to speak. 'Sir, I have followed your father since Jomora, and will obey your command, whatever that may be. But have you not seen the numbers gathering out there? An attack would be as much use as pissing on a forest fire.'

'I don't disagree, General Visp, but the city is full of freed slaves, survivors of the Mander evacuation, and civilians, camp followers. They will all be slaughtered or enslaved again when Atropolis takes the city. What an attack will do is give you and Jonotrix time to lead them all away from the city while we fight.'

'No! I will fight,' Jonotrix objected. 'We will all fight.'

Enola shook her head. 'No, you will survive. Keep the embers of our crusade alive to rise again one day in the future and finish what we started.'

'They will hunt us down,' Visp muttered.

'Not if we hurt them enough,' Enola responded. 'Now return to your troops and await my orders. Defend the walls, and remember, we are lions stalking our prey, not sheep waiting for slaughter.'

Sonaji

The sound of panic drifted in through Sonaji's window. The city folk had been told to ready themselves to flee. Every boom of the Dragons being fired sent a wave of anxiety through the streets. For two weeks the new weapons had pounded the city walls. More of the metal tubes that were being called cannons had been brought to bear on the city. Almost thirty had been counted belching smoke when they hurled their balls at and over the city's defences.

Without her generals, Sonaji had no influence and was left to her own devices. Her loyal guards were replaced with Enola's men, but they had orders to keep their ward safe, not to detain her.

Her band of followers had slunk away into the shadows as soon as she had been stripped of her power. Only the Chancellor stayed, out of some misplaced sense of loyalty. He had proved to be useful, and today Sonaji sent him on another errand.

Erwin easily avoided the guards' attention by taking the rooftop entrance leading to the rooms where Sonaji had taken residence. It was an old palace with more than a dozen entrances and only a half dozen guards.

'Is he coming?' Erwin asked, striding into the room.

Sonaji had changed into a purple swarez, the traditional Corinthian colour when mourning, but there were no tears clouding her eyes. She sat in a high-backed chair at one end of a heavy oak table, tapping its surface with her sharp nails.

'The Chancellor has gone to fetch him,' Sonaji sighed. 'Apart from the serving girls, that bitch has seen to it I'm left with no one I can trust.'

A glint appeared in Erwin's eyes. 'You can trust me, Your Highness. I am still your loyal servant.'

Sonaji explained what had happened, while Erwin listened, nodding sympathetically whenever he thought it appropriate. A maid entered carrying a plate of food and a jug. She placed them in front of Sonaji, filled a cup from the mug, and curtsied.

'Is your boat still in the harbour?'

'Thanks to your orders, it is.' Erwin stopped the maid as she passed. 'Another plate of food for me, dear.'

The girl looked to Sonaji, who nodded, so she hurried off towards the kitchens.

'Can you sail me out of here?'

Erwin held his hands up. 'Of course. Are you allowed to leave?'

Sonaji frowned. 'We will leave under cover of darkness.' She paused, her eyes filling with mischief. 'When you bring me the Lion Bitch's head.'

'Then it must be tonight. Ships are coming to attack the harbour, and there will be no way out through them.'

'Good, we don't want to be in the city when the fighting starts. From what you tell me, the Mander will kill everyone and everything.'

The serving girl returned with a plate of food just as The Chancellor arrived with Jonotrix. She looked at the small plate, then at the two extra guests, rolled her eyes, spun around, and returned to the kitchens to fetch more food. Sonaji sent the Chancellor after the girl with the instruction that no one was to return to the room until sent for.

'Thank you for coming.' Sonaji sounded charming. 'Jonytrix, isn't it?'

'Near enough,' Jonotrix replied with a sniff. 'You know you can no longer give me orders? I'm only here because your errand boy said it was a matter of life and death.'

'Oh, but it is,' Erwin interrupted.

'And who are you?' the rebel leader asked.

'I am the man,' Erwin bowed, 'who will save not only your life, but that of your brother.'

'What nonsense is this, and what does it have to do with Ranotrix?'

'Mander has a new Emperor, and he wants men like you on his side. He is offering you the city and the lives of your followers if you open the gates for him.'

'What treachery is this? He doesn't need me to open the gates for him. He's blowing down the bloody walls.' Jonotrix gave Sonaji a harsh glance. 'This is treason. Enola will have your heads for this.'

'Listen to what the man has to tell you before you do anything foolish,' Sonaji barked.

'Ranotrix is alive, and will remain that way as long as you open the gates to the city tomorrow, at dawn.' Erwin handed Jonotrix a silver armband, the type worn by gladiators, and matching the one he wore. 'Your brother's, I believe.'

'And he dies if I don't open the gates?'

'As will all your followers. Atropolis will take the city with or without your help. His ships are almost here, and when they arrive, he will attack from land and water. There will be no stopping him.'

Jonotrix took the arm ring and slumped into a chair. He twirled the silver circlet through his fingers, staring at it, thinking. He looked like a man whose world had just turned upside down. Sweat glistened on his toned body, like most people not born in Calinkerbad he found the constant humidity difficult to cope with. The Gladiator stood up to leave.

'You are to light a beacon over the gates just before dawn to show that they are open,' Erwin instructed.

The traitor's words cut Jonotrix to the quick. He turned slowly, his hand finding the hilt of his sword.

'Don't be a fool,' Erwin snapped. 'Kill me and there will be no signal to say you have agreed. If there is no signal, your brother dies. Atropolis says he will stuff him into the mouth of a Dragon and fire him over the wall. Your brother said I was to remind you of the Gladiator saying, "*Family before honour*," or something like that.'

Jonotrix's eyes narrowed, his expression murderous. He spoke through clenched teeth, 'This will play itself out, and when it does, I will find you.' He left.

'Do you think he will obey?' Sonaji sounded worried.

Erwin huffed. 'He will save his own skin. He owes no loyalty to the Avolonian vixen. I moored the felucca off the communal pier in-between the two main storehouses. I'll send word when it's time and meet you there. Don't row out to the boat alone. The waters are dangerous since the fools threw the dead into the river upstream.'

Enola

Dust hovered in the air making the late afternoon sun seem hotter than it was. Every shot from the Mander's monstrous weapons sent up more grime. A cloud of dust rose from a pile of stone where a large section of the main wall had crumbled under the bombardment. A barrier that had protected the city for hundreds of years had been reduced to powder and rubble in two weeks.

'The walls are too vertical,' Gavara announced. 'If they had been built sloping or at an angle, they would deflect or absorb much of the Dragon's power.'

Enola, Antona, and Gavara watched the bombardment from a tower standing a safe distance inside the city. From their vantage point, they had seen the Mander lines growing wider with every day that passed. An ocean of banners now spread as far as the eye could see in both directions. Enola was angry that her enemy had been able to make defences out of the leftover palisades she had ordered burned.

'Where are they all coming from?' Antona spoke his thoughts out loud. 'General Visp was right. Attacking this will be like pissing on a forest fire.'

'Come on.' Enola sounded encouraging. 'We have pissed on a fire or two in our time, and we're still here to tell the tale.'

'I wish I had your enthusiasm.' Antona gazed at the Mander horde. 'Don't get me wrong, I will ride by your side until the end.'

'But?' Enola asked, knowing there was always a "but" to follow such statements.

'But, while we are attacking them head on, warriors will come from the ships, through the city, and attack our rear. The battle will only last until that defining moment; then we will be cut down.'

'He is right,' Gavara said. 'Your only hope is to break through them and keep on going.'

Enola took a deep breath, drawing her hands over her face as she exhaled. 'That would condemn the civilians. We need to fight long enough for them to get away. If that's until we feel the blades in our backs, then so be it.'

A flock of seagulls were making a nuisance of themselves above the tower. Their squawking could be heard across the city, except when the Dragons roared. No one was sure how they knew there was food here, but the beasts had gathered in their hundreds to feed on the bloated bodies stuck in the river's banks.

Antona looked up. 'We should eat the seagulls, but no one wants to eat birds that have been feeding on our dead.' It was then he remembered something. 'Jonotrix has requested that he and his rebels be given the honour of guarding the gates. He says his men know how to defend them best.'

Enola nodded her consent. 'I will ride straight for the spike with my father's head when we attack.' Enola glared to where the heads were displayed. 'I will take back the Lion Lord's head and shove the spike down that bastard's throat.'

'You are the Lion Lord, now,' Gavara interrupted, 'and you should carry the Lion Blade into battle.'

'What?'

'You are your father's daughter, his firstborn. The title passes to you. You're the Lion Lord.'

Enola could not have cared less about inheriting a title. The insult to her father's memory by displaying his head fuelled the burning hatred in her heart and her desire to inflict her revenge on Atropolis.

'I will take the sword back when I kill the snake.' Enola turned to Antona. 'If I fall at that moment, don't let the army panic. Keep them fighting.'

Antona laughed. 'If you have fallen, I will probably be dead already.'

'Then make sure all our captains know that no matter who falls, the fight goes on.'

Gavara turned to Enola, his eyes full of sadness and regret. 'Hatred and revenge were the demons that clawed the life out of your father.' It was as if he could see the rage inside her, read her thoughts. 'Don't let them be your downfall, too.'

Another thunderous boom came from the fire tubes. There was an explosion of rubble and dust on the wall. The sound of clattering stone lingered longer than usual. When the dust cleared, it revealed a gaping breach in the wall, and the Mander cheered.

Gavara sighed. 'That will be enough to make him believe an attack will get him into the city. Oh, it will cost him dearly, and he will know it, but he will still come. It's late in the day now, so my best guess is that he will come at dawn.'

'That does it then,' Enola said, slamming her hand against the stone rail. 'We attack before they do. Antona! Inform the officers. Have the troops form up inside the front wall. They can sleep there overnight, so they are ready to stand and attack at first light. Have the civilians do the same. They need to be out and running the instant our army has cleared the gates. Come on, we have work to do.'

Enola and Antona left the tower's balcony, leaving Gavara behind.

The Pathfinder saw a small figure creep out from an alcove. 'Zac! Come here.'

The boy was startled and his eyes flicked between Gavara and the staircase Enola had gone down. 'Come here, boy.' Zac decided it was better to obey the old man and went to him. 'You're very fond of Enola?' Zac nodded. 'Do you want to be of great service to her?' He nodded again, a sparkle appearing in his eyes. 'Then come with me.'

Gavara

The first archer appeared from behind an upturned cart. A second rose from the side of a pile of battered shields. Both men had their bows drawn and aiming at Gavara. Confusion was etched on their faces. The old man had come from the city, the Emperor's half moon banner hanging from his staff. A young boy followed behind, walking as if he were a condemned man heading to the gallows.

'Take me to Atropolis,' Gavara told the archers. 'He is expecting me,' he lied.

The bowmen gave each other a confused look and then gestured towards the Mander lines with their drawn bows. Gavara trundled past them with no more concern than if he had been entering a market. Zac was more cautious. He ducked under the bows' aim, watching them all the time with a worried gaze. The Dragon Cannons fired, making the boy flinch.

Zac quickened his gait to catch up with Gavara. 'What are you going to do when we get there?'

'Gamble, my dear boy, gamble,' Gavara said, without looking back. 'Don't you like to gamble?'

'Not with the Mander.'

More guards approached them before they reached the front line. These men restrained Gavara and the boy, but did as the old man asked and took the two of them to the Emperor's compound. One guard went ahead with a message the old man had given him, assuring him that his commander would have his head if he failed to bring news of his arrival to Atropolis.

It did not surprise Gavara when an old acquaintance greeted him, an officer that had been on the failed campaign into Avolonia. Zac, on the other hand, was completely astonished when the big bearded Mander officer greeted Gavara with a smile and embraced him.

'You old wizard, what are you doing here?' Captain Moor seemed genuinely pleased to see him; then the smile dropped from his face. 'Atropolis is Emperor now. I'm not sure you are wise to come here. He will not forgive you for deserting him, and there were rumours that you served the Lion Lord. Tell me that's not true. He will kill you if it is.'

Gavara gave his old friend a smile. 'I'm afraid it is, and he may well do away with me. Let's find out. Take me to him.'

'Are you sure?'

Gavara nodded, so Captain Moor led him to where Atropolis stood, Zac following behind.

Atropolis glared at Gavara, like he was seeing a ghost. He said nothing, but his expression spoke for him. Gavara looked over at the cannon Atropolis was there to survey. The metal tube's emplacement was a hole in the ground, walled with boulders. Rope bound the barrel, and its metal was cracked.

'Too little copper in the mix,' Gavara explained, without being asked. 'It will explode if you continue to fire it. Those ropes won't help.'

Atropolis threw back his head and let out a laugh. His black leather breast plate, covered in symbols of Kush, was shaking from the laughter. The good humour stopped as quickly as it started.

'We will find out when I have your bony carcass fired from it.' Atropolis drew his sword as he approached Gavara. His intention was clear.

'Did the disciple Rhydian help you find the Questerus?'

Atropolis stopped, but kept his blade pointing at the old man's chest.

'I asked him to guide you to it,' Gavara went on. 'Not to give it to you, but to let you discover it. I knew you would place a higher value on it that way.'

'How could you have had a hand in that? No one knew I would end up at the Disciples' monastery.' Atropolis' amber eyes scrutinised his once loyal servant. 'You have come to ask for your friend's head. Well, you have wasted your time and your life.' He poked Gavara in the chest with the tip of his blade. Blood stained the Pathfinder's white robe. 'My fate is no longer bound to the Avolonian. I severed that along with his head. His skull will stay on that spike until the flesh has rotted from it and the bone is bleached. His spirit will suffer that humiliation throughout eternity.'

'No, it is not the Lion Lord's head I've come to ask for. His spirit would anger if I spoke for him. I have come to make a trade.'

'I will pay nothing for you. I have more advisers than the Avolonian ghosts I'll make when I get inside those walls.' Atropolis turned to Captain Moor. 'Have this traitor crucified in full view of the city and hang that boy next to him.'

Zac's eyes widened with fear. Moor hesitated, knowing he had to follow orders, but reluctant to march an old friend to oblivion.

Gavara was calm. 'The original Questerus written by Kush himself.'

Atropolis, who was about to reprimand Captain Moor for not moving quickly enough, now held out a hand to stay him. The Emperor narrowed his eyes, not sure he had heard correctly.

'Kill me and it is lost forever.'

'You are a snake,' Atropolis hissed. 'But a very clever one. I could torture its whereabouts out of you.'

'And you know I would probably die without telling you the truth.'

Atropolis considered his options. The old serpent was offering him the one thing he would pay anything for. He could be lying, but such a great prize was worth the risk. 'What is your price? But know this, the only way Arc's head is coming off that spike is to be replaced by yours.'

Gavara smiled. His gamble had paid off. As he had guessed, Atropolis had kept Arc's sword for himself. 'All I ask for is that sword with my blood on its tip.' He looked around. 'It's obvious you will attack soon, and then you will have the sword back. Think of it as a loan, and you will have both the sword and the Questerus.'

Atropolis bared his gritted teeth, like a leopard menacing its prey. 'What trickery is this. You ask only a sword for the true Questerus, knowing I will take it back from the cold dead hand of the Lion Bastard's pup?'

'No trickery. I am merely fulfilling a promise to Arc, to see his sword handed to his daughter.' Gavara believed the blade to be much more than an heirloom. It was one clue to the many questions of a prophecy: a prophecy that could not be fulfilled without the Lion Blade in a Lion's hand. He gave no clue as to the value he placed on Leovesica. 'I am old and not long for this world. My soul would never rest if I broke my promise. I made an oath.'

Atropolis returned to his laughter. 'You and your oaths. I assume the boy is here to take the sword back?'

Gavara nodded.

'And, I suppose the Questerus is in a place only you can take me to?'

Gavara nodded again.

Atropolis flipped the Lion Blade and held it hilt first to Zac. 'Tell the Lion Bitch I will be coming for this.'

Zac's hand trembled as he took the sword.

Gavara leaned closer to Zac's ear. 'Tell your mistress that patience beats an enemy more often than rage or valour. With this sword there is hope.' He stood straight and spoke louder, so that all could hear. 'Take the sword to Enola, and tell her I said to die well, like her sister.'

Atropolis was finding the whole thing bizarrely funny. 'Her sister died pathetically on the back of a cart.'

Captain Moor stepped forward. 'I will see the boy safely through our lines.'

Zac gave Gavara a nervous look.

The old man with his wispy white beard and hollow eyes, smiled. 'Go, you will be safe. Take the blade to Enola.'

The boy and Moor had been gone less than a moment when Atropolis snapped the next order. 'Strip him naked. Lash his back until it is raw. Then, chain him, and throw him in a cage behind our lines. There will be no rescue or comfort for him.'

Gavara showed no fear and stared defiantly into the Emperor's eyes while his robe was torn from his frail body.

'By the time I have finished with you, you'll be begging to tell me where the book of our Lord is resting,' Atropolis snarled. 'Take him away!'

Erwin

It was easy for Erwin to blend into the crowds of warriors flowing through the streets like a lazy summer river. Everyone had been ordered up to the walls either side of the main gates. They would sleep there, if they could, with their armour on and their weapons by their sides. They would attack at first light.

Erwin grinned knowingly. His new Lord and Master would already be in the city by first light, or at their walls to greet the Avolonians as they burst from the gates. There would be no escape. The Gladiator had done what was needed to save his brother. The rebels guarded the gates and would unlock them before dawn. It would be a slaughter if the Mander gained access to the city while their enemy slept or were still in the confusion of readying themselves.

It was dark when Enola left her officers with two bodyguards following her. Erwin had been keeping track of her all day, waiting for the moment when she would take some rest. He followed her back to the villa where she had been staying. Raymed was waiting in the shadows by the back wall.

'Is the Lady Sonaji by the harbour?' Erwin asked his accomplice.

'She is,' came the reply. 'Bloody nightmare getting her there, pushing through the crowds coming this way.'

'And men to guard her?'

'Four cutthroats and thieves, but all good men in a fight. They were just happy to be getting a place on a boat out of here.'

Raymed was a big man, but as much fat as muscle. He had only one eye, the other lost to a sword cut in battle. He had once been a proud warrior, now reduced to wearing a tattered tunic and a mail coat with several holes in it.

'We need to get over the walls and onto the roof. She won't sleep for long.'

Raymed chuckled. 'Can I do her before we kill her?'

Erwin rolled his eyes. 'Kill her before she wakes, or she will do the both of us, and not in a way you'll enjoy.'

The two men climbed over the villa's wall. Despite his size, Raymed was light on his feet. They used a tree to get up onto the flat roof at the back of the building. Light came from the three windows set into a step in the roof. Erwin sat by the side of the window to the far left and cautiously looked in. He watched Enola empty a cup of what he assumed was wine, then dismiss her guards. She unbuckled her sword as she blew out the candles and turned down the lamps. Enola laid her belt holding the golden sword on a small table before blowing out the final candle and collapsing fully clothed onto the large bed.

Erwin kept his eye on the sword, *'That will be mine soon,'* he thought. *'The richest sword I know of, and soon it will hang at my side.'*

Enola

The heavy wooden door to the chamber swung smoothly open on its well-oiled hinges. Artur insisted on entering the room first, diligent in his duties to ensure no danger awaited his Commander. Enola did not wait to be given the all clear, she was exhausted and eager to hit the mattress. The room was already lit by several candles and two lamps. Small alcoves were cut into the white plaster walls to hold the lights. There was a comfortable-looking bed at the centre of the room, and a small table with a cup on it.

'Gavara left you a sleeping draft,' Hurcan announced from the doorway.

Enola immediately drank the bitter tasting potion, knowing it was her only chance of finding sleep. 'Leave me,' Enola told her guards. 'But wake me well before dawn. I don't want to still be wiping sleep out of my eyes as we ride through the gates.'

As soon as Artur had closed the door behind him, Enola blew out all the candles but one and turned out the lamps. She placed the golden sword on the table, blew out the last candle, and flopped onto the bed, too tired to undress. The dark room seemed to sway as if she was on a boat, her mind going over the events of the day.

She had been right to move everyone up to the walls. It had taken all evening. If she had waited until dawn to ready the troops, it would have been noon before they could attack. During the day it was not safe by the walls where much of the cannon shot came over, shattering buildings and killing anyone in range. But at night, the Dragons fell silent. Gavara had pointed out that the cannon crews were afraid to work the beasts in the dark, and even more so using torches to light their labours. One spark, let alone any of a dozen burning torches that could fall over at any time, would be enough to blow them to smithereens.

Enola tried not to think about the coming battle. She thought of her husband, the Pirate leader Huwel. She would have liked to see him one more time. *'A good reason to survive,'* she thought. The sleeping potion took hold, and Enola could no longer distinguish between her thoughts and her dreams. Her sleep was restless, as she dreamed about the battle. A thousand faces of the dead swirling by, calling out to be saved. Another thousand swinging swords or thrusting spears, trying to cut her down.

From amongst the chaos walked a slender figure in a white robe, calm and smiling.

'Jenaliena, you have found me,' Enola whispered in her sleep.

The ghostly figure of the beautiful young woman smiled, opening her arm to show Enola across the room. Enola saw Jenaliena kneeling on her sleeping body, shaking her shoulders, trying to wake her.

'To see yourself while you are sleeping is to have seen your own ghost,' a soft voice echoed through Enola's thoughts.

She could hear a dog barking in the distance, a husky bark. Suddenly she was finding it difficult to breathe.

Instead of looking across at the ghost trying to wake her, she now felt the weight on top of her. The dog's bark grew louder. *'Wake up,'* she told herself. *'Wake up.'*

Before she had even opened her eyes, she felt the hands at her throat. A large weight crushed her chest, a hand covering her mouth. The silhouette of an enormous figure flickered into view as Enola blinked her eyes open. She struggled, but he was too heavy and her arms were pinned

There was another figure standing over her. She saw the glint of a blade in his hand a moment before she felt its cold edge at her throat. She bucked and twisted to no avail, unable to shift the weight, and the knife was starting to bite into the flesh of her neck.

Enola suddenly felt the man on top of her stiffen. He let out a groan.

'Quiet, you fool,' the other man whispered, harshly.

Enola felt blood trickle down her neck as the blade was lifted from her throat. The bulk on top of her twisted, grabbing over his shoulder, trying to reach his back.

'Assassins!' yelled a frightened voice.

The big man leapt off Enola, revealing a small figure holding a sword. The door burst open, Artur and Hurcan rushing in, lamps and swords in hand. In the new light, Enola saw Zac holding a sword, Raymed's blood dripping from the point. The boy did not have the strength to ram the blade deep enough for a killing thrust, so Raymed was still in action. The huge man threw himself at the two guards, a tornado of sword swings and thrusts. Zac jumped out of the way, the Lion Blade knocked out of his hands as Raymed bolted past.

Artur blocked and parried every swing and thrust coming at him. Hurcan calmly placed his lamp on a stand before joining the action. Artur stepped back and allowed his bigger companion to do his thing. Hurcan stopped the huge assassin in his tracks with a blow to the face. He then pressed him against the wall, ramming his blade through the man's throat. Raymed made a gurgling sound, then dropped his sword. Hurcan stepped back and let him slide down the wall to die in a pool of his own filth and blood.

While the guards had been battling with Raymed, Enola had come to her senses. She sprang from the bed to retrieve her sword from the table and trapped the other assassin in the room. Erwin only had the curved dagger he had planned to slit Enola's throat with. He grabbed Zac by the hair and pulled him in to use as a shield. Zac yelled and protested, but could not break free. Erwin placed the dagger at the boy's throat.

The room was suddenly quiet, making the rasp of Enola's blade being drawn from its scabbard sound loud. Erwin's eyes flicked between the door and the open window he had entered through.

Artur broke the silence when he came over with a lamp. 'You!' He turned to Hurcan. 'It's that raping bastard who nearly got me hanged. Erwin.'

Enola paid little attention. She was transfixed by the clasp fastening Erwin's robe. It was Jenaliena's silver lion brooch, the one she had given her. 'Spartiken turned assassin and traitor. I will skin you alive and use your stretched hide for bow practice.'

'Not if you want this boy to live,' Erwin threatened, pulling the boy's head back to press the blade harder against his throat. 'Now get out of my way.'

Enola spread out her arms to push the other two back with her. They all watched Erwin edge his way to the door, Zac tight in his grip. Once he had reached the doorway, he paused, and again pressed the blade into the tender flesh of Zac's neck.

'Give me the sword.' Erwin jerked his chin towards Enola's golden blade.

'Cheeky bastard!' Artur exclaimed.

Enola hushed him, her only concern being the boy's safety. Zac tried to shake his head, but Erwin tightened his grip. Enola's fear for the boy's safety deepened, she slid the sword along the floor towards Erwin.

'Now, let the boy go.'

Erwin kept a tight grip on Zac, as he bent to reach for the sword. 'Now, back up, all of you,' he demanded, pointing the tip of the sword to the far wall.

Artur and Hurcan did not move. 'Do as he says,' Enola told them, and all three backed towards the wall. 'It'll be alright Zac.'

When they were against the wall, a grin spread across Erwin's face. He held the boy out as if he were about to let him go, but then thrust the dagger into his back. Zac's face contorted with pain. Erwin thrust the boy to the floor, slammed the door, and was gone.

'No!' Enola cried out, rushing to the boy.

She fell to her knees, scooping the boy up.

Zac looked into her eyes. 'I was brave, wasn't I?'

Enola found the wound and applied pressure. 'You were. You saved me.' She lifted the boy and passed him to Artur. 'Take him to the surgeon. Keep pressure on the wound.'

Hurcan was already through the door and giving chase. Enola picked up the sword Zac had dropped, shocked to see that it was Leovesica, her father's blade.

Zac grabbed Enola's arm as she went past. 'Gavara sent me with the sword. I am to tell you.' Enola put a finger to her lips, but the boy would not be silenced. 'I am to tell you, patience defeats more enemies than rage. The sword is hope.' Pain forced Zac to pause. He shivered, then found enough spirit to go on. 'Gavara said, to die well, like your sister.'

Enola smiled, hiding her confusion. 'Quiet now, you sweet boy.' Zac's eyes flickered shut, and he was silent. Enola turned to Artur. 'Take him, hurry.' Then she left.

Enola saw Hurcan disappearing down an ally leading towards the docks. She followed the clatter of footsteps, her rage speeding her on. The streets were dark and empty. A pale moon gave little light, which lessened by the moment as heavy clouds drew a veil across it. Enola arrived at the harbour, panting. She was greeted by the sight of Hurcan standing his ground with three men advancing on him. They were approaching cautiously, two with swords drawn, and the third carrying an axe.

Hurrying to Hurcan's side, Enola didn't see Erwin and two others, at first. Only when she was at Hurcan's side did she notice the assassin with another man and Sonaji. Her rage boiled over, and she lunged at the man with the axe. Erwin shoved the fourth man forward, into the fight, and untied the small rowing boat by the dock.

The man with the axe put up a brave fight but fell to Enola's blade in moments. Of the two men attacking Hurcan, one was dead in less than a moment, and the other was backing away. Enola swung her blade at the man who had been pushed into the fight. He had no stomach for the fight after seeing two of his companions cut down so quickly. He turned and ran.

'Coward!' Erwin called after the fleeing man.

Enola turned her attention on the Assassin. Erwin drew his sword, approaching Enola with the menace of a wolf approaching a lamb. He had imagined this moment many times, seeing himself standing over the Lioness' bleeding body as the outcome, every time. He pounced, and there was a clash of swords, a swirling of limbs, and then one was down. But it was not Enola lying on the ground bleeding; it was Erwin. The Assassin lay on his back, looking up at Enola; his hand pressing the wound in his chest, blood oozing through his fingers. He tried to swing at Enola with his blade, but she stood on his arm.

Enola stared into Erwin's eyes, her skin crawling with hate and disgust. She looked at the lion brooch and then back into his eyes. Pursing her lips, she spat into his face.

He shook his head, a disgusted frown on his face. 'Spare me, there is much I can reveal to you.'

'What could a snake like you tell me that I don't know already?'

The grin returned to Erwin's face, thinking he had Enola's attention, and a chance at freedom. 'There is no child in the belly of the Corinthian, for one.'

'Shut up, you fool!' Sonaji snapped.

Lifting her head, Enola looked at Sonaji, and pointed her sword at her stomach. 'There's no child in that diseased womb of yours, is there?' she shouted the last two words.

Sonaji flinched, but then looked defiant. 'Men are easy to fool, and your father easier than most.'

Enola choked back her anger. 'He didn't deserve you.'

'No, he did not deserve me.' Sonaji glanced out at the harbour and saw something that made her confidence swell. 'I will still be Queen of Corinth when the Great Lion Lord is long forgotten.'

Enola curled one side of her mouth into a snarl, reached down with her blade, and nicked Erwin's jugular.

'For Jenaliena,' she said, plucking the lion brooch from his chest.

Blood flowed from the wound like water from a pump. A pool of dark crimson spread across the stones of the harbour wall, reflecting the light of the lamp held by Sonaji. Enola watched the life fade from Erwin's eyes, cursing his soul as it left his body. She spat on him again.

A scream broke Enola's trance. Hurcan had fought the last of the attackers until he had fallen off the harbour wall. Sonaji took advantage of the distraction and scrambled down the ropes to the boat below. She used an oar to push the craft away from the wall. Enola was about to jump down after her when Hurcan grabbed her arm.

The man was thrashing about in the water, desperate to reach the boat. Several wakes cut through the dark surface, all heading for the struggling man.

'Crocodiles,' Hurcan said, with a grim fascination.

The beasts had ventured into the harbour, scavenging on the bodies that had drifted in from the river. The man scrambled up the side of the boat, just as the first beast reached him, almost capsizing the craft. Sonaji clobbered him across the head with the oar, knocking him back into the water. His screams filled the darkness until the river monsters dragged him under in a death roll. The boat lurched to one side and hit a mooring post. Sonaji was flung into the water, disappearing below its dark glassy surface.

Both Enola and Hurcan gasped, watching the water bubble where Sonaji had gone in. But she did not reappear.

Hurcan suddenly increased his grip on Enola's arm. 'Oh shit, may the Gods help us.'

'Good riddance, more like,' Enola replied.

'No, look.'

Enola lifted her eyes from the bubbling water to look across the harbour. She saw what had given Sonaji a boost of confidence. The Mander fleet had arrived and were sailing directly into the port.

Atropolis

Darkness smothered the land, the stars and moon covered with a thick veil of cloud. A mist hid the Mander camp from spies on the city wall, but it did not hide the beacon burning above the city's gate. A traitor's signal of treachery and betrayal. There had been a glow of light radiating above the city for most of the night, which had long faded into darkness and silence.

Atropolis watched the flames flickering above the gates, his army advancing in silence under cover of the mist. His troops had been edging forward all night, metal bound in rags to maintain the silence. The Emperor was aware of his enemy's readiness for battle, but they would wait for the first light of dawn, and that would be too late. Much of the outer wall had been reduced to rubble over the past two weeks. It had taken all the black powder the Merovingians had brought. Without more of the lightening seeds, the dragons would remain silent.

The Avolonians still defended what remained of the walls, but there were too many breaches large enough to let an army in. It would be impossible to resist the full force of the Mander assault. Sheer numbers would win the day. If they managed to hold back the tsunami of warriors flooding their defences, they would be finished when the warriors from the ships flanked them.

'Does the fleet know we will attack before first light?' Atropolis asked his advisors.

'We sent riders to signal them two days ago,' Al-Genoa replied. 'The admiral acknowledged the message, and his ships arrived in the night.'

'Then it is time. Let us put an end to this.' Atropolis drew his sword. 'Order the attack. Blow no horns, shout nothing, we will descend upon them like the shadow of a thunderstorm crossing the land.' Atropolis looked around at his generals. 'It is our time. Now take me forward to victory, and my destiny.'

The mist was thinning by the time Atropolis crossed the ditch and climbed the embankment leading up to the gates of Calinkerbad. His head was held high, and unlike the surrounding Immortals, he carried no shield. Every man by their Emperor's side wanted to show their bravery. They took bold strides to hide their fear of arrows coming through the mist at any moment to strike them down. All remained silent, no arrows or calls of alarm came from the walls.

Atropolis followed the light from the beacon until he came upon the gates. He saw a flicker of light through a gap in the gates' centre. They were open, only by the width of a hand, but they were open. Atropolis caught the eye of a captain and nodded towards the door as an unspoken order. The officer conscripted several of his men to follow him to the gates.

'Are they still sleeping?' Atropolis thought. *'Do the fools think they are springing some kind of trap by letting us in.'* He watched his men approach the gates cautiously, expecting Avolonian Warriors to spring out at any moment. 'The Gladiator has been true to his word and opened the gates.' A smile crept onto the Emperor's face. 'Pity his brother ran

onto a sword rather than be used against his sibling. But they will be together soon enough.'

The Captain and the other Immortals pulled the gates open. The doors were huge, taking four men to push each one open. Apart from a flickering light, there was no sound or movement from within. Two warriors disappeared through the portal. There were a few silent moments before they returned, shaking their heads.

The Emperor's patience snapped. He took great strides towards the entrance, his guards hurrying to keep pace with him, holding their shields at the ready. Their eyes flicked between their leader and the top of the wall, still expecting a trap. Atropolis bounded into the city, his sword at the ready to cut his enemy down.

There was no enemy. The streets were deserted. All that waited to greet the Mandorians was a head on a post, a torch burning on either side, and a sign hanging below. Atropolis sauntered up to the display. He recognised the head; it was the assassin, Erwin. He read the notice below, written in blood.

Honour before all else

'What does it mean?' General Al-Genoa asked, arriving at his Commander's side.

'It means the Lion Bitch thinks she can gain some advantage by fighting our navy first.' Atropolis held up his sword, the flames dancing in his wild eyes. 'To the harbour! We will find them there, and crush them between our forces. Forward!' Atropolis' voice carried over the heads of his army. His order echoed by every officer already in the city. 'Kill! Kill everything, everyone, kill!'

There was no more creeping. The cry went up, Mandorians cheering as they ran through the streets to the harbour. Warriors of the New Order flowed over the wall where it had been reduced to rubble. Every alleyway was filled with warriors, a river of men twisting and turning to find their way to the waterfront. Closed gates blocked all the entrances to the port district, but they were unmanned, hammered from their hinges in moments.

Streets were like flows of lava, lit by thousands of torches set to flame as soon as there was no longer a need for surprise. Flames lit the way for soldiers hellbent on catching their enemy. The streets widened close to the waterfront, so the Mander fanned out. The front runners formed a shield wall, ready to engage the enemy; an enemy that was nowhere to be seen. The cheering died down, replaced by a hum of confusion.

The clatter of hooves drowned out all other sounds as Atropolis and his generals rode their heavy warhorses down the harbour wall. The great beasts slid and skittered to a halt, the men on their backs gazing out at the river, astonished at what they saw.

A single barge floated in the harbour's centre, a funeral pyre blazing upon it. Flames leaped high into the night sky, obscuring the view to the river beyond. A steady crackle came from the pile of logs, the shape of a body still visible in the inferno's midst. The black water reflected flames as if they were spreading across its surface. Swirling smoke and embers danced in the rising heat. Behind the flames, Atropolis could make out shapes. Wind filled sails, carrying his ships swiftly downriver, away from the city, and his army.

Epilogue

Enola

The last Spartikens clambered over the rails of the remaining ships. Huwel joined Enola on the raft where logs had been piled to make a funeral pyre for Jenaliena. The young woman's body lay on top of the wood. She was wrapped in fine silk from head to toe. Only her face and hands remained uncovered, her flesh yellow, almost gold, from the resin Gavara had used to preserve her. Jenaliena looked serene and at peace, her final expression that of a sleeping child.

'It's time to leave,' the huge Pirate told his wife.

Enola placed the silver lion brooch in Jenaliena's hands, so that it was clasped over her heart. She gently kissed her forehead. Taking the burning torch from Huwel, Enola said goodbye as she lit the pyre.

From the back of the dreadnought ship, Enola watched the flames engulf her lover. She heard the

Mander shouting as they entered the city, too late to take even one more Avolonian life. Huwel had come to their rescue. Standing like an avenging angel on the prow of a Mander ship he had stolen. And not just any ship, the Mander flagship. A dreadnought built by the Avolonians, and sold to the highest bidder by Panus, the Wolf King.

As the flames grew higher, Enola could see little of the port's side or the Mander army rushing towards the harbour wall. She felt Huwel place his strong arm around her, and took comfort in that.

'We should thank him for sending us messengers to tell us when he would attack. The fools waved their flags assuming Mander sailors sailed Mander ships.' Huwel laughed, pleased with himself. 'I had one of our Mander prisoners signal back that we understood, and would obey the order to attack in the night.'

'How did you end up with the entire Mander fleet? They were sent to stop you rescuing us. Yet, here you are using their ships to snatch us to freedom from under their noses.'

Huwel laughed again. 'I'm a thief and did what thieves do best, I stole the ships. We couldn't break their blockade or get past the fort at Ratlarbig. The arrogant bastards figured they had trapped us, and left their fleet tied up on the far side of the bluff to go ashore. We did what they didn't expect. We abandoned our own fleet, crept around them, and stole theirs.'

'And here you are.'

'Yes, here I am. We still have to get past the bastards to make it back out to sea. Where to, then? Will you carry on with the crusade or shall we make sail for Avolon?'

'Neither. We are going to find my sister.'

'Is she alive? I thought...' Huwel decided to be silent and let Enola speak.

'Vengeance and rage drove my father to his destruction. He died without knowing his youngest daughter is alive, and thinking he was to be a father again. He'll carry those lies into the next world. His spirit is condemned to walk alone through the mist of restless dreams, betrayal haunting the eternal sound of silence.'

'That doesn't sound like your father. I'm sure he will be in the great hall, drinking with the Gods and famous warriors. He will be fighting battles, happy to have his favourite warhorse beneath him again. I doubt earthly lies will ever trouble him again.'

Enola managed a gentle smile. 'He did look magnificent on Shadin. I wish you could have seen him. That's how I will always remember my father, on that black stallion, a God of War, parting the Mander lines like an axe splitting logs.'

Huwel studied Enola's face. He could still see the tempestuous young girl who had married him to defy her father, but she had changed. She was still young but he could see the lines of responsibility etching their way across her face. Her eyes no longer sparkled with the anticipation of life. Loss and responsibility had dulled them.

'Who's the boy on the stretcher you made such a big fuss about getting aboard?' Huwel nodded towards the injured boy, and the little girl knelt in prayer at his side.

Enola smiled. 'That boy saved me more than once. He has the heart of a lion. He brought me the Lion Blade with a message from Gavara. The old fool sacrificed himself to get my father's sword to me. He believes there is still hope if I carry the sword.' She laughed. 'He's a cunning old fox. He told the boy to tell me not to die like my sister.'

Huwel's brow furrowed with confusion. 'I thought you said she lived?'

'She does. The message was coded. Only he could twist the meaning of words in a way that would open a new door, and turn me away from the fight.'

'And the little girl?'

The smile faded from Enola's face. 'She dotes on Zac. He is all she has left in the world. Her mother was raped and murdered by the same reptilian monster who took Jenaliena from us. The same creature now laying in a lake of his own blood on the harbour wall.' Her smile returned. 'One nick from the Lion Blade sent him to oblivion.'

'They will send riders to reinforce Ratlarbig,' Huwel told Enola. 'It will take too long for the Emperor to march any numbers that far west. I see there are many Mander prisoners with you, too many. Will they fight for us?'

Enola sighed. 'They will. They are all volunteers, none of them forced to join us. Any that refused are locked in the harbour's storehouses.'

'You should have killed them.'

'You're probably right, but there was no time.'

'Then if they'll fight like you say they will, we can overrun the fort, and collect our fleet to add to this one. But then where to?'

'The Southern lands of Avolonia. The Black Mountains.'

Huwel whistled. 'I've never been that far south. It's cold in those parts, I'm told. A land steeped in the old ways and ruled by the iron fist of a Black Prince. Most travellers freeze in their sleep, those that don't more often than not fall prey to the slave traders. Few of your army will want to go there.'

'Those that want to return to their homes can do so after we pass Ratlarbig.' Enola sounded sleepy. 'Some ships can take others back to Avolon. The Spartikens are loyal, they will follow me to the south, and we will find Cubb.'

'There is good Mander wine and a soft bed in the cabins below. Shall we retire?'

Huwel's offer was met with nothing but silence. Enola was already sleeping, dreaming of the destiny awaiting her.

Lords of Destiny

List of main Characters Reap The Hurricane

Arc Saberlund

The Lion Warrior, lord of the House of Lions and the Lion Army. Son of Isola. the deceased commander of Highground. Stepbrother to Davos, the Eagle Warrior. Husband to Jem (Deceased) Father to Enola and Cubb.

Enola Saberlund (Fawn)

The Lioness, warrior princess of Avolonia. Daughter of Arc and Jem, sister to Cubb.

Gavara

Ligtomidies Gavara Entrmolocles
Pathfinder of the Windweaver prophesy. Guardian of the 17th Zodiac
Adviser to Atropolis then Arc and the Windweaver child

Atropolis Al-Din

The seventh chosen son of Amen Al-Din. Commander of the Mander Western Army defeated by Arc at the battle of Caputhora. New religious leader in Mander-Kush.

ABOUT THE AUTHOR

Stephen Ricketts was born and raised in the Northwest of England and now lives in Oslo, Norway, with his family. He has spent the best part of the last 34 years traveling and working around the world as a snowsports expert. Stephen's literary work combines his real life experiences and adventures in the mountains of the world, with a fascination for history.

Printed in Great Britain
by Amazon

39320205R00286